Journeyman: Honor Fades Not

Book Three

of the

Journeyman Chronicles of the American Revolution

First paperback edition April 2023

Book design by

ISBN 978-1-961486-65-2 (paperback)

ISBN 978-1-961486-64-5 (ebook)

www.frankamason.com

www.thejourneymanchronicles.com

For Deri, Always

and

For Jack Robert Pearson

Table of Contents

Chapter 1 – Remembrance

"**G**randpa, what's this old paper?"

Will Yelverton leaned back in his chair, easing his tired back, a reminder of too many years in a saddle. That, and even more years standing over a workbench in his gunsmith shop, had worn Will's lower back. "That is my commission, Kenny. Where did you find it?"

Five-year-old William Kennedy Yelverton said, "It was on top of the table in there." Kenny nodded toward the front room of the house. "What's a 'mission?"

Will smiled a far-away smile and said, "That's 'commission.' 'Tis a paper, signed by the Congress, appointing me an officer in the Continental Army. I used to have it framed, but the frame fell off the wall and broke, so I need to get a new one."

Little Kenny had big blue eyes, light brown hair, and an English complexion that matched Will's when he was the same age. "What did you do in the Army, Grandpa?"

"That, young man, is quite a question. It's a long story."

Kenny paused and looked at his Grandpa with slightly narrowed eyes, "I ain't doin' nothin' right now."

Will laughed and said, "Let's read it together, and I'll tell you what the paper says – we call it a document. Then, I'll tell you some stories about the Revolutionary War and what your old grandpa did."

A new century was dawning, and Will Yelverton would soon be 50. Kenny - William Kennedy Yelverton - was the child of his son, William Branch Yelverton, Jr. Will and Kenny sat on the porch of his spacious home in the Blue Ridge Mountains. A grand vista spread before them. Ranges of ancient, round-topped mountains marched into the distance, thunderheads crowded the skies, and the air tasted of rain. A slight whiff of ozone from a far-away lightning strike added tang to the air.

The heat of the day had broken, and a cool breeze dried the sweat on Will's neck. The clarion call of time echoed in Will's mind as his mind ranged back to 1779. Once again, he heard the jingle of harnesses and bits, smelled the stink of an army on the march, and heard the distant pop of muskets. A roll of thunder made him jump slightly. For a moment, Will had thought it was artillery.

Will took the creased, aging piece of paper from Kenny. It was nicked and tattered on a couple of the corners, foxed with speckles in several places where the acid in the cheap paper had turned brown. A few tiny holes had appeared where the document had been folded too many times.

The spidery script on the paper proclaimed Will Yelverton an officer in the Continental Army of the United States. The bottom of the page was torn off and long ago lost. The part of the page where the signature of the President of the Continental Congress was had been lost when Lt Colonel Banastre Tarleton had snatched at it in fury.

"I was only 20 years old when they made me a major in the Continental Army, Kenny. This document is the official paper that told everyone that. Actually, this one tells everyone I was promoted to Lieutenant Colonel."

Kenny's blue eyes were big, and he looked at the paper and then at Will. "You were a colonel?"

"Lieutenant Colonel, Kenny. I'll tell you all about it ..."

Chapter 2 – March 4, 1779 – The Day After Brier Creek

Will Yelverton ached in his soul. Will had just witnessed the brutal death of Noah Harris, his boyhood friend.

Noah, Sam Hawks, Dicky Caswell, and Will were inseparable growing up in New Bern, North Carolina. They hunted and fished, played marbles, and tolerated Mr. Tomlinson, the teacher at the New Bern School. Mr. Tomlinson of the hickory stick that he tapped on the floor to make a point. "Two plus two is?" *Tap, tap, tap, tap.* "Correct, Master Yelverton, the answer is four!" *Tap, tap.*

It was with a mixture of joy and concern when Major William Branch Yelverton, Continental Army of the United States, rode into the camp at Brier Creek and discovered Sam and Noah among the troops under General John Ashe's command. Joy because Will had not seen his friends in months. Concern because Will knew that General Ashe was not a strong commander.

Sam and Noah were astonished that Will was now a field officer in the Army. Lieutenant Charles Black of the New Bern, North

Carolina, Militia was even more astounded. A few years older than Will, Chuck Black bullied Will every day until Will had had enough and defended himself. Chuck's sister Martha was the object of Will's adolescent affection, and Chuck resented it. After Martha ran off with a sea captain, Chuck apologized and sought to make amends. Still, there was friction.

Will's concern about the situation at Brier Creek was based on his own experience with General Ashe. Ashe was somewhat hot-headed and not possessed of the strongest of military minds. Will had witnessed Ashe lose his temper at Fort Johnston in North Carolina many months before. Royal Governor Josiah Martin had slipped away from almost certain capture; Ashe had been furious. In a fit of pique, Ashe had burned down the fort. Not that burning down a ratty old compound made any difference to the war or Ashe's temper.

Now, Ashe commanded a mixed force of the North Carolina Militia, a few Continentals, and a small contingent of Georgia Militiamen. After a hurried march across South Carolina, Ashe arrived at Major General Benjamin Lincoln's headquarters only to be ordered onward.

Lincoln, recently appointed commander of the Continental Army's Southern Department, directed Ashe to march to the confluence of the Savannah River and Brier Creek. There, in a pie-shaped wedge of land between the two waterways, Ashe encamped and awaited the arrival of other Patriot forces. Once the forces were assembled, Lincoln would lead a march east to retake Savannah.

Instead, the skilled British commander, Lt Colonel Marc Prevost, expertly flanked the Americans and surprised them. The Patriot forces were routed, many never firing a shot. Survivors were slaughtered.

One of the many dead was Noah Harris. Though Noah died on the battlefield at Brier Creek, as did so many of his North Carolina Militia brethren, it was more of a murder than a combat death. Noah was on his knees, nearly incapacitated from dysentery, when a Scottish Highlander of His Britannic Majesty's 71st Regiment of Foot bayonetted him between the shoulder blades.

Will witnessed the killing of his helpless friend, and it sickened him to the core. He promptly shot the Redcoat Highlander, killing him instantly. *Too bad,* Will thought, *A quick death was too good for that inhuman murderer.*

Now, Will realized that such a pitiless, no-quarter fight was simply the way this war would be fought. Where Will had once been a reluctant participant in the War of Independence, now he was a Patriot to the core. For Will, it wasn't about politics. He cared little for all the political arguments. No, it was personal.

~~<>~~

Major Will Yelverton led his exhausted horse, Molly, into General Benjamin Lincoln's camp at Purysburg, South Carolina. It wasn't much of a camp, either. Though the army – both the Continentals and the various militia units – had been there for many months, the lack of money and equipment made for a ramshackle affair.

Admittedly, it was better kept than some camps Will had seen. The latrine was near the edge of the woods, its stink somewhat muted by distance. The horse line was also a little distant from the tents and makeshift hovels that sheltered the men. That kept the flies down somewhat.

Will led Molly to the horse line and found a spot with good grass. One of the men tending the horses offered to take Molly, but Will refused. He tied Molly in the shade of a tall magnolia tree that inexplicably had taken root in the field near the edge of the camp. He gave Molly enough line so that she could get to the sunshine, as well as the grass. Will took Molly's saddle and, using a handful of grass, rubbed down the poor mare's coat. He wished he had a curry comb, but grass would have to do.

Molly tossed her head and whickered. She turned to nuzzle Will and rubbed her sensitive lips against his hands, looking for a treat. Will discovered a carrot he had put in his pocket two days ago. It had been forgotten in the terrible rush of the fight and the subsequent escape. *No, it was not a retreat,* thought Will. *It was a bloody mess of a frantic escape.* Molly contentedly crunched the carrot and looked for another one.

Will said, "You are the best horse, Molly. Alas, I don't have another carrot just now, but I'll get you one from the mess tent. Assuming they have anything to eat, that is." Will patted Molly's neck and stumbled over to a larger tent in the middle of what was clearly officer country. The dust of thousands of other men marching around stuck in Will's nostrils, and he coughed. He reported in.

An officious little man wearing a captain's epaulet looked up from a sheaf of papers, "Ah, Major Yelverton. We had listed you as missing. I shall rectify that mistake immediately. Luckily, I have a billet for you. Your horse is taken care of?"

The dust in Will's throat made it hard to speak, so he nodded.

"Brier Creek was hard, was it?"

Another nod.

"We have a tent just there," said the precise little captain, waving toward the row of tents to the left. "Fifth one down."

Will put his saddle in the tent and sat on his cot. Exhaustion flowed over him, and he hung his head. The last few days had been hard. He looked at his hands. They were covered in grime – dirt, gunpowder, horse sweat, and more dirt. Worse, they shook.

9

Though he was not yet 21, Will marveled that he shook like Old Man Adams, who lived on the next farm over in New Bern. Mr. Adams had a disease that was called *St Vitus Dance*. He shook and vibrated. When he walked, he seemed to dance along. *Please, God,* Will thought, *don't let me be like Old Mr. Adams. What is wrong with me?*

~~<>~~

As a senior officer at Brier Creek, but one without a command, Will had taken on scouting duty. He spent several days riding the perimeter of Ashe's doomed command. Will killed a few deer which went into the pot and endeared him to the men. He also became familiar with the land, the creeks, and the approaches to the Savannah River.

On the morning of the Battle of Brier Creek, Will was out hunting with Sam Hawks. It was a rare pleasure to be with Sam. They had hunted together all their young lives, so this was a treat. Although it was cold, no deer were moving, triggering Will's instinct for trouble.

Something had spooked the deer. Adding to Will's concern, the few birds that he had seen the last few days were nowhere to be found.

Will and Sam spotted the approaching British forces. Despite Will and Sam trying to warn Ashe and the others, the British achieved near complete surprise. The poorly equipped and even more poorly trained Patriot forces frantically worked to distribute cartridges and form ranks but to no avail. The British were quickly upon them.

~~<>~~

Will's path to his Continental Army commission was unique. Colonel Samuel Elbert of the Continental Army had urged Will to join and accept a major's commission. This was no small thing, but Will had impressed Colonel Elbert – along with many of the other leading citizens of Georgia – with his honesty and bravery. He was barely 20 when he accepted the offer.

But it was not patriotism that made Will a soldier. No, as with so many other soldiers down the ages, it was a woman. Will had realized too late that he loved Abigail Kennedy, daughter of Alexander Kennedy. Will earned his master gunsmithing certification under the tutelage of Alex Kennedy at Bear Creek, North Carolina. Over his apprentice year, Will and Abby became close but not yet lovers.

Then Will left to seek his fortune. He planned to open a gunshop on the frontier in Tennessee or maybe North Georgia. But first, he had to procure parts, and that necessitated a trip to Pennsylvania. His trip to Philadelphia, and the outlying areas where gunmakers abounded, was a failure. Pennsylvania's fledgling legislature confiscated all gun parts and ordered all gunmakers to supply their wares to the militia. There were no parts to be had.

Compounding Will's problem, when he went in search of the parts, he was gently conscripted into the Battle of Brandywine Creek by none other than George Washington himself. Will had asked Washington for safe passage through the lines. When Washington learned that Will had a horse, he promised safe passage after Will 'volunteered' to serve as a courier. The battle turned into a hellscape of death and destruction. Will was lucky to end September 11, 1777, alive, but on the march with Washington's badly mauled army.

Even worse, after Brandywine and failing to find the necessary gun parts, Will got trapped in occupied Philadelphia. Starvation abounded in the city, but Will was fortunate to have well-off friends who kept him fed. His room at the Tun Tavern was secure, despite the demands of the occupying British for quarters.

Will also attracted the attention of Frances Montravalle, the unhappy wife of British Captain John Montravalle. Frances introduced Will to the pleasures of the flesh. Between Frances' attention and his well-to-do friends, Will was not in terrible straits.

Given that he was well-fed and well-bedded, one might imagine that young Will Yelverton was doing well in Philadelphia. And that was true until a hard-faced young British Major named Banastre Tarleton accused him of spying. Will fled across the Delaware River into New Jersey and was on the road to the Jersey Shore to find transportation south when he ran into Tarleton again. This time, Tarleton had a noose ready for Will.

Only good luck and a great horse, Molly, kept Will from dangling. During a brief tussle with Tarleton on that pitch-dark night, Will took one of Tarleton's beautiful Brander pistols. Now he carried the gun everywhere.

An eventful ride on the privateer *Beatrice* with Captain Obadiah Dawkins landed Will in Georgia and a fateful meeting with Colonel Samuel Elbert. Elbert was one of Georgia's leading citizens. Alas, Elbert immediately accused Will, a curious stranger in the Eagle Tavern in Sunbury, of being a spy. Will threatened him with Tarleton's Brander pistol.

A long and beautiful friendship began when Sam Elbert saw the tempered steel in Will Yelverton's heart and decided to trust him. Will and Sam Elbert fought side-by-side at Savannah when the British took the city.

Still a civilian and focused on a future on the frontier, Will visited Abby to ask for her hand in marriage only to learn that the Kennedys believed him long dead. None of his many letters had arrived. No word of Will had made its way to Bear Creek, a very out-of-the-way little settlement west of Cross Creek. Abby, not wishing to be a spinster, married Zeke Carter and was pregnant with Zeke's child.

His spirits utterly deflated, Will went back to Georgia and took Sam Elbert up on his offer of a major's rank in the Continental Army.

~~<>~~

At Brier Creek just a day ago, Will had witnessed the destruction of Ashe's army, and watched helplessly as Noah was murdered and Colonel Elbert captured. Will could not get to Sam Elbert to rescue him, but he did get Sam Hawks, Zeke Carter, and Lieutenant Chuck Black across the Savannah River while helping General Ashe to escape the carnage. The rout was a disaster of Ashe's own making and one which left Will disgusted.

Will Yelverton had all the trappings of a field officer of the Continental Army. But Will's orderly, Corporal Charles Cuthbert, had not been seen since the fight at Brier Creek. Will had last seen Cuth on his horse trying to get General Ashe to turn toward the river. The melee that swirled all around distracted Will for a moment, and when he turned back, Cuth was gone. Will felt sick at the thought that his one subordinate might have been killed in the needless carnage of Brier Creek.

Chapter 3 – Reunion

A completely disoriented Will Yelverton woke to the sounds of people moving around. After a moment of staring at the tent cloth inches from his face and realizing his arm was asleep from resting on the wooden rail of his cot, Will remembered that he was in General Lincoln's camp in Purysburg, South Carolina.

Will thought, *I suppose I should report to General Lincoln,* as he rubbed the sleep out of his eyes. It was still daylight, and he realized exhaustion must have taken over. It was mid-afternoon, and he had slept for at least four hours. *Must make myself presentable first.*

"Major Yelverton, are you in there?"

Will snatched the tent flap aside and, blinking in the March sunlight, saw Corporal Charles Cuthbert standing there with a big grin on his face. Will threw his arms around Cuth's shoulders and said, "Thank God! I thought you were dead or captured."

Cuth's eyes flicked into the distance. "Not many captured, I'm afraid. Lots of dead, though."

Will said, "Aye, I saw Noah Harris bayoneted in the back when he should have been taken prisoner."

"They're not taking prisoners, Sir."

"My God, what is this world coming to?"

"Don't know. I was lucky to have a horse. I saw you had Sam and that blond-headed militiaman, as well as Lieutenant Black, on horses herding General Ashe toward the river."

"Aye. Sam was on Colonel Elbert's horse, and Chuck Black was behind him. I had Zeke Carter, that's the blond fellow, on Molly's back. We were hell-for-leather to get Ashe to the river before he got himself killed. He tried to rally the troops, but that was not possible. The situation was a complete rout. What happened to you?"

"Aye, Sir. It was a rout. I was trying to follow you but got cut off by mounted militia in green jackets. No sense in dying for a lost fight, so I went into the swamp and bogged around for a while 'til the shooting stopped. Then, I picked my way to the river and found the ford. They took a couple of shots at me on my way across, but it was too far for muskets."

"I see you got nicked in the shoulder."

"Just my coat, Sir."

"I'm so happy that you got out of there, Cuth."

"Would you like me to find some water and a razor, Sir?"

"God, yes! I'm a mess. I think I should clean up a bit before I go see General Lincoln."

~~<>~~

While Will washed and shaved, Cuth brushed Will's coat and shook out the one clean shirt left in Will's saddlebag.

"I'm surprised that thing is dry, Cuth."

"Aye, you have good saddlebags, Sir. Appears little damage from Molly's swim."

"Poor Molly. She's a great horse, but I've been abusing her. I hope to let her rest for a few days before we head off to wherever the next insanity is."

~~<>~~

Will stepped up to the adjutant's desk and said, "Major Yelverton to see General Lincoln."

The adjutant looked Will over and said, "You cleaned up quite nicely from this morning, Sir."

Not trusting himself to reply to the officious little prig, Will merely nodded.

The adjutant looked inside the large tent and spoke briefly. He turned to Will and, looking down his nose, said, "The General will see you."

"Thank you."

Uncertain of the protocol, Will took off his hat and tucked it under his left arm. He stepped into Lincoln's tent and presented himself in front of General Benjamin Lincoln's folding camp desk. Will made a slight bow and said, "Good afternoon, Sir. Major William Yelverton reporting."

Lincoln rose from the desk and took in Will from head to toe. He extended his hand, "Thank God we had someone who is a fighter at Brier Creek!"

Will was speechless. He nodded and shook the General's hand. "Come, come, Major. General Ashe has told me that you saved his life and fought like a banshee as the enemy closed in for the kill." Lincoln's broad, New England accent was like flint on steel.

"Sir, I ..."

"Now, now, don't be modest. I know your background. Colonel Elbert specifically requested you be commissioned as a major because you demonstrated leadership and courage under fire, even as a civilian volunteer. You proved that at Kettle Creek and again at Brier Creek. I know you don't have a command, there hasn't been time for that, but I intend to remedy that oversight. I have written to General Washington insisting that you be promoted to Lieutenant Colonel and be given a command wherever we can find one."

"But, Sir, I ..."

"No buts, now young fella," Lincoln's broad New England accent came through even more strongly. "You'll do just fine commanding troops."

"Yes, Sir."

"Now, pending your promotion, I want you to join Lieutenant Colonel Francis Marion and the Second South Carolina Regiment at Fort Moultrie. You will like Marion. He's a hard taskmaster, but he is a warrior."

"Sir, I am acquainted with Colonel Marion. Friends, really."

"Indeed? Well, I'll be damned! Then you'll both do well! Colonel Marion will be a good teacher for you until I can push your promotion through Congress."

"Yes, Sir."

"Now, I want you to rest a bit before leaving for Fort Moultrie. Just now, the enemy seems to be quiet. Not sure how long that will last, but let's take this as a pause."

"Yes, Sir."

"Any questions for me?"

"No, Sir."

"Very well, then dismissed and, I can't emphasize this enough, my heartfelt thanks for your leadership. There was nothing to be done at Brier Creek, but you did what was possible. You are to be commended."

A confused Will Yelverton simply nodded and said, "Thank you, Sir."

~~<>~~

As Will stepped out of Lincoln's tent, he heard a booming voice in the near distance saying, "... and yay, the Lord God spake unto the Canaanites ..."

Something about the voice was eerily familiar. Will walked toward the noise. He thought, *perhaps the word of God is in order this day ...*

Will cut around a couple of rows of tents and saw a man standing on an oak stump, holding forth on God's word. *"Oh my God! It's Benjamin!"*

~~<>~~

Will stood quietly next to a tent out of Benjamin Yelverton's view. Benjamin was Will's brother. Five years older than Will and named for Benjamin Franklin, Will's brother was gifted with neither Franklin's intelligence nor industrious nature. He was, however, afflicted with active skin that made his face florid with red whelks, some pus-filled and obviously painful. Benjamin Franklin Yelverton had always been jealous of Will. He was also a drunkard and buffoon.

Almost 15 years earlier, Benjamin had tried to drown Will in a creek at Branchton, the Yelverton family's plantation in North Carolina. But last year, Will had set some men on Benjamin who convinced the poor drunkard that they were the angels of the Lord and that he must repent.

Must have taken, thought Will. For now, Benjamin was an itinerant preacher of the gospel who apparently had become the army's chaplain. *Is he official? Or did he just take up with the army and they let him stay?*

Benjamin ran out of words and energy and blessed the few men who stood listening to his sermon. "May the Lord God bless you and keep you all the days of your life. May he help you to smite our enemies and make our blessed land free from tyranny. Go with God. I shall preach here again on the morrow, my children. Do come and hear the word of the Lord, thy God."

Will thought, *he was more tolerable when he was a drunken, murderous lout*. Benjamin stepped down from the stump, glanced up, and saw Will.

"Will? Will! Is that you?" Benjamin rushed across the scant 20 feet to embrace Will in a bear hug. "Ah, my long-lost brother! And you are now a major!?"

At least he doesn't stink as bad as before. Will stammered, "I, uh, well ..."

"Tell me all about it! You always were an achiever!"

This last was with tones of admiration replacing years of derision. *Maybe he really has changed ...*

Looking at a torn place on Will's blood-spattered breaches, Benjamin said, "Good Lord! Were you at Brier Creek?"

"Yes, I rode in this morning. It was quite terrible."

"Indeed, so I heard."

Will looked at Benjamin. "How did you find your way here?"

"Oh, Will. As you might remember, last year, the Angel of the Lord came to me and humbled me before God. I was a terrible sinner, and the Angel put the fear of God in me. He made me see that I am a sorry human being. I vowed to repent and give my life to The Lord. Soon after your last visit – I think you were there for my conversion – I set upon the road to preach the gospel and help others to come to God.

"The Lord's plan for me led me across North Carolina and then to General Ashe's march south. We arrived here a few weeks ago. General Lincoln ordered Ashe onward, but they asked me to stay here. Ashe said Lincoln needed a chaplain. So, here I am."

Will thought, *Ashe wanted you gone and made up an excuse,* but instead he said, "It seems you are making a difference."

"Indeed? Do you think so? I, I mean, I hope somehow to help our fellow countrymen know the Lord and, if it pleases God to take them in battle or in sickness, then they may go with a happy heart. Battle is bad enough, Will, but there is so much sickness."

Will was surprised at the sincerity in Benjamin's words. *My God, I paid those slavers Jim and Red 50 Spanish dollars to put the fear of God in Benjamin so he might stop ruining our parents' lives. I think they succeeded. I think he's still quite mad, but now his madness is about the Lord.*

Benjamin said, "I fear for you, Will. You must tell me how you came to be an officer in the Continental Army. Last time we were together, you were heading for the frontier. Wasn't there a young lady?"

~~<>~~

Will sat wearily on his camp cot and thought about Benjamin. What a surprise, but a good one. Benjamin had been a terrible lout who stank of body odor and tobacco smoke mixed with fumes of brandy or cheap wine when he could not afford brandy. Will had detected none of those offensive scents while talking to Benjamin. In fact, he was presentable and sincere. He was happy for Benjamin.

More so, Will was happy for their parents, Zech and Mandy. Other than Benjamin and Will, Zech and Mandy had no other children alive. Who would carry on the family plantation in Halifax County, North Carolina, if not Benjamin or Will?

Long ago, Will had been exiled from the family home to protect him from Benjamin's excesses and murderous intent. As a child, Will had determined that he must make his own way, and so he became a skilled gunsmith. Benjamin had been right: the frontier was Will's future. A master gunsmith was a key member of every frontier community, and Will was assured of a prosperous future. But war and events had conspired to delay that future.

Will sighed. His heart ached for Abby Kennedy. She was now Abby Carter, married to Zeke Carter, whom Will had impulsively rescued from the terrible fight at Brier Creek. Certainly, by now, Abby had given birth to Zeke Carter's baby. In the story of Will's life, he had been just a moment too late to tell Abby of his feelings. He had prioritized his plan for the frontier over his unrecognized love for Abby. Now she was Zeke's wife, and Will was alone.

Worse, as Will and Zeke plunged into the Savannah River escaping from Brier Creek, Zeke had said, "We are brothers now!"

Will had thought, *yeah, we're brothers, all right. And I slept with your wife. I'm such a rotten human being. I truly deserve to be alone.*

Well, not totally alone. There was Mary Proctor. Mary had certainly demonstrated her affection for Will. She had visited his bed more than once and enthusiastically shown him that there was more to her than just a rich, Charlestown society girl. And he liked her. Did he love her?

An honest man would say no, Will thought. *But then, who marries only for love? I mean, people marry, have children, and die with regularity. Then, the surviving husband or wife quickly marries again. 'Tis the way of the world. Perhaps I should simply marry Mary, settle on some Carolina plantation owned by her rich daddy, have a flock of children, and live my life.* Will flopped back on his cot.

~~<>~~

The sun rose on March 6th in Purysburg, South Carolina, a place famous only for being the camp of the Continental Army and associated state militias. In short order, Will's tent became uncomfortably warm.

Will rolled over, cast off the blanket, and lay upon his back for a few moments. Then he rose and stuck his head out the tent flaps. Will had become accustomed to having Cuthbert nearby, and today was no exception. Cuth was sitting on a cut log upended to become a stool.

"Good morning, Sir. I have some warm water and a towel."

"Oh, God, Cuth. Thanks! I feel like death."

"You look quite well, Sir. When are we leaving for Fort Moultrie?"

Will said, "Soon, I think. I have to be polite to my brother, and I want to let Molly and your horse have a little more rest."

"Aye, Sir. I'll get our things together. Do you want some breakfast?"

~~<>~~

Will walked across the camp. He was looking for Sam Hawks and Zeke Carter. Instead, he found Chuck Black.

Chuck was sitting by a small fire where coffee was brewing in a tin pot. He jumped to his feet. "Will, er ... Major Yelverton! I'm so happy to see you."

"How are you, Chuck?"

"I'm alive, thanks to you."

"You were holding your own against that bunch of enemy soldiers when I saw you."

"Aye, well, 'twouldn't have been long before they overcame me."

"Maybe, but I saw the grin on your face as you were dueling, sword in hand, against four Highlanders with bayonets."

"I must admit that I had no idea that the Militia was a life for me."

"I will mention you for promotion when I see whomever is now in charge of the North Carolina Militia."

"I would be a Continental Officer, like you, Will."

"I'll mention that, as well, Chuck. We need fierce leaders who are not at all afraid to step into the breach themselves. I saw that in you."

Chuck looked around, and a blush crept up his neck. "Generous praise from a man I abused when we were small."

"Ancient history, Chuck."

"Still, I'm embarrassed for my past behavior."

Will changed the subject, "Have you heard from Martha?"

"No, but then she's at sea and …" Chuck waived a hand around the camp, "and here we are."

Will wryly grinned, "Just so. We're nowhere to be contacted, I fear. Say, do you know where Sam Hawks and Zeke Carter are billeted?"

"The men are in those wretched hovels over yonder. I wish we had tents for them."

"Aye. But the Army has no money. Every commander we've had has begged for money. But nothing has been forthcoming."

~~<>~~

Will walked toward the hovels. Each hovel was different, but all were made of branches with palmetto leaves made into thatch to keep the rain out. They were miserable, but not nearly as miserable as having to sleep in the open.

Fortunately, winter in South Carolina was unlike winter in other parts of the country. Certainly, it got cold at night, but mostly it was not so bitter and deadly. The hovels were warm and mostly dry.

"Sam? Sam Hawks? Zeke Carter?"

Both men stuck their heads out of their hovels. They saw Will and scrambled out to come see him.

Will looked the two of them over. They were dirty, and their clothes were damaged from the fight and the ensuing rush across the river.

"I've been ordered up the country to Fort Moultrie. How are you?"

Sam said, "I'm doing all right. We've eaten and been able to rest some."

Will looked at Zeke.

"I'm doing well, too, Sir. You saved my life."

Will shrugged, "I was in the right place at the right time."

Zeke grew serious, "I will always think of us as brothers. You were like a brother to my wife, Abby.

"Aye, the Kennedys are my other family. You must survive this war, Zeke, so that your baby has a father."

Will was sitting in the sun outside his tent penning a letter to Noah Harris's parents. Dust from the camp blew in the cool March breeze. There had been a drought for some weeks in South Carolina, and the swamps were drying up. So was the field at Purysburg.

Will struggled to keep the dust from fouling the ink on his letter of condolence. He thought, *everything is covered with dust, including me. I think it's time to head up the road.*

As if on cue, a Lieutenant walked up. "Sir, are you Major Yelverton?"

"Aye, I'm he."

"Sir, I am Lieutenant James Legare. I have been ordered to the 2nd South Carolina, and I must travel to Fort Moultrie. I am to take my ten-man mounted platoon and report to Lieutenant Colonel Marion soonest. It was suggested that I invite you to join us in our ride north."

"Good. When do we leave?"

"On the morrow, Sir."

"Very well, I will be pleased to ride with you. My orderly, Corporal Cuthbert, will find you and get the details."

~~<>~~

Will went to say goodbye to Sam, Zeke, and Chuck Black.

Sam said, "None of us would be here if not for you, Will."

Will said, "We were all lucky. If we had not had horses, we would be four more corpses in the swamp."

Zeke said, "I will be sure to tell Abby and the Kennedys about our exploits."

Will smiled, "Please do give all of them my love. Are you going north soon?"

Zeke nodded at Sam, "Aye, our six months are up in a few days, and this has not been working out well. So, we'll go home."

Will nodded and looked around the camp. "Aye, but the fight is not over. We'll need to throw the British out of Savannah soon. If not, I fear they will be in North Carolina in a few months. Then, the fight will be personal for all of us."

Chuck nodded. "I'm staying, that is, unless we are ordered home. God knows, I'm a terrible coward, but I love this life."

Will said, "You are far from a coward, Chuck. I saw you grinning from ear to ear, standing up to those Redcoats armed with nothing but a sword. I think you may be the senior officer in the North Carolina Militia here, Chuck. I will be sure to commend you to North Carolina leaders when I find one with sufficient authority to recommend you for promotion."

Chuck said, "Rumors among the officers is that they have recommended you for promotion to Lieutenant Colonel."

Will looked around and knitted his brow before his eyes fixed on the horizon, "Aye, 'tis true. Not that I have the vaguest idea of how to command troops."

Chuck, a bit of his old swagger coming out said, "Beg to differ, old boy, but I saw you getting the Continentals to stand firm."

Will grimaced, "Had it not been for Colonel Elbert, there would have been a worse rout. I was following his lead as best I could. My main task was to keep an eye on General Ashe, so he was not captured or killed."

Sam said, "You damn sure did that!"

Will smiled at the group. "You all keep your heads down and get home safe. Chuck, if you ever see Martha, do give her my best. Zeke, take care of that new baby. Sam, when you see Noah's parents, please give them this letter."

~~<>~~

Will walked over to the clear spot where Benjamin was preaching.

As Will walked up, Benjamin said to the small flock – several men and a few women camp followers – "Go with God. I must confer with my brother, Major William Yelverton, the hero of Brier Creek."

Will knitted his brows and looked down at his feet, "I'm no hero, Ben. I just came to say farewell. I'm off to Fort Moultrie. I've been assigned to the 2nd South Carolina Regiment."

"I shall miss you, Will. I had hoped to have time to build a friendship we should have had all these years."

"Time enough for that after the fight, Benjamin. I did want to say that I'm delighted that you are here ministering to the men. May God continue to grant you peace."

"Thank you, Will. Let us pray?"

Will nodded, and Benjamin launched into a lengthy harangue to the Lord to bless and keep William Yelverton and bless the cause of liberty and all the men and leaders of the American cause.

As Will gathered his things in his tent, he reflected, *Benjamin is a changed man. That's good. He sure is a near-apostle. I hope he continues to thrive.*

Chapter 4 – Fort Moultrie

Will, Cuthbert, and Lieutenant Legare's small troop clattered across the bridge at The Cove, a branch of the river separating Sullivan's Island from the South Carolina mainland. The several boats aligned with planks over the top to make a pontoon bridge swayed disconcertingly under the weight of the horses and men. But the floating bridge was better than waiting on a ferry and could be quickly removed in case of an attack.

Sullivan's Island was a low-lying piece of sand with scrubby palmettos dotting the otherwise barren landscape. The larger palmetto trees had been long ago cut to make log walls for the fort that had famously resisted British Admiral Peter Parker's armada in 1776. Now the fort was called Fort Moultrie in honor of South Carolina General Moultrie.

Moultrie, himself, and some 1200 Americans were south of Charlestown along the King's Highway at the Coosawhatchee River Bridge and a small settlement of the same name. On the way from Purysburg, Will and the small unit trotted through their lines, and Will had courteously called on General Moultrie.

The conversation was pleasant, and Moultrie was curious about the fight at Brier Creek and the days leading up to it. Will was careful not to blame Ashe more than the obvious mistakes anyone could easily discern.

Moultrie nodded several times and finally said, "Why anyone would camp in the forks of two waterways and then not set sentries and patrols is beyond me. That you took on patrolling on your own is commendable."

"I was hunting, Sir. Added meat for the pot."

"You can allow others to believe that, but we know differently. That Prevost flanked Ashe's position is both embarrassing and deeply disturbing. I know you did everything to get Ashe to listen."

"He had many concerns, Sir."

"Harrumph! Of course, he did. You, Sir, are a loyal officer. I also know Sam Elbert must have tried to get Ashe to listen. I hope to serve with you in the future."

Moultrie waved a hand toward the south and in the general direction of the surrounding swamps. "As for our position here, we are vexed by dry swamps. The drought of the past weeks has made passage through this area easier for the enemy should they decide to come north. Defending this bridge will not be easy.

"Then we have the Tulifinny River just up the road. That's another difficult-to-defend bridge. I have John Laurens and his men patrolling, though we disagree about burning the houses along the riverbanks. I think we should burn them, but John disagrees. Welcome to the challenges of command, Major."

Will smiled, "I can see the difficulties, Sir."

"Indeed. I must get back to the tasks at hand. Be sure to see the quartermaster about billets for your men and to get some food. My regards to Lieutenant Colonel Marion. Again, I hope to serve with you."

~~<>~~

Francis Marion hurried across the central parade ground in the middle of Fort Moultrie and extended his hand. "*Major* Yelverton, is it now? I'm delighted to see you."

Will smiled as he shook Marion's hand. "It is good to see you, too, Sir. I have a letter from General Lincoln."

Marion nodded, "Please come into my office."

Turning to his adjutant, Marion said, "See to the new troops and have their lieutenant come to see me after they are settled."

In Marion's sparsely furnished office, Marion said, "Coffee? Tea? Something stronger? As you know, I don't drink much in the way of spirits, but I can offer you a taste."

Will said, "Coffee is fine, Sir."

They sat in companionable silence as Marion read Lincoln's letter. Several times he glanced up at Will.

"So, since I last saw you, it appears you accepted Elbert's offer of a commission and distinguished yourself in the field both as a soldier and a leader. Says here you saved Ashe."

"I'm not sure I saved General Ashe, Sir, so much as followed him across the Savannah."

"Ha, Ashe is not the sharpest knife, and I suspect he would lay dead along with his command had it not been for you, Sir."

Will said nothing.

Marion went on, "I'm glad they assigned you to 2nd South Carolina. We're tasked with a critical mission to protect the approaches to Charlestown. You know this fort defended against Clinton and Parker in '76?"

"Aye, Sir. You think they'll try to force the harbor again?"

"I was here for the fight in '76. They'll think twice about coming past here again. But there are rumors of a potential fleet from the north coming this way. There are always such rumors, but we remain vigilant."

Will said, "I'm delighted to be here, Sir. I hope to learn field command from you."

"Lincoln says he's put you in for promotion to Lieutenant Colonel. Says you're command material, and I agree. Lincoln's written to Washington. You're acquainted with General Washington, correct?"

"Aye, Sir. I had the honor of acting as a courier for General Washington at Brandywine."

Marion smiled, "Well, I would guess George Washington will be only too happy to forward your recommendation. If asked, I'll be happy to add my endorsement."

"Thank you, Sir."

~~<>~~

Will checked in with Cuthbert to make sure he had good quarters and had eaten.

"Aye, Sir. I've got a good bunk in the barracks, and the horses are stabled. Molly is well taken care of, too."

Will grinned, "Good, thanks. I'll go see her, and I got a couple of carrots from the mess."

Will was good to his word and went to see Molly. Her brown coat gleamed where the stable hand had curried her. She had plenty of hay, and the stable was clean. Will smiled, and Molly nodded and whickered. Will offered her a carrot which was quickly gone. She chuffed and nuzzled Will as he stroked her muzzle. Will slipped the second carrot out of his pocket. If a horse could laugh, Molly would have giggled. Instead, she delicately took the carrot and crunched it contentedly.

Will walked into his room. As a field grade officer, Will was afforded a slightly larger room with a bed, small wardrobe, and washstand. He also had a small window that allowed for a breath of air. He was tired but not as exhausted as he had been after Brier Creek. He flopped on the bed and took inventory.

He was doing as well as could be expected, he decided. He was still shaking, but being at Moultrie offered a respite from the constant riding, fighting, and death of the past weeks. His heart was heavy about Abby, but he also felt right about having taken Zeke Carter out of the middle of certain death at Brier Creek. Abby was firmly in the past, and he was near Charlestown. Maybe he would get a chance to see Mary and continue their relationship.

Marion's adjutant tapped on Will's door, "Colonel Marion's compliments, Sir. He asks if you would like to accompany him to a gathering at Governor Rutledge's home in the city."

"Will said, "Absolutely! When shall we leave?"

"You must leave today and plan to stay at McCrady's Tavern. The gathering of the State's finest is tomorrow evening."

"Very well, I am delighted to join him and am at the Colonel's disposal."

~~<>~~

Marion nodded at Molly, "New horse?"

"No, Sir. This is Molly. She's been my horse for nearly five years, but she was resting in Georgia when last we met. I since collected her and have put her through quite a hard few months."

"Nice looking animal."

They trotted along in companionable silence. Behind them rode an escort of six troopers as well as Cuthbert and Marion's orderly. The escort was necessary because of the potential for loyalist militia patrols and the threat of bandits, a threat that had only increased in recent months.

Will and Lt Colonel Francis Marion trotted up to McCrady's Tavern in the still-bustling city of Charlestown. McCrady's was on East Bay Street, and fresh air from the Bay kept the residents cool. Will fondly recalled his stay last year. It was at McCrady's that Colonel Marion had introduced Will to books and where Will sat in the sunshine puzzling over the meaning of Homer's words in *The Odyssey*. He was still puzzled over those words, and *The Odyssey* still rode in his saddle bag.

~~<>~~

Lieutenant Colonel Francis Marion and Major William Branch Yelverton promptly presented themselves at Governor John Rutledge's home on Broad Street at 7 p.m. Elizabeth Rutledge welcomed them. She was gracious with a round face that betrayed being well-fed. Her skin was luminous, her eyes lively, and Will thought her a wonderful match for a politician.

They were on time, but the gathering was already in full swing, with the Governor squiring attractive women around the room. Continental and Militia officers chatted over glasses of punch. A few politicians were in the mix. Lieutenant Colonel Marion pointed out a couple of the notables: Rutledge's lieutenant governor, Mr. Christopher Gadsden, and Mr. Rawlins Lowndes, who was Rutledge's immediate predecessor. Marion confided that Lowndes had opposed armed rebellion. There were several others – Legare family members, Coopers, Rhetts, Somersalls, and Middletons.

Will was dazzled at being in such a rarified company. These were among the top merchants and planters of South Carolina. True, Will had grown up on his family's plantation, but the people at this gathering would have seen Will's people as mere farmers and not quite of the same planter class.

A string quartet played a minuet, and several couples danced. Will thought it looked silly. He rather liked reels and other country dances. He wryly reflected, *"But I am, to these people, a bumpkin."*

Will's heart skipped a beat when he spotted Eliza Young Wilkinson and Mary Proctor across the room. As soon as he could, he moved across the room to where the two ladies stood.

~~<>~~

Eliza Wilkinson flicked her fan closed and used it to tap her left cheek. "Major Yelverton!"

"Hello, Mrs. Wilkinson. You are looking lovely this fine evening." And she did look lovely. Her gown was a splash of crimson with cream petticoats topped off with a cream kerchief. These colors complimented her skin tones.

Mary Proctor had been facing away, but at the sound of Will's voice, she spun, and her face lit up. "Were you not going to say hello to me, as well?"

"I was going to say hello to you especially, Miss Proctor."

Mary blushed and batted her eyes, her fan fluttering near her lips. "Aren't we being formal?"

"'Tis a formal gathering," said Will.

"You mock me, Sir." Mary's face looked fierce, set against an emerald-colored gown with a cream kerchief similar to Eliza's.

"Never."

She softened, "When did you get to town?"

Will explained, "I am now assigned to the 2nd South Carolina Regiment at Fort Moultrie. Colonel Marion and I rode in late yesterday. We are at McCrady's. I have been hoping both of you lovely ladies would be at this gathering. My wish has come true."

Eliza said, "Gallant as ever. Tell us about your adventures since we last saw you."

Will said, "Ah, well, not much to tell."

Eliza said, "Harrumph! I think there's plenty. I have spies who say you are continuing to be quite the hero. And to think that I thought you a coward when we first met."

Will blushed and looked around the room.

Mary said, "Your uniform has evidence of fighting and bloody fighting at that."

"Aye, fortunately, the blood is not mine. My orderly has done everything he can to make me presentable."

Eliza said, "I hope 'tis the blood of the enemy and plenty of it!"

Mary said, "I doubt there's another man here with enemy blood on his breeches. These are mostly garrison soldiers."

Will smirked, "I'm a garrison soldier now."

Eliza said, "Not for long, I'll own. Oh, look! There's Mrs. Rutledge. I must pay my respects."

As Eliza bustled off to speak with Elizabeth Rutledge, Mary quietly said, "I have missed you terribly, Will Yelverton."

"You are too kind, Miss Mary. It is I who have missed you."

"Have you really?"

"Oh, yes. Many a time, I found myself thinking of you. I hope you have been well."

"I have been well but lonely. Not to be indelicate, but when you went to North Carolina all those months ago, it was in search of your lady, Abby."

"Yes, I was. When I arrived, I learned that Abby thought me dead. None of my letters arrived, and not wishing to be a spinster, she married. She was with child. I'm sure the child has been born by now. I wish her happiness."

Mary looked at him hard, pink spots on her cheeks flaming up. "You have no regrets?"

Will smiled a sad smile, "We all have regrets, Miss Mary. But, no, I am now content. I hope to move ahead with my life."

A small smile flickered, and the pink color in her cheeks began to diminish. Mary asked, "You said you are at McCrady's?"

"Aye."

"Why did you not call upon us? My father would be thrilled to host you and Colonel Marion."

"I did not know you were in town and did not wish to seem presumptuous."

Mary gave him a very meaningful look, "Please consider coming to stay at our home."

Will smiled, "I shall convince Colonel Marion." His loins stirred, and he realized his loneliness after Abby was also rooted in his youthful need for release.

~~<>~~

Will and Marion presented themselves at Homer Proctor's townhome door the following morning at 10 a.m. They were met by the butler, who ushered them into the first-floor parlor, where Mr. Proctor welcomed them and formally invited them to stay for as long as they wanted.

Homer Proctor was a solid Patriot and owner of several plantations. His financial contributions to the Revolution were well-known, and his support of the troops in the form of food and produce was invaluable. Proctor asked if they had horses and servants and instructed the butler to afford them accommodations.

Soon, Will was sitting in the sun in Proctor's garden, his copy of *The Odyssey* on his lap. This was the most relaxed he had been in several months. His hands still shook, but it was diminishing.

Mary's soft voice interrupted his reverie. "What are you thinking? Why are you looking at your hand?"

Will got to his feet, "Hello, Miss Mary."

"You didn't answer my question."

"Ah, I was just thinking that this is the most relaxed and calm I have been in months."

"And what causes this calm?"

Will smiled, "'Tis hard to say ... perhaps the proximity of a lovely dark-haired woman?"

Mary lowered her eyes, "Eliza is not here just at the moment."

Will looked at Mary with level eyes, "T'was not Eliza about whom I spoke."

"Ah, then who might it be?"

"I think you know."

"I would like to hear it, still."

Will gave in to the game, "Then, of course, 'tis you, my lovely lady."

"Just so." Mary pursued her earlier query, "And your hand? Why were you looking at it so intently?"

Will shrugged.

Will and Mary enjoyed a sunny walk along the bay, and Will noticed that there were still small ships and boats in the harbor. A couple of larger ships were present, a surprise with the increasingly active British naval presence offshore. Privateers abounded, and shipments by sea were always at risk.

Will kept his hands behind his back as much as possible. He found clasping them together helped keep the shaking from being so obvious.

The afternoon quietly slipped into evening, and soon the Proctor family and guests gathered for supper. It was dusk, and Will hoped his hands were not as visible in the penumbra.

Supper was pleasant: a pork roast with potatoes and some greens. Will was happy to eat food that was not cooked in a large vat with water that had twigs floating in it and handfuls of salt as the only condiment.

The company was excellent, as well. Homer Proctor was intensely interested in the fight in Georgia's backcountry, and Will did his best to relate the fight at Kettle Creek. He left out the worst details of Brier Creek. He noticed that his stomach quivered when he talked of Brier Creek. He kept his palsied hands under the table.

~~<>~~

Midnight or very near it. Will had washed and stood at his window wearing only his long shirt. He breathed in the salt air of Charlestown. It was late, and Will wondered if Mary would come as she had before. The quiet of the night encouraged reflection; the humidity wrapped its arms around Will, and his flesh stirred when a cool breeze huffed.

A slight change in the draft caused Will to turn. There, closing the door quietly behind her, was Mary Proctor. The candle guttered with the freshened breeze, and its soft, flickering light hinted at Mary's ripe body beneath the bedgown. The diaphanous cloth was the only garment she wore.

She turned and stepped into the full light of the candle. She stood hipshot, hands on hips. Her body was a question: "Do you like? Do you want?"

Will wanted to scream, "Yes! Yes, I want!" Instead, he padded across the room and took her in his arms. He kissed her – hard.

Mary's lips parted as she uttered unintelligible words, "Uh, uh. My God, uh....uhhhhhhhha." She shivered against him, and he felt her convulse. His erection throbbed against the rough cloth of his nightshirt. Her hot breath caressed his throat. His blood thundered in his ears.

He bent and grasped her bedgown at the hem and, in one motion, pulled it up over her head and tossed it aside. Her perfect body, animated by the flicker of the candle, alternated between hidden and revealed. She was beautiful, just as he remembered.

He knelt and kissed her belly, and she involuntarily gasped as her muscles under his kiss involuntarily quivered. Will ran his hand up her inner thigh and discovered that she was drenched. He ran his hands over her buttocks, and she shivered. He stood, pulled his shirt over his head, and took her to the bed where, without preliminaries, they were joined.

She whimpered, suppressing a scream of sexual excess, and spasmed under him. Will tried to remember the lessons of restraint he had learned with Frances Montravalle all those months ago in Philadelphia. Think of other things ... relax ... allow things to calm. These techniques were to no avail as he erupted in a tidal wave. His buttocks were so tight it hurt, and it was all he could do not to cry out in full throat.

Will's voice quavered as he whispered in Mary's ear, "My God!"

She said, "My God, indeed, Will Yelverton. You slay me, Sir."

"You seem quite well to me, but I shall endeavor to slay you again ... momentarily."

Mary laughed a deep, satisfying rumble.

Deep into the night, with yet another frenzied activity behind them, their breathing slowed. Heartbeats no longer galloped. Their heads buzzed with a soft afterglow, and Mary took his trembling hand and kissed it. She pressed his fingers to her chest and stroked the back of his hand.

Mary quietly said, "When you're ready, you can tell me all about it. Maybe then the shaking will stop."

Chapter 5 – Mary

Lt. Colonel Marion pulled Will aside on the third day of their visit.

"Must get back, old boy. Why don't you take a few days to rest here with these good people?"

Will started to protest, but Marion said, "Consider it an order. You need to rest. I need you to work out the shakes, Will."

"But, Sir, I ..."

"I shook like that for a month after the Battle at Sullivan's Island in '76. Getting bombarded senseless or having your friends slaughtered will do that to you. Come back out to Moultrie next week, and we'll do some training with the troops."

"Very well, Sir. And thank you."

~~<>~~

The next few days were wonderful moments of playing hooky. Will finally admitted he needed the rest. Needed the time for something that seemed like normal life to return.

He still shook, but it was getting better. He slowly stopped jumping like a startled cat when someone spoke.

Will and Mary took long walks along the shore of the bay. They talked of not much and then everything. In the night, Mary came to him and set him afire.

On Friday, they sat in the garden. It was after dinner, as the mid-day meal was called, and the early April sun was warm. Will was trying to read *The Odyssey* but getting nowhere. His head buzzed with the need for sleep. The food weighed heavily on his stomach, and the nights with Mary left him whipped, but in a good way.

Mary asked, "When the war is over, what will you do?"

"I had plans to go to the frontier and open a gunshop. My brother will inherit most of the family's North Carolina plantations. There are two holdings close together."

"Did you not want to be a planter?"

"I inherited a very nice farm from my Aunt and Uncle last year, but I sold it because there's nothing there for me. I'm not a farmer. I also will inherit my former master's gunsmith business and property when Miss Becky, my master's wife, passes on. They had a son, but he died in an unfortunate accident."

"Oh, how terrible!"

"'Tis a long story. His name was Isiah, and he was insanely jealous of me for no reason. He was, and I'm being kind to the dead, a worthless lout. Mr. Bert and Miss Becky made the decision to leave the farm, the livestock, and the gunshop to me, and that infuriated Isiah. They knew he would run the place into the ground in no time. Isiah attacked me in the stable with a loaded musket which went off and killed him instantly. Fortunately for me, Mr. Bert was present, and no one accused me of killing Isiah."

"Oh, my. You never told me of this before!"

"'Twas not the first time someone has tried to kill me."

Mary swallowed hard, "Oh ..."

Will said, "I've had a dream of living on the frontier, fixing people's guns, having a good life. Of course, 'tis dangerous on the frontier."

Mary's eyes looked into the distance, "I suppose so."

"I imagine you would find it unpleasant to live in a rustic cabin near the mountains."

"I hear the mountains are beautiful."

"So I've been told. The closest I've come is North Georgia, and we were in such a rush to get ahead of Boyd and his men that I didn't really look beyond what was right in front of us. But I did get the impression of lush hills and long vistas."

"I might like to see the mountains if you were there, Will."

~~<>~~

Saturday morning. A tired Will Yelverton walked downstairs to a very pleasant breakfast of eggs, ham, some greens, and coffee.

He was just finishing when Mary came in. She had dark circles under her eyes.

"I must head back to the fort tomorrow. I think Colonel Marion is planning training for the coming week."

Mary sighed, "Oh, yes. I suppose so. I wish you could stay."

Will glanced around to assure they were alone, "I should think you need me gone so you can rest."

Mary leered at him and half-whispered, "Hush!"

~~<>~~

Will and Mary walked along the Bay. The day was brisk, as some days in April are. Will noticed some flowers beginning to bloom. Dogwoods were in full bud, with sprays of green along the branches. Soon there would be a profusion of azaleas and white dogwood flowers, as only the South in spring can deliver.

Will quietly asked, "Shall I talk to your father?"

Mary stopped dead still. "What?!"

"Shall I talk to your father? Would you be amenable to life on the frontier?"

"If you were there."

"Then, shall I speak with your father?"

Mary tottered over to a low wall fronting the water. She sat hard and rocked back and forth momentarily, her hands on her knees. "Of course."

Will said, "I cannot promise not to die in this war."

"I know that. Several of my friends have lost husbands to either disease or to the British. Either way, they're quite dead. Eliza is one. Her husband and then her baby both passed away from a fever, and now she's a widow. Better a widow than a spinster."

"The frontier is hard, I hear."

"Of course, it is. But do you not think we're capable?"

"Aye. But 'twon't be the life you live here."

"I may surprise you, Will Yelverton."

~~<>~~

Homer Proctor sat behind his desk and steepled his fingers. "You are a fine young man, Mr. Yelverton. I must ask, how will you provide for my daughter?"

Will had anticipated this question and explained about his inheritances, provided Mr. Proctor with his letter of introduction, as well as his letter of credit, from Governor Caswell. Caswell's letter attested that Will owned over $800 in Spanish coins, a small fortune in these days of rampant inflation.

He also provided Caswell's letter of introduction to John Sevier of the over-mountain area of Western North Carolina. Also called Tennessee, that frontier was bustling with settlers, and Sevier was their leader. Moreover, Caswell and Sevier were investors in the land, and Will would be able to invest in land as a friend of Caswell. His future was bright.

Homer smiled, "For a young man, you have means. Not rich by any stretch, but quite an impressive stake. You know that Mary has expensive tastes?"

"Aye, Sir, I do. She understands that the frontier will not be easy."

"That, young Sir, is an understatement. But, of my seven children, Mary is the one who will survive anywhere. I knew she had picked you out last year when you visited. I predicted this outcome then. And, my boy, even then, I thought it would be highly acceptable. Welcome to the family."

"Thank you, Sir. You're sure you don't have a problem with a son-in-law with gun grease under his fingernails?"

"No. The gentry hereabouts looks down on people who work for a living. They are willing to let others fight their war over taxes, slaves, and commerce. But they will soon learn that everyone bears the costs. I fear the British will entice our slaves to revolt, and that will crush the planter class. When we win this fight, as I believe we must, there will necessarily be taxes to pay. That won't sit well either, but there it is."

Homer continued, "These old-money planters look down on me and mine because we are also merchants. So, you'll be joining a family that's seen as 'second' anyhow. And I couldn't give a damn if you have dirty hands from working. 'Tis honorable."

Will grinned. "Very well, Sir. I care not what people think but did not want to cause you discomfort."

Homer Proctor grinned, "Funny, I don't really care what they think, either."

Will liked Homer Proctor immensely.

~~<>~~

Mary rested her head on Will's shoulder. Tonight, their lovemaking was less frantic and more contemplative. Will attended to Mary in ways he knew would satisfy her and leave her limp.

She said, "We shall be happy, Will."

"I know that."

She said, "Alas, these days, with the war, our wedding will be something of a quiet affair."

Will said, "Aye, but all I care about is that the day is happy for you."

Mary reflected, "Are you sure that three weeks from now is acceptable? April 24th?"

"Of course, my darling. I'm sure Colonel Marion will be happy for us to have a few days, and he'll provide an honor guard. He will be pleased to be my best man for the service, I'm sure."

Chapter 6 – Vows

April 24th dawned beautiful and clear. Charlestown's air was swept clean by a fresh breeze, and Will felt very good. Today he would marry Mary Proctor and begin setting his future on track.

Will hoped the war would end soon. Perhaps a decisive victory over the British would end the fighting, and his life might get back on track. He silently dreamed that he and Mary would go to the frontier, find a good piece of land, and create a future where they might raise their children to be strong, independent, and good.

The war was sure to continue for the immediate future, and Will was committed to winning it. Will was now a believer in the imperative of liberty and independence from Great Britain. He also knew that he was committed because of Noah Harris's death and the capture and imprisonment of Colonel Samuel Elbert. These wrongs must be righted. Will was an absolute believer.

The banns had been read in St Michael's Church at the corner of Broad and Meeting Streets. Homer's influence had pushed up the schedule for the reading of the banns, forcing it into the bare minimum of three weeks. That and the war drove the hurried reading of the banns before the congregation. The banns having been read, today was the day of the actual ceremony, and Will and Mary would become husband and wife.

Will was jittery. He smiled to himself that he had not yet been scared going into battle, but today he was deeply concerned about whether he would do well. It was a fear he had never felt.

Will knew he loved Mary. Not like he loved Abby. No, no one would ever touch his soul as Abby had. But life must move on. And Mary occupied his thoughts and his soul. He was content that he honestly did love Mary.

So, Will Yelverton, Major, Continental Army of the United States, marched resolutely into St Michael's Church and, with his friend and commander Lieutenant Colonel Francis Marion at his side, repeated the vows before God and became husband to Mary Proctor.

The April sun was bright. His darling, who had made her interest clear from day one of their association, was now his wife. For the moment, nothing could put a shadow on the day.

That night, as far as everyone else knew, they slept together for the first time. But for Will and Mary, the lovemaking was even more powerful than it had been. It signaled commitment, love, promise, sharing, and true intimacy. Sated, Mary wept quiet tears. Will slept the sleep of a contented man.

Will's hands no longer shook.

Chapter 7 – Threat

Lieutenant Colonel Marion received a message that General Lincoln had pulled north from Purysburg, heading toward Augusta. Marion said Lincoln was going to cross the Savannah River and move toward Savannah. The next morning, Francis Marion returned to Fort Moultrie.

As he mounted his horse, Marion said, "Enjoy a few days with your new bride, Will. Then, come back to the fort. We shall soon be quite occupied. I believe Lincoln's move will provoke the British. More likely, they'll see an opportunity and come north. I think Lincoln has unwittingly opened the door to South Carolina."

~~<>~~

Will and Mary enjoyed two days of quiet, wedded bliss. But on the third day, a rider from Fort Moultrie brought the message that the British had crossed the Savannah River and were marching north toward Charlestown. Lincoln's move toward Augusta had, indeed, had the effect of opening the door to South Carolina's low country.

Will sent a servant to tell Cuthbert to get ready to ride. Will quickly packed his saddlebags and hurried to the carriage house and stables to get Molly. Cuthbert was already there.

"Saddle your horse, Cuth. I'll saddle Molly. Best load our weapons, too. Colonel Marion was right; the British have crossed the Savannah and are coming north."

Cuth said, "Aye, sir. Are you loading buck and ball?"

"Aye. Never know what we'll run into on the road to Sullivan's Island."

Will took an apple from his pocket and held it out for Molly. She crunched happily while Will put her blanket and saddle on.

Will brought his rifles, his English dragoon carbine, his Brander pistol, and the ancient horse pistol that rode on Molly's saddle. He quickly ran a swab down each gun's bore, making sure they were clean and unloaded. Then, he set about loading each weapon.

First, he loaded the Brander and the carbine with a slightly heavier powder charge and the .62 caliber ball mixed with a few swan shot. The ball was deadly, but should the ball miss, the swan shot would shred flesh. The horse pistol was next to get a load of buck and ball. The pistols and the carbine were close-in weapons.

Next, Will loaded his older rifle that he made from parts when he was apprenticed to Mr. Bert Koontz. The .45 caliber rifle was highly accurate, and Will had carried it everywhere for the past five years. He carefully measured the powder and selected a ball that was as perfectly round as he could find. The ball, at .45 of an inch in diameter, was smaller than the carbine and pistol rounds, but it would pack a punch at quite a range.

Will had killed game – and men – with it at ranges over 200 yards. He carefully rammed the ball, wrapped in a thin piece of deer hide, down the rifled bore. It was difficult, because the edges of the rifling – the grooves in the barrel – bit into the ball. He left the priming pan uncharged.

Then, he drew Josie from her soft deer hide scabbard. Josie, Will's .40 caliber hand-made long rifle, rode in the soft deer hide scabbard that Abby Kennedy had made especially for Will. Will and Mr. Alexander Kennedy hand-forged the barrel and worked the tiger-maple stock to a fine gloss. The work took the better part of a year, but the outcome was brilliant.

Will had picked Josie as the name for the rifle, and Josie was Will's presentation masterpiece. He didn't know why the rifle was Josie, it just was. A masterpiece like Josie was required of a gunsmith to earn the master designation, and Kennedy had been excited to confer the master on Will. The initials WYB were engraved on a small piece of coin silver inlaid on the stock. The Y was slightly larger than W and B – they stood for William

Branch Yelverton. Will smiled at the thought of the future, *Perhaps 250 years from now, someone might see these initials and wonder who I was.*

Will carefully measured the special powder he carried for Josie. Again, he found the perfect .40 caliber ball and wrapped it in the finest deer hide to ram it gently down Josie's bore. As with his .45 rifle, Will left off priming Josie. No sense in having fouled priming or an accident.

Will looked up from his intense concentration to see Mary standing at the door of the stable. Her brows were knit together, and her eyes were wide.

"Are you leaving?"

"Yes, Sweetheart. The British have come across the Savannah and are on the march north. I must go immediately back to the fort. I know not what will happen next."

Mary's cheeks flushed and her mouth made a perfect O. She turned and hurried into the house.

Will put his weapons on Molly, patted her neck, and said to Cuthbert, "I have to go change into my uniform and console Mary. I'll be down in a few minutes."

Cuthbert looked up from ramming a cartridge down the bore of his musket. "I'll be ready to go, Sir."

~~<>~~

Will walked into the bedroom to find Mary lying on the bed. She was curled into a ball, and she snuffled into a handkerchief. Her shoulders shook.

Will sat on the edge of the bed and stroked her hair. "Now, darling. You knew this was bound to happen."

Mary wiped her eyes. "Yes, but I had hoped we would have time to say goodbye."

Will said, "This is just a brief parting. I think that this British incursion may be just a probe. I do not know what this will bring. I do know that Fort Moultrie must be manned against a naval invasion."

Mary nodded, her face red from crying. "I must look a mess."

"No, my love. You look beautiful as ever."

Mary sat up and flung her arms around Will. "Do you have to leave this very minute?"

"I must first change into my uniform."

Mary had a sly grin. In a shy little voice, she asked, "Then, you will, of course, have to disrobe?"

Will smiled, "Of course, I will."

Mary ran her hand across his cheek, "Should I leave so you can have privacy?"

~~<>~~

An hour later, Will and Cuthbert mounted their horses. Mary stood in the courtyard doorway of the Proctor townhouse, her face pink from exertion.

Mary said, "You both look so fierce!"

And they did. Will's officer's sword hung from the left side of his saddle. His .45 rifle and Josie rode in their scabbards on the right side of Molly's saddle, close to hand. The horse pistol was in its leather bucket holster on the right side of Molly's saddle. Will wore crossed belts over his shoulders. One was a white baldric modified to accept Uncle Ewan's Scottish dirk on Will's left. The other carried Will's shot pouch and powder horns on the right. The Brander pistol was tucked into Will's belt, and he carried the English dragoon carbine in his right hand, its butt resting on his right thigh. He was, indeed, fierce.

Cuthbert was similarly equipped. He did not have long-range rifles, but he had an English fusil in his hand and a French-made Charleville musket in a scabbard. The fusil was a shortened officer's musket. A pistol was tucked in his belt and a razor-sharp, thick-bladed English dragoon's saber hung from a baldric on his left side.

Will said, "I will be back as soon as I can. I will send letters as often as I can."

Mary ran down the six steps to the yard. She threw her arms around his right leg and pressed her cheek against his boot. "You better come back to me in one piece."

Letting go of Will's leg, she turned to Cuthbert. "Cuth, don't you dare let him do anything dangerous."

Cuthbert grinned, "I'll do my best, but the Major is quite uncontrollable."

"That's why I asked you to keep him out of trouble."

Cuth swept his hat from his head and bowed from the saddle, "Depend upon me, My Lady."

Will smiled and said, "Adieu, my darling,"

He nudged Molly with his knees, and she trotted out of the courtyard and onto East Bay Street. Molly turned left, instinctively heading toward Hibben's Ferry.

~~<>~~

Will and Cuthbert trotted along the heavily traveled dirt street to the ferry landing at the hard beach off Market Street near Mr. Charles Pinckney's magnificent home. They paid the fare of 62 and ½ cents each for man and horse and waited. Soon, the flat-bottomed ferry arrived, skidding to a stop as it beached. The ferry was a horse boat instead of the large canoes for passengers without horses or livestock. It had a flat ramp on each end, and Will and Cuthbert walked their horses aboard and down the three feet into the flat-bottomed hull.

After her unpleasant two weeks in the hold of *The Beatrice*, Molly did not like boats. She tossed her head and rolled her eyes at Will. Her sad face begged for the solace of dry land. Will patted her neck, "Easy, girl, we haven't even pulled off the sand yet."

Molly stamped her hoof and nodded. She chuffed and made a distressed sound. Will played his trump card. He offered Molly a juicy apple. She took the apple with an eye roll of trepidation. Will talked to her quietly in gentle tones as the boat shoved off and bobbed in the light swell of the harbor. Molly caught her balance and settled down as the crew of four slaves began to row. They set a steady rhythm that would soon eat up the nearly two miles of water between Charlestown and Haddrell's Point on the other side of the Cooper River.

He drew in the slightly chilly late-April wind on the water. Soon it would be May, and sweat would flow down woolen-clad backs. But today, it was pleasant, maybe even cold. Will planted his feet like he had learned aboard *The Beatrice* and looked across the water to see Castle Pinckney on Shuts Folly Island.

He idly wondered why it was called Shuts Folly. He thought, *"Alas, I probably will never learn the answer to that riddle."*

Will and Cuthbert trotted away from the ferry landing at Haddrell's Point on the East side of the Cooper River. They turned east and trotted along in companionable silence. Just ahead was a collection of houses and a couple of wharves – Mount Pleasant. Will thought the little settlement lived up to its name.

The road from Mount Pleasant to The Cove, before Sullivan's Island, was isolated scrub and dune land. Perfect for a bandit ambush. Will primed the carbine and both pistols. Cuthbert followed suit, and they separated slightly so that they rode about five feet abreast, with Cuth slightly behind and to the left. This left a clear field of fire for each man, with Cuthbert having to be careful because Will was to his front. The distance was not more than a mile, but Will was cautious.

Will and Cuth trotted along, with Will looking in all directions for any suggestion of a possible ambush. Cuth kept a lookout to the rear. They did not rush because rushing could mean getting into the midst of bandits before recognizing any indications of trouble. No, best to proceed with caution.

Will watched the seabirds. Seagulls floated lazily on the wind. A great blue heron angled into the wind, dropped its feet, and flared its wings to land delicately near the water's edge. Will watched as the heron quietly searched the shallow water. In a burst of motion, the heron darted its needle-pointed bill into the water and emerged with a fish. The fish flapped frantically, but in seconds the heron had turned the fish and swallowed it headfirst.

Will thought, *"We must become better soldiers. The British are like that heron, and we are but minnows."*

Half an hour later, Will and Cuthbert rode down the causeway, clopped across the pontoon bridge onto Sullivan's Island, and hailed the fort. The sentries recognized both Will and Cuthbert and waved them through into the parade.

~~<>~~

Francis Marion stepped out of his office. "Welcome back, Will. You look good."

"I feel good, Sir." Will lowered his voice, "The shakes are gone, too."

"Good. Now, don't get comfortable. I want you to ride to Moultrie and ascertain the situation. It's not a liaison. Rather, I want you to observe Moultrie and Laurens' command methods and absorb them. Lincoln's letter recognized your leadership and natural abilities. It directed that I be sure you are trained so that when you are promoted, you will be prepared in the military arts."

Will nodded. "Aye, Sir. I'll get the rest of my things together and leave right away."

Marion said, "First thing in the morning will be fine. Get an escort of ten men. Maybe that young lieutenant Legare? I'll give you a letter to Moultrie."

Chapter 8 – Coosawhatchee

Molly was excited at the preparations. She knew she would be on the road again. She pranced a little and tossed her head. Her ears twitched and constantly turned to hear every sound. Will gave her a carrot he had filched from the fort's mess.

While Molly crunched the carrot, Will tightened the saddle girth so it was comfortable but snug. He also checked the mountings for the rifle scabbards, his sword, and the horse pistol. Will primed all the weapons this time and made certain the lock covers were in place to prevent moisture from dampening the primer powder. Will checked the straps that held his bedroll and saddlebags. His water bottle was full, and the fire starter kit he always carried was in place. Lastly, he drew Uncle Ewan's Scottish dirk and checked the edge. The dirk was an heirloom, outlawed in Scotland but smuggled to North Carolina with the many Highlanders who were pushed there after Culloden. The age-old blade was now entrusted to Will. He was ready.

It was still dark when Will, Cuthbert, Lieutenant Legare, and his ten troops mounted and trotted out the gate at Fort Moultrie. With Legare on his left, Will led the small band across the pontoon bridge and down the spit of land to Mount Pleasant and onward to Hibben's Ferry.

The ferryman looked Will and the troops over and asked, "Weren't you just here, Sir?"

Will said, "Aye, heading back."

The ferryman accepted this noncommittal response. "There's no charge for a military unit, Sir, but it'll take me two trips to get everyone across."

~~<>~~

Will walked Molly off the ferry first and stood on the sand. Legare had remained with the second group.

"Cuth, you're in charge of these troops. Don't let them wander. I will ride quickly to Mary's and bid her farewell."

Cuth grinned. "Tell her I sent you."

Will smirked, "She'll never believe that!"

In the near distance, the church bell at St Mathew's struck six. Will said, "I'll be back in two hours. It'll be that long for the boat to go back and forth."

~~<>~~

A rather worn-looking Major Will Yelverton trotted up to the ferry landing. St Mathews' bell was striking eight, and the troops were just disembarking from the ferry. Will turned to

78

Legare and said, "Let's water the horses and let the men stretch a minute. Then we'll be off."

Soon, the small band of Continentals, their horse furniture jingling, rode up the Charlestown Neck and trotted toward the Ashley River Ferry. Toward 10 am, the detachment arrived at Stoney Point, a low-lying phosphate rock outcropping that formed the Northeast landing of the Ashley River Ferry.

Will saw the ferry boat on the other side of the river, some 100 yards away. Several black men, almost certainly slaves, pulled the rope to move the ferryboat across the water. The boat was a wide, flat craft with ramps like other ferries Will had ridden. As with Hibben's Ferry, the Ashley River Ferry accommodated half the troops.

Will and Cuthbert rested their horses on the Southwest bank of the river while the boat brought the second contingent of men and horses across. Ashely Ferry Town was a thriving little berg with a tavern. Will learned that the town on the other side of the road was called St Andrew's Town. He thought, *"I'll never learn why the whole area has two names."*

Will and Cuth tied up their horses next to the Ferry House Tavern's trough and bought hay for the detachment horses. The detachment went into the tavern and ate some stew with fresh ale. Not the greatest food Will had ever eaten, but it would be better than the camp fare that awaited. Mr. Legge, the proprietor, accepted a warrant for the food.

Soon, they were on the King's Road. If the weather held, they would be halfway to the Tullifiny Bridge by nightfall. No reason to believe the weather would go bad, either. The dusty road attested that the drought of the past weeks continued. Will was glad he had water in his bottle.

He asked Legare, "Do your men have full water bottles?"

"Aye, Sir. We also brought jerky and some cornmeal. I know that General Moultrie's camp will have food, but 'tis a good idea to be prepared."

"Cuthbert packed us some of the same. I always carry a fire-starting kit and a waterproof bedroll. I've spent some miserable nights in the cold and wet, but the woolen blankets and oilskin have kept me warm and dry."

~~<>~~

The next afternoon, Will reported to General Moultrie.

"Back so soon?"

"Aye, Sir. I have a letter from Colonel Marion."

Moultrie scanned the letter. "So, he wants you to observe command, eh? Well, you'll get your chance these first fine days of May. We have reports that General Augustine Prevost is just a few miles from here, marching north with 2,400 troops. He obviously means to take Charlestown. I believe you are familiar with the good general's younger brother, Lieutenant Colonel Marc Prevost?"

Will said, "Sir, I had the unfortunate experience of killing his horse at Midway."

"Killed his horse?"

"Aye, Sir. T'was a sad accident. I was aiming at Prevost when his horse shied and put its head in the way just as I touched the trigger."

"Pity about the horse."

Will's eyes were turned down as he replied, "Aye, and I observed him commanding the 71st Highlanders in slaughtering our people at Brier Creek."

Moultrie stared into the distance, not really seeing anything. "His brother is no better. I regret to say that General Augustine Prevost is an excellent commander."

"I have heard that as well, Sir."

"I'm going to put you with Lieutenant Colonel John Laurens. Laurens is a dam' fine commander to observe. I've sent him forward to this side of the Coosawhatchie to relieve the small detachment I placed there to guard the river crossing. He has some 250 men of our 1,200. As you can immediately apprehend, we're outnumbered here two to one. The defensive value of the two rivers will be in our favor. Laurens is to remain on this side of the Coosawhatchie. After contact with Prevost's troops, he is to fall back and bring the 100 men of the crossing guard."

"Yes, Sir. I am briefly acquainted with Colonel Laurens. I had the pleasure of meeting him at Brandywine."

"Did you, now? Damn, Sir, but you do continually surprise."

Will smiled in self-deprecation. "I was trying to make my way through the American lines when General Washington gently conscripted me as a courier and scout. I had a horse, you see. Colonel Laurens was one of Washington's aides-de-camp."

"Ha! Well, General Washington can be most persuasive. You'll observe how Laurens places his troops and when he decides to fall back."

~~<>~~

Will and Cuthbert trotted down to Laurens' position. Lieutenant Legare and the other troopers were left with Moultrie.

Will remembered John Laurens as an affable man in his mid-20s. Not much older than Will, he had a pleasant face with the shadow of a heavy beard below expressive, intelligent eyes. No powder nor wig for Laurens, his dark hair was pulled back and tied with a simple ribbon. He affected a simple look that Will liked. But it belied the heart of a lion. Will recalled the Marquis de Lafayette saying that Laurens was somewhat reckless in battle. Will hoped this was no longer true.

Laurens looked up from a map he was studying. "I know you! You were a civilian at Brandywine. Now you're a major! I'm sure there's a story in all that."

"Aye, Sir, 'tis a pleasure to see you again," Will said as he handed a note from Moultrie to Laurens. "I shall be glad to tell the rather lengthy story when this business is over."

Laurens read quickly. "Observe, eh? Very well. But I see you're armed to the teeth. There's a story in that, too, I imagine."

Will nodded, "I've had a few scrapes."

Lauren's grinned, "Looks like you're about to have another. I think we shall see Prevost on the morrow."

~~<>~~

The morning sun dazzled as a pop of musket fire announced the arrival of Prevost's 2,400-man army. Skirmishers approached the Coosawhatchie Bridge in mid-morning. The brief, staccato exchanges of fire served as an alert to Moultrie's command.

The 100-man detachment of river guards had done their job of warning of the British approach. Moultrie gave Laurens the nod to retrieve the detachment. Moultrie sent a note saying to advance with 250 additional troops to guard the flanks and bring back the detachment.

Swinging into his saddle, Laurens grinned at Will. "This is going to be great fun, old boy."

Laurens nodded to his aide, Major John Barnwell, and waived to the troops that had quickly assembled. "Foooooorrrward!"

As the 250-man contingent stepped off, Will looked at Cuthbert with one eyebrow raised. Cuth smirked and looked the other way.

Laurens, his aide, Will, and Cuthbert trotted quietly down the road toward the little settlement of Coosawhatchie and its critically important bridge.

The distance was not far, and Laurens' light infantry covered the distance in short order. The small force arrived and quickly crossed the Coosawhatchie bridge before forming the line of battle.

Will quietly said to Cuthbert, "This will not go well. Laurens was ordered to bring the detachment back, not engage the enemy."

At that moment, British artillery opened fire. From the sound and the range, Will thought they were six-pounders, and the rate of fire suggested six guns. A second barrage of artillery ripped through the air, splintering trees, cutting brush, and killing two men. Laurens fell from his horse, landing with a hard thud. The horse collapsed, dead from artillery shrapnel. Laurens tried to stand and sagged against his dead horse. He looked around until he spotted Captain Thomas Shubrick.

"Maintain this position, Shu." Looking at Major Barnwell, Laurens said, "Go get medical help. We have wounded. I fear some are dead."

The artillery battery was some 250 yards away in a small clearing with trees on either side of the line of guns. Will could see a captain marching back and forth, commanding the battery as the disciplined British troops loaded the guns. Will reached down and drew out his .45 rifle. He primed the pan and set the trigger.

Will took careful aim at a sergeant who stood at rigid attention behind the second gun. He touched the trigger, and the sergeant looked down at his cross belts before sinking to his knees. The sergeant's arms sagged, then he flopped on his face.

Will returned the .45 rifle to its scabbard and drew Josie from her deer hide case. He primed her pan, set the trigger, and took aim at a gunner on the third gun. WizCraaaak! Josie thumped Will's shoulder, and the gunner died. His body flopped over the gun before sagging to the ground.

Pandemonium struck the artillery battery. Two men dead in less than 30 seconds, and the source was not clear. Certainly, no one from the Patriot lines could be firing accurately at this distance. Could they? The artillery stopped as men milled about, their discipline broken by the confusing circumstances.

Will calmly reloaded Josie. He primed the pan, set the trigger, and took aim at the one brave soul who continued to try to rally the gun crews. Perhaps a sergeant? Unknown, but that man joined the others in death, a .40 caliber ball lodged in his heart from at least 250 yards range.

Will put Josie back in her scabbard and looked to Laurens, whose face was gray with pain. John Laurens would live if an infection didn't kill him. The wound was shrapnel-torn skin in his shoulder. Will thought it must hurt terribly, and Laurens' face betrayed shock.

Will looked at Cuthbert, "We need to get him out of here."

Cuth nodded and swung off his horse. Will got down, and between the two of them, they got Laurens up and onto Cuth's horse. Will helped Cuth onto the horse behind Laurens and said, "I'll be right behind you."

Will looked around and found Captain Tom Shubrick. "Are you going to hold this position?"

Shubrick said, "Colonel Laurens left me in charge, and you, Sir, are an observer. Therefore, the decision is mine. I will withdraw, as the artillery will certainly start firing again soon. 'Twas amazing to watch your shooting, Sir. But I fear that was only a momentary respite."

Will said, "Aye, good decision, Captain."

~~<>~~

Moultrie was in a snit. "What the hell was that? Why in the world would anyone cross the river and set up a line in a less advantageous position?"

Will shrugged. So did Major John Barnwell, who said, "I have no idea what Colonel Laurens was thinking, Sir. Perhaps we crossed the bridge because skirmishers were coming forward. I am not certain if Colonel Laurens was aware of the artillery."

Will said, "I believe there were six guns, and they're six-pounders. I also believe I saw the uniforms of the 71st Regiment of Foot. I did not see any militia. I was unable to count the enemy, but there were fewer than 2,400."

Captain Shubrick said, "We were lucky, Sir. Major Yelverton put on a display of shooting. He killed three of the artillerymen and suppressed the artillery fire. That permitted our withdrawal."

Moultrie looked at Will hard. "You were to observe."

Will nodded, "I was, Sir, but our people were under serious threat. It seemed wise to make the artillery crews think twice about marching around like they were on some parade field in London."

Moultrie nodded. A tight smile played on his lips, "It appears that worked. Gentlemen, we shall withdraw up the King's Road toward Charlestown. We have too small a force to defend this bridge. I'm certain the British would quickly find fords up and down the river and flank us. I hope we can gain time for General Lincoln to about march and come in this direction. I have sent a messenger to Lincoln asking that he do so."

Moultrie looked at the small group of officers. "Any questions? No? Very well, we march immediately. I mean to be gone before General Prevost can get across the Coosawhatchie and cause us trouble."

Chapter 9 – Ashley Ferry

Once again, Will found himself trotting along with a retreating army. The stink of men, horses, dust, and dung assailed his nose. He smiled that he was senior enough to ride close to the front. Those at the rear had all the misery of marching and walked in the spoor of those in the lead. Will smirked to himself, *It is always this way.*

The Americans quickly pulled out of the camp at the Tullifinny River, destroyed the bridge, and marched off up the King's Road. Moultrie was good to his plan, and the men marched briskly northeast toward Charlestown. Two hours up the road, Moultrie pulled out of line and trotted back to Will.

"You certainly distinguished yourself this morning, Will. I'm aware you have been in several battles. Marion's request that you observe military tactics is a good one. 'Tis clear you are an excellent leader, so 'tis important I find ways for you to observe good decisions. Sadly, Colonel Laurens' decision this morning was not a good one. Crossing the Coosawhatchie and engaging the British created several problems. Can you tell me what you think those problems were?"

"Aye, Sir. Not to speak ill of Colonel Laurens, but I understood your orders were to retrieve the troops guarding the crossing and not to engage."

"Aye, that's right. What did the engagement do?"

"Gave away our position, strength, abilities?"

"Aye. Exactly. And ...?"

"It kept us in place when we should have retrieved the guard, destroyed the bridges, and marched immediately. We should be some ten miles further along this road."

"If you had been in command, what would you have done?"

"Sir, no criticism of Colonel Laurens, but I would have obeyed your orders and moved the troops away from the Coosawhatchie without engaging. That said, we did learn that the British have at least one battery of six-pounders."

Moultrie quietly considered for a moment. "True, we did learn that they have considerable artillery. Anything else?"

"I saw no evidence of cavalry, Sir."

"Yes, I believe if they had cavalry, we would have been flanked while Laurens was tied up being shot at."

"We do have a rear guard, Sir."

"Aye, that's where I'd like you to go now. I want you and your ten troops to join the rear guard, my compliments, of course, to Major Barnwell. Barnwell is a good man, comes from an old Carolina family, and has a military background. We must be on our guard against possible British cavalry. I don't think they have much in the way of cavalry. It appears they didn't bring the mounted militia, else we would have seen some green jackets this morning."

"Yes, Sir. I will collect Lt. Legare and seek out Major Barnwell."

"Good. Laurens is well-placed politically. His father is the President of Congress, you know. So, John's hotheaded mistake of this morning will not be characterized as such. In fact, though my report won't say it, John will be counted as a wounded hero, and so on. Must keep the peace among the politicians, my young friend. That's a leadership lesson for you as well. Avoid raising their ire. Even when you're right, they will exact vengeance that is not good for the cause."

Will nodded. "Yes, Sir. I understand. I was present at the utter collapse of our forces in Savannah when the British landed. Colonel Elbert begged General Howe to put heavy defenses at Girardeau's plantation. Had we done that, perhaps the city would still be ours."

"Aye. And Brier Creek?"

"Lost friends there, Sir. And, yes, 'twas a disaster from the start. Again, Colonel Elbert begged General Ashe to pay attention to the possibility of being flanked."

"Unless I miss my guess, Will, you were the person who scouted all the potential approaches?"

"Aye, though Colonel Elbert rode with me several times. We tried to convince General Ashe that the British could march around Brier Creek to the west and then get across a flooded creek. But Ashe would not listen."

Moultrie ran his hand over his face; he was clearly tired. "Aye, and now many lay dead."

"My friend from childhood, Noah Harris, was bayonetted as he tried to crawl away. He was sick."

"You saw it?"

"Aye, and the Redcoat who killed him died seconds later."

"Shot him, did you?"

Will nodded and looked off into the scrubby woods they were passing. "Aye, ended his miserable life. Gave me no pleasure."

"Good. If we took pleasure in killing, we would be no better than animals."

Will nodded, his mouth turned down and his eyes full. He looked away from Moultrie so his tears would not be seen.

Moultrie glanced down and quietly said, "I've lost people, too, Will." Brightening up, he said, "Well, off with you to the rear guard. Here's a note to Barnwell."

~~<>~~

Will spent the next two days riding with John Barnwell. He found he liked Barnwell immensely. A no-nonsense leader of enthusiastic militiamen, Barnwell knew the country from his birth.

Will sat on Molly next to Barnwell as he supervised the burning of the bridge at the Salkehatchie River.

Barnwell said the British a bit."

Will said, "I didn't see any mou, "I hate to burn all these bridges, but it must be done. The Salkehatchie – some call it the Saltketcher – is deep, and 'tis hard to find a good ford. Destroying the bridge should slow down nted militia at Coosawhatchie, but Prevost would be a fool to leave them in Georgia. I'm sure they're out scouting for crossings."

Barnwell looked at Will. "Aye, but they won't be coming from the east. Swamp everywhere there. So, we'll concentrate on any western approach. Shouldn't be much, I think. These swamps and roads will tire them."

Will said, "I think our people will be tired too."

"Aye. They have been in the woods and camped at Purysburg for weeks. The food has been not so good: grits, rice, some beef, and occasional venison when some of the men hunt. That's been it. Not that there's much else to be had anywhere else. Still, t'would be nice to be at home and have food at the table. Still, they are in good spirits, and 'tis not yet so hot as to make this march any worse than it already is."

Will nodded. "Aye, I understand. My people are in North Carolina. I haven't been with them in months."

"Isn't that your brother, the chaplain?"

"Oh, aye, that's my brother, all right."

Barnwell grinned, "I think there's a story there."

~~<>~~

Two days of hard marching drew the Americans within a few hours' march of Ashley Ferry Town and the ferry across the river to Charlestown. Will smiled to himself. He glanced at Cuth, "Weren't we just here?"

Cuthbert snorted, "Aye. Coming and going, Sir."

The next morning, Moultrie ordered the building of defensive positions outside Ashley Ferry Town and St. Andrews Town. These two towns sat astride the King's Road, and defending this area was critical to protecting Charlestown. Bacon's Bridge was to the west, but that was several miles of a detour. Moultrie sent a small detachment in that direction to watch for any British approach.

An express rider came into the camp that afternoon with word from General Lincoln that the main American army was now marching toward Charlestown. Moultrie gathered the officers and shared the news.

"Thank God we got word of the severity of this threat to Lincoln, and he has responded. I don't know how long it will take him to reach us – maybe seven days? 'Tis a long march cross country from Augusta. While we wait, we shall prepare to receive General Prevost. I believe the British are no more than two days behind us."

John Laurens, recovered somewhat from his shrapnel wounds, asked, "Sir, have we alerted the people of Charlestown?"

Moultrie said, "Aye, and they're vigorously fortifying The Neck. Should Prevost push past us and cross the river, he will find quite a hornet's nest on t'other side of the water."

~~<>~~

Moultrie's assessment was accurate. Two days later, lead elements of the British advance popped out of the woods and appeared along the King's Highway. A light crackle of musketry from Moultrie's outlying scouts and British skirmishers heralded Provost's arrival.

Will checked the prime on his pistols, the English dragoon carbine, and his two rifles. He and Barnwell had seen no British scouts or advanced parties, and now he thought things might heat up. Will considered quietly, *If I were the British commander, would I press my advantage and take the Ashley River Ferry?* He answered his own question. *Absolutely, I would. And I would rapidly put troops across to secure the crossing. Then, I would flood the other side with men. I would also rush Bacon's Bridge.*

The crackle and pop of muskets got louder and more intense as Moultrie's patrols gave ground slowly to British skirmishers. Moultrie called a council.

When all were present, Moultrie said, "We will cross the river and burn the boats. It will take a while, so we must start now. We have some 1,200 men, and the boats will take perhaps 75. Less the 100 men I sent to Bacon's Bridge, this means at least 15 trips. Add the horses and other equipment, and I think we'll see 20 trips. The best we can hope for is three trips an hour. That means some six or seven hours to move everyone. I fear we may have waited too long to cross."

Skirmishing continued throughout the morning and into the early afternoon. Will and Barnwell trotted to a low rise in the woods where they could observe. Clearly, the main British units were not yet positioned.

Will looked around to Cuthbert, "Cuth, ride back to General Moultrie and tell him that Major Barnwell and I have a strong belief that the British have not yet massed to attack. But we must make haste in crossing because we see more Redcoats arriving. It is possible that Prevost is resting the men out of our sight, which is what happened at Brandywine."

Barnwell nodded, "Compliments to the General. I concur with Major Yelverton. Once they've gathered and rested, all hell is going to break loose."

Half an hour passed before Cuthbert quietly walked his horse up to Will and Barnwell's lookout. "The general said our patrols have orders to continue falling back. We have perhaps half a dozen trips across the river left. He says when you see the patrols moving back past here, we are to return to the crossing."

Another half hour and Will could see South Carolina Militia and other militia clad in hunting shirts and leggings beginning to filter out of the next tree line toward the British position along the King's Road.

Barnwell said, "I'd like to know what those patrols are seeing."

Will nodded. "Can we get closer?"

Barnwell grinned and nudged his horse to a walk.

Will followed suit. "Cuth, stay here and report to the general if this goes badly."

Cuthbert's eyes narrowed, "Let's not do anything rash, now ..."

Will grinned, "No, we're just getting a better look and finding out what the skirmishers know."

~~<>~~

Will and Barnwell hurried back across the field and slowed just enough to shout for Cuthbert to join them. They cantered the half mile to Ashley Ferry Town, where Moultrie had set up his headquarters in the tavern. Moultrie's aide sat on the porch with a folding field desk, quill pens, and inkpot, keeping track of the troops moving to the ferry. Some 100 men remained, not to mention the skirmishers.

Will and Barnwell dismounted and hurried up the three stairs and did not observe courtesies of asking permission to enter. They walked briskly into the tavern.

Moultrie looked up from a page indicating which troops were embarked. "Yes?"

Will looked at Barnwell, who said, "Sir, we think the main body is no more than a mile down the King's Road. We may have an hour before this becomes a general engagement."

Moultrie looked at Will, his face a question.

"I agree, Sir. Perhaps they'll rest before attacking, but that's unknown. At Brandywine, the British made a long, flanking march and rested for an hour before attacking."

Moultrie said, "We have three more trips at least, probably more. That's at least an hour, assuming all goes well with loading and unloading. We can only hope that the boat continues to operate well. Major Barnwell will command the rear guard, and you, Major Yelverton, will be his second.

Barnwell trotted off to collect the 100 troops that would form the rear guard. Will and Cuthbert returned to their lookout. It was well protected by a berm made when a rice grower dug an irrigation ditch. With the drought, the ditch was dry. By standing their horses in the ditch, they were out of view but had good sight lines over the berm.

Soon, Barnwell marshaled the troops into position along the ditch and behind the berm. As the remaining skirmishers drifted back, they joined the others behind the berm. Then, they waited.

They did not have to wait long. The British skirmishers began drifting out of the tree line about 100 yards away. Will let his English dragoon carbine dangle from its shoulder strap. Reaching down, he drew his .45 rifle out of its scabbard. He primed the rifle carefully and rested it on his hip as he watched the tree line.

Soon, a Redcoat with stripes on his sleeve stepped out and cautiously looked around. The Redcoat sergeant stood fully upright and turned to wave his troops forward. That was a mistake. Will's .45 cracked, and the sergeant flung his arms out before sagging to his knees.

A few moments passed before a Redcoat cautiously darted out of the trees to check his sergeant. Another mistake. While the Redcoats were looking for the shooter who had killed their sergeant, Will handed the .45 to Cuth to reload while he primed Josie. WizCraaaak! Josie killed the Redcoat who was examining his sergeant.

Pandemonium ensued among the British. They were frantic to find the deadly sniper. The .45 boomed again, and another Redcoat died. Josie cracked, and another Redcoat clutched his shoulder and stumbled into the trees. Now, Will and Cuthbert were in a rhythm of load, prime, fire, load.

A dozen Redcoats started hurrying across the open field. Will shot three before they reached musket range for the Patriots. Barnwell shouted, "FIRE!" And the berm erupted in flame, smoke, and gunpowder stink. "RELOAD!"

A couple of the Redcoats fired their muskets toward the berm, but the gunsmoke from the Patriots' volley obscured targets. A few more Redcoats drifted out into the field and cautiously moved forward. Will shot one, and the other darted behind a small bush.

Barnwell said, "I'm sending half these men to the ferry."

Will nodded, "I don't know how much longer we can keep this up. They're bound to mass some troops and charge across that field. I don't think we can survive a bayonet charge."

Barnwell grimaced. "This is the best position we will get. I'll get the ones back to the Ferry Town and set up a defense near the tavern."

~~<>~~

Will watched Barnwell gather the 50 troops and hurry them down the road and into the town. Will turned and cracked another .45 round at the British lines, just to keep them guessing.

Cuthbert had just finished reloading the .45 when Will saw about 50 Redcoats stand up at the edge of the woods, fix bayonets, and begin to walk purposefully forward, muskets leveled waist high. An officer on a horse stepped out behind them, waving his sword and issuing orders. A .40 caliber bullet from Josie flicked the officer off his horse.

A sergeant took over. He was easily recognized because he carried a spontoon, a long spear-like weapon used to marshal the troops. Will shot him with the .45.

Neither of these losses slowed the professional Redcoats who marched forward resolutely. Will recognized the red and white checkerboard band on their headgear as the 71st Highland Regiment of Foot. They were the same bastards who killed Noah and captured Colonel Elbert. Will shot two of them before they reached musket range.

Will looked right and left up and down the berm. Patriot militia were all leaning against the dirt, muskets primed and ready. He looked over his shoulder and saw Barnwell galloping back from Ashley Ferry Town.

Will shouted, "We will fire one volley and immediately withdraw in good order down the road to the town!" He paused for a moment to shoot another Redcoat. "FIRE!"

The berm erupted in smoke and flame. Some dry rice stalks in front of the berm started smoldering. The Redcoats picked up their pace.

Will shouted, "WITHDRAW!"

Turning back to the British, Will flicked the cock back on the .45 rifle and shot another Redcoat. Too late to reload, he slid the still smoking .45 into its scabbard and put the carbine butt on his thigh. Will nudged Molly, and she turned and daintily stepped up on the road. Will ignored a musket ball that whizzed past his head.

Cuthbert was already a few paces down the road, and Barnwell was hurrying the withdrawing troops along. As the Redcoats topped the berm, two green-coated Loyalist Militia on horseback rushed across the 100-yard gap and burst past the berm on the road. One held a carbine, and the other brandished a wicked-looking dragoon sword. They veered toward Will. The leader of the two swung the dragoon sword around his head and bared his teeth in a killing grimace.

Will shot him point-blank with the carbine. The carbine's load of buck and ball was devastating at this range. The ball hit the militiaman high in the chest, and the swan shot shredded his shoulder, neck, and face. The militiaman sagged in the saddle before tumbling into the dusty road, a puddle of blood turning the dust into mud.

Will ignored the dead man and turned to meet the other Green Coat with the carbine. The second militiaman's carbine cracked, and Will felt a tug as the ball clipped his coat. In one fluid motion, Will dropped his carbine to dangle from its shoulder strap and drew the horse pistol from the bucket holster on Molly's saddle. He jerked the cock back and pointed the pistol at the Green Coat, who threw up his hands and said, "Please, Sir."

Will would not shoot an unarmed man. But Cuthbert's pistol cracked, and the Green Coat's white shirt turned red with his blood to match his scarlet collar and cuffs. As the militiaman joined his dead comrade in the dust, Will, Cuth, and Barnwell turned and galloped toward the town.

As they arrived, the last of their men were clambering aboard the ferry, and the ferryman was just about to cast off. Cuthbert swung down from his horse and kept moving quickly as he boarded the ferry. Will and Barnwell quickly dismounted and led the horses aboard. The ferryman cast off, and the boat bobbed some with the weight of people and horses. Exhausted slaves hauled on the ropes as the boat moved sluggishly across the 100 yards of the Ashley River.

Will patted Molly's neck. She whinnied and nodded. Her eyes rolled, and she stamped nervously. Will looked back across the river. He saw redcoats popping out from behind the houses. Flames licked at the roof of one of the houses along Ashley Ferry Road. Will hoped the British would not burn the town in frustration.

The Americans had escaped again.

Chapter 10 – Stono

Will and Cuthbert trotted into the American lines late in the day on May 10th. Will looked around and was surprised to see the diminutive Count Kazimir Pulaski, now a Brigadier General, and his makeshift cavalry unit encamped along with several hundred other rebel units behind the hastily erected defenses. The rebels had dug ditches, created redoubts, and dragged abatis into place; their sharpened stake limbs pointed menacingly outward at any foe foolish enough to attempt to climb them.

Will was pleased to see the colors of the 2nd South Carolina Regiment. Lieutenant Legare and his ten 2nd South Carolina Regiment troops were already at the encampment. Will waved at Major John Barnwell. It was clear that Barnwell had reunited with his small cavalry unit after he and Will formed the rear guard at Ashley River Ferry. Will smiled because he had lost track of Barnwell in the haste of clearing the ferry boat and moving toward Charlestown.

Will recognized Colonel Owen Roberts and his second-in-command, Lt Colonel Bernard Beeckman, of the 4th South Carolina Artillery. It was good to know that sufficient artillery would blunt the enemy's advance.

Will asked a private for directions to Lt. Colonel Marion's tent and made his way to report.

Marion was in good form, pacing up and down on his short legs, his piercing black eyes missing nothing, his hook nose pointing at each discrepancy like a saber. He glanced up and saw Will. "Good! You're back from the wars."

Will grinned, touched his hat in salute, and said, "Good evening, Sir. I see you brought the entire regiment."

Marion's voice crackled with dry humor, "Aye. Couldn't let Moultrie have all the fun."

Will said, "Hasn't been much fun so far, Sir."

"No, of course not. I suspect it will get worse shortly. We had a rider a few minutes ago saying Prevost is busy crossing the Ashley River. I know you burned the ferry boats after you got across. It's deep water there, so I must believe Prevost found boats somewhere."

Will said, "I fear that not everyone is a Patriot. It's impossible to burn all the boats up and down the river. I'm sure there were volunteers to take troops across. Laurens wanted to burn every house on the Coosawhatchie. I was not present, but I'll bet he advised Moultrie to burn everything around the Ashley Ferry Crossing.

Marion's voice dripped with sarcasm, "That would win the hearts and minds of the people, I'm sure."

Will grinned, "Yes, Sir. I did see one house burning in Ashley Ferry Town. I suspect it was set ablaze by British fire."

~~<>~~

Will watched the next day as Pulaski led a force of rebel cavalry and infantry out to build outlying redoubts. Will thought, *Guess they plan to slow the British down. Either that or get them into a fight and draw them into some sort of ambush.*

A few hours later, Will heard the unmistakable crackle of musketry and a couple of sharp reports of small artillery. *They must have gotten into a fight. I hope Pulaski's cavalry are winning.*

Soon, Pulaski and his bedraggled cavalry unit trotted back into camp. It was easy to see that Pulaski's sally to create redoubts and challenge the British was not a success. Will was not a career military man, nor was he a cavalry officer. But he knew a beating when he saw one.

Marion said from over Will's shoulder, "That one will get himself and his men killed one day. Boldness is one thing; impetuosity is quite another."

~~<>~~

The following day, British forces began arriving. They paused and began to deploy outside the range of Colonel Owen Roberts' freshly emplaced artillery. They could be seen marching around, establishing unit positions, and pitching tents. Soon, cooking fires could be seen. Clearly, the British were planning a lengthy siege.

Governor Rutledge called the senior officers to a council. Will went along with Lt. Colonel Marion. When they arrived, Rutledge, Moultrie, Pulaski, Roberts, Marion, and several other commanders stood in a circle, with Rutledge leading the discussion.

Rutledge said, "I propose to send a letter to General Prevost asking his terms."

Marion squawked, "What?!"

Moultrie raised his eyes to heaven. "Of course, Your Excellency, you're not serious."

"Oh, I am quite serious," replied Rutledge. "'Twill buy us time for Lincoln to get here."

Marion said, "So, we ask terms of our enemy without the honor of honestly considering them?"

Roberts said, "I'd rather employ a bit of deception than heat the barrels of my guns. Besides, we only have sufficient powder for a brief defense. The British don't know that, of course, but there it is."

The next morning a lieutenant mounted his horse and trotted out toward the British lines, carrying a white flag.

Two hours later, the lieutenant returned across the gap between the lines bringing Prevost's reply. The reply was terse and indicated there would be no terms.

Toward dusk, an express rider from General Lincoln arrived. Having skirted the British lines, the rider had news that Lincoln was approaching and was a day away.

~~<>~~

Dawn broke with the clear evidence that the British had broken camp and departed. South was the only way they could go, having maneuvered themselves into the jaws of Charlestown's hastily erected defenses and Lincoln's 4,000-man army. Lincoln's men would be tired from their hasty march across South Carolina, but they now threatened the British rear.

Prevost had been willing to take the risk of charging up the Low Country from Savannah on the off-chance of taking Savannah while Lincoln marched toward Augusta. Now, Prevost found himself in quite a pickle. Will watched from an elevated redoubt to see a dust cloud marking the British march toward the ferry.

Marion walked up. "Left, have they?"

"Aye, Sir. Seems like."

"We're fresh; they're tired. We have Lincoln at their rear; they have nowhere to go but south. If this were my army to command, I'd send Moultrie south by Johns Island to cut them off, and we'd sally out there immediately and jump on them. I'd send a note to Lincoln to attack with dispatch. We would grind up that bunch of Limey bastards!"

Will nodded. "Alas, I don't see that kind of bold action coming, Sir."

"No, you bloody well don't. Not from this crowd of clodhopping ninnies!"

Unmolested, the British marched down the King's Road and crossed the Stono River. They were headed southeast. Even to Will, it was obvious they intended to make their way to Beaufort. There they could effect a seaborne evacuation, probably back to Savannah.

~~<>~~

With the British withdrawn, Lincoln had come forward and joined with the rest of the Patriot forces. Will went with Marion to another council of war with Rutledge and the commanders.

Lincoln, his New England accent even more evident from being weary, said, "We must take this opportunity to pursue Prevost. It appears he's moving south toward Beaufort. If we catch him, we can destroy his army before he pulls off a Naval rescue."

Moultrie looked around at the assembly. "I would be happy to undertake that mission, General."

"Aye, but I want you to lead troops to Johns Island, where you will secure that area from any secondary British troops. If you get the chance from there, you may be able to cut off Prevost. Our scouts report that the British have created a bridgehead at the Stono River. Clearly, that's a rear-guard for their main force."

"The schooner *Rattlesnake* is sailing to come up the Stono River to engage when we attack. For the main army, we will plan a force of some 1,200 under Generals Sumner and Huger, with me as the overall commander. General Pulaski's cavalry will ride in support. We march in the morning."

Later that night, Marion's aide came to Will's tent. "Colonel Marion's compliments. He says General Lincoln has requested you accompany him south as a courier and general's aide. You leave at dawn."

Will said, "Very well

. My compliments to Colonel Marion. I shall prepare to depart."

After telling Cuthbert that they were marching in the morning, Will lay on his bedroll on the ground. Blessedly, there were no tree roots, nor was the ground soggy. He thought about Mary. He was sad he would not see her during this brief visit to Charlestown. That would have to wait.

As he dosed off, Abby Kennedy stole into his dreams. She smiled at him. He smiled back but saw that she held a baby and stood next to Zeke Carter. His smile faded into a sad empty feeling. As he fell into an exhausted sleep, a small voice said, *"You should be ashamed of thinking of Abby and not Mary."*

~~<>~~

Cuthbert said, "Are you up, Sir?"

"Aye, Cuth. I slept for a while but then woke up and couldn't get back to sleep."

"I've got you a basin of water for a wash and shave. There's coffee at the campfire as well as some bacon and grits."

They went to the campfire and ate. The bacon was undercooked and slick with rancid fat, and the grits were watery and tasteless. Everything was laden with salt, the only bonus of the breakfast. The British had embargoed salt from the Caribbean, making it hard to find and used sparingly. If the food didn't sour their guts, it would sustain them for much of the day.

Will and Cuthbert tended to their horses and prepared to ride. Molly tossed her head and stamped her hooves. She was excited to be going somewhere. Will often wondered if horses knew they were going into harm's way or if they just did their duty to carry their rider. Molly, for her part, nuzzled Will and snuffled at his pockets, looking for a carrot or an apple. Of course, Will always tried to have something, and today was no exception. He produced a rather large, somewhat wilted carrot. Molly tore into the soggy carrot with gusto.

The two men checked their weapons. Will loaded his .45 rifle and Josie with his usual extra care. He wanted every shot with the rifles to be deadly accurate.

He put his customary load of buck and ball in the English dragoon carbine and both the Brander pistol and the horse pistol. As always, Will wore Uncle Ewan's Scottish dirk and his powder horns and shot pouch.

Will hung his sword on Molly's saddle and tied his bedroll behind. His saddle bags were, unfortunately, heavy. He had jerky, a pound of flour, and his fire starter kit, as well as a water bottle and his gunsmithing tools. Homer's *Odyssey* still rode in one saddlebag along with some other reading material – Paine's *Common Sense* was one – and a map of South Carolina.

Cuthbert loaded the fusil and the French cavalry pistol he carried. Both got buck and ball loads. Cuthbert hung his heavy British dragoon saber on his horse's saddle and checked his bedroll. Will smiled at Cuth's preparations. He had become an excellent companion and a reliable man to have in a fight.

Soon, men were forming up for the march, and Will reported to Marion, telling him goodbye.

Marion, never an emotional man, said, "Be cautious that some fool doesn't get you killed."

Will understood that 'some fool' meant any commander not named Marion.

~~<>~~

Will and Cuthbert trotted to where General Lincoln sat his considerable bulk on his horse, watching as the army assembled. Lincoln's New England accent was more muted after some rest, "Ah, Majah Yelvahton. I have been meaning to mention to you that General Washington was pleased to learn that you ahre now a Continental officer. The Commander-in-Chief graciously forwarded your recommendation for promotion to Congress. Alas, I know not how long the Congress will take with their deliberations. Until they do, I'm pleased to have you with us, and I am vigilant for a command position for you, Will."

Will blushed, "Thank you, General. I am privileged to be with you and deeply honored that you recommended me for promotion. I won't let you down."

Although they would never be as professional as the British army, the men marched off in something that resembled good order. They were mostly militiamen but willing to do their part. As they marched out of the camp, Will saw Benjamin standing on a stump, blessing the troops.

Benjamin's voice carried across the camp, "And yay! Mathew said, 'Verily I say unto you, except ye be converted, and become as little children, ye shall not enter into the kingdom of heaven.' And Jesus said, 'Suffer little children to come unto me, and forbid them not: for of such is the kingdom of God.' Know then that ye must all become little children, and Jesus will accept ye all into his bosom. Now go, my children! Go with God and smite our enemies!"

Will simply prayed that the men would fight better than they marched.

Will and Molly trotted along in General Lincoln's entourage. Once again, it was good to be in the lead of an army on the march.

The route was littered with trash from the retreating British army. The June low country heat began to take a toll. A few British soldiers were taken captive when, either sick or exhausted, they gave up.

One of the prisoners told interrogators that Prevost was heading for Beaufort. That confirmed Lincoln's suspicion. Confirming scouting reports, another prisoner told them that Prevost was leaving Lt. Colonel John Maitland and several hundred troops behind at the Stono River Ferry.

The march was not lengthy; the distance to the Stono River was not more than eight miles. But the column strung out, with many stragglers slowing progress. Five days later, late in the day, Lincoln's force paused for the night.

As he rolled into his bedroll next to Cuthbert, Will understood that the dawn would bring a fight. Throughout the night, Will heard the tromp of Americans arriving from the strung-out column.

As the American Army assembled before daybreak, a scout hurried back to Lincoln's staff with reports that Maitland had constructed three redoubts on the north side of the river. The redoubts were circled by abatis and manned by Highlanders from the 71st Regiment of Foot as well as Hessians and Loyalist militia troops. The estimates of about 900 enemy troops were confirmed. Worse news was that there was an armed British galley in the river. The galley's canons would be a dangerous factor in the coming hours.

At dawn, the army advanced in two wings. Sumner and his Carolina Militia were on the right, with two guns. Huger and his Continentals were on the left with four guns. Huger's light infantry would range ahead. This would be a difficult approach through thick woods and boggy terrain as they neared the water.

As the sun broke the horizon, Huger's light infantry made contact with the Highlanders and Hessians manning the redoubts. Will and Cuthbert sat on the road behind the cover of trees. They were with Lincoln's staff and observing the battle.

It was an engagement of small arms with artillery support. The Americans did quite well. After about an hour, a messenger reported that the Highlanders were down to about a dozen men and the Hessians had broken.

The same messenger reported that the American units were at the abatis and were asking for more ammunition. A few minutes later, another messenger reported that Americans had taken the redoubts and were again asking for more ammunition. The British and Hessian troops were falling back.

A victory was in Lincoln's grasp when another messenger reported British reinforcements coming up to join the fight.

Lincoln looked around at his staff and asked, "Do we have extra ammunition?"

A staff major shook his head. "Alas, Sir, no. 'Tis the bane of our existence, the lack of powder and shot."

The British river galley began firing on the Americans in support of the reinforcements. Huger's guns were sited on the high ground overlooking the river. They opened fire on the galley, and the boat quickly moved out of range. Huger's artillery shifted to fire on the Hessians but had difficulty depressing their guns, and most of the rounds fell long. The British reinforcements marched forward and used small boats to cross to the north side of the river.

Lincoln slapped his saddle. "Damme! We must withdraw. Without ammunition, I cannot leave the men to be slaughtered, and we seem unable to stop the reinforcements from getting across the river."

He looked around, and his eyes fell on Will and another courier named Daniels. "Major Yelverton, my compliments to General Huger. Please ask him to withdraw in good order to this road and thence northward. Major Daniels, my same compliments and orders for General Sumner."

~~<>~~

Will and Cuthbert cantered up to Huger's position on the high ground on the left. Colonel Owen Roberts' artillery continued to blaze away but with little effect. The schooner, however, was having some success in blunting the British and Hessian advance.

"General Lincoln's compliments, Sir. He orders immediate withdrawal in good order to the center road and then northward. There is no ammunition to provide to our troops, and the British are advancing despite our artillery."

Huger looked at Will hard. "Don't I know you?"

"Aye, Sir. Major Will Yelverton. We were at Savannah together."

"Ah, yes. You were with Elbert. I seem to recall that you were a civilian volunteer. Aside from Elbert, that fiasco was another example of inept leadership. The uniform looks good on you. Well, shan't tarry. My compliments to the general. We shall begin withdrawing immediately."

"Thank you, Sir. The general sent similar orders to General Sumner, so you may expect him to join you on the road."

Huger nodded. "Very well."

Will turned Molly's head as a small caliber ball whizzed by. Clearly, it was a rifle shot at this range. He looked across the water to see a Loyalist ramming a ball down the barrel of a rifle.

Will drew the .45, primed the pan, and set the trigger. He ran his thumb across the edge of the flint. It was sharp. He raised the rifle and aimed at the Loyalist, who had just finished ramming the ball down his rifle and was priming it for another shot. It would not do for Huger or any of the other leaders to be killed.

WizCraaaak! The .45 hammered Will's shoulder, and the Loyalist rifleman pitched backward, his rifle firing harmlessly into the air.

Huger glanced around in alarm at the sound of Will's rifle. "Damme, Sir! But you startled me!"

Huger's aide said, "He shot a rifleman across the river."

"But that's at least 200 yards!"

"Aye, Sir. I believe the Loyalist was trying to kill you, Sir."

"Indeed? Indeed? Well, thank you, Major Yelverton. Will, is it? I shall stand you a drink when next we meet."

Will tipped his hat, slid the .45 back into its scabbard, and trotted off toward Lincoln's entourage.

Cuthbert smirked, "That got his attention."

They trotted back to Lincoln, who raised an eyebrow. "Couldn't stay out of the fight, eh, Major?"

"Couldn't allow them to stand about unmolested whilst shooting our generals, Sir."

"Do remind me to keep you around, young Sir."

~~<>~~

Soon, Generals Sumner and Huger, with Roberts' artillery in the middle, were marching briskly up the road to the north and away from Stono Ferry. The *Rattlesnake* schooner provided covering fire. Still, a good many British troops had crossed the river and were forming up to pursue the withdrawing Americans.

Lincoln watched from the side of the road and turned to Pulaski. "Count Pulaski? Sir, I would be grateful if you would do the honors of stopping the British from their pursuit?"

Pulaski's little mustache twitched as he smiled. His black eyes narrowed as he said, "Wiz pleazzure, Cheneral." Drawing his saber, Pulaski spun his horse and galloped toward his cavalry force. He whirled the saber about his head, a diminutive figure full of fight and near-insanity to get at the enemy.

Will saw the reserve cavalry all draw sabers and crowd in behind Pulaski. Led by a Frenchman named Vernier, they were a mixed bag of men from a variety of nations. Their officers were Poles and Frenchmen, and one American named Bedkin. Pulaski's infantry legion marched smartly to assist the cavalry and become a rear guard. Will smiled. *This is what the new nation of America is about. So many different people, all inspired by freedom.*

Will and Cuthbert trotted along behind Lincoln. Will thought, *What a sorry end to what could have been a victory and opened the door to seriously damaging Prevost. As it is, we've no ammunition, and thereby lies the tale of yet another lost opportunity.*

Two days later, Will and Cuthbert reported to Lt. Colonel Marion. When he heard the news of the withdrawal due to limited ammunition, he furiously stomped about his command tent in frustration. "Jesus, Joseph, and Mary! Is there no end to the idiocy that runs this Army?"

Will smiled; at least he would get to see Mary.

Chapter 11 – Charlestown

Lieutenant Colonel Marion gave Will and Cuthbert a four-day furlough to rest after their travels. It would have been more, but Marion was sure Lincoln was returning to his quest to re-take Savannah. Soon, the army would march.

A tired Will Yelverton and Molly trotted up to the carriage house at Homer Proctor's townhome. A stable hand named Tom stepped out, grinned, and said, "Welcome home, Major."

Will thought, *I guess that's true. This is home.*

It made him feel good to have someplace to call home. True, his parent's farm near Halifax, North Carolina, was a kind of home. But he had left there at age six. For the next six years, he lived with his Aunt Pat and Uncle Ewan at their farm in New Bern, North Carolina. Then, he apprenticed with Bert and Becky Koontz until he was about eighteen.

Since age eighteen, wherever he slept had been home. Bear Creek with the Kennedys for a year, Philadelphia for a year, Georgia for a year. Now Charlestown. He hoped this would be permanent. But with the war, who knew what might happen?

Mary rushed out the door. Hiking up her skirts immodestly, she ran to Will, her well-turned ankles flashing in the bright June sun. She bulled into Will, throwing her arms around his neck and kissing him with passion. Servant opinions be damned, Mary Proctor Yelverton loved her husband.

She stepped back and assessed Will from head to toe. "You're filthy! A bath is required, and cleaning your uniform is an absolute must. More, I insist we get you a new uniform! We shall visit the tailor tomorrow." She took his hand and dragged him toward the house.

As he was trotting along behind Mary, Will called over his shoulder, "Cuth, take care of Molly and my rifles."

Cuth grinned his agreement as Will was dragged into the house.

~~<>~~

Will fell back in the steaming tub that Mary's housekeeper, Mam'Janey had prepared. He felt the Turkish towel against his back, a luxury he had never known until he married Mary.

"Is your father in residence?"

"Yes, he's here. I talked him out of going to the plantation. It's too close to the road to Savannah, and that's become bandit country."

"I'm glad he's safe, but I had hoped we would have the place to ourselves. If he goes anywhere, he should go up the country toward the plantation at Camden. Safer there, I think."

Mary cut her eyes and snickered. She was sitting in a chair beside the tub. She was nude except for a pair of white woolen stockings that were very thin – almost gossamer – and tied up with bright red bows at the top. She stood.

Will took in her body. Slim but womanly, she had heavy breasts and a flat stomach. Her hip bones protruded on either side of her dark patch. Light hair on her thighs was visible in the sunlight that intruded from the windows on two sides of the room. She stepped over into the bath, her butt wiggling slightly from the effort. Facing Will, she slowly lowered herself into the water. As she settled into the water, her legs parted invitingly, and Will grew burstingly erect.

Mary took him in her hand. She leaned forward, her breasts swaying as she tugged him. Will closed his eyes and leaned his head back. He felt Mary move, and soon she straddled him. Will thought, *How could I be so lucky?*

Will awakened after an afternoon of sexual excess interspersed with laughter and sleep. He was rejuvenated. He didn't care if Homer Proctor heard.

~~<>~~

"Oh, POOH! You're leaving so soon?"

Will explained that he had a four-day furlough pending a march to Savannah. It was the last day of June, and he knew General Lincoln was set on taking Savannah back from the British. Leaving the city unmolested meant allowing the British a foothold in the South and a place to mount an invasion.

Will explained to Mary that, so far, Prevost only had the 3,000 or so troops, and these were mostly bottled up in Savannah. Because of the poor American showing at Stono River, Maitland had settled in at Beaufort. Lincoln hoped to lock him there with his 800 troops. Some Loyalist Militia were running around in the Georgia backcountry, vigorously hanging Rebel militiamen and innocent farmers who failed to bow to London.

Regardless of the British intentions and the present lack of fighting, the Americans had to move against Savannah and deny it to the British.

Will also had silent, personal reasons for wanting to go to Savannah. He liked the town and its people. Moreover, his discussions with Lincoln's staff while riding to Stono Ferry had revealed that Sunbury was the place where interned Georgia leaders were held. This included Samuel Elbert. Will intended to rescue Elbert from captivity. He kept this quest to himself. But he was excited to get moving to rescue Savannah and, more importantly, Samuel Elbert.

Just before the Fourth of July, as the society people of Charlestown were planning a celebration of the Declaration of Independence, British General Henry Clinton signed a proclamation aimed at undermining the economy of the southern colonies.

Whereas the enemy have adopted a practice of enrolling NEGROES among their Troops, I do hereby give notice that all NEGROES taken in arms, or upon any Military Duty, shall be purchased for the public service at a stated Price; the money to be paid to the Captors.

But I do most strictly forbid any Person to sell or claim Right over any NEGROE, the property of a Rebel, who may take Refuge with any part of this Army: And I do promise to every NEGROE who shall desert the Rebel Standard, full security to follow within these Lines, any Occupation which he shall think proper.

Given under my Hand, at Head Quarters, PHILIPSBURGH the 30th day of June, 1779.

H. CLINTON

Charlestown society all relied upon slaves as the engine of production on their plantations. The upper levels of society in

127

Charlestown were made up of old money planters and merchants. While Homer Proctor and his family were welcomed, they were not quite the top level of all society. Old money. Old plantations. Old families that had been Charlestown inhabitants since the earliest days looked at others as lesser beings.

On the third day of Will's visit home, Homer invited him to have a glass of brandy in his study. The study was paneled with dark wood and lined with books. Homer Proctor had an elaborately carved desk of teak wood brought from the orient – Asia – by one of his ship captains. Homer and Will sat in the pleasant room with sunlight streaming in from tall windows.

After some discussion about the war, Homer got down to the topic he wanted to address.

"This proclamation is most disturbing, Will. The slaves will surely run away, and our plantations will go fallow."

Will said, "I don't know how anyone can prevent this from happening, Sir. There are so many slaves and so few slaveowners. There are not enough people to keep the slaves on the plantations. It is a terrible situation because the economy will fail, and while it sounds good to slaves to be told they are free, how will they survive? They will have to find food and shelter.

"My father freed two of our slaves, but secretly father had taught them to read and cipher. They are surviving as freedmen in Philadelphia. But if they had no learning, what would they do?"

Homer nodded. "I am a slave owner. And now, Mary is one. 'Tis not a comfortable thought, the owning of another human being. I have always tried to treat the slaves with compassion. But, nonetheless, the slaves belong to my family and me. My plantation near Purysburg will fail without the slaves."

Will said, "Aye. 'Tis not an easy topic. Sooner or later, we will have to free the slaves. Smarter men than I must plan for that day."

"Will, that kind of thinking is why I'm deeding this house to Mary. The deed comes with the provision that her mother and I can continue to come here for the remainder of our lives. I also am deeding her the slaves and other furnishings and £1000 a year to keep the house running."

Will said, "That's very generous of you, Homer. I'm sure Mary will be most grateful."

"Ah, but Will, what it really means is that the house is yours. Our laws are clear: the wife's property belongs to her husband. I hope you will be a good steward of this townhome and know it truly is your home. Of course, the caveat that her mother and I retain use rights means the property cannot be sold, not that I expect you would do that."

Will said, "Sir, I do not intend ever to act as though this home is other than Mary's property. I am honored that you trust me but know that I will always act with integrity regarding this wonderful home."

"I know that, Will. It's the reason that we – Mrs. Proctor and I – decided to deed the property to Mary."

Will said, "The £1000 is most generous to keep the house operating in the style you've kept, Sir."

Homer's face became serious. "Will, death lurks everywhere. You could be killed in battle. Mary could die of some fever or other. Hell, her mother and I could be dead tomorrow! I knew that you were the right man for Mary. Even if, God forbid, Mary should be taken from us, you are part of our family, and the house would become yours."

Will nodded. There was not much left to say. "I am most honored, Homer. May God keep us all and may we all live here happily for years and years. May God grant the United States the freedom and liberty we fight for. May we all live to see the day the British sail out of Charlestown Harbor."

Homer soberly said, "Amen, and amen."

Chapter 12 – Jasper

"**M**ajor Yelverton, this is Sergeant Jasper."

Will said, "Sergeant Jasper, it is an honor to meet you."

Jasper blushed, "Ach, Mein Herr Mayor. Der pleasure iss all mine."

Lieutenant Colonel Francis Marion, Commander of the 2nd South Carolina Regiment, smiled and said, "Sergeant Jasper is the famous hero of the 1776 invasion attempt on our little fort here. It was called Fort Sullivan, then. Now it is Fort Moultrie. I thought we should have named it Fort Jasper."

Jasper blushed again, "Ach, Mein Herr Oberst Leutnant, I am nothing."

"Nonsense! Major Yelverton, our flag was shot down by British cannon fire. Sergeant Jasper climbed the ramparts with the flag tied to a cannon rammer. He placed the flag for all to see that Fort Sullivan still stood. 'Twas quite a heroic feat. The governor presented him a special sword in tribute."

Will said, "I had heard this story, but until now, I did not know we had the honor of having Sergeant Jasper in our midst."

Marion said, "Which brings me to the point of this meeting. I want you and Sergeant Jasper, as well as Sergeant Newton, to go to Georgia."

Will cocked an eyebrow, and Jasper stood straighter. Will said, "Indeed? To Georgia?"

"Aye, the mission is to find some prisoners who can tell us the state of the British defenses of Savannah. We also need to know the disposition of British troops outside Savannah – the town of Ebenezer, for instance."

Jasper nodded. "Und, ze Herr Mayor iss in charge?"

Marion said, "I believe this is an extraordinary mission. The Major will make decisions of a strategic nature. For example, if you find yourselves in a situation where withdrawal is required, the Major will make that decision with your advice.

"On the other hand, tactical decisions, such as where to go to get into the enemy camp and which prisoners to take, will be made jointly by you and the Major. Will, er Major Yelverton, you'll need to lean on Sergeant Jasper's experience and work with him. I want you to learn how he does what he's now famous for doing – infiltrating enemy lines and taking prisoners."

Will said, "I'm happy to work with you, Sergeant Jasper. I'm happy to learn from you."

Jasper nodded. "Ich bin at your service, Herr Mayor."

The next day, Will, Jasper, and Sergeant John Newton trotted out of Fort Morris. They were accompanied by Lieutenant Legare and his ten troops, as well as Corporal Charles Cuthbert. The small entourage was to provide an escort for Will and the two sergeants as well as camouflage the secret nature of the mission. People would have wondered if a continental major and two sergeants were seen trotting along a road without any troops.

As usual, Will carried his rifles, his English Dragoon carbine, and two pistols. The carbine and pistols were loaded with buck and ball. Molly carried Will's bedroll, a cooking pot, some meat and flour, and the fire-starting kit. Will left his officer's sword in his quarters. Few of the men in the fort noticed that Will wore his hunting pants and moccasin boots instead of his officer's breeches and riding boots.

Once away from Charlestown, Will and the two sergeants would change from uniforms to common clothes. Will's rough-hewn linen hunting shirt and his wide-brimmed hat were tucked into Molly's saddlebags.

Will and the two sergeants carried papers that indicated they were farmers from the backcountry and traveling to visit relatives in Burke County, Georgia. Which, in the case of Jasper, turned out to be true. Will considered that these papers were too transparently fake and would fool no one, but they were better than nothing. He had a few flashbacks of riding Molly through the backwoods of New Jersey, no idea of where he was going beyond a hand-drawn map, staying one step ahead of Major Banastre Tarleton and a British noose.

~~<>~~

Once again, Will rode the ferry across the Cooper River. He desperately wanted to see Mary, but this mission was too urgent. Will knew stopping might also reveal the secret of his trip to Georgia. He reluctantly trotted through Charlestown and onto the Ashley River Ferry. Once across the ferry, the group stopped at the tavern for food and some small beer.

The Ashley Ferry Town Tavern owner recognized Will and Cuthbert. "Back again?"

Will replied with a grin, "Aye. Taking these miscreants to Purysburg."

The tavern owner smirked, "Isn't everybody going to Purysburg these days?"

Will smiled. No need to disabuse the taverner of his assumption. And it was true, they were going to Purysburg, but only long enough to drop off Legare and his troops and Cuthbert and then move on quietly, just Will, Jasper, and Newton.

~~<>~~

The July heat beat down on the little troop as they moved along the dusty road toward Purysburg. The road was mostly a sandy dirt track with weeds and sand spurs growing in the middle. Dust whirled up from the horse's hooves, clinging to the riders' teeth and clogging their noses.

The sweat dampened the troopers' faces creating a wonderful opportunity for the dust to become a fine layer of mud on their skin. Soon, each looked like some species of a medicine man, intent upon incantations or other rituals enhanced by mud-covered skin and dusty hair.

Will and Jasper, their horses abreast, trotted along. Will said, "Tell me about yourself, Sergeant."

"Plezz, mein name iss Wilhelm, but here all call me William, Herr Mayor."

"Well, William, my name is also William. My friends call me Will."

"Ya, Herr Mayor."

"What I meant was, please call me Will. If we are to succeed, we must drop our military rank so we don't make a mistake and get caught."

"Very well, Herr ... uh, Will. We shall be William und Will."

"Good. That's settled. We have a difficult mission. But I hear you've done this before."

"Ya, Herr ... uh, Will. John and I haff been to this part of Georgia und taken captiffs. In April, ve here come und take two Brite Offizer. Zey gif goot information."

"How do you do this so successfully?"

"Ve look like ve are nicht threatening. No guns. Farmer clothes. Und, ve quietly await zem. Vhen zey are not looking, ve take ze unsuspectink. Ze two Britishe Hauptman ve took in April ver not schmart. Zey trink too much in ze tavern und ven zey go piss, we take them. Ve wear no uniform, zo if we are captured, ve hang."

Will nodded at this last. He asked, "How did you come to be here?"

"Ach, zat is ein long story."

"We have a long ride."

"Ach, zo. Ich was ein poor mann in Deutschland. Ich sign az a servant to here com von Deutschland. Und I come to Philadelphia. I met mein frau in Philadelphia und ve leave. Ze indenture vas unfair und zo I run to the south. Here compt von Philadelphia mit no money. Zo, I choin der Army."

"Is that the only reason you joined the Army?"

"Nein! Ich bin ein Patriot, und ze boot heel of der Britishe ist no better than in mein home. I vould be free! Und, zu, Herr Mayor?"

"It's a long story."

"Ach, we haf ein long ride."

Will laughed. "Fair enough. I trained to be a gunsmith. I went to Philadelphia to buy gun parts to provision the shop I planned to have on the frontier. There were no parts to buy, and I was trapped in Philadelphia when the British took the city. Friends helped me to escape to New Jersey.

"Along the way, I was accused of spying and threatened with hanging. I ran as quickly as I could to the Jersey shore and got passage on a privateer. The privateer dropped me in Georgia, where I met Colonel Elbert. He convinced me to join the Continental Army. Here I am."

"I zink zere ist much more to zis schtory, mein freund."

"Of course, as there is with your story."

Jasper laughed, "Ve haf zis much in common: I ran von Philadelphia und zo did you."

Will said, "I spent several months in Savannah and the surrounding area. I think Marion and General Moultrie thought that might be of value. I'm not sure, but I'll do what I can."

"Ja. Ve must find a Britische offizer to take. Alzo, ve schuld get into Savannah und see ze defenses."

"I think we should go to Zubly's Ferry after Purysburg and make our way to Ebenezer. We could pose as going to Burke County."

"Zis iss ein gut idea. What after Ebenezer?"

"We cut cross-country to a road I know and approach Savannah that way. It would not do to go back past the defenses in Ebenezer so quickly."

"Ja. Sehr gut."

~~<>~~

The small troop arrived at Purysburg and stayed overnight. Lieutenant Legare was told to wait for word from Cuthbert, who would accompany Will and the two sergeants. Once the three men changed into civilian clothing and went into character as simple farmers, Cuthbert would wait on the South Carolina side of Zubly's Ferry.

Will and the others trotted off the road and well into the nearly impenetrable woods about a mile short of Zubly's Ferry. They found a small clearing and quickly changed clothes. The three men soon looked just like the farmers they were impersonating. Now to move out without appearing to be military.

Will left his rifles and English dragoon carbine with Cuthbert. He took his horse pistol and the Brander pistol tucked into his belt. He left Uncle Ewan's Scottish dirk with Cuthbert. It killed him to do so, but a simple farmer would carry a utilitarian knife like the one he now put on his belt.

Will looked around the clearing. There was evidence of habitation.

Cuthbert said, "Probably this was a maroon camp. Escaped slaves had to find safe camps along the roads so that they could lay up during the day on their way to Florida. We used to find camps like this near Sunbury."

Will quietly said, "Cuth, don't mention it to anyone else, but after we complete this mission, we have been asked to go to Sunbury and find out about the treatment of high-ranking prisoners there. They include Colonel Elbert and Colonel George Walton. You have civilian clothing?"

Cuthbert nodded. "It might be dangerous to travel to Sunbury during the day, it being so far south of Savannah, but I know the way in the dark."

Will said, "We'll be back, with prisoners, I hope."

~~<>~~

The late July heat was oppressive, even at dawn when Will, Jasper, and Newton led their horses out of the thicket and mounted up for the short ride to Zubly's Ferry. Insects were already buzzing around the various plants. Birds flitted from tree to tree, frequently flying down to catch an interesting bug. Somewhere a squirrel barked a warning. There was no breeze.

No one asked anything as they paid their penny fare to ride the ferry boat. Each horse was also a penny. Molly shook her head as Will led her onto the boat. She nuzzled his face, and her sensitive lips dragged on his three-day beard growth. Will had intentionally let the dirt stay on his skin, especially his neck, ears, and the backs of his hands. Years of gunsmithing had created respectable callouses on his fingers and palm, so his claim of being a farmer would at least be believable.

The three trudged on foot toward Ebenezer. The heat made it unfair to ride the horses, and the three spies wanted the horses fresh in case they had to run. So, with sweat trickling down their backs, they walked. The sweat left trails in the dirt on their skin, adding to the effect that they were poor men. A knowledgeable person would have noticed that their horses were far better than animals most farmers could afford. But that couldn't be helped.

A Loyalist corporal in a green jacket with scarlet cuffs and collar stepped out of a lean-to near Ebenezer's outlying redoubt. "Who might you be?"

Jasper spoke up, "Ve are going to Burke County to zee mein cousin who iss zick. Hiss frau needs our help to tend ze fields."

"What's his name?"

"Johann Weiss und hiss frau Barbara."

"Don't know him."

"Ach, I don't know everyone either."

John Newton said, "We camped off the road a few miles back. We've been on the road from Orangeburg for days. Saw lots of rebel activity."

"Did you, eh? Well, they best think twice about coming this way."

Will said, "Looks like you're ready for a fight here."

"Aye. More than ready. Brown's Rangers – they keep changing our name – are ready. Bloody rebels! Half of them are country boys with fowling guns, and the other half are dumb as mules. They'll get a lickin' if they come this way."

Will spat on the ground. "Give 'em hell!"

The corporal looked at all three spies. "Be careful in Burke County. Rebels there have been hard to control. We don't have enough men to manage the entire backcountry. That, and there are *banditti* running around, acting like militia, but they're mostly common thieves."

~~<>~~

The three spies padded through the half-deserted German village of Ebenezer. Jasper passed easily because there were a good many Germans in Georgia, and the existence of a cousin named Johann Weiss in Burke County was completely believable.

They walked well out of sight of Ebenezer, and then Will said, "William, this little track on the left goes over to a back road that will bypass Ebenezer and take us to the outskirts of Savannah."

"Ja. Gut."

The three spies walked a little more briskly now. The sun beat down, and Will was glad of the wide-brimmed country hat. He frequently drank from the water bottle that dangled from Molly's saddle. They also stopped at every water hole to let the horses drink. It would be an all-day walk to Savannah, but the horses would be fresh.

The day wore on to become a blur of heat, dirt, sand, dust, biting insects, and swamp. Birds flitted, squirrels barked, and the occasional buzzard circled, waiting for some poor animal to breathe its last. And still, the spies plodded on, a torment of salty sweat dripping in their eyes.

Toward dusk, the trio slowly led their horses to a sentry box near the outskirts of the town. Two Redcoats sitting on a log stood up and hefted their muskets. A sergeant stepped out of the sentry box, picked up his spontoon, and held it across his body. "In the name of the King, Stop!"

The three spies all stopped. Weary from their travels and coated in dirt and sweat, they were not a threatening bunch.

"Ere, now. Wot's yer business in Savannah?"

Jasper spoke, "Ve haf been to Burke County to visit my cousin who is zick. Ve helped viz der crops. Und now, ve go back to Carolina."

"Carolina's that way."

"Ja. But we look for a tavern. Ze one in Ebenezer ist closed."

The sergeant looked at the three in disgust. Their collective odor was quite rancid. "Aye, yer needs a wash, I'll own. Tondee's Tavern is closed, but there's an inn on this road. Walk straight ahead, and you'll see it. Has a sign with a Negro woman on it."

Jasper nodded, "Danke, mein herr."

The three spies walked past the sergeant. They kept their heads bowed in exhaustion as well as to avoid the sergeant's eyes, the better not to be remembered.

~~<>~~

Jasper went into the tavern to get a room while Will and Newton took the horses to the stable. They groomed the horses, and Will produced three carrots stolen from the Purysburg mess. Newton, a man of few words, grinned and fed the carrots to his horse and Jasper's. Will took care of Molly, who stamped and whickered in delight at getting her carrot.

Tondee's Tavern being closed, the inn on Augusta Road was a lively place. Plenty of British officers were disporting themselves playing a skittles game called Aunt Sally in the yard. Aunt Sally involved a small manikin of a Negro woman with exaggerated features. The object of the game was to knock the Aunt Sally figure off a pedestal by flicking a wooden rod at it.

For some reason, this outrageously silly game caused peals of laughter and drunken encouragement from fellow competitors. Betting on the outcome appeared to be a major pastime. The Aunt Sally figure explained the inn's sign of a Black woman with exaggerated features.

Will had enjoyed some of the games at Tondee's but decided to avoid the crowd lest he be drawn into a conversation. Will walked into the interior of the inn and paid for a hot basin of water, and went to wash. Three British officers were sitting around a table drinking and playing a game of cards that Will did not recognize. That explained the Ace of Spades on the sign next to the Black woman.

While he washed at a small stand behind the inn, Will watched the comings and goings of the British officers and a few citizens whom he recognized from his time in Savannah last year. He kept his face averted, but since he was poorly dressed and dirty from the road, he didn't get a second glance from the better class of citizens. He did not shave; better to look rough and not attract attention.

Jasper and Newton had gone to the room the three had rented. They ate jerky washed down with small beer they bought from the tavern. The jerky merely added to Will's thirst, and he was glad the small beer was not intoxicating.

Jasper said, "Those drei idioten playing cards are perfekt. Ve must select zwei iss all."

Will said, "When shall we do this?"

Newton said, "Toward late, just before closing. I'll saddle the horses, and you two wait for them to go to the outhouse. I'll quietly bring the horses to the outhouse. We'll knock them on the head and throw them on horseback. William, you'll lead the way, and Will and I will each ride with a prisoner across our saddles."

Will said, "I'm going to quietly walk around the streets to see what is going on. I'll be back before 11. We can do it then."

The others nodded, and Will quietly went down the stairs, avoided the main room of the tavern, and stepped out the back door. He hurried up Broughton Street and made his way to the burying ground, where he saw British soldiers' tents pitched among the graves. This affront to human decency infuriated Will. He thought, *How can civilized people do such a thing?*

He wandered onward. Fortunately, the town was not so large that he could not cover it in a two-hour walk. Near the barracks where the Americans had been routed so ignominiously last year, he saw units of the British Army encamped. He saw some general improvement in the defensive positions, some ditches, walls, and abatis. Will's best guess was the defenses were some 50 yards from the edge of the city. Aside from the few notable improvements to the defenses, the city seemed to sleep.

A small group of Redcoats marched down Bull Street. Probably heading to mount guard for the midnight-to-dawn rotation. Heart pounding, Will stepped into the shadows to let them pass. Sweat trickled down his back, and it was not from the heat. A mosquito whined in his ear, but he didn't slap at it. A sharp movement might have drawn attention.

Will concluded that the British were well-disciplined, and there were about 3,000 of them. Keeping to the shadows as he returned to the tavern, Will walked with a purpose, like a man of business who was not engaged in subterfuge. Still, the sweat trickled, and his legs felt weak. He had the Brander pistol in his belt under his hunting shirt, but realistically he could not have withstood a challenge from an armed patrol.

If he were caught, he'd face the noose and no question. It would not matter that he had done nothing overt. That he was a Continental Army officer in mufti would be sufficient for a hanging.

~~<>~~

Will walked into the stable yard behind the Aunt Sally Tavern to see Newton holding the horses next to the watering trough as though he was giving them a drink. Jasper was in the shadows next to the privy. Will joined Jasper.

Will said in a quiet conversational tone, "What cheer?"

Jasper smirked. "Nothing yet. But zey haf not had a piss in hourz. Und zo, it vill not be long."

"And the plan once we have them on horseback?"

"We mount and quietly trot ze horses until we are close to the sentry. Zen, we gallop past ze sentry box as fast as we can go until we are out of musket shot. Zen, we go past Zubly's to ze ford I haf used before. Zen off to Cuthbert and on to Purysburg."

As Jasper finished, the back door to the tavern opened, and two British officers stumbled out. One did not bother to walk across the yard to the privy but simply let fly a stream of urine against the back of the building. The other officer, a major, laughed uproariously as he stumbled to the privy.

Jasper jerked his chin at the captain pissing against the building, and Will nodded.

The major entered the privy, and Will walked with purpose toward the captain, who was singing some silly ditty about a serving maid. He started on the second verse, a lusty tale of a maid impaled when Will hit him hard behind the right ear with the butt of the Brander pistol. The captain dropped like a stone, half in his own puddle.

Will hissed quietly, "Shit. Now Molly's going to stink of piss."

The major stepped from the privy and instantly apprehended what was happening. "I say ..."

His words were cut short when Jasper clobbered him with a small wooden truncheon.

The major said, "Ow! Damn you!"

Jasper hit him again, and he collapsed in a heap.

Newton quickly walked the horses over, and he and Will boosted the piss-drunk captain up on Molly's saddle. Then Newton quickly grabbed the major by his scarlet coat and dragged him to the second horse. Both men were draped over the front of the horses' saddles, and the three spies mounted and trotted out of the tavern stable yard.

A left turn and the spies were soon quietly walking the horses in the shadows on the left side of the street. There was a full moon, and that aided in seeing the way. The light was welcome as the streets were pocked from lack of repair since the rebellion. The frequent potholes were perfect for breaking a horse's leg. Of course, the well-lit countryside also made the horsemen more visible.

In the shadow of a building about 100 yards from the sentry box on the Augusta Road, the three stopped. Jasper dismounted and went about expertly tying the British officers' hands and feet. Then he ran a rope under the horse and tied the officers so they would not fall off.

As Jasper finished, the major made a noise. Jasper clobbered him again with the truncheon. Will hoped the major would not die unnecessarily. Will was not being altruistic. All the trouble of taking him prisoner would be for naught if he were dead.

Jasper re-mounted, and they quietly trotted around the building and into the road. As they walked the horses toward the checkpoint, all three spies were alert for any movement from the sentries. 50 yards … 30 yards … 20 yards. One of the sentries saw the three horsemen in a moonbeam and stood up.

"'Alt! 'Oo goes there?"

Will said, "Three travelers going to Bethlehem."

The sentry's voice was thick with sarcasm, "Right, Bethlehem? Are you the bloody wise men?"

By this point, they were almost on top of the sentry, whose eyes went wide as he saw British officers draped over two of the horses.

"'Ere! Wot's this?" He swung his musket up just as Jasper kicked him hard in the chest.

The sentry flew backward, and the musket flopped in the dirt. The second sentry and the sergeant, now alerted by the commotion, both burst upon the scene as the three spies spurred their horses to a gallop and rushed into the night.

A shout and a musket shot cracked the quiet of the night. Will not so much heard but felt the musket shot as the ball whizzed past his head. And then the trio of spies were out of musket shot and soon around a bend.

"We kannst nicht stop now. Zey vill get ze cavalry."

The three roared down the road, thankful for the moonlit night, as they rushed away from Savannah. The moonlight and the white sandy road made for quicker travel with less chance of breaking a horse's leg. Will thanked God for that because he could not stand the thought of Molly being hurt.

Daybreak found the three spies trotting toward the ford that Jasper knew above Zubly's Ferry. Here, they could cross undetected. Besides, Zubly's loyalty was ever in question, so they could not have trusted him if they took the Ferry.

The idea of taking Molly into the Savannah River again disturbed Will. She was a great horse, and she was his loyal companion. He knew the last crossing in the frigid water and into the deeper part of the river where the horses had to swim had been terrible for Molly and Will. *Is it Molly I worry about, or is it truly me?*

~~<>~~

The three spies and their captives made it into Cuthbert's camp about three hours later.

Cuthbert was visibly relieved that they made it back. "Welcome back! I see you were successful."

Will said, "Hello, Cuth. I'm glad to see you. We had quite an adventure."

Will pulled Jasper aside. "William, I have a further mission in Georgia, so Cuth and I will be going back. I will write a report and draw a diagram of Savannah's defenses that you can take back to the higher-ups."

Jasper looked at Will quizzically. "You do not neet mein help?"

"Cuth knows the way for this job. So, no. Besides, getting the two prisoners back to be interrogated was the main mission."

"Ja, Herr Mayor!"

Will smiled. "It's still Will."

"Gut. Back come safely to ze Fort Moultrie, Ja?"

"I will."

The British major began to thrash some, and Will could not blame him. Being flopped over a galloping horse all night on top of being drunk and disorderly must have been most uncomfortable.

Jasper and Newton got the two officers off the horses and gave them water. The prisoners were still bound hand and foot.

Will said, "I think we should search them and confiscate any currency and papers."

"Ja. Und you are writing a report for us?"

Will said, "Yes. Also, when you get to Purysburg, tell Lieutenant Legare I want him to wait for us for no more than five days before returning to Charlestown. If we are not back in five days, we've been taken, and he is to return to Fort Morris."

"Ja. Sofort."

Will sat down with a pen, inkpot, and paper and wrote his report. He drew a small map of Savannah with British camps annotated. He concluded that about 3000 troops, Redcoats,

Hessians, and Militia, were in Savannah. He mentioned that Brown's Rangers, also called The King's Carolina Rangers, were at Ebenezer manning three stout redoubts. He mentioned there were visible fortifications around Savannah but that these had not been greatly improved.

Will recommended an immediate assault, if possible. He mentioned the guard's comment that the British had insufficient forces to hold the backcountry in Georgia. Finally, Will included a paragraph commending Jasper's leadership and Newton's bravery in the face of certain execution if captured.

Two hours later, Jasper and Newton put the captives on horses and walked out of camp headed toward Purysburg.

Will looked at Cuthbert, "Tomorrow at dawn, we'll go to Sunbury."

Chapter 13 – Sunbury

An hour before dawn, Will and Cuthbert walked their horses quietly out of the thicket that had become their forward base outside Savannah. They walked the horses down the road. The heat of the last few days continued, and Will and Cuthbert wore loose shirts, pants, and boots. No hunting shirts or coats: the heat was too oppressive.

Will carried all his weapons on this trip. Still, he did not flash the rifles but left them under a horse blanket draped over their scabbards. The English dragoon carbine rode along with the rifles rather than resting on Will's hip. Uncle Ewan's dirk rode in a saddlebag. Better to be unobtrusive. Will carried the Brander pistol in his belt, and Cuthbert carried his pistol on his hip, tucked into his belt.

Will and Cuth made their way north to Hudson's Ferry and crossed the Savannah River. This put them north of Ebenezer, and the Loyalist outpost there. They threaded their way southeasterly along a back road. Their destination was Samuel Elbert's country estate and farm.

Will said, "Cuth, you seem to know this area very well."

"Aye, Sir. My people owned a plantation outside Savannah. We used to come here a good bit."

"I thought your people were from Sunbury?"

"Aye, they are. But we have relations in Beaufort, and there's the old plantation outside Savannah. My father moved the family to Sunbury a few years back. He had become quite a merchant and the plantation business was very costly. He believes in his bairns making their own way, so when I heard you needed an apprentice gunsmith, I jumped."

Will said, "Aye, gunsmithing will pay your bills all your life, Cuth. At least, I think so. I was planning to set up my shop on the frontier, but 'tis only a dream until this war is over."

"I hope to do the same. My family is well off, and I'm sure father will help me get a start. But we have to win this fight first."

"You never said, but isn't Cuthbert a Scottish name?"

"Oh, my people go back to Castlehill near Inverness. I'm told someone was a Laird in the 1300's. I don't know if that's true. My mother says Cuthbert comes from St Cuthbert, who was some saint in the days of early England."

"Well, your lordship! Or should I call you Saint Charles?"

"Ha! I think I shall be lucky to be a gunsmith in this new world of ours."

~~<>~~

The day wore on and the heat rose along with the ascent of the sun. The buzz of insects and bird song made the day noisy. A complete lack of wind made for a long, sweaty plod for man and beast. Every hour they stopped at a water hole or creek and poured water into the horses as well as themselves. They dumped buckets of water over their heads which brought only brief relief.

A bit before dark, Will and Cuth plodded into Samuel Elbert's farmyard. Elizabeth Rae Elbert flicked the curtains aside from a window at the front of the farmhouse.

"Will? Is that you?"

"Yes, Ma'am."

Liz Elbert, a diminutive woman with short dark hair and small shoulders, ran from the front door and threw her arms around Will's neck. All convention for a married woman aside, she was thrilled to see him.

Liz Elbert said, "What's this ma'am stuff? Didn't I tell you to call me Liz?"

"Aye, you did. But I didn't want to presume."

"Presume? Hell, you're almost my son. And who's this?"

"This is Charles Cuthbert."

Cuth said, "I have the privilege of being Major Yelverton's orderly, ma'am."

Liz said, "Well, I'm not a ma'am to you either. If you take care of Will, you're high in my book, as well."

Cuth blushed. "Thank you, ma'am ... er, Liz."

Liz looked at the two of them, "Come in. I think there must be a story here."

Will said, "Aye, we're on a bit of a mission."

~~<>~~

Will, Cuthbert, and Liz Elbert sat at her modest dining table.

Liz's dark eyes were both beautiful and penetrating, "You didn't come all this way, walking, behind the British lines, to sit and chat with me."

"While I love to visit with you, Liz, our mission is to go to Sunbury to learn how the British are treating our senior prisoners. In particular, we want to know if there is possible any escape for people like Sam, er, Colonel Elbert."

Liz put her hand to her mouth, "Will, 'tis very unsafe to be here. Worse, 'tis terribly dangerous for you two to go to Sunbury."

"Why is that, Liz?"

"Because Sam has given his parole, he may be punished if they learn he has talked to you."

"But our information is that the British have not upheld their version of the paroles of the senior officers. Thus, they should be released from the obligation of their parole and should be free to escape."

Liz looked sick, "Oh, God. I can't stand the thought of Sam being put in a position that he might be hanged for a lack of honor."

"'Tis not dishonorable to escape when the enemy has not been honest in their treatment of a prisoner on parole."

"You and I might agree on this, Will, but the British hangman might have another opinion."

Will looked pained. His eyes squinted and he looked out the window of Liz's pleasant little farmhouse dining room. "I shan't talk the Colonel into a breach of his honor or into doing something that would give the British an excuse to mistreat him."

Liz's shoulders slumped. "Will, Sam Elbert is all I have. The rotten British have undoubtedly taken our home at Rae's Creek and are using it for who knows what purpose. This little farm property is all we have that we can be sure of. So far, they have not molested me here, but that is not a certainty."

Will said, "We will be most circumspect, and Sam will have the last word."

Liz said, "I know I can trust you, Will. Ephram will show you to your rooms. I have asked the kitchen to put on extra food. We shall have a pleasant feast."

~~<>~~

Dinner was simple, but as promised, it was a feast. The main course was a piece of beef, braised to fall-apart tenderness, mixed with a few potatoes and some carrots. Deer tongue fennel gathered from the nearby swamp mixed with some greens called poke salad made a green vegetable. The greens were stewed for hours with a chunk of smoked pork. Will had eaten poke salad before and knew it must be cooked multiple times and rinsed before the final cook, or else it was poisonous. This meal was perfect. It certainly was better than the muddy, half-cooked meat and grits that was military fare.

After dinner, Liz, Will and Cuthbert sat on the front porch of the Elberts' farmhouse. Mosquitoes whined, and the air was thick but cooler. A light breeze dried the sweat. Liz asked the kitchen servants to bring some chilled cider. The cider was not truly chilled. It was more like cool from being kept in a spring house where water flowed through, reducing the temperature.

After a while, Cuth said, "Please excuse me, Sir, ma'am. I will retire."

160

And Will and Liz sat alone in quiet contented friendship.

Liz said, "Last I saw you, 'twas about a woman you were fretting."

"Aye. She is married and now has a child. She couldn't wait, you see."

"I think you told me that. Did you have time to bid her adieu?"

"Yes. She came to me at her parents' home."

"And ... ?"

"And, what?"

"Do come on, Will."

Will smiled in the dark. It was a sad smile. "We said goodbye."

"You took her, didn't you!"

"I had no choice."

"Of course you didn't. She will always be your love. But she's married and now you are alone."

"Not entirely. I married Mary Proctor."

"You DID! Good for you, Will Yelverton! She is Homer Proctor's daughter?"

"Aye."

"Well, I am certain she's a happy young woman. You're quite a man, Will."

"Oh, I'm not so much of anything, but she is special, and I love her."

"Good. And she loves you?"

"Oh, yes, I think so."

"Then I am content that your life is good. Miss Charlotte Jones wanted you desperately."

"Aye, she made that clear."

"Did she now? Damn! I had no idea."

Will said, "We gentlemen try very hard never to betray the confidence of a young lady."

Liz threw her head back and brayed a laugh.

~~<>~~

The morning dawned just as hot as the day before. July in coastal Georgia was hell, and this was no exception.

Will and Cuthbert trotted out of Liz's farmyard on the way to Sunbury, a half-day ride. They each pulled a spare horse along as they trotted down the road. Will would have rather spared Molly the effort of carrying his weight, but speed was critical to getting to Sunbury and then getting back. The spare horses were for Elbert and whichever Patriot leader who might want to escape.

Will thought, *This is a fool's errand. But Lincoln and Marion demanded I do this.*

The two men trotted along in the heat that was too hot to permit conversation. Frequent stops at anything that resembled water kept the horses from collapsing. Will's shirt was soon brown from the tea-colored tannin-filled water. He did not care. It was pleasant to soak the shirt every few miles of dusty, sweat-laden travel.

At half the water holes, startled moccasin snakes rushed away from the travelers. Will thought, *Just as well. I don't need to get bitten.*

At one hole, a 10-foot alligator dozed a dozen feet away. Will and Cuth watched the gator with caution as they got water and quietly left.

Cuthbert said, "We're about a mile from Sunbury, Sir. I think it best to dismount and walk the horses from here."

Soon, the men and the horses came within sight of the small seacoast town of Sunbury. Will noticed it looked worse for wear from the last time he saw it. In the distance, he could see the burned-out hulks of the Georgia Navy's galleys beached on Sapelo. The ribs and blackened frames of the *Washington*, *Bulloch*, and *Lee* were sad testaments to the British triumph over Georgia. No ships were in port. When Will had been here last year, the wharves had been full and there were ships waiting for a chance to dock and offload cargo.

Will scanned over to Fort Morris where he saw damage from a brief bombardment. The barracks building where he had lived for several months was blackened and nothing but a couple of sagging walls of brick. Some Redcoats walked around in the parade ground of the once-proud little dirt fort.

Will leaned over and spat on the ground. He said, "I wish that fool Howe had listened and moved some of the guns from here to Savannah and put them at Girardeau's. We could have stopped the British in their tracks before they ever set foot on land."

Cuthbert said, "Aye, we were denied the things we needed to save Savannah. Sir, if you will wait here in this thicket, I shall visit my family and learn where the captives are kept."

Will, angry to his core over the foolish leadership at Savannah last year, nodded.

Cuth walked off toward the town, quietly keeping to the trees all the way until the last hundred yards to one of the homes. He was gone for a while. Will expected this exact situation as Cuth's family were probably thrilled to see him. Will just prayed that none of Cuth's relatives were loyalists who would hurry to betray Cuth to the British.

The minutes passed as slowly as molasses in winter.

Cuth exited the back of the house and walked through the small garden and up the slight hill into the woods where Will waited.

"They say that Elbert and some of the other captives are living in houses in the town. They occasionally take late-afternoon walks for exercise and to also exercise a small amount of freedom."

Will said, "Any idea of where they go for their walks?"

"Aye. We're standing very close to the path they usually take. Just over there is the burying ground and then the military cemetery for all the poor soldiers who came south and died in the heat."

Will said, "Then let's just wait here and see what happens."

Cuth nodded. "I hope today is one of their days for exercise."

~~<>~~

The day wore into twilight and the heat broke. A light onshore breeze brought relief from the mosquitos and the smell of the marsh reminded Will of his months in Sunbury. A few minutes later, Will saw the familiar figure of Colonel Samuel Elbert step out the door of one of the houses in the village.

Elbert walked with a purpose toward the woods and the path that was some 30 feet from where Will and Cuthbert stood behind the trunk of a stout oak. Will and Cuth had left the horses some 50 yards back down the path.

Soon, Colonel Samuel Elbert of the Continental Army, Brigadier General of the Georgia Militia, walked up the path with purpose. Sam Elbert only did things with a purpose. As was Elbert's habit, he wore his full uniform, polished boots and all. His hair was powdered and arranged in a que down his back.

In brief moments, Sam Elbert rounded the oak tree to face four Indians who silently stood up from the thicket across from Will and Cuth.

One of the Indians raised a musket, jerked the cock back, and aimed at Elbert's chest.

Elbert stopped short. His mouth hung open in an O shape, his surprise complete.

Another Indian who seemed to be in charge, said something unintelligible to Elbert who replied in the same language. Their tones were tense, edgy. The fourth Indian moved to keep Will and Cuthbert in view.

Elbert had not seen Will and Cuthbert, who froze stock still. Will understood that an overt move toward his pistol would result in a tremendous firefight that would leave Elbert dead, and very likely Will and Cuthbert dead, too.

Will softly said out of the side of his mouth, "Don't move."

Cuth's gently snorted breath acknowledged this command.

Elbert stood steady and focused on the Indians. They exchanged heated remarks in the Indian language. Will thought the Indians were Creeks, but he was not certain. Soon, the Indian leader made a sharp remark, and the brave with the musket lowered the barrel and uncocked the hammer. The brave watching Will and Cuthbert relaxed a bit, his posture was less tense.

Elbert and the Indian leader exchanged several more comments in rapid-fire Creek language. Will had no idea what the words were.

In a flash, the four Indians turned and quickly disappeared into the darkening woods.

Elbert's shoulders drooped and he breathed out a deep shuddering breath.

Will and Cuthbert stepped around the tree to an astonished Elbert, who blurted, "What are you two doing here?"

"We came to rescue you, Sir," Will said.

"Harrumph! Fine job of that! Those Indians were hired to kill me, but they recognized who I am. I used to be an Indian agent and they know I am an honest man. I spoke with them about who sent them. T'was the British. They thought I would be better dead, but they could not kill me themselves since I accepted British parole as their prisoner."

Will said, "So the British want you dead, in spite of your accepting parole? Why?"

"Because they somehow think me a threat, obviously."

Will said, "Well, that's good because we brought a horse from your farm. We can be gone in a trice and have you home to Liz in a day. From there, we can take you to Charlestown and you can be part of the army. It won't be long before we take Savannah back from the British."

"Ha! You actually think the buffoons who run the Continental Army are capable of taking Savannah?"

"Sir, I hope they can do that. If not, I fear the British will come south and use Georgia as a base from which they will take the Carolinas. Then, God help us."

"Will, you have become quite a strategic thinker. And I believe you are right, but I can go nowhere!" Elbert exclaimed.

Will said, "Why not? The British just tried to have you killed."

"Aye, Will. But just because the British have no honor does not mean I can't have any. Honor fades not, Will. Either one has honor, or one does not. I shan't go back on my parole."

Will stood with his shoulders stooped. "I wanted to help you, Sir."

"I know that, Will. You are a good man, and I agree with you. If this were just a matter of Sam Elbert getting on a horse and riding to Charlestown, then you'd be 100 yards behind me all the way there. But I have given my word. Honor is all we have. Besides, what would happen to men like Walton and the others who are here if I broke my parole and ran?"

Will nodded miserably.

"Look, Will. I would give anything to go with you. I know you also risked yourself and young Cuthbert here to come to find me. Your courage is appreciated."

"Liz desperately wants you home, Sir."

"Aye, and I want to see her. She is a fine woman. You should find such a girl, Will."

"I have, Sir. I married Mary Proctor in Charlestown."

"Indeed! When?"

"Just last month."

"I'm delighted and congratulate you on an excellent match." Elbert looked at Cuthbert, "Your family is here."

Cuthbert nodded, "Aye, Sir. One or two of them are loyalists, so I had to be careful in coming here."

Elbert looked troubled, "Yes, I was going to warn you of this. You two must leave and soon. Will, I shall do everything in my power to be released from my parole and return to the fight. Give Liz my love and please give my warmest best wishes to the commanders of our army. I hope the coming fight for Savannah is successful."

Will said, "I will tell them all, Sir. Know that Liz thinks of you all the time and asked me to tell you that she waits for you. She is at the farm in case you didn't know."

Elbert nodded, his eyes shining in the growing gloom, "Honor fades not, Will. Honor fades not. Remember that."

Chapter 14 – The Rescue

Will and Cuthbert rode along, heading back toward Hudson's Ferry. The British assigned control of the backcountry to the militia, so Will constantly was on guard for a Loyalist militia patrol. Fortunately, the Loyalist militia had neither sufficient men nor funding, and there were few militia patrols. Still, the ride was nerve-wracking. Will constantly scanned for escape routes.

The heat continued with threatening clouds piling high in the sky every day until, at about 5 o'clock, Will could smell the ozone and humidity of a storm somewhere. The storms seemed to catch against the river, thus the drought on the South Carolina side. The Georgia side of the river was wet. More than once these past few days, Will and Cuth had been drenched. The road was wet and boggy from a massive gusher of rain the day before. The muddy road made hard walking for the horses.

Will and Cuthbert discussed skipping Hudson's Ferry to avoid patrols and going somewhat south to Jasper's secret ford. But the weather had swollen the river and the dozens of creeks that fed it. So, it would have to be the ferry.

They ambled toward the ferry road, the horses walking and picking their way around water holes that might be deep. Will was content with their slow progress because a broken leg for a horse was a death sentence.

They had left the extra horses at Liz Elbert's farm when they told her that Samuel would not break his parole. Liz tried to be stoic but lost her composure and sobbed into Will's filthy shirt. Her tears added to his sweat. He held her and let her cry, her shoulders wracked with sadness.

Finally, she pushed away. She wiped her reddened face on her apron and said, "I know I look a mess, and that was quite a display for you to have to endure, Will."

Will said, "Not at all, Liz. I was just as disappointed when he refused to come with us. But Sam's quite stubborn when it comes to honoring his word. He told me, 'honor fades not.' I think the British have not honored their part of the parole bargain. I have also heard of the British changing the terms of parole and then hanging the poor parolee for some trumped-up violation. I understand it is terrible in the backcountry."

Liz nodded, "I have heard the same, Will. This is the backcountry, but it's not quite Wilkes County. I heard that around Augusta, the Tory militia hang any man who refuses to sign a loyalty oath."

Will and Cuthbert stayed the night at Elbert's home and moved on in the morning. Now it was late day, and a sudden shift in temperature warned that the big clouds Will had watched all day were about to burst and provide yet another drenching.

A sudden chill gust bent the trees, followed by a crack of thunder, and then rain. Large droplets left pockmarks on the surface of the road. The rain was so hard it stung exposed skin, and the two riders left the road to shelter under a giant oak. The oak was so big that its spreading limbs touched the ground in several places. The area under the tree was large and dark. The tree did provide some shelter from the downpour, at an increased risk of being struck by lightning. The riders took that chance.

An hour of pouring rain and cracking thunder ended with a whimper as the storm moved on. Will grinned at Cuthbert, "We keep this up, we won't need a wash when we get to Purysburg."

Cuthbert smirked, "Speak for yourself, Sir. I can't wait to get this road grime off me. I stink."

~~<>~~

Will and Cuthbert trotted around a curve, their horses' hooves spraying mud with every step. They cleared the curve, and a rider stepped out from the woods some 50 yards ahead. Usually, Will would have known someone was there, but with the heavy rain just passed, there were no birds to flush and no noises to pick up on. Will and Cuth were trapped!

The rider raised an arm that held a musket. Something was familiar about this man.

It was Sergeant Jasper, "Ach, zo, Herr Mayor! Guten tag."

"Hello, William. What brings you here?"

"I haff visited mein bruder who here lifs. He is ein loyalist, but he does not holt mit hanging ze Rebels. He tell me zey are taking prisoners to Savannah. Rebels. They will hang them when they arrive in the city."

Will said, "I'm surprised they didn't hang them right away."

"Ja, but maybe zey want ze spectacle uf ze Rebels dangling. I kannst nicht let zem do zis! I vill save zem if I can."

"And you want Cuth and me to help."

"Ja. I haf been waiting fur you to here kom."

Will said, "How did you know we would come here?"

"You are nicht hard to track, Herr Mayor."

Will smirked, "I thought we were better than that."

"Ach, ja. You fool der Britiche but not Jasper."

"What are we going to do to rescue the prisoners?"

"Ze are held in ein cabin nearby. I habe ein plan."

Jasper had scouted out the cabin where the prisoners were being held. It was an old, disused farmstead abandoned when the revolution started. There were two guards outside the cabin, one on the door and one in the narrow lane leading to the small farmyard. The lane was now overgrown by weeds and volunteer plants. No plot of land in Georgia stays fallow for long. This plot was now becoming a thicket. *All the better for Jasper's purpose*, Will thought.

The moon had waned, and heavy clouds obscured the remaining moonlight. There was just enough light to move about without running into a tree or falling into a ditch. A candle in the cabin provided some light, the chinking between the logs had fallen out long ago and allowed light to escape.

Jasper, Will, and Cuthbert stood with the horses about 100 yards downwind from the cabin. Jasper and Will quietly edged into the brush and began circling the farmstead. The plan was that Jasper would take the guard closest to the door while Will took out the guard in the lane. Cuthbert was to wait in the road until he saw flickers of the candle and then bring the horses to the lane. The three men carried pistols, and Will had the English Dragoon carbine. Everyone was loaded with buck and ball. Uncle Ewan's dirk dangled from Will's belt. He hoped he would not need it.

Will left his powder horns and shot case on Molly's saddle. He carried three paper cartridges in a pocket. He hoped the three extra shots would be more than he would need. If he needed more, it would mean things had gone very badly, and there would be no time to reload. Instead, he and Jasper would be frantically running through the woods to escape the Tories' wrath. If things did go badly, Cuthbert was briefed to hurry back to the spot where they split up and wait as long as he could before mounting and riding off. No sense in all three being captured to dangle alongside the prisoners they hoped to rescue.

The night was deathly quiet as Will crept through the forest. It was more a thicket than a forest since it had once been a farm field. Reeds, bushes, and a canebrake had taken residence in the field. The reeds and cane were miserable to negotiate with stealth. More than one tiny branch stuck in Will's face. One narrowly missed his eye, stinging the flesh on his cheek. Another bush, this one full of thorns, raked Will's arm, digging through his shirt and threatening the mission by wiggling precipitously. Will stepped back and gingerly pulled his sleeve out of the thorn bush. His sleeve was damp. *Blood,* Will thought.

A few more steps and Will could see the candlelight seeping through the cracks in the cabin wall. Silhouetted against the faint light from the cabin, Will saw his quarry and the other guard. Will also saw the faintest glimmer of Jasper in the shadow of the cabin. Will barely turned his head and got a slight whiff of horse. Cuthbert was in position. All was ready.

Will watched and waited. Jasper was to make the first move.

With a swiftness that belied his tall, lanky frame, Jasper took one step into the light and smacked the guard in the head with his club. It was the same club he had used on the British major in Savannah.

Will did not hesitate. When he saw Jasper move, he stepped into the road and hammered his guard with the buttplate of the Brander pistol. Will's guard dropped like a stone. Rolling the unconscious guard over, Will threw a length of rawhide around the guard's wrists and ankles. Then, he shoved a piece of linen into the guard's mouth. Another length of rawhide tied the gag in place, and Will hurried toward the cabin.

Jasper waited by the door. His guard was dead. Will cocked the carbine and stood to the other side of the door. They nodded to one another: one, two, three! Jasper spun and kicked the door open as Will rushed into the only room of the dilapidated house.

A militia captain was sitting at a broken-down table. He looked up in utter shock and reached for his pistol.

Booooom! Will's carbine deafened everyone in the small room and killed the captain, who took the ball in the chest and had his face and left shoulder shredded by the swan shot.

Will dropped the carbine to dangle from its sling and drew the Brander. He thumbed back the cock and looked around the room.

A militia sergeant was trying to stand up when Jasper's pistol cracked beside Will's ear. The sergeant staggered backward, caught a foot on a discarded chunk of pottery, and dropped like a stone. Jasper looked around the room for other guards.

Mouths open and eyes wide, the astonished prisoners all tried to talk at once.

"Ve must go quickly. Is dis der only militia?"

One of the prisoners said, "There are two guards outside."

Will and Jasper looked at one another. Will said, "They're not a worry, now."

Will whipped out the dirk and cut the ropes binding each prisoner's hands and feet. "Let's go."

They stepped out into the darkness and saw Cuthbert standing holding the three Patriots' horses. Jasper rushed around the back of the cabin and came back with four horses—one for each prisoner.

"Ve must hurry. The shots vill haf alarmed someone. Ve go to ze Hudson's Ferry, sofort."

~~<>~~

The seven men trotted along in silence. Jasper was in the lead, and Will brought up the rear. They hurried but avoided galloping because this road was slick with mud and just as severely pocked as all the others. They let the horses pick their way while urging them along. Will could tell Molly was tired from the several days on the road.

Dawn was breaking as they reached the ferry. It had been four tense hours of riding, but they dared not stop. Gunfire could carry a long distance in the quiet of the night. A Loyalist troop from Ebenezer could have easily ridden to intercept them if they heard the shots.

The group boarded the ferry, and the ferryman reluctantly accepted a warrant to pay for the passage. That was not unreasonable. The Rebels were not winning any of the fights, and the situation did not promise to improve. Worse, the warrants would not be honored for many months, even years.

Will took his last carrot from the saddlebag and fed it to a very tired Molly. Molly chunked on the carrot and stamped her hoof. Will patted her neck and talked to her quietly until she settled down for the ferry ride.

Will stood at the rail, looking out at the river. The river water moved in a timeless flow to the sea.

Will considered the past few weeks. He had fought at Coosawhatchie, Ashley Ferry, and Stono Ferry. He was bone tired from the last month of constant riding in Georgia, doing spy work that guaranteed the noose if he were captured. He was pleased that he had helped to get vital information and to save these men from hanging. He was disappointed in not being able to get Elbert to escape, but Elbert had been right. Honor was all that Elbert had, and when Will thought about it, it was all he had, too.

Jasper stepped up to the rail next to Will. "There vill be more of this before der victory, Herr Mayor. Und, you must be part of it."

Will nodded and watched as the copper water rushed to the sea.

Chapter 15 – Brief Respite

Will and Cuthbert trotted into the Patriot camp at Purysburg. Jasper and the four prisoners they had rescued brought up the rear of the little formation. Will thought, *'Tis lucky there were only four prisoners, and the four guards all had horses. We would never have made it this far on foot.*

Glancing about the camp, Will saw that it was the worse for wear. Not as many Patriots were present, the others having been pulled back to Charlestown when the British came north. Legare and the small troop were still present, per Will's order.

"Ho, Lieutenant Legare! I'm glad you're still here."

Legare said, "Welcome, Sir. We were planning to leave tomorrow if you had not arrived, Sir. I'm glad we waited an extra day. One of the men was sick, and I thought we could let him rest another day."

"Good. Is he well now?"

"Aye, Sir. Touch of dysentery. He's better now." Legare made a wry face, "The thing is, we shouldn't drink the river water. 'Tis brackish when it's not flowing in spate from rains. But when there's been rain, the water is contaminated with filthy runoff from cows and such up the country."

"Can we ride north tomorrow? I'd like to rest the horses a day, as well as my bones. I'm not yet 20 years old, and still, I hurt like an old man."

"Aye, Sir. We'll prepare to leave. First light?"

"Aye. I want to get to the regiment's camp by the day after tomorrow if we can do it. 'Tis a long ride."

Later, in his tent, Will lay back. He let his back and hips relax for the first time in days. He also let his mind wander to the events of the past several days. Capturing two British officers and walking the streets of Savannah in the dark was both dangerous and nerve-wracking. The ride out of town past sentries was certainly exciting.

Will ran his mind over the discussion in the woods with Elbert. Will hoped Elbert did not think less of him for coming to talk him into escaping. Elbert said, "Honor fades not," and he believed he must honor his parole.

Will thought, *But the British provoke dishonorable behavior like slave rebellions. 'Tis true the Negroes should not be held as slaves but provoking disorder to keep the colonies paying and supplying the British is not honorable. 'Tis also not honorable to put people on prison ships and feed them nothing, as I have heard about in the north. I believe in being honorable, but 'tis not fair to insist upon honorable oaths that men cannot keep. They would hang those men we rescued for not keeping an oath they were forced to swear. They would hang Samuel Elbert merely for speaking with me in the woods. Of course, that was after British agents almost certainly set those Indians to kill him.*

Will drifted off to his first solid sleep in a fortnight.

~~<>~~

Cuthbert, God bless him, cleaned the rifles and drew their charges. Will re-loaded them with the meticulous care he always took. Will gently ran his hand over Josie's stock and touched the deer hide case Abby Kennedy had made.

With the rifles cleaned and loaded and equipment checked, Cuthbert brought a clean bowl of warm water for Will to wash away some of the road grime. Involuntarily, Abby popped into Will's thoughts. As Will washed, he remembered the day Irene Kennedy had sent him and Abby to the creek to wash off after they cleaned the two turkeys Will and David Kennedy had killed. Abby had asked Will to stand behind a bush and keep a lookout while she disrobed and washed. He saw her nude in a ray of sunlight, the brisk autumn air raising gooseflesh on her perfect skin. Embarrassed at his betrayal of her trust, he quickly turned away. That day was two years gone now, but it still haunted his thoughts and dreams.

Despite his delight in being married to Mary and his certainty that Mary loved him, Abby came to his thoughts in these unguarded moments. He thought, *Such thoughts are truly dishonorable!*

In two years of war, more, considering 1776 and Moore's Creek, many miles were behind Will. Miles made him a traveler, a journeyman. He often wondered, as a gunsmith, *"Am I more of a tinker? Riding all about fixing things like a tinker fixes pots? Have I somehow become the army's tinker? It seems I have been everywhere there is some danger, something needing to be fixed."*

Washed, Will still wore his hunting garb. He did not want to soil his uniform further. He hoped to get into Charlestown to see Mary. He missed Mary, and he sincerely wanted to retrieve his new uniform ordered from the tailor on his last visit. But mostly, he needed rest.

Feeling depressed, Will settled into Molly's saddle for yet another long ride on the battered, pot-holed King's Road to Charlestown. As usual, his rifles and various equipment rode on Molly, and she didn't seem to mind. Will smiled to himself, *Molly is such a good horse. Cuth is the best friend I have here, and I'm lucky to be married to Mary. I should cheer up!*

~~<>~~

Two days later, and once again covered in dust and road grime, the little unit of twelve troops trotted onto the Ashley River Ferry. Will wondered how the ferryman had magically conjured up another ferryboat after Moultrie's men had burned the last one.

Will and the troops found their way to Lincoln's camp and received directions to their billets. Tents and lean-tos abounded. A couple of poorly located latrines stank in the hot August breeze. As a field officer, Will was granted a tent with a cot. The tent did not reduce the latrine stink. As soon as billeting arrangements were complete, Will sought out Francis Marion.

Lieutenant Colonel Francis Marion was sitting on a camp stool in the shade of a large oak, leaning back against the tree and smoking a clay pipe. The pungent tobacco wreathed his head, making him look either like an angel or a gorgon. This was a rare moment for Marion. Will had learned he rarely relaxed. One of his lieutenants, in an unguarded moment, had commented that Francis Marion was the toughest, most driven son-of-a-bitch he'd ever encountered.

"Welcome to our sumptuous accommodations, Major Yelverton. I see you're still wearing spy garb."

Unintimidated by this mild sarcasm, Will said, "Aye, Sir. The road is terrible for grime. Oddly, 'tis wet on the Georgia side of the river. I have much to report, so I came straight away."

Marion laconically said, "Well, do tell."

Again, ignoring Marion's sardonic tone, Will did.

When Will got to the part where Elbert had refused rescue, Marion snorted. "Guess he's afraid they'll hang him if he escapes. Bastards will hang him if they can think of a reason. Doesn't matter a damn about his honor."

Will said, "Yes, but I understand him."

"Oh, aye. We all have the commitment to honor. But of late, the British make up their definition of honor as it pleases them. They don't see it as dishonorable to clap people into prison ships that are wet, stinking hulks laden with disease. They don't see it as dishonorable to feed the prisoners less than half a ration that will keep a man alive. They don't see it as dishonorable to run around the backcountry burning peoples' homes and hanging men because they won't join the loyalist militias. I could go on about bloody honor!"

Will nodded. "Aye, Jasper enlisted our help rescuing four prisoners destined for the gibbet in Savannah. Their crimes were, if I understand it, violating loyalty oaths they were forced to swear under threat of being hanged. 'Tis hell if you do, and hell if you don't."

Marion nodded, "My point, exactly." Changing tack, Marion asked, "Your report stated that Savannah is poorly defended?"

"Aye. They have made some minor improvements to the defenses. 'Twas dark, but I saw only a few changes to the defenses we had in place last year when the British took the city. It looks like they pulled down many buildings near the edges of town and have used the timber and brick to make a couple of redoubts, and shore up a ditch or two. But 'tis not much."

At this, Marion cocked an eyebrow.

Will continued, "I can't say it would be easy to take Savannah back, but the two officers we abducted let slip that sickness abounds, and only about a third of the three thousand troops are fit for duty. The water is bad. Last year I learned from the citizens of Savannah that the river water is dangerous to drink. My guess is there is not sufficient well water to supply the people and the troops."

Marion glumly said, "'Tis something for us to consider as well. We have considerable sickness here. I don't think we have sufficient troops to march on Savannah. Even if everyone were well, most of our forces consist of backwoods clodhoppers with ducking guns that don't work well. We have few bayonets and fewer troops trained to use them. Brier Creek should have made it clear that we can't go up against trained, professional troops with our half-trained militia. But go we shall. 'Tis a matter of time before someone decides we must troop off to Savannah and hurl ourselves against whatever defenses they have put in place."

Will said, "I thought we gave a good account of ourselves when they came to Charlestown."

Marion stared into the distance, "Will, I think they were testing our defenses and commanders. They were learning the lay of the land and determining how they will beat us when they want to. I will be greatly surprised if they don't put a huge army ashore hereabouts and take Charlestown in a week."

Will said, "You seem gloomy, Sir. Much more than if we were simply facing defeat from the British."

"Aye, 'tis hard to listen to unreasonably optimistic ideas and plans. I can depend upon you to say what you think is true. You don't paint a cheap piece of pottery with shiny Japanese lacquer and proclaim it a treasure. You are wonderfully honest."

Will said, "Oh, I was unaware that others didn't tell the truth."

"Oh, they tell the truth or at least their version of it. Many curry political favor and are bootlickers telling the generals what the generals want to hear."

"How can we win like that, Sir?"

Marion's eyes tightened, "I should think the answer is obvious, Will."

Will's face fell, and Marion said, "'Tis above our ranks to attempt to correct the toadying and sycophancy."

Will nodded, but he really didn't understand.

Brightening, Marion said, "Take four days' furlough to visit your wife and put your affairs in order, Will. I fear something is brewing. The British officers you and Jasper took let slip that the British plan to take all of the South. That is not a surprise. They've wanted to dominate the South since 1776. After all, the Southern colonies are the basis of the American economy."

Marion looked into the distance, reliving the past, "Our success at Fort Sullivan turned the British back and disappointed them. They will come north from Savannah when they can get more troops. This almost certainly means a fleet coming to land and march on Charlestown."

"Where will they land, Sir?"

"When is actually the question, Will. As long as the British have Maitland sitting in Beaufort with several hundred well-trained, experienced troops, I would bet they will land somewhere near there. I think a landing on John's Island with support from Maitland in Beaufort, and their southern flank covered further by Savannah would be the correct military choice. But, when?

Well, I think when is merely a question of their transport and supply. When they believe they can get sufficient ships to transport the troops and provide supplies once they land, they will come."

Marion continued, "I wouldn't give us a chance in hell of taking Beaufort at this stage. Maitland is too good a commander to fall to this bunch. Thus, we must take Savannah to deny them an operating base and to threaten their southern flank should they bring an army and land on the Carolina shore. The problem we face is that we have mostly militia troops, and I think we might be able to muster 1,000 to march to Savannah. The British have 3,000 in Savannah, so they outnumber us 3 to 1. Knowledgeable military men know the ratio must be some 3 to 1 in the other direction to have any chance of overcoming an entrenched defense."

Will said, "This seems pretty bleak, Sir."

Francis Marion dragged on his clay pipe and exhaled pungent smoke. "Indeed, Will, indeed. But for now, I'm sitting here under the shade of this magnificent tree, enjoying my pipe, and taking the air. The smell of the latrines is especially piquant this time of morning."

~~<>~~

The next morning, Will rode Molly to the house on Bay Street. Cuthbert came along; he had earned a four-day furlough, too.

They trotted into the stable yard in front of the carriage house to the delighted squeals of Mary as she burst from the house.

"Will! Cuth! I'm so happy to see you." She threw convention to the winds and threw her arms around Will, and kissed him passionately.

Cuthbert turned and led the horses into the carriage house.

Mary whispered in Will's ear, "You shall be rewarded handsomely for coming home in one piece. That is, right after we wash the stink off of you."

Will grinned, his loins stirring at the thought of whatever might be meant by 'handsomely rewarded.'

He said, "'Tis only four days, but I'm so happy to be here. The last month has been quite exhausting, and I have missed you."

Mary lowered her eyes, and a blush crept up her throat. "I have missed you, too. Some of my dreams have been quite ... inappropriate."

~~<>~~

Will's bath was almost as good as the sex. And the sex was intense and fulfilling.

Will lay with his face buried in a pillow, the smell of goose down mingling with sheets that had been air-dried and ironed to crispness. He smiled, *I've never had luxury like this. All those years I slept in the Koontz's kitchen, I thought it was luxurious to be in the room with the fire … well, at least in winter. Sleeping in my own little room in the Kennedys' stable was also luxurious, I thought. I mean, who has their own private room? Even though the stable stank of horse shit, it was wonderful to have my own room. But this! This is more than I deserve. I am so lucky!"*

Mary interrupted his thoughts by kissing his shoulder blades as she ran her hand up the inside of his leg.

Will was instantly erect and rolled over to face her.

~~<>~~

That afternoon, Will and Mary sat on the piazza enjoying an intermittent breeze that flicked the leaves on the trees and cooled post-coital sweat.

Will said, "You and your parents should get out of Charlestown."

"Whatever for?"

"Marion thinks the British will come in force next time and take the city almost instantly. He believes they will land in Carolina – perhaps Johns Island. They hold Beaufort and Savannah. It will be hard to dislodge them from those two places, and they can bring quite an army to land on our shores. 'Tis a short march to Charlestown."

Mary said, "Harrumph! We are protected by the rivers. They couldn't cross the river without taking huge losses."

"Not true, my darling. They followed us across the Ashley River like it was nothing. We burned the ferryboats, but Tories helped them with boats, I'm sure. Moreover, just last week, I crossed the Ashely River Ferry, and the ferryboat had already been replaced. I'm pretty sure there are more boats than we know about. Laurens wanted to burn every house along the Coosawhatchie to reduce the chances of Tories helping the British to cross. Moultrie wouldn't let him do that. Laurens is a firebrand, but I can see Moultrie's point."

Mary stared out to the bay. "I shan't leave here, Will. So long as you are coming back here from the war, I will be here. I will wait on you every day."

Will said, "But if the British take the town, they may not treat the citizens with honor."

Mary did not look up from her needlepoint, "I'll have to take that risk."

Will sighed heavily. "Still, I think you should go. Don't go to the plantation near Sheldon because the British and others – *banditti* like that slime McGirth – might come north through there. I think you should go to Procton. It's upcountry near Camden and out of the way of an invading army."

"Perhaps. Daddy's gone there now. Something about the Negroes all running away. He will return soon. I shall ask his opinion. But I shall stay here as long as possible. I can't abandon this home as long as you will be here, however short your visits might be."

They sat in companionable silence. The slight breeze made the August heat tolerable, but just barely. Will tried to read *The Odyssey*. He wondered if Mary was his protector like Athena protected Odysseus.

He looked at Mary as she worked on her needlepoint and thought, *Does she have divine powers to protect me? Or is she putting herself in danger to be here for me?*

Will tried a different tack. "Have you considered getting the smallpox inoculation? I hear it is hard and makes you sick, but then you won't catch the deadly pox and die."

"No, I have not. But then, there's not much smallpox in town."

"Yes, but 'tis more likely to get smallpox where there are many people. At least, it seems that way. The army always has a number of cases, and we keep them separate from the healthy men. Nonetheless, soldiers still catch the disease and die. I hear 'tis a horrible death."

Mary said, "Ummm," as she ran another stitch.

Will turned back to *The Odyssey*.

Chapter 16 – The March

Will and Cuthbert returned to the 2nd Regiment routine of formations and marching. There was no target practice because there was no extra gunpowder. So, the troops paraded, marched into formation for volley fire, and pretended to fire and reload. The small concession to realism was that each man was given one cartridge. The powder in that single cartridge was used to prime his musket so that the flint ignited the prime and created a small cloud of smoke. At least the soldiers could be experienced in the puff of smoke, and officers could tell if a soldier's weapon misfired.

Will was not a commander and had no direct responsibility for troops. Seeking to be useful, he volunteered to oversee the small group of gunsmiths – some contractors, some militiamen, a few Continentals – in repairing the many weapons that were in poor condition. Soon, the misfire rate dropped considerably.

Those soldiers who had muskets with bayonets participated in bayonet practice. Other soldiers waited a turn to use the same muskets in bayonet drill, hoping they might someday capture an enemy musket and bayonet. It was the best that the rebels could do.

August wore on, and a variety of illnesses added to the misery of the heat. Most well-to-do people had decamped to their plantations outside Charlestown. Malaria and other diseases seemed to be brought by the heat and the miasma in the air.

Scattered throughout the camp were small pits where soldiers burned corn cobs and green sticks. These items smoldered and gave off clouds of smoke that the soldiers hoped would dissuade the hordes of mosquitos that constantly feasted on flesh. Some soldiers from northern colonies sickened and died, while southerners seemed unaffected by the heat.

The officers fared well; most were billeted in comfortable rooms in Charlestown. But the poor soldiers lived in tents and hovels – lean-tos, really – that did not keep the rain out. Heat and illness were a constant. Sanitation was limited, and dysentery was common.

Smallpox was not as common as dysentery, but the fatality rate from smallpox was high. As a result, Lincoln commanded some 3,000 troops, but he had only 1,000 effective soldiers.

Smallpox was the bane of an army. The ordinary form of smallpox was more common. The victim experienced high fever, vomiting, pustules forming in the mouth and other mucus membranes, and pustules on the skin the size of a pea with a dent in the middle. Despite the physical and emotional discomfort, most of the victims of this form survived to display scarring on their bodies for the rest of their lives.

The more malevolent form of the disease was less immediately visible, but then the victim suffered hemorrhages under the skin, internally; systemic collapse and death were frequent. Often, the victim was fully conscious and lucid until near the very end of the eight-day hell that was hemorrhagic smallpox.

The physicians were at a loss as to how to treat smallpox victims. The victims often suffered mostly alone, and those that died frequently met a lonely and isolated end. The only people who could help the smallpox victim were former sufferers who had acquired immunity, a few inoculated souls who were also immune, and the limited number of physicians who braved the dangers of entering the presence of a victim. Smallpox sufferers either died or did not. When they died, they were buried quickly at great risk to others who might venture to attend a funeral, regardless of how brief such a rite might be.

Smallpox occasionally popped up in the city. Pregnant women were more susceptible to the terrible death of hemorrhagic smallpox. As with the soldiers, citizens who caught smallpox suffered with little in the way of therapy, and they, too, often found a grave in the soggy, low-country soil. The ones that survived had the scars to prove their bout with the deadly disease.

~~<>~~

The first of September continued the heat and misery. The drills continued. Men died from diseases. A few deserters escaped; a few were captured and publicly hanged at guard mount on the morning after their brief court-martials and convictions.

And the French sent a fleet to Savannah.

Lincoln called a meeting of all field officers.

Lincoln surveilled the group: "Gentlemen, I have a message saying that the French under Count d'Estaing have been spotted off Tybee Island. There are a great many ships, and clearly, this is an invasion force."

The assembled officers all shouted, "Huzzah! Huzzah!"

Lincoln smiled a rare smile, "We have hoped for this, and we shall prepare and march immediately. I have also sent a letter to General McIntosh in Augusta to march with all haste toward Savannah. I will send scouts to determine the British positions in the vicinity of Savannah."

Marion asked, "Sir, what shall we do with Maitland and his troops at Beaufort? Will we attack them?"

Lincoln replied, "I have sent scouts to determine the position of Maitland and his troops, and then we shall see."

Lincoln's New England accent became thicker, "We have few troops ready for battle. Sickness and whatnot have reduced our numbahs. As a result, I prefuh to attack Savannah directly and bypahss Maitland."

An officer on the far side of the gathering said, "Sir, wouldn't Maitland present a threat to our rear?"

Lincoln replied, "Aye, 'tis true. But we must not tarry. Savannah has ineffective defensive works, and the British soldiers are as sick as ours. I know not how many troops d'Estaing brings, but an immediate combined assault should succeed. If we delay we give them time to mount a credible defense."

Another officer asked, "Do we not have spies? What do they tell us?"

Lincoln replied, "Oh, aye, we've got spies. And some of the officers here have actually been in Savannah of late." He looked directly at Will, a small smile played at the edges of his lips. "Some of these things are not certain – the number and disposition of d'Estaing's troops, for instance – but we must not tarry in anticipation of perfect information. Now, everyone back to your units and make ready. I want to march two days hence. If there are no further questions, dismissed."

~~<>~~

Will and Cuthbert rode a couple of lengths behind Lt. Colonel Marion, who had quite a sturdy horse. The horse was not a big mount, but instead was lower to the ground and not as heavy as a cavalry horse.

Will observed, "That is an impressive horse, Sir."

"Aye, 'tis a Marsh Tacky. They've been breeding these tough little horses for a very long time hereabouts. I'm told they are descended from horses left behind by the earliest Spanish missionaries and their military protectors. They are very sure-footed and don't spook when guns are fired when other horses shy and rear. This is Able, and he's quite a good ride. Not fast like your horse, Will. Fast enough and fearlessly steady."

Will nodded, "Aye, Sir, I can see that. Molly has been utterly fearless, even when the bullets were flying and she got grazed, she never spooked. I know, first-hand, the value in that."

They trotted along in the stultifying heat. Insects buzzed in their faces, and the horses' ears and tails flicked constantly. The heat made sweat pool, and that rubbed their thighs and groins raw from the damp cloth grinding against their saddles. Will wore his linen hunting trousers and left his uniform breeches in his saddlebag. The linen was less irritating, but still, the ride was miserable. It seemed to drag on forever. Will thought, *I'd like it to rain, but then it would be even worse with the humidity.*

~~<>~~

It was nearly dark on September 11th when Lincoln's army of 1,500 troops, baggage and supply train, camp followers, sutlers, and other hangers-on, arrived at Zubly's Ferry and began crossing to Ebenezer. The King's Rangers had abandoned Ebenezer and relocated to Savannah, leaving the outer edges of the city unguarded. Thus, there was no fight at the river, but the crossing was arduous and slow.

It took four days to get all army elements across the Savannah River and settled into a camp at Ebenezer. While the army camped at Ebenezer, Brigadier General Pulaski and his legion ranged out to find the French.

Cuthbert found hot water and brought it to Will with a cake of lye soap and a rag. Scrubbing off the dirt and sweat from the days on the road was welcome, and Will flopped on his bedroll with the rare pleasure of being clean. Well, cleaner. There was no getting all the grime off, it was ground into every crevice of his body. Will knew the army would march again in the next day or two, Savannah was still some 40 miles away. The sweat and grime would be back.

Still, Cuth was a good man and always looked out for Will. Will also thought, *He's making an excellent gunsmith, too. I was nominally in charge of Charlestown's gunsmiths, but Cuth made it all work.* The warm afternoon and the exhaustion of the march, combined with the comforting personal odor of his own bedroll, conspired to put Will to sleep.

~~<>~~

September 15th saw the Army on the move again to Cherokee Hill. McIntosh's brigade was encamped at Miller's Plantation, just 3 miles from Savannah. The next day, Major General Lincoln and several of his officers rode to Miller's Plantation to meet with Brigadier General Lachlan McIntosh.

As the officers tethered their horses, a rider galloped into the camp. The rider swung down from the saddle and rushed to McIntosh's tent. Clearly, there was news.

Lincoln and his entourage gathered with McIntosh to hear the news. The rider was from Pulaski's Legion. He handed a message to McIntosh and stood to the side while McIntosh read it.

McIntosh, his Scots brogue strong, belying his Highlands birth, said, "It seems Coont Pulaski and tha' French charged a British picket and took prisoners. Our losses were two men and a horse. The prisoners were interrogated. It seems our French allies," the word allies was spat out with disgust, "hae allowed a truce these last days durin' which the British hae strengthened their defenses. Noo there's quite a wall and ditch aboot tha' toon and several redoubts. They've also felled aboot half a bloody forest to make abatis."

One officer asked, "How did they do this with many of their troops sick? If our people are sick, so are theirs."

McIntosh's sarcastically drawled. "Tha' British ha' made liberal use o' slaves in diggin' tha' ditches. I suppose they're the verra same slaves they promised ta' set free if they would just run awa' to tha' British."

Several officers tittered at this laconic humor.

McIntosh sobered, "General Lincoln, this is yer party, Sir. D'ye na' hae orders?"

Lincoln smirked, "Aye, I do have orders." His New England accent nearly as broad as McIntosh's brogue, "We will encamp and set pickets. I will meet with d'Estaing. I think we should plan to attack the enemy quickly, but I do not know what d'Estaing thinks. I worry that we're in the midst of hurricane season, and setting a lengthy siege will merely expose the troops and the French Navy. That is untenable."

~~<>~~

Will and Marion trotted along abreast. Marion said, "This will not go well."

Will said, "Sir?"

"I said, this will not go well, Will. As I mentioned before, we have a small army of clodhoppers armed with ducking guns. It appears the French took several days – more than a week – to disembark somewhere south of Savannah. I heard Beaulieu Plantation, where there's a good landing. Then, they marched around for days and finally camped. I heard they had no accurate maps. We should have sent someone from Georgia who knew the roads to guide them. My God, they were probably so arrogant that they wouldn't have asked for a guide!"

Marion wiped sweat from his face. "Meanwhile, Prevost has gone completely mad with preparations. One of the spies said they have sunk British warships in the river to stop any incursion of our Navy, such as it is. Of course, they took the guns off those ships, and now they have that many more guns on their wall. A wall that, you saw for yourself, did not exist just a few weeks ago. Consider that a warship might have 30 guns. Two warships means sixty... sixty (!) ... guns added to their defenses."

Will said glumly, "This makes me sad."

"I just hope it does not make you dead, Will."

Chapter 17 – Savannah: The Siege

Lt. Colonel Marion's orderly presented Marion's compliments to Will and asked that he visit the colonel. It was early morning on the 20th of September, and it had rained every day.

Aside from the rain, nothing much had happened at Savannah. Nothing, that is, unless you count Pulaski's harassing actions against the British pickets and the Negroes who were busily bogging in the mud digging fortifications all around Savannah. Pulaski accomplished nothing other than making the British and the poor enslaved Negroes even more miserable than just being wet and exhausted from digging.

Will thought that the appearance of action was satisfying to Lincoln and McIntosh, as well as Huger and the other commanders. Maybe it impressed the French, but there was little contact between the Americans and their French allies. Arriving at Marion's tent, Will learned that this situation was about to change.

Marion said, "God knows what's going on, Will. The French are digging ditches – sapping toward the British lines. Pulaski is running around waving his saber. And the British continue digging in. They control the river. The galley *Congress* attempted to get in amongst their ships and was driven off. There have been a couple of other minor naval skirmishes. The British sank two of their ships in the deep hole in the river's bend just before the city. The guns from those ships have now been emplaced in the redoubts."

Will nodded. "Yes, Sir. We may have missed the opportunity to attack while the enemy was not yet well prepared."

Marion's black eyes narrowed, and his long, hooked nose appeared to wiggle with each word. "That is an understatement, Will. The French took days to get off their ships, and now they're setting up for a classic siege. I fear the weather will get worse, and we'll run out of time and supplies before we finally assault the city."

Will looked quizzical, "They're well supplied?"

"Yes. The British are well-supplied, and we are not. 'Tis a true inversion of the usual siege situation where the defenders are ultimately starved out. That won't happen here. We've been stripping the farms here about, but the British control the harbor and the ocean, so they want for nothing."

Will said nothing, but the corners of his mouth turned down in a mask of despair.

Marion said, "I want you to go to the French and observe what is going on. Report back of course, but more importantly, find out what we can do to push this situation ahead."

"How will I do that, Sir?"

"I'll get you a letter to d'Estaing from Lincoln asking that they work with you. We need to know what the French need from us to be ready to assault the British works. This constant rain is making a muddy mess of everything. Our supplies will be eaten up quickly while the British sit snug behind their defenses. We cannot wait."

Will said, "Yes, Sir. If I understand it, you want me to learn what the French need to get them to move ahead with an assault. If we give it to them, then they have no excuse but to attack."

Marion nodded, his face a mask of weary resignation. A half-smile played on Marion's lips, "Got it, exactly, Will."

~~<>~~

Will and Cuthbert trotted down the muddy road toward the French lines. Knowing the French were quite formal, Will had donned his complete Continental Uniform, including the sword. He hated the sword but wore it because it was expected of a field officer, and the French were sticklers for this kind of detail.

The rain came and went, and Will was thankful for an oilskin cloak he had thrown into his saddlebag at the last minute. Cuthbert was similarly attired and had a cloak as well. The two were the envy of many allied officers who stood stoically in the rain, water drizzling from their cocked hats into their eyes and down their necks.

Will left the horses with Cuthbert and went to report to Admiral d'Estaing. Formally, the admiral was Jean Baptiste Charles Henri Hector, Comte d'Estaing. He was a slight man in his early fifties, his salt-and-pepper hair swept back from a slightly receding hairline and woven into a long queue that hung down his back.

Despite the heat, humidity, and constant wetness, d'Estaing wore his woolen frock coat with its high collar and cravat. Will was surprised that the count did not seem to sweat. Comte d'Estaing's youthful face was unlined and open. His eyes were dark and penetrating, and his nose was short and almost feminine.

Will presented Lincoln's letter. "General Lincoln's compliments, *mon Admiral*." Will called d'Estaing *mon admiral* because he had been instructed to do so.

D'Estaing ran his eye over the letter and looked at Will appraisingly. His English was excellent. "*Merci*. You are quite young to be a major."

"Aye, Sir. I have been fortunate."

"General Lincoln's letter says otherwise. 'ere 'e says you 'ave fought ze Goddams – ze English – with great courage and skill. Ze general say you are young but very dependable. 'E ask zat you observe and learn what is needed to be ready to run ze Goddams out of Savannah."

Will nodded and said, "Yes, Sir. General Lincoln hopes we can assist in whatever way we can."

"You can see for yourself, *mon ami*, but I can tell you zat we must have tools to dig. As you can imagine, ze naval ships do not carry hundreds of shovels and picks. We have no wheelbarrows to move ze soil. We also need wood to shore up ze trenches as we sap closer to ze British. Where ze Goddams have ze luxury of tearing down houses for wood and bricks, we are left with sticks and logs, and must cut trees to get them."

D'Estaing's smile was genuine, "I 'ave asked *Capitaine* de Terson to show you our works and explain our needs. I'm sure you will see zat we are working wiz dispatch. Welcome to France, *Majeur*. Please let me know what you need from me."

Will made a slight formal bow and said, "Thank you, *mon Admiral*."

~~<>~~

Capitaine Phillipe Seguier de Terson, commander of a company of grenadiers, was a pleasant, avuncular young man who was frank about the situation. "We 'ave brought cannon from ze ships. Zis would be good, but we do not know how to mount them. Ze are on ze ship gun carriages, and we do not have wooden platforms on which to mount zem. Zey are useless in ze mud. We must get wood that is squared so the few carpenters we have can build ze foundation for naval carriages."

Terson and Will bogged through the mud—soft, slimy mud made worse from the digging and rain. Thunder crackled overhead as they surveyed the trenches. Many of the trench walls were slumped. Several of the trenches – saps that zig-zagged toward the British defenses- were filled with water. This was because the rainwater had nowhere to go, the water table was high, and the allied lines backed up to swamps.

Will glumly looked at the mess, hoping to find some ray of hope. He found none.

Terson and Will mounted and rode around the French camp. When they got to the Jewish Burying Ground, Will was surprised to see several hundred blacks wearing uniforms and carrying muskets. Well, most of them sheltered from the rain in lean-tos, hovels, and tents. But these men were soldiers, and they were not enslaved.

Will noticed the French camp stank worse than the American camp, which was not saying much. All military camps faced sanitation problems. The proximity of the swamps led troops to ignore latrines and simply visit the swamp when the need arose. After two weeks of occupation, the swamps were giant cesspits. The stink was multiplied by the heat and thick humidity. The rain made the swamp water encroach further on the camp.

Terson pointed at the various French siege works. "Ze men are become exhausted *Majeur*. Zere is little rest. Men spend every third night in ze trenches digging. We would do more if we had more tools. I must emphasize ze need for ze digging tools."

The next day Will and de Terson bogged through the mud to the forward trenches. The captain explained, "If we can mount ze cannon, we will be able to fire at the British trenches and redoubts. But we will have to keep the rate of fire slow because we have little ammunition. I fear this is not the case for the British."

Will looked at a French soldier's musket. "May I?"

Terson nodded tersely.

The musket was in poor repair and dirty. Will said, "I am a master gunsmith by trade."

Terson sniffed at the admission that Will was not a nobleman. "*Oui?*"

"This musket will not fire. The pan is fouled, and the weapon has not been cleaned." Indicating the soldier's cartridge box, "May I?"

"*Oui.*"

The cartridge box was wet and there was no doubt that the cartridges would never fire. "Is this the same for all the soldiers?"

Terson spoke rapid fire French to the soldier who replied diffidently, visibly shaking. Terson said, "He said zat the rains have made it impossible to stay dry and no soldat has dry cartouches. 'E said ze musket is dirty because 'e 'ave no cleaning tools zat are not foul from ze rain and mud."

Terson looked away and muttered, "Zis is mos' unfortunate and we shall pay dearly."

Will nodded and said, "We do what we can, *mon ami.*"

Terson's face was long, and his mouth turned down, "*Oui*, but eet is not enough. Zis will go badly. My God, but ze men – ours and yours – 'ave plundered the countryside for food and anything else zey can steal. It is most dishonorable!"

~~<>~~

That night, Will ate an excellent meal with the French officers. One French major said, "*Alors*, ze food your troops eat is not fit

214

for ze pigs, *Majeur*. Zis grog zat everyone trink is thick and too sweet. It make you drunk, but it is not pleasant. It make me, 'ow you say, spew."

Will said, "I assure you, *mon Majeur*, I don't drink the grog either. I much prefer your fine wine."

This got Will applause from the company of French officers. The French major said, "Zere is 'ope for ze Etats Unis!" This brought another round of laughter and applause.

Three days later, Will visited Count d'Estaing to report that he was leaving for the American camp. "I will inform General Lincoln that you need as many tools as we can find, as well as that we must assist in finding farms and houses that we can tear down for the lumber."

"*Bon!* Please tell General Lincoln zat I hope to begin bombardment of ze Goddams in a week. Thank you for visiting, and *bonne chance* in ze coming battle. I'm sure we shall see one another on ze field."

~~<>~~

Will stood in front of General Lincoln and his assembled staff. "Captain de Terson explained that the cannon cannot be mounted without wooden platforms. The ground is so soggy that the heavy cannon sags and then rolls over. The French artillery commander insisted that such a situation would never

215

allow for the guns to fire more than once before they have to be wrestled back into place."

"I'm sure Admiral d'Estaing has already requested digging tools so they can speed up the saps toward the British lines. He and Captain de Terson asked that I repeat that request. I also believe the Admiral has already stated he believes bombardment of the British works can begin in a week. I believe that means 4th October, Sir."

General Lincoln looked around the table. "Questions? No? Very well. Thank you, Major Yelverton. Your report certainly agrees with earlier reports we have had and restates d'Estaing's dem...uh...*requests*."

Will said, "General, the French weapons are in deplorable condition, and many of the troops I saw had wet cartridge boxes. Their officers admit an attack just now will not go well if it depends upon the poorly maintained muskets and damp powder."

McIntosh's face was red. He blurted, "We should nae ha' waited this long to attack! The bluddy French piddled about getting from ship to shore and then let the British ha' a bloody truce, fer Goad's sake. Worse, you tell us that their bluddy guns are in disrepair, and they've bluddy well got wet cartridges! This bluddy well won't do."

General Isaac Huger spoke up, "Thank you, Will, for this report."

Turning to Lincoln, "I had the pleasure, though brief, of serving with Major Yelverton here in Savannah when your predecessor failed to listen to Will. At the time, Major Yelverton was Mister Yelverton and had a better sense of the military situation than most of the rest of us wearing the uniform. Will begged Howe to pull guns from Sunbury and put them at Girardeau's Plantation. Elbert pushed the same idea, but Howe refused. Today, we are at this pass because Howe did not listen to this young man."

Huger turned to Will, "What do you recommend?"

Will glanced at Marion and then Lincoln. Marion nodded, and Lincoln made a resigned motion with his hand.

Will said, "Sir, I think we should consider withdrawing. The French are unprepared, and the British have had several days to erect defenses that were not here two months ago when I walked the streets of Savannah. Certainly, it was dark when I walked around, but the defenses of Savannah two months ago were nearly non-existent. Of course, we all know that the British have strengthened the defenses and are working daily to make the city harder to take."

Will paused. Looked around the group and saw some nods. Taking a deep breath, he plunged on, "I understand that we had

Maitland trapped in Beaufort, but the 24-hour truce allowed by Count d'Estaing gave Maitland the opportunity to march south and cross the Savannah under cover of the British Navy. I think, gentlemen, we should withdraw and set up strong defenses in Carolina. It makes me sad to say it, but I believe Georgia is lost."

Will blushed and looked down.

Marion interjected, "I agree with Will. This situation is untenable ..."

Clearing his voice, Lincoln glared at Marion. "We should have bottled up Maitland in Beaufort. That failing is my fault. I observe that he pulled off an impressive military maneuver in crossing many marshes and creeks on foot before being brought across the river on boats. He is a formidable commander."

Lincoln looked around the table. "My God, gentlemen! This young fella has given us something to think about. Major Yelverton, you may be dismissed with all our thanks. We shall consider your recommendation."

~~<>~~

Will sat on a stump, his face glum. He sighed heavily. He had said too much. *Well, I didn't have a military career anyway, and they asked. So, I told them.*

Marion walked up. "What the hell is your problem?"

"I fear I let you down, Sir."

"Not at all, Will. They asked, and you told them. You told them exactly what I think, too. Sadly, we cannot withdraw. For months, Lincoln begged the French envoys to mount an invasion and support our efforts. Now, they have, and honor demands that we fight alongside our allies."

Will spat out, "Honor? Honor? Damn all honor! Elbert remains captive because he won't violate his parole because of honor. We can't withdraw because of honor. We must stay here, hurl ourselves against a robust defense, and get killed. But we'll damn sure have our honor!"

Marion sat on an adjacent stump. "Aye, 'tis all about honor. But Will, without honor, what do we have? I mean, we might be alive and be able to do day-to-day things. Still, we'd always know we walked away when we should have tried."

"Sir, trying against an insurmountable force when we can step away and find another way, seems foolish to me."

"'Tis foolish, but 'tis also foolish to allow the British to have free reign here and have a fully defended southern flank. A larger army would be here in a trice to press an attack on Charlestown and soon hold all of the south."

Will looked bleak, his face white in the light of the fire, "They'll do that anyway, Sir."

"Perhaps, but we have our orders. And, in the end, we shall have our honor, Will."

Chapter 18 – The Battle

Will lay sleepless in his bedroll. Crickets chirped in unison, a rhythmic chorus that roared all night long. Insects sang in his ears, and he snuffed a persistent mosquito away from his nose. At least Cuth had found them a piece of dry ground away from the latrine stink of the swamps. Cuth had also found some disused pieces of wood and a few bricks that he used to create a kind of platform for their tents. The frequent cloud bursts soaked everything, but Will's oilskin bedroll and his makeshift tent floor were dry. He quietly thought as he rolled over, *Thank God for small favors.*

The sky began to haze with the milky dawn creeping through the trees. The insect song of the night was silenced, not by the dawn but by a sudden bursting, thundering, rolling cannonade. The French and American guns opened fire on the city of Savannah. The ground under Will's tent quaked while the trees all around the Allies camps shook, sending a cascade of trapped water as though the cannonade had torn a hole in the very heavens.

Will had known the bombardment would start soon. He thought perhaps it would have started yesterday. Count d'Estaing claimed the French would be ready by the 4th of October, and he was good to his word.

221

Will pulled on his boots and clamored out of his tent. He stood for a moment getting his bearings and looking across the plain toward the British lines. He walked to where he saw Marion standing in the orange glow of brightening dawn. Marion handed him a spyglass. "See what you think."

Will looked through the glass and scanned from left to right. He looked at the lines in the dim light and then raised the glass to look at the town. "We're destroying the city, but the lines are intact, Sir."

"Aye. We're not making a dent in their defenses, our rounds are going long, and I don't see much effort to correct that. I regret to say you were right about our ability – us and the French – to reduce the British defenses."

~~<>~~

Will had little to do for the next three days. He merely rolled with the continuous slamming of guns and the sporadic return fire of the British.

Twice a ship wore in close to the near shore of the Savannah River, perhaps 300 yards from Will's tent, and opened fire. Round shot smashed through the trees shattering trunks and raining splinters. Will learned the ship's name was *Germain,* and her captain was none other than John Mowbray.

Will grinned a wry smile to himself. Last year he had encountered Mowbray twice. The first meeting was when Will, a civilian aboard the privateer *Beatrice*, was involved in a running Naval fight off the Carolina coast with Mowbray's ship, the *Rebecca*. *Rebecca* was a dangerous coastal raider flying the British flag and operating from St Augustine, Florida. As the fight started, Will used Josie to shoot Mowbray's plumed hat from his balding head. Mowbray threw a tantrum and tried desperately to capture the *Beatrice*. Fortunately, Mowbray failed, and the *Beatrice* safely made port at Sunbury, Georgia.

The second engagement was when Will, a civilian volunteer aboard the Georgia naval galley *Washington*, met the *Rebecca* and Mowbray in the Frederica River. Mowbray recognized Will and, despite bullets and cannon fire, had doffed his hat in salute. Mowbray and the British lost that fight, too, and a badly damaged *Rebecca* became a rebel prize.

Will thought, *I'd shoot more than his hat this time.*

Friday, October 8th, dawned soggy but clear. Will hoped it would stay that way. He ate a hard biscuit and a piece of dry ham that Cuth had managed to scrounge. It was terrible but not as bad as most others were eating. Marion sent his orderly to advise Will of an officer's call. The cannonade continued, with most of the town shot through, but the British lines appeared largely undamaged. The mud before the earthen walls simply absorbed round shot with nothing more than a spray of dirt and foul water.

Marion waited until the 2nd South Carolina Regiment's officers were assembled. Will nodded to several. He stood toward the side with Lieutenants Bush and Hume. Will noted Sergeant Jasper was in attendance, a sign of the respect Marion had for his abilities. Will smiled at Jasper, who nodded with a tight smile.

Marion cleared his throat, and the group became quiet. "Gentlemen, we attack at dawn tomorrow. We will form columns at 4 am. The French will form three columns on the left and we will form two columns on the right. The main objective is Spring Hill Redoubt, directly on the road, or what's left of it. Some elements will move left to take the flanking redoubts."

"General Pulaski will conduct a demonstration before the British on our far left, and he will charge the smaller redoubts when opportune. General Huger will conduct a demonstration in front of the central redoubt to our far right and to the right of the French. Huger's forces will attack first to distract and draw the enemy's attention to the right."

"Be sure your men are fed and check their muskets and cartridge boxes to make sure their powder is dry. Tomorrow will be hard going with the mud. Men must first take the abatis out of the way and then rush the walls. I expect we will have many wounded and hope every man will do his duty. Any questions? No? Then, dismissed."

Will stood behind a small dirt mound that afforded some protection from the British counterfire. He looked over the enemy lines. Lines he and Marion would attempt to take in the morning.

The British lines extended along the ridge that Savannah occupied. Yamacraw Creek formed an impenetrable boundary. The lines were a chain of redoubts with cannon batteries linked with dirt walls. Abatis fronted ditches all along the front.

In the center of the line, Huger's objective was a formidable battery made of dirt and brick where a large public building of brick had stood. Will realized Huger was not expected to take this strong position but rather to make it appear that this redoubt was the main objective of the Allied assault.

Will scanned to the left and looked at the Spring Hill Redoubt. This was the objective for the 2nd South Carolina Regiment tomorrow morning. The redoubt commanded Yamacraw Creek, with two smaller redoubts and an armed galley adding to the defenses on the extreme left. Pulaski was to attack these smaller defenses to the left, and Will wished him luck. He would need it.

Will thought that the British had done an excellent job of building defenses that were extensive and made the best use of the few men they had. Tomorrow morning would be hell.

He sat on his bedroll and pulled out a scrap of paper from his saddlebag. He wrote his name on it and added a brief last will and testament of William Branch Yelverton, Major, Continental Army of the United States. He had few possessions to will to anyone. He left his beloved rifle, Josie, to his good friend and mentor, Lt Colonel Francis Marion. His personal effects were to go to Corporal Charles Cuthbert, his loyal orderly and friend. He left some $700 in Spanish silver and other small effects to his dear wife, Mary. His Scottish dirk was to go to his friend Richard Caswell, Junior. He could think of nothing else other than Molly his beloved horse. Molly was to go to Mr. and Mrs. Bert Koontz of New Bern, North Carolina, where he hoped Molly would live her days in peace and the joy of a quiet pasture and comfortable stable. For the purpose of feeding and caring for Molly, Will left the sum of 100 Spanish silver dollars to the Koontzs.

He could think of nothing else to do, so he took another scrap of paper and wrote to Mary.

Savannah, 8th October 1779

Mrs. Mary Proctor Yelverton

Charlestown

Dearest Mary

If you are reading this, it means I am either dead or captured. Tomorrow, we will assault the British, and it looks most daunting. I will be in the lead elements with Colonel Marion.

I love you, Mary. Know that I hold you in my heart forever. If I do not return, I want you to find someone to love you as much as I do, and I want you to love him back. I wish you great happiness.

To your parents, please tell them that I have been honored to be their son and that I appreciate being made a member of your family.

May God hold you in the palm of his hand, my darling.

I am, your loving husband,

Will

Will thought a long time about the next letter. Finally deciding that he must write it, he took another sheet of paper and wrote,

Savannah, 8th October 1779

Mrs. Abigail Kennedy Carter

Bear Creek, North Carolina

Dear Abby,

If you are reading this, it means I am dead or captured. I wanted to say adieu and let you know that I think of you often. I am married to a wonderful woman and consider myself very lucky. Zeke Carter is a lucky man. May God watch over you and your child.

I am, and always was, your friend,

Will

He warmed some sealing wax and closed both letters, writing the addresses on the outside of the paper. He placed each letter in the oil skin pouch that kept his copy of the Odyssey dry and placed them carefully in his saddlebag. Then he set to cleaning and loading his English dragoon carbine and his two pistols. He would not carry Josie or the .45 rifle tomorrow. The carbine and pistols, all loaded with buck and ball, would have to do. He would not take the damned sword, rather, he would carry Uncle Ewan's dirk. He was not a hand-to-hand fighter, but he thought the dirk would serve in a desperate pinch.

After careful consideration, he removed his uniform breeches and high-topped boots and replaced them with his backwoods hunter's close-fitting leggings and moccasin boots. They were more comfortable, and if he were to die, let it be in clothing he liked. Then, he looked in on Cuthbert.

"Cuth, I want you to stay with Molly and be prepared to help with the wounded."

Cuthbert looked up from what he was doing. "I had expected to go with you, Sir."

"Aye, I know. But someone has to stay behind. Er, if I don't make it, there are letters in my saddlebag with my book that I'd like delivered. Can you see to that?"

"Certainly. It would be my honor. But you are going to be safe, and no doubt about it, Sir."

Will smiled. "If I don't make it back, know that I have truly valued our friendship, Cuth. I wish you the best of everything."

"Thank you, Sir, but that won't be necessary, I'm sure."

"I wish I were sure, Cuth. Good night."

Will didn't really sleep. He half dozed, mostly dressed except for his uniform coat and his cocked hat. Soon, it was time to rise from his hard wooden bed. He had no troops to command, but his place was with Marion, and that's where he would be.

He looked around the camp and was met by Cuthbert, who had clearly not slept.

Cuthbert said, "I'll take care of your things, Sir, if that is necessary. But it won't be."

"Thank you, Cuth. I hope to see you soon."

Will walked over to Marion. "Good morning, Sir."

"Not much good about it, Will. At least it's not pouring down. The mud is already bad enough."

They walked over to where a group of officers stood. The officers all stood to attention and Marion said, "Please be at ease, Gentlemen. We're under the command of Lt. Colonel Laurens this morning. Ah, here he is now."

Laurens sauntered up and glanced around the group. "Morning, Francis! Will, pleasure to see you again. Gentlemen, good day! Today we shall extract revenge upon the Englishmen! Now to business."

Laurens went over the 2nd South Carolina and other units he commanded, explaining that the regiment would be on the right of the American columns. They would begin marching soon, and the officers were released to give instructions to the sergeants who would marshal the troops.

Marion quietly said, "He's dangerous, Will."

Will, just as quietly, replied, "Oh, aye, Sir. I was with him at Coosawhatchie where he damn near got 200 men trapped by disobeying Moultrie's orders and going ahead to confront the British. He was wounded and was taken from the field. Barnwell salvaged the situation."

"Aye, I've known Barnwell a good many year. He's a good man."

~~<>~~

The sergeants formed up the 200 men of the 2nd South Carolina and began a march to align the unit in its position. This was followed by two hours of marching and countermarching in the dark. Will and Marion tried to manage the mess that this created, but to no avail.

Marion swore out loud, "God *damn* it! This is the worst damn mess! Our men are well drilled, but every other fool on the face of God's green Earth is out here tromping around in the mud about turning and oblique marching and every other damn thing! Soon, it will be dawn, and we will still be bumbling about while the British laugh their asses off."

Will nodded. He was not much of a marching man, but he could tell that the units were blundering into one another in the pitch dark. The attack was a shambles before it had even begun.

~~<>~~

Dawn broke to a terrific cannonade opened upon the British. As had been the case all week, the shells flew long, mostly landing in the town.

The infantry units were soon aligned, but it was fully light, and any element of surprise was long lost. Will looked toward the British lines and saw that they were holding their fire. The well-disciplined gun crews of the Royal Artillery stood easy by their guns, but he could see smoldering linstocks in the gunners' hands.

Looking toward the French columns, Will could see d'Estaing. In the distance, Will saw his friend, Terson. It was almost 6 o'clock when Will heard firing, and various other battle sounds from the center of the British line. General Huger was attacking.

Marion said, "They're late. The sun is up, and the British will surely see that Huger's attack is a feint. The feint was supposed to be done in the dark to draw the British attention as we swept forward from here. Of course, it doesn't matter because this mess," he angled his chin toward the French and American troops, "has not yet congealed into the utter catastrophe I expect it will become."

Laurens rushed over. "The French are ready to move. We're going to move ahead also."

Will looked at Marion questioningly.

Marion muttered, "Oh, aye. Let's do plunge ahead without any organization to accommodate the bloody whim of the French!"

The American unit, some 700-strong, with Laurens in the lead, stepped off. Marion said, "No need to have any organization, Will. Just fling us onto the abatis and die with honor!"

As they began to march forward, Pulaski's Legion trotted through the column heading toward the far left of the American line.

Marion spat, "What a damn sight that is. The Pole, his half-assed Hessian deserters, and whoever else he could cobble together are charging forward with élan ... and our unit be damned!"

Lauren's column was supposed to charge the Carolina redoubt but veered right and marched straight at the Spring Hill Redoubt, the strongest position along the entire left of the Allied lines. The men hurried across the plain until they reached the abatis and the ditch.

British guns opened a withering fire, and, as men reached the abatis, musketry from the redoubts began to crackle with devastating effect. Dead men hung from the abatis, lay in the mud by the dozen, and others struggled to drag the abatis aside. The abatis were heavy tree trunks bristling with sharpened limbs which dug into the mud. Men died trying to create a hole in the thicket of abatis.

Will went over an abatis, tripped, and landed headlong on a pile of bodies. One man he recognized had half a face, the other half shattered by a ball. Another man gasped for air, a huge hole in his chest sucking air and taking his life by degrees.

Will pushed himself up from the pile of bodies and hurried forward toward the Spring Hill Redoubt. He lost track of Marion but could see the 2nd South Carolina blue flag waving a dozen ranks ahead. Lieutenant Bush had the flag and was pushing forward.

Will watched as he pushed forward himself, musket balls and canister shot flew by, making whizzing sounds. Zzzzpt! Something flicked past his ear. He felt a tug on his right shoulder and looked down to see his epaulet was missing, replaced by a neatly rent hole in his coat. He shoved his hand under the cloth and brought it back, expecting to see blood, but it was dry. He muttered a silent prayer and kept pushing ahead.

The man next to him made a gagging sound, and Will looked to see what had happened. The man was no longer a man. He was in two parts, upper body split in half from the lower body. His legs still standing as his lifeless torso flopped into the mud and quivered. The legs stood, mute testament to the death of their owner.

Will felt like vomiting but was soon distracted by the scene in front of him. Lieutenant Bush reached the redoubt and began a climb up the dirt wall. Others behind him were bogging in the ditch as the British defenders fired down on them.

Will saw the defenders were the British 71st Highland Regiment of Foot. Just yesterday, the American officers had been briefed that this redoubt was defended by militia. Clearly, that was wrong, or the British had put veterans in place to reinforce this crucial position. Regardless, these men were professionals and masters of the bayonet. Will reached the ditch and saw Bush and the flag flying off the rampart to land dead in the ditch.

Jasper was suddenly there and grabbed the flag. He looked around wild-eyed and shouted, "Ach, zo! Kommen Sie mit mir!"

Jasper began to climb the rampart of the Spring Hill Redoubt, the blue 2nd Regiment color in his hand, his gray hair flying in all directions, a determined look on his face.

Will struggled in the mud to follow Jasper. Random thoughts flicked through Will's mind. *A sergeant ordering officers to follow, and they're doing it.*

Jasper gained the top of the rampart and used the flagpole to bash a Highlander out of his way. He jammed the flag into the soft mud of the rampart and looked around triumphantly at his comrades of the regiment when a ball slammed into him, and he fell backward off the rampart. His hand was still on the regimental colors, and the flag flew off the wall with him. Jasper landed on a pile of bodies, his face as gray as his hair.

"Was macht?" he muttered.

Will said, "You are shot, my friend. I'll take the color." Will dug in a pocket and produced a handkerchief. He thrust it into the musket ball wound in Jasper's chest and grabbed Jasper's hand. "Press this here."

Jasper looked at him and said, "Danke. You are a brave man, Will. Kill der Brite schweine!" Jasper's eyes fluttered, and he passed out.

Will dragged the flag out of Jasper's hand and turned to the rampart. He had the color in his left hand and his English dragoon carbine in the other. Will staggered up the rampart digging the flagpole and the carbine butt into the ground for balance as he reached the top. A Highlander lunged at him with a bayonet, and Will shot the man in the face and upper body with the carbine. The carbine ball killed him, but the swan shot pulped his face, making him unrecognizable.

Will dropped the carbine to dangle from its sling and drew his Brander pistol. Lieutenant Gray, whom Will had briefly met the night before, said, "Allow me, Sir," and took the flag to plant it. A Highlander shot Gray in the chest with his musket, and Gray went backward off the rampart with the flag.

Will shot the Highlander with his pistol. The buck and ball load knocked the Highlander backward to sit on his rear, a puzzled expression on his face as he looked down to see he was mortally wounded. Will put the Brander back in his belt and dragged out the horse pistol.

A British lieutenant stepped forward, whipping his sword about expertly. The lieutenant's challenge to Will was clear. He expected a fellow officer and gentleman to engage in honorable combat. But Will Yelverton was not a gentleman, and he did not have a sword. So, he shot the young British lieutenant with the horse pistol resulting in the untimely and dishonorable death of the young gentleman.

Will felt no remorse as he jammed the horse pistol into his belt and reached for Uncle Ewan's dirk. The Highlanders stormed into the redoubt. Will saw them coming and knew he would die any second.

Oddly, Will looked across to the Carolina redoubt to see a young woman tending a fallen Continental officer. Their eyes met for a moment. She was a lovely, dark-haired beauty with strong features and a determined look. Will saw a half-smile from the young woman. It made his heart glad to be alive.

Something hit Will in the chest, and he fell backward off the rampart to land in the ditch. He put a hand on his chest and felt for blood. He looked at his hand and saw there was no blood. Will quizzically wondered what had hit him that did not kill him.

Will rolled over onto his face and tried to get up when a body landed heavily on him, crushing him into the mud and water at the bottom of the ditch. Will panicked, he did not want to drown. The time that Benjamin tried to drown him in the creek at Branchton flooded back into his memory. Will tried to get the body off him, but another body landed on that one, and Will was pressed inexorably downward. He strained with every fiber of his being to get up the side of the ditch and keep his face out of the muddy water.

Will found it increasingly hard to breathe. As when he was just six years old, and Benjamin was drowning him in the creek, Will found himself floating above the chaos. He saw himself in the ditch, the bodies piled on him. He heard sounds like pops and bangs. Thumping sounds. Will calmly watched his own death from a distance.

Blackness closed in. Will hoped his letters would be delivered to the two people he most loved in the world.

Chapter 19 – Aftermath

Light. Soft light floated into Will's field of vision. Well, his right eye's field of vision. His left eye was jammed into the mud, and when he tried to open it, the burning from the filthy, blood-infused water made him whimper. A soft hand touched his face, and he flinched.

A voice said, "I'm trying to help get the bodies off you, Sir."

Will ranged in his mind. That voice was feminine, but it was neither Mary nor Abby. He found himself in quite a quandary. Who was that? His limited field of vision did not help anything.

Will thought, *Where am I? I thought I was dead.*

He heard his own voice croak, "What happened?"

The soft, feminine voice – clearly an angel – floated to him. "You were covered with bodies in this ditch. I thought you were killed."

A great weight was lifted off Will's back, and he could suddenly breathe freely. *Air! Jesus be praised! Air!*

Will croaked, "How did I get here?"

The soft voice hardened, "You, Sir, are a disgusting rebel. One of our men slammed you in the chest with the butt of his musket, and I saw you fly backward off the rampart. By rights, you should be dead, and I should let you die here."

Will tried to lift his head.

"NO! Keep your head down. They will come bayonet you!"

Will croaked, "Why are you doing this if you hate me so?"

The soft voice said, "I do not know. Maybe it is because you have the most beautiful blue eyes and looked at me with such humanity in the middle of the fight."

Will spit out some nasty, bloody ditch water. "That was you? The beautiful angel who was helping a wounded man?"

"Yes. The poor man died. His name was Martin Coleman. He asked that I convey a message to his sister, but I shall never meet her. Perhaps I might write to her when we have ended this foolish revolution."

Will was at a loss. He managed to speak, "'Tis a conundrum. We fight one another, but we are of the same country. We love people who think differently than we do. Some people are killing their loved ones. I am here by a series of accidents. I had planned to be a gunsmith on the frontier and wanted no part of this war. But here I am." He thought for a moment, "and you are truly the most beautiful woman I have ever seen."

The soft voice said, "Do you have someone?"

"Aye, I am married to a woman I love very much. Truth to be told, there was another that I shall love to the grave. But she is married to another. She married him when I was forced away by this war. She thought me dead and did not want to be a spinster."

"Ah, so you have two women?"

"Nay. I have but one wife who is the best woman I know. But the other will never be truly gone."

"I understand. I wish I knew you better, but you are my enemy. I am here to help you out of my Christian duty. Do not move here until it is dark. Then, crawl in the direction your head is pointed. Do not stand. They will shoot you. If you move during the light, they will bayonet you."

"Thank you. My name is Will Yelverton."

The soft voice said, "My name is unimportant, but it is Elizabeth. Remember me as Betsy. I shall never see you again. I wish you well. Honor me by being a good man, Will Yelverton."

Will said, "Betsy. That is a nice name. Thank you."

Will waited. "Betsy? Betsy?"

But Betsy was gone, and Will was alone in the sun. In the distance, he heard the angel's voice saying, "They're all dead, rebel scum! Don't bother going down there. Here, I have some water."

~~<>~~

Dark slowly stole into Will's vision. He was desperately thirsty. His angel had not given him water. He figured out that the British would have known he was alive if she had. Then they would have bayonetted him. His face was still stuck in the mud, and his left eye was plastered shut.

Every so often, Will heard a soft moan nearby. Apparently, another rebel soldier was wounded and dying nearby. Will hated that he could not help.

Will waited until the sky was completely black. Crickets began to sing. The British lines were quiet. Will thought, *Of course they're quiet. They are as exhausted as we are.*

Slowly, with great deliberation, Will flexed his fingers and wiggled his legs. He tried to move his knees and elbows. They worked! He dragged his left knee up to waist height and pushed. He found no pain, and he squished forward two feet. Soon, he moved his right leg in the same way and pushed forward another two feet.

Please, God, don't let them see me.

Will repeated the process. And again. And again. His face was still smashed against the dirt. There was no grass, so every inch was abrasive. Still, he dragged a left knee then a right, then a left.

An hour went by. Left knee, right knee. Drag and ache. Will thought, *I must do this for the angel I will never see again. I must do this for Mary. And Abby.*

~~<>~~

A voice said, "Bloody hell! What is this?"

Another voice said, "Looks to be an officer crawling."

The first voice said, "Perfect to see one of those bastards crawling."

"Shut it. Give me a hand getting him up."

~~<>~~

Marion said, "Well, well, look what the cat dragged in! We thought you quite dead, Will."

Will looked up, his vision still foggy from the left eye being grubbed in the dirt for hours. "Is that you, Colonel Marion."

"Aye. Damned if you didn't almost plant that flag. I saw you on the rampart before we were pushed back. You tried to take the entire Spring Hill Redoubt single-handed, Will."

"I did?"

"Aye. We were pushed back, and I looked up and saw you standing atop the rampart with our flag. I saw you shoot three of the enemy, and plant the flag. Well, actually, Gray took the flag out of your hand and was killed."

Will's mouth felt like cotton. "Jasper?"

Marion's voice was bleak. "Jasper is dead. That's a great pity. He was worth 20 men. We got him back to the lines, but his wound was mortal. He was a good man. He asked after you."

Will moved his tongue around his dry lips. "I tried to stop his bleeding. Handkerchief."

"Aye, he lived several hours because of that. But he was shot through the lungs, and there was nothing that could be done. What the hell happened to you, Will?"

Will croaked, "A beautiful angel came to me and dragged bodies off me. She called me rebel scum but warned me not to move. She said if I moved, the British would bayonet me. I believed her because I'd seen that at Brier Creek. She told me to crawl when it was dark. So, I lay in the sun until it was dark. Then I crawled. I'm desperately thirsty."

Marion helped Will to drink water. Then he said, "T'was a terrible debacle, as we thought it would be. There have been meetings all day, but no one thinks we should try the defenses again. Our plan was flawed, and d'Estaing refuses to accept any responsibility. Pulaski was badly wounded riding around in front of the British defenses. I think it will be a mortal wound. They took him to a ship off shore. I think we're done here, Will."

Will nodded. "I will be up and around soon, Sir."

"Rest, Will. Cuthbert is here. He'll help you."

Will smiled, "Cuth! Thanks."

~~<>~~

The next day, Will was able to walk some and, with help, drank what he thought must have been an entire bucketful of water.

The camp doctor said he was dehydrated. The doctor said it was a miracle that Will did not die from lack of water, and he must drink at every chance. The doctor said Will would know when he was hydrated when he urinated clear liquid every quarter hour. Finally, about supper time, he staggered to the edge of the camp and pissed copiously. His heart felt better. Half the time the last two days, his heart seemed to be beating slowly as though it were pushing molasses through his veins.

~~<>~~

Will asked Cuthbert, "You didn't send those letters, did you?"

"No, Sir. I didn't have the chance before you crawled back into camp. I was too busy feeling down over you being killed. Everyone was sure you were dead."

"'Tis good those letters are still in my saddlebag. I shall burn them. No sense in anyone getting a letter saying I'm dead."

Cuth grinned. "You're not anywhere near dead, Sir. Thanks be to God."

~~<>~~

The leaders of the Allied coalition continued to squabble. Lincoln insisted that a better plan would result in the capture of the town. D'Estaing stated that his naval commanders were dancing from one foot to the other to be gone from the coast of Georgia. Hurricane season was deepening, and the chance of a devastating storm was high.

Admiral Count d'Estaing prevailed in this logic, and the French began to decamp toward the landings at Beaulieu Plantation.

Lincoln threw his hat in the dirt and shouted, "God damn the French!"

Will flinched along with several other officers. Lincoln's New England accent was broad and strong when he said, "We have no bloody choice but to withdraw across the river and then move north to Charlestown."

Lincoln scanned the room. "Make all plans to effect that action immediately. We must quickly withdraw before the British see that we are moving and sally to attack us."

Everyone stood. Before they began to file out, Lincoln said, "Make no mistake, Gentlemen. The English will come north and soon." He made a dismissive gesture with his hand and reached to pick up his hat.

~~<>~~

The next morning, Marion's orderly came to Will's tent to inform Will that Marion had called the regiment's officers to a meeting within the hour.

The meeting was brief. Marion said, "We are marching north tomorrow. Our orders are to encamp at Sheldon Old Church. We will be a blocking force in case the British come north."

Will looked around the assembled officers. The number was greatly reduced from the several dozen once assembled. The carnage at the Spring Hill Redoubt had reduced the regiment from some 700 men to about 200. Many of the losses were wounded and not dead, but still the losses were huge. Will was pleased to see Lieutenant Legare present. In the tumult of preparing for the assault, Will had lost track of the young man.

The morning came, and the regiment, minus its blue regimental colors ignominiously captured by the British at Spring Hill, marched northwest toward Ebenezer. The 200 men embarked on Zubly's Ferry and made the crossing.

Will and Cuthbert rode in Marion's lead element, and Marion waived Will up to talk. "We made a shambles of the entire siege. The assault was an utter cock-up if I've ever seen one. My God! What did we expect? We sent a rag-tag bunch of clodhoppers with ducking guns against a trained, well-equipped army of professionals. And we got beat, Will." Sarcasm dripped from Marion's voice, "What a surprise!"

Will said, "Aye, Sir. I hoped we would have a better showing."

"Aye, well, hope in one hand and spit in the other. See which one gets wet!"

Will snorted a laugh. "That's true."

Marion said, "We begged the French to come to fight the British, but there was no plan. The French simply showed up and set the terms of the entire siege. As you reported, they didn't have sufficient equipment to conduct a siege, but we pressed ahead anyway. The morning of the battle, and I think you saw this, confusion was everywhere. I learned that d'Estaing rearranged the units in his column at 2 in the morning. That confused the French more than they already were."

Will's eyebrows shot up, "Why did he do that, Sir?"

"God only knows, Will. I mean, you dealt with the French. They groused about the food and the lack of wine and every-other-damn-thing. Who knows what they were thinking?"

Will smiled. "The one I worked with was quite a professional soldier, Captain de Terson. He was as frustrated as you are, Sir."

Marion said, "We managed to add to the idiocy. I'm sorry that Pulaski got wounded. I hear he died onboard a ship out in the mouth of the Savannah. It appears he was riding around in the swamp waving his saber and finally could stand it no longer and charged the redoubts over by the river. Got shot for his trouble. I liked him. He was small but had the heart of a lion."

Will said, "I had not heard he died until just now. I was at Brandywine when he begged Washington for permission to lead a cavalry charge to slow the British. That was foolhardy but brave."

Marion smirked, "Aye. I'm not sure which is worse for a military unit: foolhardy or brave. Put them together, and you get a combination that results in dead people, not victory."

Will said, "How will we continue our fight for liberty if we keep losing like we just did? I mean, looking at our regiment, Sir, we have a quarter – fewer actually – of the men we charged the redoubt with."

Marion scanned the sky and trees in thought, "We're going to have to think about other ways to fight. Fight like Indians. Hit and run. Standing up in a field, or marching across a plain like yesterday, and shooting at one another won't work for us. Hell, you heard all the stories of Lexington and Concord where the British shot up our militia on the village green but then got shot to pieces trying to get back to Boston. Our boys are woodsmen and hunters. The Concord Militia hid behind trees Indian style, killing the British like a turkey shoot."

~~<>~~

They marched the remaining 50 miles over the next five days to arrive and camp near the ruins of Sheldon Church. Once again, Will was delighted to be an officer and ride a horse in front of the stinking dust cloud created by horse dung and unwashed men with various maladies, including dysentery. There was a baggage train that didn't have much in the way of supplies. The inevitable wives and children were trudging along at the very rear, trying to avoid the horse manure, muddy potholes, and sick soldiers squatting in the brush along the side of the track that passed for a road. Along with everyone else, Will was dirty and tired. Reaching Sheldon Old Church was most welcome.

The damaged church saddened Will. Clearly, it was once a magnificent building. Will didn't know what the style was, but he could tell the building was meant to be like some classical building from ancient Greece. There were imposing columns with brickwork abounding. Vaulted openings formed cloisters down the sides of the church. Will knew that in the colonies, brick was the most costly and the church must have been the most important place to someone. The stink of burned wood hung over the building, but the brick columns and cloisters remained. Will gritted his teeth when he realized that Prevost's forces burned the building just last year.

Marion did not allow a rest but demanded that the fallow farm fields adjacent to the church become a training ground. The unit formed and marched, drilling to preclude the potential for a repeat of the chaos at Spring Hill.

Will found himself sleeping well and becoming lean and hard. But being in a remote camp away from Mary and any other distractions wore on Will. Will found himself dreaming of Mary and their times together in the soft, goose feather bed at what was now Mary's house in Charlestown. Will remembered her skin and her textures. Her sounds of both gently voiced conversation and passion. He had missed Mary before, but now it was much more acute.

Every other day, Will took Molly and rode to the forest to hunt. As usual, he had good luck, and his rifle brought back deer and turkeys. Will used skills he developed as a boy to set snares to bring home several rabbits every other day. Cuthbert was a decent hunter, as well, and he killed his share of game for the pot.

Other soldiers foraged and found an abandoned mill. There were sacks of flour and grits which were appropriated. Soon the camp was functioning like a little city and things were going well. At least the troops were fed and there was no fighting. Marion kept up a picket line well out from the camp.

Despite the rest and relative comfort of camp life at Sheldon, Will found himself longing for a march north to Charlestown and the stable life of the garrison at Fort Moultrie. He knew it was a fantasy, but it gave him hope.

Chapter 20 – Promotion

Marion's orderly presented himself at Will's tent with compliments of Colonel Marion and a request that Will report to the colonel. Will quickly donned his shirt, cravat, and coat and marched across the battered churchyard to Marion's command tent.

"Sir, you wanted to see me."

Marion looked up and smiled, "Ah, Colonel Yelverton."

Will said, "I beg your pardon, Sir?"

"You heard me, Will. You knew General Lincoln sent your name to Congress with Washington's enthusiastic endorsement. You have been promoted. Which makes me happy and sad at the same time."

Will said, "How exciting! Why does it make you sad, Sir?"

Marion said, "You are so refreshingly unaware of the military. I'm sad because I will lose you to your own command. No one is promoted to lieutenant colonel who is not believed to be ready for command."

Will said, "I'm not sure I'm ready for command, Sir."

Marion's face grew serious. He asked, "Are you calling into question Lincoln's judgment? Washington's?"

Will looked stricken, "Uh, no. Sir, I uh, well ..."

Marion looked stern and then grinned. "Ha, had you there! Of course, you're concerned about being a commander for the first time. Who wouldn't be? Command is a daunting responsibility. But you must know that every man placed in command must grow to it. Few are born to the responsibility."

Will relaxed and said, "Thank you, Sir. I am humbled."

"There's more good news. I am demanded, uh, I mean *requested*, to visit Charlestown to meet with the generals. Things have been quiet, and everyone is becoming quite skittish. They're all like horses ready for a race. I am to bring you with me so Lincoln can personally promote you with appropriate great ceremony."

Will said, "My goodness, but I hope my uniform is acceptable. I have a new one."

Marion said, "I'm certain it will be perfect. We leave in the morning."

~~<>~~

Will and Marion rode north to Charlestown with Lieutenant Legare and his troopers. Cuthbert and Marion's orderly brought up the rear of the column that totaled 13 riders.

Marion said, "Thirteen well-armed, well-trained Continentals should give any bandits pause. If that fails, we'll have to help them understand the folly of attacking us."

Will grinned. "Hope it doesn't come to that. Last time bandits attacked me, it took a Lumbee Indian with a knife to keep me from dying."

Marion snorted, "I'm sure there's a tale there."

The detachment trotted along in the November sunshine. The air was soft, and the occasional breeze from the north brought a strong hint of winter. Still, the ride was pleasant enough. Will thought it was much better than the ride south in the late summer heat. Two days later, the group crossed the Ashley River Ferry and trotted into Lincoln's camp outside Charlestown.

Cuthbert saw to Will's accommodation while Marion's orderly did the same. Legare and his men found appropriate tents, and Marion told them that they had the run of the town for the next five days. That brought grins all around, and Marion said, "Don't make me come get anyone out of the jailhouse."

Legare said, "Depend upon me, Sir. We shall be the utmost of decorum."

Marion said, "That's what I'm afraid of."

This last was met with a round of laughter.

Marion and Will found Lincoln in a rare, good mood. "Ah! Look who's here, the man of the hour!"

Will involuntarily glanced over his shoulder, causing great peals of laughter from the normally taciturn Lincoln. "No, young fella! You, Sir, are the man of the hour. Are you yet 21? And the Congress has reposed great confidence in you to promote you to Lieutenant Colonel. We shall have a parade of the Army where we will promote you. You are married, I understand? Yes? Well, your lady is most welcome to attend. Then we shall have a small gathering of the senior officers to congratulate you."

Will said, "This is most kind of you, Sir."

"Nonsense. I have had report after report of your courage and leadership. I understand you climbed the wall at the Spring Hill Redoubt and personally tried to plant the colors. I heard you were knocked off that wall and left for dead. That you are still alive and here is a tribute to your moral strength and courage, Will."

Will blushed and managed to say, "Thank you, Sir. T'was just my duty."

Lincoln looked at him hard, "Would that everyone had your sense of duty."

~~<>~~

Will and Cuthbert trotted into the stable yard at the Proctor home on East Bay Street. Will had barely dismounted when Mary burst out the door and ran full tilt across the mews to throw her arms around his neck.

"Oh, Will, Will! Oh! You're alive! Oh, God, but I thought you must be dead. I have heard nothing, but the reports were that so many were killed!"

She turned to Cuthbert. "Cuth! I'm so glad you are here, too." She hugged Cuthbert hard, making him blush.

Turning to Will, Mary said, "You both need a bath. My God, but you stink! Did they not have water in Georgia?"

Will blushed. "My darling, we've had no creature comforts for months. Cuth has taken good care of me, but hot water was hard to find, and soap was nowhere to be had."

Mary made a face, "You both shall have baths. Cuth, I will have the servants draw you a bath and attend to your every need.

Will, come with me. I need to supervise to make sure you are fully cleaned."

Will said, "That's Lieutenant Colonel Yelverton now, my dear. And this is Sergeant Cuthbert."

Mary said, "What?!"

Will said, "Yes, my dear. You are invited to attend a parade of the army the day after tomorrow where General Lincoln will make me a lieutenant colonel."

~~<>~~

Mary said, "I am so proud of you, Will. I cannot tell you how I knew it, but the moment I met you at Eliza's home last year, I knew you had substance. Eliza was so cruel to you about not being in the army, but I knew from your eyes that you would prove her wrong."

Will said, "My darling, I could not be luckier. You are my life and my love. You make my heart happy."

They were sitting in a deep tub full of foamy, hot water. Will had washed twice and still felt nasty from the weeks in army camps. Mary helped that situation by washing him with a cloth impregnated with good-smelling soap that she used to scrub every inch of his body. The first wash had produced a tub of grimy water and a blackened cloth that both had to be replaced.

Will leaned back, his wet blond hair plastered to his skull. Mary leaned forward, "You are the most wonderful man, Will Yelverton. And because you are so clean ..." She bent farther forward, lifted his hips, and engulfed him in her mouth.

Will nearly fainted. Only Frances Montravale had ever done this, and then only once. The time that Frances had done this Will had not been able to control himself, and the exquisite sensation resulted in a quick end.

This time, because he trusted Mary and was surprised, he relaxed and enjoyed the powerful sensations. This was something Mary had never done before, and Will loved it.

But he resolved not to be selfish and merely lay back and be served. He gently pulled Mary up to kiss her, and she straddled him. Soon, they were joined as Mary rode him like a horse. The hot water of the bath began to slosh back and forth as though the bath were a harbor in a storm with waves slamming against a wharf. Mary put her hands on his shoulders and, leaning her head back, shuddered deep into her soul. Will responded and let go. His body, unattended for these months, erupted deep inside Mary.

Soon they regained their senses. Both were exhausted as they crawled from the tub, dragged a towel over their wet, foam-covered flesh, and collapsed into the bed.

It was late the next morning when Will floated back to consciousness to see the most beautiful woman next to him. Mary was sleeping, her beautiful young face was unlined and unconcerned with the death and destruction of the world. Will looked at her as she slept.

An involuntary thought flitted through his mind. He was on the rampart at Savannah for a moment, looking across the battleground and meeting Betsy's eyes. He heard her soft voice in his ear saying that he had the most beautiful blue eyes. A brief, utterly disloyal thought floated through Will's mind. In his mind's eye, he was pushing Betsy down into a soft bed such as the one he now occupied with Mary. He saw Betsy, his guardian angel, nude. Her perfectly white body and rosy-tipped breasts rising up under his touch made him grow erect. At that moment, Mary's eyes opened, and she smiled. Will's faithless, impossible dream ended, and he reached for Mary.

~~<>~~

Two days later, Will and Mary rode in Homer's carriage – really, Mary's carriage, now – pulled by a beautiful bay horse out to the Army's campground. They arrived, and Will escorted Mary into General Lincoln's tent.

Lincoln doffed his cocked hat and made a half bow, "Good day, Mrs. Yelverton. 'Tis my great pleasure to make your acquaintance."

Mary simpered prettily behind her fan. She snapped the fan shut and said, "Please, General, do call me Mary."

'Ah, Madame. My friends call me Benjamin, and I hope we are now friends."

Will could see that Mary was flattered by Lincoln's attention. She said, "Thank you General ... uh, Benjamin. You must come to dinner at our humble home soon."

~~<>~~

Will stood on a small platform on Major General Benjamin Lincoln's left. To Will's left was Lieutenant Colonel Francis Marion. Other officers, Moultrie, Huger, and Laurens, to name a few, were on the platform. Arrayed before the platform were the battalions of the Continental Army in Charlestown. Mary was afforded a pleasant chair where she sat wearing her nicest dress and bonnet, watching the proceedings. Will thought the situation was much more than he deserved. He also thought that Mary was the most beautiful woman in the world.

Lincoln stepped forward and projected his voice. "The Congress of the United States of America, having placed great confidence in the loyalty and abilities of Major William Branch Yelverton, promotes him to the rank of Lieutenant Colonel of the Continental Army. I hold here the document, signed by the President of the Congress with appropriate seals hereto appended."

Lincoln stepped back and beckoned to Mary, who stepped forward. Lincoln turned to an aide who held a tray with two silver epaulets of Will's new rank. Lincoln took one and inclined his head toward Mary. The aide stepped across to Mary and offered her the remaining epaulet.

Lincoln nodded as he stepped to Will's right side, and Mary stepped up to his left. They removed Will's gold epaulets and replaced them with the new silver ones. Lincoln turned to the assembled battalions, "Hip, Hip!"

The battalions responded, "Huzzah!"

Three times the multitude shouted "huzzah" in response to Lincoln's prompt. All the while, Will blushed, and Mary glowed.

When the cheers had died away, Lincoln stood to attention and commanded, "PASS IN REVIEW!"

Fifers and drummers began a lively march. One by one the battalions faced and marched across the small plain, made column movements and soon drew abreast of the platform. A piping command of "Eyes ... right" rolled out of the lead rank, and the lead battalion snapped their heads to their right in salute. Lincoln and Will both saluted as the battalion marched past. Soon the colors marched past, requiring another salute. The remaining battalions marched by, saluting the reviewing party on the platform.

It was the most moving moment of Will's life. He had never had such a rare, personal honor. He had never considered himself anything special, but this official confidence and honor of his new nation made Will's heart feel as though it would burst. He blushed crimson in embarrassment, knowing that others lay dead in the dirt of Savannah while he stood here receiving the salute of his fellow military members. Jasper was dead, and Will was being honored. It simply did not seem right.

That night, Lieutenant Colonel William Branch Yelverton bedded his beautiful wife. Mary's face was pink with joy at being the woman of such a celebrated man. As the physical pleasure took her, Mary threw her head back, cords in her neck straining with effort and soft sounds escaping her throat as she lost herself in the moment boosted by the events of this joyous day.

An exhausted Will drifted off to sleep. His mind was at peace. But he heard a tiny voice belonging to Betsy, the woman whom Will had met as he lay dying in a ditch before the Spring Hill Redoubt at Savannah.

She whispered softly: "Be careful how you exult in today's happiness, for sorrow is always just around the corner."

Chapter 21 – Joy

A messenger from General Lincoln arrived at Will's house in Charlestown. It was two days after the ceremony promoting Will to Lieutenant Colonel.

"Is Colonel Yelverton at home?" the messenger asked Will, who answered the door himself. Will wore casual breeches, riding boots, and a linen shirt.

"I am Maj ... er, Colonel Yelverton," Will replied. "Please come in."

The messenger was a young lieutenant. "Thank you, Sir. General Lincoln sent this message, Sir. He asked that I wait for your reply."

Will took the sealed letter and said, "Do come in. Would you like some refreshments? 'Tis warm for November."

The lieutenant said, "Thank you, Sir. My name is John Huggins. Something to drink would be very nice, if that's not too much trouble."

Will smiled, "Lieutenant Huggins, I'm not some scary old man. Relax. And some near beer is no trouble at all."

Huggins grinned and relaxed some. "Thank you, Sir. That would be very nice."

Will said, "Please come sit on the piazza. It's most pleasant this morning. I'll ask the servants to bring you some near beer. Please excuse me while I read the General's letter."

Will left Huggins relaxing on the piazza where a brisk November breeze made for a pleasant place to sit. A little cooler would be unpleasant, but today was nearly perfect with the morning sun warming the piazza.

Will stepped into Homer's study. Will thought, *"I guess it's my study, now. How odd that feels!"* He unfolded Lincoln's note:

"I would like for you to become a member of my staff and learn how higher command works, Will. Of course, it means you would have to leave the 2nd SC Regiment and Lt Colonel Marion. I know this is hard because you feel loyalty to Marion. But becoming a member of my staff means you will contribute to liberty. I continue to look for a command opportunity for you. Please consider my offer and reply by Lieutenant Huggins (who is a good man)."

"On another note, please offer my congratulations to your orderly, Corporal Cuthbert, upon his promotion to sergeant."

B. Lincoln, Maj Gen'l

Commanding

266

Will read the letter twice. Then he walked up the stairs to find Mary in the bedroom doing some needlepoint. She sat by a window, taking the pleasant morning air. Her skin was pink in the cool breeze, and her eyes were shining with joy at seeing him.

Mary saw his face and said, "You look serious, Will."

"General Lincoln has asked me to join his staff. 'Tis an opportunity to learn how senior staffs work. The general continues to look for a command for me."

Mary said, "Oh, Will! How wonderful! He recognizes your ability!"

Will smiled, "I think he recognizes your beauty and thinks you and I are somehow connected in South Carolina society."

Mary snorted. "Well, Daddy is somewhat connected, but he's no Ioor nor Ashley. We are certainly not Rhetts or even Somersalls. We are simply planters with some holdings."

Will said, "What shall I tell the general?"

Mary looked at Will, "Oh, Will! I think you must accept. T'will be good for you as an Army officer. I think it will give us time together. I had accepted that we would be mostly separated. Now, maybe, we can be together a bit more."

Will said, "Marion already said that he would lose me from the 2nd South Carolina."

Mary said, "Aye, Francis is quite pragmatic."

Will said, "Very well. I'll send a note back accepting the General's offer."

Mary jumped up, her needlepoint flying. She threw her arms around Will's neck and said, "You shall be rewarded handsomely this evening, Sir." Her hands roamed down his back, and she cupped his buttocks.

Will grinned. "Careful what you wish for ..."

Mary pushed away from him, her face pink with excitement. "My God! I shall actually have a husband. Oh, happy day!"

Will went downstairs to tell Lieutenant Huggins that he would write a brief note to the General in reply.

~~<>~~

The next morning, a tired Will Yelverton swung into his saddle and trotted out of the small mews behind his home. As he trotted down the street, he marveled that this was his house. Will gave Cuthbert – now a sergeant – the day off. No need for Cuth to ride out to the camp when Will wouldn't need anything. Thirty minutes later, Will reported to General Lincoln's tent.

Lincoln looked up from a paper he was examining. "My God, but the costs of keeping an Army, Will!"

Will said, "Yes, Sir?"

"God knows the men need to be fed, and we need arms and ammunition, but the costs for horse fodder, and every other possible commodity, is astounding."

Lincoln saw Will's look. "Oh, don't worry. We have clerks to manage this. I shan't expect you to take on this painful duty!"

Will grinned. "Thank you, Sir. What would you like me to do?"

"I want you to become the Army's Inspector of Arms. I do NOT want you to become the gunsmith to the army. Rather, your expertise in arms and the related sciences means you are perfect for overseeing those maintaining our arms and keeping the powder and shot safe in the magazine. Is that acceptable to you?"

Will smiled, "It will be an honor to serve in any capacity, General. But this is in my area of expertise, and I shall work diligently to improve our arms."

Lincoln said, "I knew this would be a perfect match, Will. Let me know what you need. That said, alas, we have little extra. But I'll do what I can to remedy any problems you might find."

Will bowed and turned to leave. Lincoln said, "Oh, and because the armory is in town, you may continue to reside at your home in the city. Your orderly may also remain in town."

Will smiled, "Thank you, Sir. My wife is delighted that I am remaining in Charlestown. She sends her best wishes, Sir."

~~<>~~

Trotting to the city's magazine, Will set to work. He was delighted that he could walk to work each day, thus giving Molly a rest. He found that there was a great store of powder in the city's magazine. Other aspects of the Army's munitions and weapons disturbed Will. A junior clerk stood at attention when Will entered and sweated copiously when asked about simple information.

These lapses in supply and management caused Will to set to work inventorying every detail. As a gunsmith himself, Cuthbert was a wonderful help, and his new rank of Sergeant gave him authority over the junior men.

Muskets were in various states of disrepair. A limited supply of bayonets and gun flints was an immediate concern. Some powder seemed damp, and one room in the armory had obvious high humidity, causing Will to worry about the powder's viability.

Will spent three days and prepared a report for General Lincoln.

"Damn!" Lincoln said as he read the report. "I knew you were the right man for the job, Will. What shall we do?"

Will said, "There's not much we can do about the building. I recommend we find a better building that is dry for powder storage. The gun flints are not as big a problem because there is a ready supply of flint at the harbor. Ships from England frequently carried flint as ballast, and the flints were thrown overboard when the ships loaded for the return trip. We can assign a company of men to retrieve the flints and cut those stones to fill our needs. The bayonet situation, as the General knows, is a conundrum."

Lincoln thought for a moment. "This is good, Will. Look for a dry warehouse away from the wharves where it will be less vulnerable. I will have one of the companies of the 4th Regiment down to the wharves to begin retrieving the flints. That, young man, was a brilliant solution to a major problem."

Will said, "My next duty, Sir, will be to oversee an inspection of every weapon. I have confidence in the gunsmiths I have met. They will be required to repair weapons as needed. My orderly, Sergeant Cuthbert, is a passible gunsmith himself, so he will aid in overseeing the work."

Lincoln nodded absently, "Good. I knew we would get this in hand."

~~<>~~

The duty was not demanding, and Will spent time with Mary. They often walked down to the point where batteries were under construction. Sometimes they walked out to where some of the troops and assembled Negroes were digging defenses across the Charlestown Neck. Will looked at the ditch, the redoubts, and the beginnings of a major stone hornwork in the center of the line that stretched across the neck. He saw Negroes dragging chopped-down trees clearly intended to be abatis.

Mary said, "How wonderful! The British won't ever penetrate that!"

Will smiled. He thought the defenses were adequate, but he wondered if the rebels could defend Charlestown as well as the British had defended Savannah. He didn't explain this to Mary. No need to scare her.

Will was delighted with their relationship. Mary was kind and gentle and very loving. She made it clear at every opportunity that she was smitten with Will. Every afternoon they had the chance, they made love.

~~<>~~

In mid-December, Mary was sitting on the bed one morning when suddenly she lurched over to the commode cabinet and vomited into the chamber pot. After a moment, she vomited again.

Will was aghast. "Are you all right?"

Mary wiped her mouth and tottered back to bed. "Yes, must have been something I ate last night."

Will nodded. Mary seemed all right, and they made passionate love. Afterward, Mary vomited again.

Will asked again if she were all right. She nodded but looked wan.

The next morning was a repeat of the vomiting. Will noticed that Mary had brought a clean chamber pot to the bedroom in anticipation of the possibility of another episode. Each day for the next week, leading up to the week before Christmas, Mary had this sickness in the morning.

Finally, Will said, "My darling, this is not usual."

Mary said, "Oh, 'tis completely to be expected, Will, when a woman is carrying a baby."

Will was stunned. "Are you telling me you are with child?"

Mary nodded. "I hope you are not angry."

"Angry? Of course not. I'm delighted!" Will jumped up and danced around the room.

Mary laughed at Will's antics. He looked silly, especially because he wore only a nightshirt that had ridden up, and as he danced, his member flopped around. Mary laughed until tears ran down her face.

Will was immediately concerned. "My darling! Why so sad?"

"Ha, I am not sad. I was laughing at your flopping willie as you danced. It was adorable. I'd like to see that again."

Will said, "I'm afraid it won't flop satisfactorily in this condition."

Mary looked down and laughed. "No, 'tis quite stiff and not at all floppy!"

Chapter 22 – The Departure

Christmas passed with quiet joy – at least as much joy as a sparse wartime Christmas could bring. Mary was glowing, but she was often sick, especially in the mornings. Will felt bad for her, but he smiled every time he considered becoming a father.

Although the entire world was on alert for British activities, Charlestown's people enjoyed some festivities. The fare was not what it was before the revolution, but Charlestown society ignored the threat and behaved as though things were normal. The various social clubs held parties and dinners. People dressed up more than usual and promenaded when the weather permitted. The mood was as festive as possible.

Mary loved social occasions and even had a new dress made. The newest fashions from Europe were unavailable, but she had some nice scarlet fabric appropriate to the season. The dress was magnificent on her, and Will was delighted to squire her to the upper-crust affairs.

Most of the attendees were pleasant and welcoming to Will. A few were unfriendly, making it clear they considered Will a plowboy who had married above his station and was lucky to be in their company. Most of the unfriendly people were men who were neither in the army nor the militia. They were slow to recognize that only the military stood between them and the British. Many professed to be patriots, but Will thought them opportunists.

A constant topic of conversation was the outbreak of smallpox in the city. So far, it was localized to a few city sections, but more sections seemed to be involved each week.

Will chatted with a pleasant gentleman named William Somersall at one of the social club gatherings. Will had briefly met Mr. Somersall, who was a neighbor of the Proctors.

Somersall said, "Colonel Yelverton, I am delighted to see you joining us. I hear you have been quite the hero at Savannah and before."

Will smiled, "I assure you, Sir, I am no hero. I have just occasionally found myself in the middle of desperate situations."

Somersall grinned, "I think that must be how heroes are made, Sir."

Will smiled in acknowledgment of the compliment. He asked, "How came you to Charlestown?"

"'Tis a good question. Like you, I came by accident and made it my home. My family owns property in Bermuda and St. Kitts.

We have sugar plantations. I came here to sell sugar and stayed."

Will nodded. "'Tis a very pleasant place to be, although I must say I hear the West Indies are beautiful."

Somersall chuckled. "Aye, the islands are lovely, and the sea is beautiful and blue. But Charlestown is a much more accommodating place for business and general living. Sadly, this lovely city is often diseased, as we see with smallpox. One of our sharper wits said the city is a paradise in spring, hell in summer, and a graveyard in winter."

Will smiled. "Would that were not true."

Somersall said, "Aye, were it not for yellow fever in summer and this smallpox, t'would be the finest town in the colonies, er, the Nation, I mean. 'Tis a major center of commerce, and I fear the British will come north with a vengeance. We will be hard-pressed to defend against an all-out assault."

Will nodded. "I have seen our defenses, and while they are well constructed, especially the horn work, we don't have fully trained professionals like the British. As always, we are short of supplies."

~~<>~~

The new year dawned bright for Will and Mary. Will reflected that last year he was pushed out of Savannah by British forces and spent a soggy New Year's Day celebrating with nasty weather, a tired horse, and several hundred defeated and exhausted Patriots withdrawing to South Carolina.

Will reflected on 1779 as being a year of torment and delights. Battles and deaths, the love of his life married to another man and pregnant with his child, Elbert nearly killed and now captive, Noah Harris killed at Brier Creek and the senseless confusion and loss in Savannah – twice. He did consider that 1779 had its delights in that he had been successful as an Army officer, an unexpected turn. And, of course, his marriage to Mary had made so many things better. He thought that though he had lost Abby, which hurt his soul, Mary was a wonderful woman and the best wife. He counted himself lucky. Now he was to be a father, and he hoped that 1780 would be better than 1779.

Optimism aside, Will soberly feared this year would be worse.

~~<>~~

January was quite chilly, and the damp wind off the bay certainly made the chill that much colder. Will continued to check weapons, oversee repairs, and attend to Mary. She was feeling better with less morning sickness. Cuthbert was growing as an assistant to Will, more than just being his orderly.

Will met with Colonel Owen Roberts, Commander of the 4th Artillery Regiment. Roberts' former deputy, Colonel Bernard Beeckman, was present as commander of the Charlestown Artillery Brigade. "Gentlemen, I am not here to tell you how to command your artillery. It is merely my function to find ways to help. I also am to identify weapons that need repair and attempt to effect those repairs.

Roberts said, "You are most welcome, Colonel. I know we have so little extra, anything you can help with is valuable."

Beeckman nodded. "Aye. I think we're well prepared, but another set of eyes is always welcome."

Will looked at the condition of the cannons and was happy to see that they were all well-maintained. Individual members' muskets were also in good repair, and Will reported to Roberts that all was in order. He also promised to find out if there were other sources of powder.

Beeckman said, "Our preparations of defenses continue, Will, but I worry that it will not be enough. I have guns on the main line across the neck. I also have guns on the various batteries lining both riverfronts and the bay. We have quite a problem in supplying all those guns. Will, I fear the British will sail into the harbor and up the rivers and brave our guns, at the same time, they will show up in thousands in front of the line across the neck. I despair over how quickly we might become overwhelmed."

Will said, "I understand, Sir. I have no answers."

Beeckman looked glum, "Sadly, neither do I."

~~<>~~

At the beginning of the second fortnight in January, Will reported to Lincoln.

"Sir, I have reviewed all the weapons in the city and our area here. I believe I should now go south to Sheldon Old Church and check the weapons there."

Lincoln said, "Very well. You can take dispatches to Colonel Marion. When do you propose to leave?"

"I leave tomorrow if that will be acceptable, Sir."

~~<>~~

Mary was distressed. "I thought you were going to be here!"

"I am, my darling. I will be gone for only a few days. Two days to ride down to Sheldon, and two days back. Five days there to inspect weapons."

Mary wailed, "So you'll be gone for ten whole days!"

Will took her in his arms. "Yes, only ten days. We have endured worse. I will be home very quickly, my dear."

Mary nodded resignedly. "I will miss you terribly." She patted her still-flat stomach, "Little Will also will miss you."

Will grinned. "You think we're having a son, then?"

"Oh, yes! I can tell even now that he is very much the same man you are."

~~<>~~

Will and Cuthbert trotted down the street and into the American camp outside Charlestown. Lieutenant Legare and the usual troop of ten men were ready to head for Sheldon.

Legare said, "Colonel Yelverton, good morning, Sir."

"Lt. Legare, 'tis nice to see you this fine January day. How are you? You have family here, I believe. I think I met your aunt who is married to Mr. Somersall?"

"No, Sir. My Aunt Sarah was married to Mr. Somersall, but she died a few years back. Sarah was the mother to my cousins Stafford and Thomas. I believe the confusion is that Mr. Somersall's new wife is also named Sarah. She was Sarah Crossthwaithe before they married."

Will said, "Oh, my, that is confusing! James, I'm sorry about your aunt. I didn't know there was a Sarah before the current one."

Legare said, "'Tis the way of the world. A great deal of death from disease. Aunt Sarah died giving birth to Thomas."

Will nodded. "I am sad about that. My wife is with child, and I fear the birth may be hard. 'Tis our first baby, and I understand those can be very trying."

Legare said, "I have no wife, but I know many women are lost in childbirth. I wish you and Mrs. Yelverton the very best. Please accept my congratulations on becoming a father."

~~<>~~

The small troop trotted into the familiar environs of Sheldon Old Church. Will carried the dispatch case with information and directives from Lincoln to Marion and the other commanders at Sheldon and Beaufort.

He spotted Marion observing his troops marching in the fallow farm field near the ruined church. Dismounting, Will kicked his way through the overgrown grass and weeds to where Marion stood. Even though it was getting late in January, Will broke a light sweat in the harsh winter sun.

"Will! Welcome back! I see that dispatch case, so Lincoln must have sent you."

"Aye, Sir. He made me Inspector of Arms, and he asked me to bring dispatches since I needed to come to look over the weapons here."

Marion said, "I think our weapons are in good repair, but I'm glad you're here to check."

Will said, "I see you're still drilling the troops. How are you doing otherwise?"

"We need a skilled hunter like you," Marion grinned. "The food's been a little monotonous. I do believe we're better soldiers after the last two months of drilling, and we're away from the city with its distractions and sickness. I did have to hang a few deserters. That has not been a terrible problem. There are not many places to go for someone running away."

Will spent the next two days checking weapons, inventorying powder and shot, and checking cartridges and cartridge boxes. He reported to Marion that everything looked good, only a few muskets had required minor repair. Cuthbert had attended to those.

Will thought he might spend a day hunting to put some meat in Marion's pots and then head home. He smiled that he would be able to help his friend with better food and still surprise Mary by being home a day or two early.

Will was mounting Molly and heading to the woods when a rider cantered into the camp, obviously an express messenger. The rider dismounted, threw his reins to a guard, and rushed into Marion's tent.

After a moment, Marion emerged, squaring his cocked hat on his head and looking all around the camp. Marion spotted Will and waived him over. Will dismounted and walked to where Marion stood.

"Sir?"

"Will, the rider delivered two messages. First, we are to march to Savannah leaving behind only 200 light cavalry to act as a screening force. The British have arrived in Savannah Harbor in force with a great fleet."

Will nodded and glanced at Molly. "We can be ready to ride immediately."

Marion's face was sober. "Will, there was also a message for you." Marion handed Will a folded paper that was not sealed.

Taking the paper Will said, "Oh?"

He unfolded the paper and read the words in a scrawl he did not recognize.

Charlestown

30th January 1780

Lieutenant Colonel Yelverton,

Sir, I regret to inform you that your wife, Mrs. Mary Yelverton, is very ill with smallpox. She was taken ill on 25th Inst and has not improved. I fear the worst. If possible, you should return to Charlestown immediately.

I am, Sir, your most humble obt svt,

Noble W. Jones, MD

Will was at a loss. His vision was a tunnel, and the sky that had been blue a moment before was now a strange gray color. He reread the note to be sure he had not misunderstood. But, no, the meaning was clear. Mary was sick, and former Savannahian Dr. Noble W. Jones, feared the worst.

Will looked around him. Marion was saying something, but Will could not hear. There was an odd buzzing sound in his ears. An orderly ran up with a small folding camp chair and held it while Marion helped Will to sit.

Moments later, Cuthbert was at his side. "Sir, I'm so sorry to hear this. Miss Mary is such a lovely and kind lady. I am at your service."

Will nodded dumbly. He was looking at everything and trying to make sense of the world at this most confusing moment. He remembered Dr. Noble W. Jones from the trek to Charlestown after the loss of Savannah a year earlier. During that frantic time, Will had escorted Dr. Jones, his wife, and his daughter, Charlotte, in a rushed escape from Savannah to Charlestown.

Charlotte had made her interest in Will very clear, and Dr. Jones had been most pleasant. Other than Jones' treating Marion's ankle, Will had not seen them in months, but that was no surprise with his various travels. Now, Jones was telling him his wife was dying and Will could do nothing.

Well, nothing except mount Molly and ride to Charlestown as quickly as possible. Will thought, A*nd do what? What shall I do? Can I save her?*

Will looked up, and Marion was saying something. Will struggled to focus. "I have sent an orderly to tell Lt. Legare to gather his troops and be ready to ride immediately. Cuthbert is loading your horse with your personal gear. You can leave as soon as you feel able to ride."

Will nodded dumbly. *Mary ... our baby ...*

Legare and his troops came around Marion's command tent, leading their horses. He handed his reins to one of his troopers and walked over. He said, "Sir, we are at your disposal."

Will nodded, his eyes not really seeing his surroundings.

Marion squatted beside him. "Will, 'tis not the time for you to worry about the war, but the British have arrived in great force in Savannah Harbor. We don't know where they will land. Don't concern yourself with this, just go to Mary. But you must know that things with the war will become very concerning, and quickly. I have given Lt. Legare a message for General Lincoln that we will march on the morrow and hope to arrive in Charlestown in five days, sooner if the weather holds. Now, are you able to get on your horse?"

Will nodded. "Yes, Sir. I am able to ride. I have to go to Mary ..." he trailed off.

"I know, Will. I wish there were more I could do."

Will said, "Thank you, Sir. I hope to arrive in time."

~~<>~~

Midday the next day, February 1st, Will and the troop cantered into Lincoln's camp. Will had spoken no more than a dozen sentences in the past 24 hours. The troop stopped only for brief rest breaks and to eat. Cuthbert insisted that Will eat and got some grudging response. Twice, Will leaned over from the saddle and vomited the little food Cuthbert had gotten him to eat.

The troops stopped at Lincoln's camp while Will and Cuthbert went on to Bay Street and Will's home. They hurried down the street but could not gallop without endangering people. They cantered into the stable yard at Will's house, and Will swung out of the saddle before Molly fully stopped.

Rushing across the stable yard to the back door, Will put his hand on the knob, but the door was locked. He turned and ran around the house to the front door only to find it locked. Will did not have a key because he had never needed one. Before, there were always servants at home to let him in. Now the house seemed empty and locked up.

Will was wild-eyed, frantic with worry as he raced back to the stable yard. He looked about with fanatic, almost possessed, focus on finding someone to let him in the house. He darted up the stairs to the second floor of the carriage house. There, one of the servants, an enslaved Negro woman, was sitting in a chair looking out the back window. "Rebecca? Rebecca? Where is everybody? Where is Miss Mary?"

Rebecca turned slowly. She looked at Will with curiosity. Recognition dawned. "Oh, Mr. Will. Oh ... Miss Mary ... she ... she ... she dead. I'm so sorry. Miss Mary, she dead!"

Will stumbled to a rough bed against the wall and sat heavily, elbows on his knees, his head hanging.

Tears streaking her face, Rebecca wailed, "Oh, it was terrible, Mr. Will. She got smallpox and it went all over her. She had blood under her skin. She died quick, Sir. They had to bury her right away. Smallpox is terrible and you can catch it even if someone has passed."

"Where is she buried, Rebecca?"

"Oh, there's a family plot at St Michael's."

"Where is everyone else, Rebecca?"

"They all left to Mr. Homer's plantation. They were afraid of being in the house with the sickness."

Without a word, Will stumbled out of the carriage house and tottered toward the street. Cuthbert hurried to ask what Will had learned. Will told him as he was walking toward the street.

Cuthbert said, "I'll go with you."

Will waved a hand in reply, a reply which could have meant anything.

~~<>~~

Will and Cuthbert stood in St. Michael's churchyard looking at a mausoleum with Proctor engraved over the door. Will knew he could not go inside, and to reinforce the point, there was a bolt and stout lock on the door.

Overwhelmed, Will sank to his knees and bent forward until his forehead rested on the ground. "Please God! Please tell me what

I am to do. Ah, God! God! God!" Will's voice was raw, and soon he could say no more. He stayed on his knees for quite a while.

Finally, he slowly stood up. He looked around and saw Cuthbert sitting on a low bench a few feet away. "Thank you for coming with me, Cuth."

Cuthbert made a dismissive gesture. "Of course, I came. Now, Sir, we must find a place to stay."

Will soberly said, "Aye. I suppose we cannot stay at the house until it is aired out to remove the bad air that brought the illness. We'll go to McCrady's. Tomorrow I will find who might let the air out and rid the house of anything that might be infested. I must also see Doctor Noble Jones and inquire about the circumstances of my darling's loss."

Cuthbert said, "'Tis not time to worry about it, but there is the matter of the British."

They were standing on Bay Street, and Will looked across the water. "Yes, we have our duty. I shall report to General Lincoln tomorrow, as well." Will shifted his eyes to Cuthbert, "Thank you for helping me, Cuth. I don't know what I'd do without you, my friend."

Chapter 23 – The Landing

Will woke up in a strange bed in McCrady's Tavern. He looked around the room, trying to get his bearings. The respite of sleep quickly drained away, allowing the fact that Mary was dead to crash in on him with a vengeance. He tried to make meaning of this sudden change in his life. His heart hurt. His eyes ached. Will was exhausted, and he felt empty in his soul.

The rush to get to Charlestown from Sheldon Old Church had been sleepless as he relentlessly pushed poor Molly and Legare's men to get him home and help Mary. The reality that he could not have helped was lost on Will. He knew in his mind that he would not have been permitted to be in the room with Mary, but his heart said he must try. Despite this conflicting knowledge, he pushed and pushed to get to Charlestown on time.

That Mary was dead and already entombed with her family was a strange, disconnected finality. It was as if Mary and the baby had somehow vanished into thin air. No goodbyes, no chance to understand what was happening. Nothing. Just the bloodless, harshly blunt words in the letter from Dr. Jones announcing Mary's illness.

Will had seen plenty of death – four years of it. At Moore's Creek Bridge in February of 1776, Will killed his first man, a Highlander who was intent upon killing him and his friends Sam Hawks and Noah Harris. That death was harsh in Will's memory, as was Noah's death at Brier Creek just a year past. All the killing and deaths, including Noah's, should have hardened Will to death. But Mary's loss was a dagger of ice jammed into Will's heart. Will knew that the ice dagger would never melt.

Added to the bright, insatiable pain of losing Mary was the loss of the baby she carried. Will's baby. Will had already begun to think of the baby as Little Will. And now Little Will was gone. Will cried hard as he considered that Little Will would have been a happy baby with a wonderful future in America, a land of liberty. What would Little Will have been? A gunsmith? A farmer? An adventurer? A merchant? A seaman? Now, Will would never know his child, never see him grow, never see him become any of those things. The sense of lost opportunity was an empty hole that was just as vivid as the icy pain of Mary's loss.

~~<>~~

Will was sitting on his bed, his head in his hands, when someone knocked on his door. He shuffled from the bed to the door. Expecting to see Cuth standing there, Will raked a hand through his disheveled hair and opened the door to find Benjamin. Benjamin's face was a mask of sadness and pain.

Will said, "Hello, Benjamin. Come in."

Benjamin said, "I came to pray with you, Will. I am so sorry for your loss."

Will sat on the bed, and Benjamin put his hand on Will's shoulder. Benjamin raised his other hand to the heavens, "Lord God, your son William is in pain. We pray for the eternal soul of his wife, Mary, and their unborn baby. Please take them in your loving hand and hold them to your bosom. Give Will strength, Oh Lord, to endure his suffering. Lord, please forgive me for the years of mistreating my brother, Will. I do not expect forgiveness from Will, for I have treated him terribly. Give me the strength to help Will in his time of need. May this tragedy at least offer reconciliation for your two sons, who are brothers and need your love and guidance. We ask in Jesus's name, Amen."

Will said, "Thank you, Benjamin."

Benjamin pulled a small chair away from an equally diminutive desk. He sat facing Will. "I meant that, Will, that God may help us heal from all my bad behavior. I know you are suffering. Please tell me what I can do."

Will said, "Not much right now, Ben. I don't understand any of this. But thank you for praying for Mary, the baby, and me. I had not yet turned to the Lord. Mostly I've been stunned. You helped me to remember the higher power of God."

Benjamin said, "Well, know I am here when you need me."

Will looked at Benjamin. "I don't hate you, Ben. Nor do I have any resentment. 'Tis all in the past. Would you like to stay at my house?"

Benjamin thought for a moment. "I suppose 'tis your house now. How hard that must be to go there."

"Yes, but I must. I must have it aired out first. Whatever bad air is there must be allowed to escape, else all who stay there will become ill."

"Well, I would say yes, but my place is at the camp, Will. You and the other officers don't always need to be there, but the chaplain is needed at all hours. So, I must decline. But I will call on you, if that's all right."

Will smiled. It was his first smile since three days ago when the news of Mary's illness reached him. "Certainly, you are always welcome. All the servants left for Homer Proctor's plantation up near Camden. There is only one Negro woman there. So I can't offer you much in the way of hospitality – meals, and so on. I suppose I'll have to hire someone."

"Oh, I quite understand. Thank you for letting me visit today, Will. Let us pray, 'Lord God, your daughter Mary and her baby are in your hands. Take care of your son, William, so that he might soon be strong enough to smite our enemies. He is a warrior for liberty in your name. In Jesus's name, we pray, Amen.'"

"Amen."

Benjamin hugged an astonished Will and left. As he closed the door, Will smiled again. It was a sad smile. He would, indeed, need strength. He thought, *I will visit Homer and Sarah if I can get out of Charlestown. And I will do everything I can to honor Mary and Little Will by redoubling my efforts to be a good man and officer. Please, God, help me make that so. Amen.*

~~<>~~

That afternoon, Will roused himself from his torpor and walked down the hall. He tapped on Cuthbert's door. Cuthbert opened the door immediately. It was as though he was waiting for Will. Perhaps he was.

"Hello, Sir. I'm glad to see you. If I may say so, you have looked better, but we shall work on that."

Will gave a half-smile. "I'm sure I don't look too good. At least I slept. Well, to be honest, I collapsed, Cuth."

Cuthbert nodded, "As did I."

Will said, "I could not be less interested in food, but my stomach is growling. Let's go eat downstairs."

They ate in McCrady's dining room and sat looking out the open windows that let in the early February air. The room was pleasant.

McCrady came over to the table, "Colonel Yelverton, please accept my condolences. I cannot imagine your pain."

Will rose and took McCrady's hand. "You have been kind to me every time I have come here, Sir."

McCrady made a dismissive gesture. "You are Colonel Marion's friend, and it is my honor to have you here. The same goes for you, Sergeant Cuthbert."

Cuth smiled and said, "Colonel Yelverton has suffered a terrible loss, but your wonderful establishment is the only place we would consider his home away from home."

McCrady said, "This is your home, Will, Cuth. Let me know what I can do."

Soon a diminutive Negro girl wearing a pinafore and a white apron came to the table with two slabs of apple pie. "Mr. McCrady say this is for you. He hope you are better soon."

Will said, "What is your name?" The little black girl looked fearful. Will said, "I only want to tell McCrady what a wonderful waitress you are."

The little girl visibly relaxed, "Dey calls me Maisie, Sir."

Will said, "Well, Maisie, thank you for the pie. I shall tell Mr. McCrady that you did a good job."

~~<>~~

Will asked Cuth to find who might air out the house on Bay Street. Meanwhile, Will mounted Molly and rode out to the camp. He had to do something other than sit in a room at McCrady's and mope.

Will dismounted in front of General Lincoln's tent. He walked to the tent and waited a moment. Lincoln personally burst out the door of the tent and extended his hand.

"Will! My God, but I'm sorry! I cannot imagine your pain. Do come sit."

They sat in the shade of the tent. Lincoln said, "What can I do to help, Will?"

Will thought for a moment, "Sir, there is nothing that will bring back my dear wife and our baby. So, I must throw myself into our cause. That will be my salvation. Please treat me like any other officer. The sooner I find solace in work and duty, the sooner I shall be better."

His voice roughened by emotion, Lincoln said, "Will, er, Colonel Yelverton, I shall respect your wishes. We are facing the British who have, as I think you know, arrived in Savannah. 'Tis as I feared. Savannah is now the anchor of the British to the south.

297

I think the British will land somewhere near Charlestown, but they won't challenge us directly, at first. They learned their lesson at Sullivan's Island in '76. I think they'll land to the south and march on us. I shall need you, but since you don't have a command as yet, I want you to be available to command special missions. I am not sure what those might be."

Will said, "I am at your service, General."

Lincoln looked into the distance, "I hope the missions I might need you for are not too arduous. But I fear you will be called upon for some dangerous tasks."

Will rose, and made a slight bow. "I, Sir, am honored to be your servant."

~~<>~~

Will looked across the plain toward the west in time to see Francis Marion and his units marching toward the camp. He stood watching the progress of the troops and in a few minutes, Marion trotted up. He was covered with road dust and his horse was obviously tired.

"Will! I didn't expect to see you."

"Sir, Mary died, and I was too late."

Marion dismounted and walked to Will. He extended his hand and put an arm around Will's shoulders. This, for Francis

Marion, was the most open and emotional that anyone would ever see.

"God, but I'm sorry, Will. I knew when you left that things were bleak. Smallpox is terrible, but some survive it. I hoped that would be true for Mary."

Will said, "Aye, 'tis a sad thing that women with child are more at risk of the deadly variety. Poor Mary died quickly, I'm told. Three days."

Marion said, "We can only thank God for the favor of a quick end. Smallpox is painful."

Will nodded. "Aye. I only wish I could have been here for her. Alas, I doubt they would have let me into the house."

Changing the subject, Marion nodded. "What does Lincoln say?"

"He thinks the British will not challenge Fort Moultrie but will land somewhere less formidable. I think he means Johns Island or south."

Marion said, "We're weak there, and it will be easier for the British to come ashore somewhere around Beaufort. We don't have the forces to threaten them. So, 'twill be a defense of Charlestown in close. I believe they will come overland from the south and take time to create a siege. Their Navy will ultimately force the harbor. The city is lost, but I imagine the city fathers will whine and cajole us into sticking it out. We shall be expected to expend blood and treasure to make them feel better before they throw the gates open to welcome the British. God damn their worthless souls."

Will said, "The British?"

Marion smirked, "No, Will. I mean the damn city elders who will act with total perfidy."

~~<>~~

Will went back to town to find Cuthbert. He finally found him at the house on Bay Street. As usual, Cuth had found people to open the house and let the brisk breeze rush through the windows, corridors, piazzas, and rooms. Cuth had gotten Rebecca, the only remaining servant, to help empty Will and Mary's room. Cuth had dragged the mattress off the bed and down the stairs to burn it behind the stables. The house was deemed safe for habitation, and Will would stay there. Still, it would be sad, and every corner would be filled with memories of Mary.

Will worried that Homer and Sarah did not know that Mary had died. He pondered how to get this sad news to them. Alas, he had no good idea. It was impossible to send a rider with the British threat.

Stepping across the street, Will spoke to William Somersall, who said, "I have business near Camden with my own plantation. A rider will be going this week. He could deliver a letter."

Will said, "That would be most appreciated, Sir. I shall write a letter this evening if that is acceptable."

~~<>~~

The next day, Will rode out to the camp. Lincoln had no special duty for him, so he checked in on the repairs to weapons and examined the powder stores. This took him two hours and yielded no beneficial results. Still, it was something to do.

A rider galloped into the camp as Will was getting ready to go into town to eat at McCrady's and then go home to his empty house. The rider dismounted and hurried to Lincoln's tent. Will was intrigued by the urgency and waited.

Soon, the rider rushed out and, mounting his already lathered horse, trotted out of camp. He was headed to the Ashley River Ferry and clearly returning south. Will hoped the poor horse would have a rest.

Deciding that the rider's message was none of his business, Will was about to mount Molly when Lincoln walked out of his tent.

"Will, do you know where Marion is?"

"No, Sir, but I will find him."

"Very well. Also, if you please, find Huger and Laurens, Owen Roberts, and Colonel Beeckman. Ten minutes in my tent."

Will nodded and made a half bow. He hurried to Marion's tent where Marion was sitting on a camp stool, looking at the day's entry in his order book.

Marion was puzzled at Will's rush, "Will?"

"Sir, General Lincoln says please meet in his tent in 10 minutes. He's asked me to find General Huger and the others."

Reaching for his hat, Marion said, "Something's afoot."

Soon, everyone was in Lincoln's tent. Lincoln surveyed the group.

"I just had an express from Colonel William Washington. His scouts report that the British fleet in Savannah Harbor has not disembarked troops. Further, there seem to be many goings-on of loading supplies, water, and other preparations. Colonel Washington believes the British will soon weigh anchor and move. He is not certain where they might go but expecting them to move north seems reasonable. That they have not unloaded at Savannah adds weight to the notion that they will soon move north."

The assembled officers all nodded and exchanged looks. Huger said, "I think we should step up training and drills. We have garrisons at Fort Johnston and Fort Moultrie. We should also consider relocating some forces to Johns Island and monitoring the area around Edisto."

Lincoln looked around the group. "Anyone else? No? Very well. I concur that we should move some small units down to Johns Island and include patrols near the Edisto River."

~~<>~~

On February 10th a rider from Colonel Washington at Sheldon Old Church raced into camp with the news that the British fleet had weighed anchor and stood out of Savannah Harbor into the open Atlantic. Lincoln sent an immediate express to Johns Island patrol units as well as to Forts Moultrie and Johnston.

On the 12th, a rider rushed into camp with the news that the British had anchored off Simmons Island, near the mouth of the Edisto River. Lincoln immediately called a meeting of the senior officers.

While the officers were meeting, a second rider hurried in to report that the British were disembarking on the south end of Simmons Island. It was clear they would complete their landing in the next couple of days and perhaps begin a march north.

Marion said, "Sir, I think we should immediately march south in force and make them miserable as they try to get off Simmons Island. Meanwhile, we'll need to leave sufficient men here to manage the final installation of defenses. In particular, we need to complete the ditch across the neck and flood it. We also need to finish all the redoubts and the horn work."

Lincoln looked around the assembled group. "No comments? I am hesitant to dilute our forces here, gentlemen. Let us wait until the enemy makes a move. Once they commit to a march, we can hurry to a place of ambush and blunt their approach there. I do concur with Colonel Marion that we must finish the defenses with attention to the elements he mentioned."

Lincoln paused, "If there are no questions, everyone can go back to their units and make preparations for both a defense and a march. Dismissed."

~~<>~~

Will and Marion walked toward Marion's tent and were out of earshot when Francis Marion burst out, "Damn! Damn and blast! We'll dither and wait. Then t'will be too late! Christ! It sounds like I'm reciting poetry, but you get my meaning, Will."

Will nodded, "Aye, Sir. But one must admit you are a fair poet."

Marion made a rueful grimace. "I wish I were a better poet. I'd write a love sonnet to stupidity while we wait to get our asses fair kicked."

Will snorted a brief laugh. Later, he realized he had not laughed since Mary's death. Perhaps he might survive after all.

Chapter 24 – Charlestown: The Storm Gathers

The next day, February 14th, Will worked with the Continental Army's Quartermaster of the Southern Department, Tacitus Gaillard, and his deputy, John Hall. They planned the distribution of shot and powder to the defenses. As Inspector of Arms, Will's function was to ensure the weapons were functional, which he had already done. So, he lent a hand to the Quartermasters as they listed units and apportioned powder and ball. Will was glad he had already put in such meticulous work on the weapons, for to try to do it now would be too late.

Gaillard was from old Charlestown money. Not the oldest money, but his family stretched well back into the 1600s. Gaillard's grandfather, yet another Huguenot, had come to the colonies from France in 1647 and had done well as a planter and merchant. Hall's people stretched nearly as far back. But his people were workers – farmers who worked hard to make a life in the sandy Carolina soil. Will felt he fit in well with these men. Will's parents owned a small plantation in North Carolina, and he had grown up apprenticed as a gunsmith. His family was not wealthy, but they were well respected among the planters of Edgecombe County, North Carolina.

The work of inventorying the shot and powder was hard, but if Charlestown was to be defended, it was necessary. Worse, insufficient supply meant every ounce of powder and every cannon shell or musket cartridge counted. As the three men finalized the list, Marion's orderly came to ask Will to visit Marion.

~~<>~~

As Will walked across the encampment he saw the oddest sight: Major General Benjamin Lincoln was helping to dig a ditch! Will walked up to Marion's regimental headquarters tent just as Marion stepped out into the sunlight.

Will doffed his hat in greeting. "I see our general is proving he's not above physical labor, Sir."

Marion grinned, "Ah, yes, someone once told me that a commander should never ask his men to do things he wouldn't do himself."

Will's eyes squinted a bit, "Aye, but digging seems a bit extreme."

"He doesn't think so."

Marion changed the subject, "We have reports that the British are landing something on the order of 10,000 men at Simmons' Island, and they have already invested Beaufort. I am certain that they'll come north in the next few days. Things will get hot and heavy here very soon."

Marion smirked, "So, of course, Alex McQueen has decided that we need an officer's call at his home. Just what we need before a fight, a night of drunken revelry."

Will smiled, "Well, I think the rector at my childhood church said something like, 'eat and drink for tomorrow we may die.' He was known for revelry."

Marion smirked, "I think that's in the Book of Isaiah, and the rest of it is that God said we would never live down that sin."

Will grinned. "I take it we're going?"

"Oh, aye. McQueen throws a fine party, and it promises to be a good time. You know I don't imbibe more than a taste, but I think we should enjoy the fellowship. Probably a good meal, and the last such for some time, I fear."

Will asked, When is this?"

"Next fortnight. March 3rd. 'Tis a Friday. That will allow the weekend for everyone to get over the drunk."

Will looked into the distance, his eyebrows knitted. "I'll have to learn who can clean my uniform. Mary took care of that for me..." He trailed off.

Francis Marion, never a sentimental man, softened, "I know 'tis hard, Will. 'Tis why I have never married. Men marry and then their wives die – and the opposite is true, leaving the wife with debts and farming, and children. I wish I could help you, but grief is a solitary thing, I fear."

Will nodded, "Aye. 'Tis hard, but the British have provided a distraction. Still, I miss her every day."

~~<>~~

Early the next morning, a small boat sailed from Wappoo Creek on James Island, just south of Charlestown. The boat grounded near the ditch across the neck and a lieutenant with a dispatch case hurried toward Lincoln's tent. Soon, runners hurried to the senior American officers ordering that they join General Lincoln. Although Will did not yet have a command, as Inspector of Armaments, he was expected to attend.

As the senior officers gathered into the tent, Lincoln stood looking at a map, his bulk noticeable in the gloom. He had dirt on his breeches and muddy shoes from working in the trenches. Though the tent was large, it was crowded with Continental officers and militia commanders.

Lincoln looked up at the group. He came to the point with no preliminaries, "The British have crossed onto James Island and are pressing north. I believe they will be opposite Charlestown

310

by March 7th. That's less than a fortnight, gentlemen. Our task is clear: we must complete the defenses and be ready."

There were quiet murmurs among the attendees.

Lincoln looked to Colonel Barnard Beeckman, Commander of the Artillery Brigade, "Report on the preparation of the batteries?"

Beeckman pointed to the map of Charlestown that hung from a frame. "Sir, the batteries along the waterfront around the peninsula have been completed. The south-end battery's sixteen guns are mounted and sighted. Along the Ashley Riverbank, six small redoubts each mount between four and nine guns. Along the Cooper River, seven redoubts are complete, each with three to seven guns. In the estuary, Forts Johnson and Moultrie have been repaired, and the guns checked. In all, we have some 361 guns."

Beeckman looked a bit grim. "Sir, we have not fired the guns. That was to preserve shot and powder. The horn work in the middle of the line across the neck is nearly complete, and we have a bit of work left on the other batteries along the line."

Lincoln nodded. "I don't need to ask how the training is going with the units. I've seen it myself, and I'm satisfied. I do remind everyone here that we are tremendously outnumbered. Reports are that the British have some 13,000 men, including the sailors on the dozens of ships. Accordingly, return to your duties. Dismissed."

Will and Marion walked back toward Marion's headquarters tent.

Marion said, "This is going to get very bad. I fear the British will come north, cross the river, and confront us head-on at the neck. Before they do that, they will force the entrance to the harbor. We will be surrounded – ships in the harbor with guns and an Army to our front. The situation will become intolerable quickly and surrender is inevitable."

Will said, "Why are we building all the defenses and flooding the ditch from river to river across the neck?"

Marion had a rueful smile, "To satisfy Rutledge! He designed the damned hornwork and insists upon defending the city. Lincoln has talked to him several times about evacuating the army and most of the well-off citizens. Rutledge and the rest of the government won't have it. Gadsden and several others style themselves as generals. 'Tis true that Gadsden was a general officer when he could chew, but now he has neither teeth nor star."

Will snorted a laugh at Marion's harsh witticism. Gadsden's mouth had fallen in and his lack of teeth was quite notable.

Marion continued, "If we stay, the army will be destroyed. Rutledge doesn't care about the army; he cares about his governorship. He knows if we evacuate, he's no longer governor, and he can't accept that. He is also a patriot and does not want to see South Carolina fall to the British. But fall it will. If we lose the army in the process, then we shall have to go to the swamps."

Will glanced at Marion. "The swamps?"

"Aye, Will. I will fight on. If the army is lost, I shall collect those who will fight and use what means we have to harass and intimidate the British and the loyalists at every turn. We can hide in the swamps and strike when the British are not expecting it. I shall make them hate their lives in the sweating, mosquito-infested swamps of South Carolina!"

~~<>~~

A few days later, Lincoln summoned Will.

"I want you to take a small detachment and ride out to Moncks Corner and the general area and report back on how passable the roads are. I need to know about the security of that area. Can we operate there? Have the British or loyalists taken major intersections? You understand what is needed, I'm sure."

Will said, "Yes, Sir. May I take Lieutenant Legare and his small troop?"

Lincoln's New England accent was strong. "Perfect, Legare is from here and knows the country. Frankly, Will, we need to know about routes to escape the peninsula should we decide to withdraw. If we stay, I need to know if we can place troops at Moncks Corner to guard that approach. Moncks Corner is also critical because Biggin's Bridge is there. 'Tis a major crossing for the Cooper River. If the British force that crossing, we shall quickly become trapped on this peninsula."

Will nodded, "Yes, Sir. We will seek out every bit of information we can find."

Lincoln said, "We need to know quickly. I think the British will come over the Ashley River within the fortnight. Then, things will get tight for us."

Will said, "We'll leave at first light, Sir."

~~<>~~

The morning was brisk as Will and Lieutenant Legare, along with the small troop of 10 Continentals, trotted out of the camp and headed north toward Goose Creek. Will wore a black, high-collared cloak over his uniform. His sword hung from Molly's saddle. *"Infernal damn thing,"* he thought.

As usual, Will had the Brander pistol tucked in his belt. His Uncle Ewan's Scottish dirk hung from a baldric on his left side while his bullet pouch and powder horns hung from his right.

He carried his English dragoon carbine in his right hand, its butt resting on his right thigh. Both the Brander and the dragoon were loaded with Will's customary buck and ball with an extra dash of powder. They were deadly.

Equally deadly at close range was Will's old horse pistol, also a gift from Uncle Ewan and also loaded with buck and ball. Ewan had taken a great risk in owning the old pistol while still in Scotland. Such items as guns and swords were outlawed for Scotsmen. But Ewan persisted and brought both the pistol and the dirk to the Colonies when he left Scotland behind. Ewan had given them to Will when Will first contracted with the North Carolina Militia as an armorer at age 17. Uncle Ewan was gone now, along with Aunt Pat. Will treasured his memory of the people he lived with for six years of his childhood and equally treasured the dirk and the pistol.

Carefully loaded and installed in scabbards on the right side of Molly's saddle were Will's .45 caliber long rifle and Josie. He often thought of Josie as a living being.

Will thought carefully about his mission – a reconnaissance – and hoped not to have to use any of the weapons. He considered that his orders were to examine the roads and report on their condition for marching an army.

Will thought, *"Tis hard to believe I have been riding with armies on the march for four years now. God knows I've seen enough roads to know if a road will accommodate five thousand men, horses, supply wagons, and a horde of suttlers, other merchants, whores, wives, and children walking along behind."*

He was also mindful of his other orders, which were to assess Moncks Corner as a likely defensive post for General Huger to emplace troops.

Cuthbert was equally prepared, and his officer's fusil rode on his right thigh. Cuthbert's horse was prancing with excitement.

Will asked Jim Legare, "I thought to cross the ferry, reconnoiter the roads out toward the North side of the Cooper River, and then cross Biggin Bridge at Monck's Corner to assess that area.

Legare thought a moment and said, "Aye, Sir. If we're to evacuate Charlestown I would think quickly putting the Cooper River between ourselves and the British would be the best maneuver. Monck's Corner is on this side of the Cooper, so setting a defense there would likely be a good policy as well. We should go across Clement's Ferry and thence north, Sir."

Will nodded, "Very well, let us cross at Clement's Ferry."

The small group was ready for any potential attack. Following Will's lead, they were armed to the teeth. Will smiled to himself. *"These fellows are capable and trustworthy. I've ridden with*

them this whole year, and they have done well. Legare is a
good man and knows this area."

~~<>~~

The group trotted past 4 Mile Tavern and then to a tavern on
the banks of the Cooper. The tavern had a sign that read, *Dover*.
Will wondered about that, but there was no time to tarry. The
horse boat was just taking on a small carriage and pair of horses
and preparing to leave the dock.

Will and the troops dismounted and began to board. Will gave
the ferryman a warrant for their fare, and the oarsmen began to
pull. The ten Negroes quickly got the ferry out into the channel
of the Cooper River. Then they pulled hard for the far shore.

Will paused to make notes in a small journal. He had observed
the roads from Charlestown to be high and dry, with only a few
places where mud might impede the army. He also noted that
the roads were narrow. It might be useful to send a road crew to
cut some trees in several spots. Wagons could pass, but the road
was only one wagon wide in many places.

Will also saw there were two ferryboats capable of carrying
horses on the south side of the river. He would look for more
such boats on the other side of the river. He did see six canoes
that were three planks wide in the keel. Each canoe looked like
it would accommodate twenty men.

As they thumped against the north dock at the mouth of Clouter Creek, Will saw two more horseboats and three canoes. They had passed two canoes on the river. Will noted that the trip had taken one hour. He had never enjoyed arithmetic but this time, it was necessary to do ciphering. He jotted down a total of 11 canoes that could each carry twenty men. Four horse boats might each carry as many as ten horses and their riders plus a wagon. The round trip for a boat was two hours if all went well and the weather was good as it was this day.

Will's ciphering indicated:

Canoes: 11 X 20 = 220 men

Horse Boats: 4 X 30 men and 10 horses = 120 men and 40 horses

Thus, each two-hour trip would yield 340 men and 40 horses across the river.

The disappointing news was that an army of 5000 men would require some 15 trips or 30 hours to cross the river. That did not include all the baggage train and any other animals. Not included in the calculations were women, children, and other camp followers.

Will would report that the crossing would require two full days of near-perfect weather, fully functional boats, and plenty of manpower to haul on the oars. He would recommend scouring the rivers to confiscate every boat available. This last would not set well with the people, but the only way to shorten the crossing was to get more boats. Or send some of the army across Hibben's Ferry, but that was quite a detour.

The group walked their horses off the ferryboat and up the slight bluff to pause at the Calais Tavern. Will raised an eyebrow at Legare, who said, "'Tis a bit of humor – Dover yonder and Calais here. I suppose the river is seen as the English Channel."

Will grinned. "I have heard that there are white cliffs at Dover. All I see hereabouts is mud and marsh grass."

Legare hooted at this and said, "May I suggest we take a bit of refreshment in Calais? Closest I'll ever come to France."

~~<>~~

The troops all sat in the gloom of the Calais Tavern and drank small beer except for Legare, who asked for coffee. The serving girl was a Negro slave who had nothing to say. She wore a ragged dress and no shoes. Will thought her feet must hurt from the cold this late February day and from walking the rough pine floors. She did not complain.

Legare glanced around and spotted the proprietor, a stout man of about 50 years. Legare quietly said to Will, "John Clement, not the most affable of men." Turning to Clement, Jim Legare said loudly, "Mister Clement! I do declare! Last time I saw you

I was with my late grandmother, Mrs. Ioor. She's dead these last ten years. Has it been that long?"

Cement scowled. "And you, Sir, are?"

Legare muttered, "He knows full well who I am," but spoke up and said, "Why, Mr. Clement, I'm Jimmy Legare."

"Huh, didn't see in the gloom. Can't say as I remember Mrs. Ioor."

Legare murmured, "Yes, you bloody do." To Clement, he said, "Small woman, gray. Dutch accent."

Clement pretended to think and then said, "Ah…yes. The accent is what I remember. What brings you this way, sonny?"

Legare let this last jibe slide by without comment. "Why we're simply soldiers out for a pleasant ride."

"Won't be pleasant for long, I hear. We had riders through here in the last few days saying the British are marching toward Charlestown."

Legare said, "Really? Hadn't heard that. What else do you hear? I'm sure being a taverner, you get lots of people by every day. A clever man like yourself certainly makes friends with all." Legare muttered, "I'll bet you play both sides against the middle, you bloody turncoat."

Will sat in the shadows and watched as Clement walked over to the table. Legare did not invite him to sit. That was a good thing, for Clement's aroma preceded him like a bow wave. The stink washed over Jim Legare and Will.

Clement croaked a conspiratorial whisper, "They wuz two fellers through here jes yesterday. Their cloaks looked normal, but they had what looked like British officers' boots and rode good mounts. That's a surprise since I heard from other riders to hide any horses I might have. Seems the British lost so many mounts during their sea passage, they're out to confiscate any old bag of bones that might be ridden."

Legare feigned disinterest. "Huh, couple grandees out a'ridin' their property, no doubt."

"No, Sir. No, Siree. They was well spoken, but not from around here. One of them had a hard face, too. Missing two fingers on his left hand. Scared me a bit, and I am not afraid to admit it."

Legare said, his voice an air of casualness, "Oh? Scared you? My, my. You seem a hard man to frighten, Mr. Clement."

"Oh, aye. In my youth, I took no guff from any man. But this one...this one was a killer, and no doubt. He was riding a white horse and his mate was riding a bay. A nice bay like this gentleman's mare out front."

Will inclined his head but did not speak.

Legare said, "Well, we must be on our way. Oh, by the by, are the other ferries running?"

Clement said, "A poor lot they are, and no competition there. But, yes, Bonneau's Ferry up the east branch and Strawberry on the west branch are running, last I heard. Of course, my ferry is the most convenient of them all."

Legare stood and donned his cocked hat. He said, "Aye, and your ferry has the best boats and is well-maintained. I think you have more boats, too."

"Aye. And thankee for sayin'. Bonneau's has as many boats, but they leak. Don't know about Strawberry. We also have rooms to let, though I have no trade just now."

Legare turned toward the door and then paused dramatically. "May I look at your rooms, Mr. Clement? Perhaps on our return trip we will need accommodation."

Clement beamed. "Of course, please do. They're just up the stairs."

Legare said, "Thank you kindly. You have a stable? Yes? My friend is most particular about his horse. May he have a look?"

Clement nodded and bowed and waved a hand in the direction of what was obviously a stable. "Please."

~~<>~~

Will and Legare rode stirrup to stirrup and discussed the visit to the Calais Tavern.

Will said, "The stable has seen some heavy use of late. The dung has not been mucked out for several days. Cuthbert wandered the property while we were in the tavern. Saw some fresh tracks. He thinks there are more horses hidden away. Clement obviously doesn't want them taken."

Jim Legare nodded. "The rooms have not been cleaned and there was evidence of several guests."

They both were lost in thought for a moment before Will said, "Men with quality horses despite the British confiscating any decent mount available, heavily used stables despite the same, recently used beds...good many horse tracks."

Will continued, "We had some heavy rain a few days back, and the ditches are full. Look at the tracks on this road. A good many horses have been this way. Can't speak to the quality of the mounts, but this road is well traveled."

Legare looked around and said, "I'm not sure what to make of this information."

Will was pensive, "Neither am I, but I think it means others have been doing what we're doing."

Legare nodded. "It also means we could ride into an ambush."

Will said, "I agree. I think we should put two men out front and two men well behind."

Legare nodded, "Sergeant Wilkins? Put two men 100 yards in front and two 100 yards behind as a rear guard. The colonel thinks there's the possibility of an ambush."

Wilkins, a stoic man of few words, nodded and said, "Yes, Sir."

Will said, "To review what we've learned, it seems the road from Charlestown to Clement's Ferry Road is good. Clement's Ferry Road needs some clearing but is mostly high and dry. Clement's Ferry will take two days to cross. It appears agents – possibly British or loyalist – are out and about gathering information as we are."

Legare said, "Aye, Sir. I think we should look at Bonneau and Strawberry Ferries."

"Agreed, I think we should pick up the pace, as well."

Chapter 25 – Tarleton

Will and Jim Legare led their troops northwest along roads that would ultimately get the army to the Peedee River area or even into North Carolina. They were fortunate to find a couple of taverns to stable the horses, eat, and sleep overnight. Will gave the tavern keepers warrants for the cost. One or two tavern keepers were reluctant to take the warrants, but they were equally reluctant to refuse. Will did not care. He knew many people were sunshine patriots, as Thomas Paine called them.

Will recorded the roads were passable and, in many cases, wide and well maintained. Will realized that he was not a cartographer. But he had a map and marked it identifying fords and ferries. On the third day, Will asked Legare what he thought of their mission accomplishment.

Legare said, "Sir, I think we have found pathways for the army should the generals and politicians decide to evacuate. If the army gets this far, scouts will find the rest of the way to the general's objective."

Will said, "Aye. Exactly what I think, Jim. Let's go to Moncks Corner and scout that. On the way back to Charlestown, we can check the ferry at Bonneau and the Strawberry Ferry."

~~<>~~

The detachment clattered over Biggin Bridge just Northeast of Moncks Corner. They rode southeast to the little crossroads that was Monck's Corner. Will quickly noted there was not much to see but that the small settlement was strategically located astride the major escape route out of Charlestown. Swamps intruded on both sides of the road leading to the Biggin Bridge. Will jotted notes that Biggin Bridge was defensible because the single avenue of approach was the road itself.

Will and Legare left the troops to water their horses and rode out from the settlement toward the south. It was late afternoon, and the coming month of March was living up to its reputation for coming in like a lion. The air was chill and brittle. The breeze was becoming more of a strong north wind. It would likely become a nor'easter. Will knew that harsh, bitter cold would drive down from the north. Perhaps by nightfall, certainly, by morning, this ride would become knife-edge cold misery.

They approached a small rise and saw two men trotting along the road coming in their direction. One rode a white horse. Will looked at Legare and took off his cocked hat, shoved it in a saddlebag, and pulled out a plain tricorn. Legare did the same with a felt hat that would ward off the cold breeze. They backed their horses down further below the crest of the hill. They watched as the two riders came closer.

There was something about the man on the white horse. The way he carried himself. Perhaps it was the way he sat the saddle. His bearing screamed English aristocracy. Privilege, power, influence, an edge of cruelty. Will knew this man, but from where?

Will and Legare checked the prime on their weapons. Legare, skilled with a sword, loosened his blade in its scabbard.

Will said, "I think this is trouble. I think they're British officers scouting the countryside. I wonder where their troops are?"

Legare shrugged. "I agree, Sir. 'Tis a big area southeast of here. I'd say they may be as far as the Tullifiny. But 'tis strange that British officers would be scouting on their own. Then, maybe they don't have mounts for their cavalry. The losses from the ocean voyage must be as bad as we've heard."

"Aye. I heard the same thing. I think we shall take these two prisoners."

They watched as the two riders trotted toward Moncks Corner. Will kept an eye out in case there was a larger force than the two men. Will and Legare quietly walked their horses to a thicket next to the road and waited in ambush. The two riders drew abreast of the thicket, and Will and Jim Legare walked their horses out behind them.

Leveling his English dragoon carbine at the man on the white horse, Will said, "Halt. I am Lieutenant Colonel William Yelverton of the Continental Army, and you are my prisoners."

The two riders stopped but did not turn. Will could see they were considering their options and whether a horse race was possible.

"I will shoot the first man who twitches his reins or moves a boot to spur his horse. Now, drop your reins and kindly raise your hands."

The two men did as ordered.

"Now, my lieutenant here will kill whichever of you moves as I walk my horse to speak to you face to face as gentlemen."

The man on the white horse snorted, "Gentlemen. Ha!"

Will moved to face the two riders, keeping his carbine leveled on the man on the white horse.

"Good afternoon, gentlemen. As I said, I am Lieutenant Colonel William Yelverton, and you are my prisoners. I would be obliged if you would tell me your names."

The man on the white horse said, "I believe you know me, Sir. My name is Lieutenant Colonel Banastre Tarleton of His Majesty's Forces. I have the honor of commanding the British Legion, the true American patriots."

Will said, "Indeed, I do know you, Sir. You threatened to hang me, Sir."

Tarleton snorted, "I should have done it, too. But it required a trial, and you slipped away."

It was Will's turn to snort, "I believe you set it so that I would escape allowing you to kill me and accomplish your purpose without the inconvenience of a rope."

Tarleton inclined his head, "Perhaps not quite the bumpkin, I thought."

Will said, "I'll have your other Brander pistol, Sir."

Tarleton started. "You! You blackguard! Do you have my pistol? I thought it lost in the dark that night."

Will said, "Mine, now. And the other one."

Tarleton said, "You were a damn spy, and I was right!"

Will said, "Nay. I was never a spy. I was merely a boy far from home, stuck in Philadelphia. You called me a spy for the sport of seeing me hang. Tell me why I shouldn't hang you, Sir."

The color drained from Tarleton's face. "I am no spy."

"Oh? You wear no uniform and show no sign of a British officer's rank. Why should I not truss you up and take you to Charlestown, where General Lincoln might determine your fate? Or, as I am the senior officer in this area, perhaps I shall convene a court in the morning. I'm certain to find you both guilty of spying and hang you myself. Plenty of good trees hereabouts."

Tarleton's face flushed red. "You scoundrel! It is I who will see *you* hang."

Will sniffed, "Tried it before, old boy. Now, I'll have the mate to *my* pistol. And be very ginger about how you hand it over."

"Bahstid! You complete bahstid! Here's my bloody gun, and be damned to you, Sir."

Will said, "Thankee kindly, Sir. Now, then, let's discuss why you are riding hereabout."

"I should think it obvious."

"Oh, aye. But as opposed to when you accused me of being a spy when I was not, you, Sir, are clearly spying."

"I am not! We are merely scouting the countryside. If you must know, I hoped to buy horses and did not want to reveal my identity in the bargain."

"Oh, that's what you were doing at Clement's ferry. The Calais Tavern? I suspect you've been to the real Calais and enjoyed it better."

"Aye. Clement is a pig. He had no horses to sell and stank worse than a hog."

"On that, Sir, we agree."

Tarleton looked bored. "What will you do with us?"

Will pretended to consider. "I should drag you to Charlestown and watch you hang. Or, as I said, hang you here. But those are both needless provocations. As I am a gentleman, and you have kindly given me your pistol as an act of good faith, I shall allow you to go."

Tarleton's eyes bulged. "Let us go? Damnme, man, but that's a humiliation!"

Will said, "Indeed, but I imagine it's less humiliating than shitting your pants at the end of a rope."

Tarleton made a face. "Vulgar, too. You're no gentleman."

Will said, "Tisk, tisk, Sir. I've just given you your life. Do try to make something useful of it."

Tarleton spat, "Guttersnipe! You're nothing but a gunsmith with grease under his nails."

"Oh, aye, I do have grease under my nails. 'Tis honorable work, fixing weapons with which to fight for our freedom."

Tarleton deflated somewhat; then, he drew himself up. His hard face was even harder than the time Will had seen him riding toward Eastpoint in Pennsylvania. "I shall kill you one day, *Mister* Yelverton."

Will laughed. In a tired voice, he asked, "Do you see this rifle?" inclining his head toward Josie.

"Aye."

"Well, Sir, you'll have to get closer than 300 yards to kill me. Now, do turn your horses and trot along home. There's a good boy. Oh, better men than you have tried to kill me, Sir."

Tarleton and his companion, who had remained silent the entire time, turned their horses. As they did, the companion smiled at Will and said, "I am Lieutenant Colonel John Simcoe, Sir. I think you are more of a gentleman than my companion does. Be aware, Sir, he is a terrible enemy to have."

Will tipped his hat with his left hand, the carbine still level on the British officers. "So am I, Sir, so am I. I bid you both a pleasant evening."

~~<>~~

Legare asked, "Why did you let them go?"

Will said, "Because it would be much effort to keep them prisoner and take them to Charlestown. We learned everything we needed from them. They're short of horses and scouring the countryside for mounts. Their main force is not here, at least not yet. I also was not going to hang them. That would have caused a major incident. But I did humiliate them."

"Damned if that's not true, Sir. The one named Tarleton was enraged."

Will grinned as he tucked the second Brander pistol into his belt, "Yes, and I have both his pistols now. I look a proper pirate, don't I?"

Legare looked up at the trees beginning to whip in the wind, "I fear you shall see him again, and it won't be pleasant."

Will nodded, "I'm sure of it."

Chapter 26 – The Party

Will and Legare trotted along toward the defensive line. Their mission was complete, and they would brief General Lincoln as soon as they reached the camp.

Will said, "The only thing that disturbs me about our confrontation with Tarleton and Simcoe is that they suggest working with your hands is lower class. I've never felt that."

Legare said, "Sir, that is the difference between them and us. We value industry and success, which I will say you have in abundance. They value birth and descent, which is no recommendation for a man other than perhaps to open doors. Even so, in Charlestown society, there is a level a man may not rise above because the nobles who came here first have walled it off. For example, my grandmother, Catherine Ioor, came here from Holland. She was well off but was not accepted at the highest levels because our people were not among the first to come here. In turn, I will never be accepted at that level. 'Tis a carry-over from England. Among the first people to come here were Cavaliers, displaced noblemen. That and Huguenot nobles are fleeing Catholic France. I often smile that they were poor as church mice. Still, somehow their birth made them the upper crust."

Will smiled an enigmatic smile, "I never aspired to the upper crust."

Legare said, "Your humility makes you appealing to the highest levels of society, Sir. I know you have had tragedy, but if you wish to stay, you will be welcome. We will never be at the highest levels, but industry and effort will carry you a long way."

Will smiled. Jim Legare had become a good friend.

Will and Jim stood before the map with General Lincoln. Will had explained the various challenges of moving the army, including the ferry limitations. Legare explained that the roads would be passable but narrow, as Will had observed. They told Lincoln that Moncks Corner was a critically important strategic location. They recommended occupying it immediately to prevent British incursions from that direction and preserve the road as an escape route should the army need to evacuate.

Will said, "Sir, we also recommended confiscating every boat up and down the Ashley and Cooper Rivers. There are two reasons. First, we must deny the British those boats. Second, we may need them to cross the river should we withdraw from the town."

They touched on the confrontation with Tarleton and Simcoe.

Lincoln asked, "You did not tie them up and bring them in?" His voice dripped with New England accent, a sign Will had learned meant the general was irritated.

"No, Sir. We couldn't try them as spies in the field. There was too much risk of their troops arriving and turning the tables. Had that happened, our small detachment would be swinging from a tree at Moncks Corner, and the mission would have failed."

"I decided that bringing in high-ranking prisoners would put you in a compromised position. We would have been distracted by a trial and a public hanging. The British would have seen it as a dishonorable thing. Repercussions would have been wide. I decided to send them on their way."

Lincoln said, "Harrumph. I can't fault your thinking. I'm not sure what I'd have done in your place."

Will said, "I know, Sir. Tarleton is dangerous, and so, I understand, is Simcoe. But we couldn't risk our mission of finding the best paths for an army to withdraw. To bring those two along would have given them critical information about what we intended."

Lincoln looked at Will hard. "Difficult choice. But you made the best of it."

~~<>~~

337

Will got to his home and found that Rebecca had been cleaning and straightening. She had some food on the fire.

Rebecca said, "Oh, Mister Will. I'm glad you're home."

Will grinned, "I had an eventful trip. Is there some way I can get a couple of pots of hot water so I can take a bath? I stink."

Rebecca nodded and said, "I'll get some water going. You are probably hungry. I got collards and fat back in that pot. I had some onions so that the collards would taste like something like a couple of sweet potatoes from the root cellar. Nobody has much meat, but the fatback will fill you up. I got a pot of rice, too."

He ate the collards and rice and enjoyed the sweet potatoes with some hunks of butter melted into the flesh. Will grinned. He was home.

Yes, he was home. He climbed the stairs to the bedroom where Rebecca had gotten the tub set up. Will and Cuthbert hauled the hot water pots up and dumped them in the tub and then hauled cold water to mix in.

Sitting in the tub with the hot water and a bar of soap – a luxury he never had growing up – Will thought about the last time he sat in this tub. He and Mary had shared the hot water, and she had scrubbed the road dirt from him. She had also smiled at him and whispered her love. They had made love and, Will thought, conceived little Will. Little Will, the child who would never be. The ache was so strong it made his chest hurt. Hot tears trickled down Will's cheeks, their tracks camouflaged by the steam rising from the hot water.

Yes, he was home, but home was empty.

~~<>~~

The next night was Alex McQueen's officer's call. McQueen's home on Broad Street was opulent. But then, McQueen was wealthy. His wife was Elizabeth Fuller, a well-to-do woman in her own right.

At 7 O'Clock, Will walked the few short blocks to McQueen's home. His dress uniform was clean. Cuthbert had cleaned it carefully. He wore his black cloak against the heavy chill. The high collar was comforting against the blowing nor'easter. Will had become accustomed to the dangling sword and managed it easily with one hand on the hilt. He smiled because he had gloves to ward off the cold, and the gilt metal of the sword was freezing.

Will mounted the stairs without catching the sword between his legs. He considered that to be a major success. *Infernal bloody thing...*

He was met by a Negro footman who asked his name. The footman opened the door and preceded Will into the interior.

He spoke briefly with a second footman who conducted Will to the second-floor ballroom where dozens of officers were gathered. Madeira was already flowing like a river.

The footman whispered to a Negro butler who tapped the floor with a rod. Will smiled – the rod tapping on the floor reminded him of his schoolmaster Mr. Tomlinson. The butler announced, "Lieutenant Colonel William Yelverton."

Faces turned. Will saw smiles; many junior officers inclined their heads respectfully. Senior officers had looks of respect. One or two had the hungry look of jealousy.

Will felt like a fraud. *How did I get this rank? And I'm now wealthy from my poor departed wife.*

Will glanced around the room. The furniture consisted of elegant white and gold Cabriole sofas and chairs covered with blue and white silk. The window curtains matched. Will saw another set of sofas and chairs covered with black and yellow figures of nuns working in silk. There were inlaid commodes, card tables, and servers. He saw a superb India cabinet and a magnificent rosewood desk and bookcase. There were Chinese paintings on glass and an elegant large organ. Will's eye was drawn to a fine musical clock by Ellicott, mounted in Ormolu.

He thought, *My God, but McQueen is more than wealthy. He's fabulously rich. Now I do feel like a fraud!*

He was relieved to see Marion standing awkwardly in the corner.

Will said, "Colonel Marion, I'm glad to see you here."

"I, for one, wish I were anywhere else, Will. And do call me Frank. We're equal rank now."

"I fear I shall always see you as Colonel Marion, Sir."

"This is a bloody foolish activity, Will. We should be preparing for the assault. Better, we should sally out, find some decent ambush locations, and attack the British as they march north. Why, for God's sake, would we allow them to casually stroll up here, set up a siege, and take this city for a walk?"

Will said, "I think they're scouring the land for horses and food. They will be here before long, I fear."

"Aye. And these fools are acting as if there were not a damn thing worth worrying about, all the while getting bloody drunk as a wheelbarrow."

~~<>~~

The dinner convened at a set of long tables set up with salat, a surprising amount of roast chicken in a sauce with curry powder, currants, and other delicacies, and of course, Madeira. The group was seated, and the host, Major Alex McQueen, rose from his seat at the head table and said, "Gentlemen, this mess

341

is convened! And what a mess it is. Just look at this assembled multitude of sorry humanity!"

There was laughter all around, and a couple of the members tapped their spoons on the table in appreciation.

A captain of the infantry rose and said, "Major McQueen, I propose a toast."

McQueen said, "Let us pause a moment, Sir."

McQueen looked toward the footmen. "Please lock the doors."

The footmen locked the doors and stood, hands behind their backs guarding the locks.

Satisfied, McQueen said, "You are recognized, Captain Mason."

"Sir, A toast to the free, independent, and sovereign States of America!"

The entire assembled multitude rose, raised their glasses, and shouted, "To the States!"

They drank. Negro servants immediately refilled the now-drained glasses.

"Major McQueen, I propose a toast!"

McQueen scanned for the speaker. "Yes, Captain Roux."

"Sir, A toast to The Great Council of America-may wisdom preside in all its deliberations!"

The multitude rose and shouted as one, "To Congress!"

The servants recharged the glasses.

A tall man with graying hair stood and said loudly, "Major McQueen, I propose a toast."

McQueen glanced around, "Major Vanderhorst?"

"Sir, a toast to the 4th of July, 1776. Down with the king!"

The multitude shouted, "Down with the king."

Will muttered to Marion, "I guess that's why they lock the doors?"

"Aye, locking up precedes the revolution. T'was a precaution against being arrested."

Another captain rose and raised his glass, "Sir, I propose a toast."

"You are recognized, Captain Subrick."

"Sir, a toast to General Washington!"

The gathered officers rose and raised their glasses.

"To the Commander in Chief!"

Another officer proposed the next toast to the American army and navy-may they be victorious and invincible. Another toast was to the fallen soldiers and sailors of the United States.

A youthful lieutenant rose and squeaked, "Major McQueen, I propose a toast."

McQueen lurched to his feet. "Do enlighten us, Lieutenant...what the hell is your name anyway?"

The lieutenant was pink-faced, "Lieutenant George Dray, Sir."

"Enlighten us, Lieutenant Dray!"

"I propose a toast to our senior officers."

Will started to rise, but Marion put a hand on his arm. "'Tis a toast to us, Will. We remain seated."

The officers rose and shouted a wobbly, "Huzzah, Huzzah, Huzzah!"

And so the evening went. At some point, the toasting slowed enough for everyone to eat the chicken. Despite the trove of liquor, no one wanted to waste the food. Marion said it was a Low Country dish called Country Captain. Indian curry spices inspired the flavors, and Will thought it delightful. He had never had curry, and he rarely had currants mixed with anything. There was a Low Country chutney to go with the chicken. He used a piece of bread to mop up the juices.

Marion murmured, "I really would like to get out of here, Will."

"How do you propose to do that, Sir? I mean, the doors are locked."

Marion said, "I shall give it some thought."

~~<>~~

Marion rose and wandered off. Will thought he had gone to urinate, as so many others had done. Several had urinated out the open windows where chill air blew. Most of the officers were smart enough to piss through the windows on the downwind side of the house. As Will had learned during his weeks on the *Beatrice,* pissing into the wind was a bad idea.

A few minutes passed, and Marion was not back, so Will went looking for him. Marion was nowhere to be found. Will became concerned and finally started looking out the windows. His search was finally rewarded when he saw Marion on the ground below an upwind window.

Will leaned out and hissed, "Frank, what the hell are you doing?"

"I jumped out the window to get away from all the folderol. I missed my landing and cracked an ankle. I'm having a bit of trouble getting up and walking."

Will said, "I'll be right down."

~~<>~~

Will hurried to McQueen and said, "I need to get out the door. Colonel Marion has fallen out a window and is hurt."

McQueen blanched. "Fell out the window?"

Will said, "Well, jumped, to be more exact. He's hurt his ankle. I need to get him to his house and get a doctor to treat him."

McQueen said, "I'll get some fellows."

Will shook his head. "Marion would be mortified. I'll help him; just get your man to open the door."

~~<>~~

Marion was hurting. "Damn! 'Tis too bad I didn't drink much. I need something to numb the pain."

Will grinned and said, "Let's get you lying down rather than putting weight on that foot."

Marion said, "What a damn fool thing to do. I thought I might simply hang from the windowsill and let go to land ten feet down. I thought I could land lightly as I did as a youth. Alas, I don't have the flexibility that I once did."

Will said, "I know you don't like spirits, but I think a jot of brandy is in order."

Marion waved a hand in vague agreement, and Will handed him a beaker of amber brandy.

Marion made a face, "I jumped out a damn window to avoid this!" He downed the spirits anyway. Soon Marion was softly snoring, and Will sought out a servant to keep an eye on him until Will could find a doctor.

It was sunrise the next day, a Saturday when Will finally roused Dr. Noble W. Jones to come to look at Francis Marion's injured leg.

Jones put his hand on the ankle and said, "Broken. Well, cracked is more accurate. T'will take some time to heal."

~~<>~~

Monday morning, Francis Marion was stumping around his house with splints on his leg and a single crutch. Marion grumbled that the crutch grinding in his armpit was worse than the leg. And he said the ankle hurt like hell.

"What's worse is I still have a hangover from that damn toasting."

Will grinned as he helped Francis Marion hobble to the mounting block and get on his horse. They rode out to the camp, where Marion had trouble getting off his horse. A servant was needed to keep him from falling. Will helped him to stump into his tent. Marion sat heavily, his leg sticking straight out and propped on a peach crate.

"Damn and blast, Will! This won't do. I don't know what to say to Huger or Lincoln. They'll think me a fool."

Will grinned, "Well, t'wasn't the most glorious moment...."

Few people could speak to Francis Marion so plainly, and soon they were both laughing.

"Damme, Will. This was silly, and I shall have to rig a sling for my saddle to command troops. 'Tis a terrible time to be injured."

~~<>~~

The next morning a courier rushed into the camp with the news that the British were crossing Wappoo Creek on the south side of the Ashley River. Will mounted Molly and trotted to one of the batteries on the Ashley.

As Will tied Molly up, Captain Tom Heyward, Commander of the Hornwork Battery, trotted up and dismounted.

"Good morning, Tom."

"Good morning, Colonel Yelverton. I hear the British are across the river now. Thought I'd come to have a look."

"Aye, I heard the same. I'm looking for them myself."

They peered across the water in the hopes of seeing first-hand the enemy maneuvers. The distance was too great.

Heyward sniffed, "Hoped to see more, Sir. I give it two weeks at most before we can see them up close on the neck."

Will said, "Aye. I think they'll hurry north toward the Ashley Ferry and hope to cross there. I don't know if we've burned the boats. I understand Huger and about 500 mounted troops are heading to Moncks Corner. That will be a crucial position to hold."

Heyward nodded. "Aye, Sir. If I had to guess, I'd say we're going to stay right where we are until there's no escape for the army. Begging your pardon for speaking bluntly, Sir."

"Oh, I think you're right, Tom. The British will move quickly and demand a surrender which we'll not do."

Heyward smiled, "Well, back to my little fiefdom."

Will liked him. Heyward was plain-spoken and smart.

Will knew there was little chance of getting the army to withdraw. They would sit in Charlestown and stew until the end was inevitable.

Chapter 27 – The Ring Tightens

March 30th dawned chilly but bright. The wind from earlier in the month had now laid down. Work on the defenses continued, and sweat began to pop in the sun. The last fortnight they had seen British movement, with the King's forces occupying Drayton Hall and Middleton Plantation just last week. Perhaps today, they would cross the Ashley River and begin taking up positions on the Neck. The ring was tightening.

Marion was still hobbling around. He hated the crutch but could not yet do without it. Mounting and dismounting was a major challenge, but Marion persisted. Dr. Jones said his ankle was healing, but it would take time. Will smiled when Jones admonished Marion to stay off his leg. Will thought, *That won't happen. Ever.*

A runner came to Marion's tent just as Will was mounting Molly to go trot around the couple miles of the neck not yet occupied by the British. The runner said, "I have messages for you, Colonel Yelverton, and for you, Colonel Marion."

Marion raised an eyebrow and took the slip of paper. The runner handed up a small wax-sealed paper to Will. He saluted and hurried off toward his next delivery.

Will and Marion broke the seals and read the words:

Gen. Lincoln had issued an order: *"Effective 30 March 1780: all supernumerary officers, and all officers who are unfit for duty, must quit the garrison and retire into the country."*

Scrawled across the bottom of Will's message was a postscript from Lincoln himself.

Will, your service has been exemplary, but I do not have a command for you. This makes you supernumerary, and I don't want to risk your death or capture for no reason. Accordingly, I want you to take a small troop – Lt Legare comes to mind – and escort Colonel Marion out of the city. I regret losing you at this juncture, but you are too valuable to risk.

After you situate Marion, if it is feasible, return for further orders.

I remain your friend and hmbl, obt, svt, B. Lincoln, Maj Gen'l

Marion's face was purple with rage. He sputtered, "Goddamn it, Will! This will not do. I'm a better commander with a bad leg than the rest of these fools with both pins working."

Will dismounted and showed Marion his note. Marion shrugged and said, "I find myself agreeing with Lincoln on naming you supernumerary. We don't need to lose officers who are not in command positions."

Will said, "Aye. I think you should take your own counsel, Sir. Let us go to your home at Pond Bluff and consider what to do next."

Marion spat, "Damn and blast! I feel like a fool for jumping out that damn window. Now I am subject of defenestration from my command."

Will asked, "What does defenestration mean?"

"It means being thrown out a window. I guess I threw myself out the damn window."

The statement was so ridiculous that Will started to snicker, and soon Marion joined him.

Marion stopped laughing and said, "Very well, we shall go to Pond Bluff."

Will said, "We'll leave in the morning. I will find Legare and alert Cuth to pack."

~~<>~~

Will looked around the house on Bay Street. His house, technically. It was strange to have nostalgia about the house, for Will had not lived there long. He would miss this place. There were things here that both were warm and painful at the same time. Mary haunted the house in Will's mind. Everywhere he looked, he saw reminders of Mary.

Will found Rebecca in her carriage house. "Rebecca, the general has ordered that I leave Charlestown."

Rebecca looked stricken. "Is you comin' back, Mr. Will?"

Will had a rueful look, "I do not know. Things might get bad here."

Rebecca started to sniffle. "What can I do?"

Will said, "Stay here in the carriage house and keep an eye on things. I can't take you with me because I'm going on a military mission. I can't take you to Mr. Proctor's upcountry plantation home."

Big tears streaked down Rebecca's cheeks. "I don't want to be alone here with them British comin'!"

Will said, "I'm sorry, Rebecca. I can't do much. Here's some money to buy food and other necessities. Close up the main house. If things get worse, go find Mr. Somersall across the street or find Dr. Noble Jones."

Will handed her a note he had written and had notarized. The note was addressed to anyone interested and stated that Rebecca Proctor was his slave and she was doing his business. It also stated that in Will's absence, Mr. William Somersall was to be the guardian of the said Rebecca, the slave woman. She was to follow Mr. Somersall's directions but otherwise have freedom of the town, and she was not to be molested. At the bottom of the page, will wrote, *"In the event of my proven death, Rebecca Proctor is to be freed of her bondage and allowed to remain so for the rest of her life."*

Will said, "I posted a bond with the city's ordinary and gave him a copy of this which he has duly filed. I also wrote out a last will."

Rebecca looked stricken, her voice quavered, "What does it say?"

"It says if I'm killed, you're to be freed and allowed to remain free for life."

"I don't want you to die, Mr. Will."

"Neither do I, but I can't leave you without a master and no options. You might be mistreated. Don't lose that paper. Do you know who the ordinary is?"

Rebecca shook her head.

Will said, "He is the man who keeps records like wills and such. I wrote his name on the paper for you as well."

Rebecca put her head in her hands. "I can't read. What I'm gonna do?"

"Stay here. If they bombard the city, go to Mr. Somersall. If you can't find him, hide in a low place out of doors where nothing can fall on you. Keep your head down so you don't get hit with flying splinters and the like. Get behind a horse trough or in a ditch and lie flat. Something like that."

Rebecca began to wail. "Ahhhh, God!"

Will said, "You are free to live with other servants – Mr. Somersall's – if you like. Just please keep an eye on the house."

Rebecca sobbed and threw her apron over her head. She ran to the other room in the carriage house.

Will did not know what to do, so he quietly left.

Cuthbert was waiting in the yard. "I bet that didn't go well, Sir."

"No. I feel terrible, but it's the best I can do with the war. At least she has a roof over her head and some money for food. I appointed Somersall her guardian and asked him to have his butler look in on her."

Cuthbert nodded glumly, "Aye. She deserves better, but that's the best you can do."

Will nodded, his eyes downcast, "We best go." Will knew he'd feel shame about Rebecca for a long time. But, then, everyone was paying the price for this war.

~~<>~~

Will and Cuthbert stopped at the camp to collect Marion and the others. Will patted Molly on the neck and gave her a carrot.

He secretly had an apple for her for later. She sniffed his pocket where the apple was. He smiled, "I guess I can't keep a secret from you, girl."

Will, Marion, Cuthbert, Marion's personal Negro servant, Oscar, two other supernumerary officers and their orderlies, and Legare's troop trotted out of the camp. They headed up the road toward Upper St Johns and Marion's plantation called Pond Bluff.

Legare's troops fanned out two in front and two behind as rear guard. Each man, including the officers and their orderlies, was armed with a variety of pistols and swords. As usual, Will carried his English dragoon carbine resting on his thigh. Tarleton's second Brander pistol now augmented his usual weapons. As with its mate, the new Brander was loaded with buck and ball tamped on top of an extra dram of powder. Will's useless sword dangled from Molly's saddle.

"How did you come to own Pond Bluff?" Will asked Marion as they trotted along.

"I bought it seven years ago from John Matthews. He bought it from the original owner's son, Mr. William Flud. 'Tis a nice spread, not far from Eutaw Springs. I've acquired a good many acres – upwards of 1000. The house is a decent accommodation – two stories, made of cypress. It might not be brick, but cypress will never rot."

357

Will said, "You know the British will probably come this way."

"Aye. Our stop at Pond Bluff may be the last I see of the place for a while. I hope it's not destroyed."

"What will you do with your slaves?"

"What does anyone do? I will be surprised if they haven't already run off. And who can blame them? The British keep enticing them with promises of freedom. False promises they are, too!"

Will nodded. "I had no choice but to leave the only servant at the house in Charlestown. Owning the house has made me a rich man, but I'd rather not have that burden. I did not know what to do with Rebecca. So, I gave her a paper saying that she's free if I'm killed."

Marion said, "Poor thing. What will she do with freedom?"

Will said, "I don't plan to die, for one thing. But if I do, freedom for her is better than some slaver selling her to the highest bidder. I do feel miserable for leaving her in this way. Seems cowardly."

Marion nodded. "Tis a fact of our lives, Will. We have naught but responsibilities and little to accomplish them with."

~~<>~~

The group trotted along the road adjacent to the Cooper River. The outriders now included a pair of troopers riding on the left of the small column. Will and Marion rode stirrup to stirrup, with Lieutenant Legare just ahead. All three kept an eye on the road ahead, looking for any possible ambush.

Will tried to distinguish any hoofprints in the road from the fresh ones left by the two troopers well out to the front. He could see where Huger's 500 troops had ridden earlier in the month on their way to occupy Moncks Corner. Not all Huger's men were mounted, and those prints were smoothed off from rain and wind. No, Will was looking for newer prints that would still be fresh but not as sharp as the ones made by the two outriders. Fresh prints would mean possible trouble ahead. Will saw nothing. Even when he examined the grass on the verge of the road and the plants that grew between the road and the farm fields, there was no trampled grass, broken branches, or other signs of travelers. Twice he saw fresh wagon ruts with mule prints. Those disappeared after the column passed a side road that was not traveled by more than a wagon. Clearly, this was farm activity.

Still, Will watched and looked for any hint. Birds suddenly flying, trampled grass, a field with broken stalks but not yet harvested, mud on the road deposited from horses riding through farm fields. Fresh horse dung. Anything. He watched the horses' ears for sudden perked-up interest toward the front. Nothing.

The small group plodded into Moncks Corner, where Will had been just a month before. It was unchanged except for the dragoons camped near the edge of a swamp east of the crossroads. The encampment was on either side of the road, with people approaching Biggin Bridge. As was always the case, the troops had fouled the land with tents, horse lines, and trash piles. The swamp stank like the cesspit it had become when men began to use it for a toilet. Will wondered if there was sickness in the camp. Shitting where you drink is unwise.

In the distance, past Biggin Bridge, Will could see another encampment. That appeared to be Huger's infantry. Will wryly thought, *No doubt they're fouling that swamp, too.*

They paid a courtesy call on Brigadier General Isaac Huger.

At first, Marion resisted getting off his horse and being seen limping on a crutch.

Will said, "We should maintain good relations. It won't take long. We'll pull the horses up close to Huger's tent, and you can put the horse between you and the camp. That way, they won't notice your infirmity, Sir."

Marion thought for a moment. "Very well, that's a good solution. I've noticed you have that ability, Will. You figure out how to manage situations like this."

The meeting with Huger was cordial and passed quickly.

Will asked Huger, "Have you seen any British activity, Sir."

"No, Will. We've been on the lookout, but nothing."

Will said, "I had an unpleasant meeting with Lt. Colonels Tarleton and Simcoe just over that ridge a month ago. They were cordial – perhaps because I was pointing a carbine at them. They let slip that they are looking for horses. I worry they may stage an attack on you here, Sir. Your horses are a tempting target."

"Aye, Will. We've thought of that."

Will, let the matter drop. He had done his duty in mentioning the threat of Tarleton and Simcoe.

Cordial goodbyes and well wishes completed, Will and Marion, trotted out of the camp at Moncks Corner, and the little column headed toward Pond Bluff.

~~<>~~

They arrived at Pond Bluff to find that most of the slaves were still present. The house was being kept up, and the fields were at least tended.

Marion glumly looked around. "T'won't stay this way."

Oscar got the kitchen going and stewed three chickens. He killed a hog and got the servants to dig a pit to smoke the meat. At least the detachment would eat well for a few days. Collards from the field, a cold weather crop, were abundant, and Oscar started stewing those with a ham hock, chopped onion, a dash of sugar, some vinegar, salt, and pepper.

Will smiled, "Now the only thing we need is cornbread!"

Oscar grinned, "I got that goin', too!"

~~<>~~

Will and Marion sat on the porch after eating a wonderful meal. They were both stuffed, a condition neither had enjoyed in weeks. Food in Charlestown had already become scarce; now, things were becoming dire. But the outlying areas where Pond Bluff Plantation was situated were still well stocked with food and livestock. Chickens abounded in the yard of most of the plantations, and eggs were available in wonderful quantities. Will was delighted to eat Marion's fare.

Will said, "I see you have quite a large spread here. There are other plantations nearby?"

Marion said, "Aye, my brother's plantation is over that away. Gabe died a couple of years back, but the house is a bit like this one, but bigger. His place is called Belle Isle. His widow lives there. I often visited there before the war."

Will said, "My parents own a plantation on the Roanoke River in North Carolina. I understand plantation life. We often did pigs like your man Oscar is doing. Nothing better."

Marion nodded. "We are lucky to have such places. I fear the war will destroy everything we have built."

Will nodded. "My parents' place was built by their hard work, their ancestors' hard work, and the labor of slaves. There is only my brother, Benjamin, and me. One of us will inherit, and, in all honesty, I do not want to be a planter."

"Your brother is quite a zealot."

"Long story, that."

"I imagine so, Will. Perhaps one day I shall get you drunk, and you will tell me everything."

"Ha, well, since you don't imbibe much, I believe I shall be on my guard when you propose drinking."

Marion threw his head back and hooted a rare guffaw for such a taciturn man. "You are clever for such a young man, Will."

It was late in the day on April 13th when a courier cantered into the yard. He had a message for Will. The British were pressing ahead with constructing siege works. Lincoln wanted him to immediately return to Charlestown with his escort for an important mission. His message warned that Will needed to return to Charlestown on the east side of the Cooper River.

Will shouted for Cuthbert and Lieutenant Legare. He informed them of the situation, and they set off to prepare to ride as soon as the horses were ready.

Will and Marion conferred about the orders. Marion speculated, "Something is about to happen. The British are going to attack; our forces will withdraw, or some combination of those."

Will said, "I hope they've come to their senses and are withdrawing. Maybe Lincoln needs me because Legare and I scouted all the avenues of escape. Clearly, it's urgent, so I have to leave."

Marion nodded. 'Tis important that you leave immediately."

Half an hour later, Will and Legare's troop rode out of the yard at Pond Bluff. Marion waved goodbye.

Will did not know it would be months before he would see Francis Marion again. And the next time would be under even more dangerous circumstances.

Chapter 28 – Moncks Corner

O nce again, Will found himself on the road with Cuthbert, escorted by Lieutenant Jim Legare and his small troop of Continentals. It was well after noon, but Will wanted to make it to Charlestown the next day, so the group left Pond Bluff immediately. They would stay overnight at Moncks Corner with General Huger's troops and leave for Charlestown at first light.

The troop cantered rather than riding at a more comfortable trot. Will wanted to be at Moncks Corner before full dark. Guards were notorious for shooting in the dark, and Will wanted no casualties. As usual, Legare posted two out riders in front, two behind, and two out to the south side of the Cooper River. Everyone watched for potential ambushes.

It was fully twilight when the little entourage cantered into the crossroads and spotted Huger's dragoon camp near the swamp that backed to the river. Will wondered if American commanders would ever learn not to camp with a swamp to their back. Memories of Brier Creek and the slaughter there rushed back in. That slaughter was followed by many militiamen bogging in the swamps next to the Savannah River. The British didn't chase them, but many ended up face down, lost forever in the black water of a Georgia swamp. Will shook off the thoughts that these 500 troops might suffer the same fate.

Huger was accommodating. "I'm glad to see you again, Will. I have no extra tents, but of course, you're welcome to a spot on the high ground yonder." Huger lifted his chin at an open ground near the road to Charlestown. It was surrounded by wiregrass and some scattered pines.

Will nodded and said, "Thank you, Sir. That is most kind of you. We'll head out at first light." Secretly, Will was happy not to be offered a campsite next to the boggy swamp.

"Lincoln sent for you?"

Will said, "Aye. He hinted at a special mission."

Huger said, "When I left, the debate was raging about whether to evacuate the army and plan to fight another day. Of course, Rutledge and his ilk were all for keeping the army in the city. Damn fools."

Will nodded. "I think you probably know that General Lincoln ordered all officers who were infirm or without command to leave?"

"Aye. I wish he'd withdraw all the troops to the north. We should be up at the PeeDee River area. I think North Carolina has a good many troops and supplies. To join those forces would provide us a much more sizeable army, and we might be better able to face the British."

Will said, "Aye. It would stretch the British supply lines. They're dependent upon the Royal Navy, and 'tis quite a way up toward Charlotte Town."

Huger said, "You're turning into quite a military thinker. If you want my guess about the special mission, Will, I think Lincoln will ask you to escort some government people out of Charlestown before the ring closes to the point of no return."

Will nodded. "I'm taking the ferry at Bonneau and approaching the town from Clement's Ferry. I hope they're still working."

Huger nodded. "Aye. 'Tis unlikely this road will be open for long. If they haven't already cut it close to town, they will. My mission is to keep this crossroads open, so there's a withdrawal route. Candidly, it's a fool's errand. They'll overwhelm this area in no time. But we set pickets and hope to hold this position long enough to permit a retreat."

Will asked, "Have you heard anything about British movements?"

"No. Nothing. I have patrols out, but they've reported nothing."

~~<>~~

Will and the troops shared in the fatback and beans that was the ration for Huger's 500 men. They made a makeshift camp in the wiregrass. Will looked at the sky in the last glimmers of light and thought, *"At least it won't rain tonight."* He left his bedroll on Molly's saddle.

Will and Legare conferred. "'Tis cruel to leave the horses saddled, Jim, but I think we should be ready to leave at first light. Also, Tarleton is in the area – or was. When we saw him, he was desperate for horses. I don't think that has changed."

Legare said, "Aye, Sir. I think I'll have a couple of men stay with the horses and put a man toward the road. The general has pickets out, but I worry about being surprised."

Will nodded and squinted at the sky, "Let's try to get some rest."

Will gave Molly a carrot he had saved and patted her on the neck. "I'm sorry, girl. You'll have to wear that saddle tonight and maybe tomorrow night. Can't have a mean old Britisher steal you away, can we?"

Molly nodded her head and whickered. She nuzzled Will's hand and then sniffed, looking for another carrot.

"Now, now. Can't eat all the carrots at once, can we?" I will patted her again. He took a light blanket a few feet away and pulled grass into a pile for a bed. He threw the light blanket over the grass and settled down.

I don't know about this, he thought. He stood up and went to Molly. He checked the prime on his two rifles and the horse pistol in its bucket holster. Returning to his grass pallet, Will checked the prime on the English dragoon carbine and Brander pistols. He smiled at the small victory of taking not one but two of Tarleton's pistols. Certainly, that made Tarleton an enemy, but he already was an implacable foe of America, so what of it? Will dozed off in the deeply satisfying knowledge that he had cheated Tarleton of two such precious items.

~~<>~~

The loud bark of half a dozen muskets and desperate shouts cracking in the darkness woke Will from a fitful sleep. Instantly fully awake, Will sat up, rolled over, crouched, and cocked the carbine. Unburned gunpowder and flint sparks had combined to make a fire in the grass a dozen yards away. Will could see troops running in all directions.

Legare was suddenly beside him. "Sir, I have ordered our men to their horses."

Will said, "Aye. But we should stand and fight."

Legare said, "Sir, this is already out of control. I was not yet abed and wandered over to the main fire. The British fell on the camp in large numbers, and Huger and his staff were forced to retreat to the swamp."

Will felt sick. "Then, there is nothing to be done."

Legare said, "We're fortunate. This tall stand of grass and sparse trees has concealed us. But t'won't last. The fires are catching up all around, and soon 't'will be quite bright."

Will glanced around one last time, "We'll leave."

Cuthbert hurried up. "The horses are ready, Sir. I untethered them.

Will, Cuthbert, and Legare hurried to the horses. Will mounted Molly, who stamped around some and nodded. She made soft whickers and pranced a couple of steps. She hated fire.

Legare looked around at his troops. "Troop, at the canter, Forward!"

Two men hurried out in front of the small group while two others faced toward the camp, a rear guard awaiting the rest of the troop to canter into the darkness along the road to Charlestown.

Loyalist-mounted militiamen burst out of the darkness. Legare's point man snapped a musket shot at one. The other paused and leveled a carbine at Legare. Will shot him with the Dragoon. The ball took him high in the chest, and the buckshot tore into his face as he toppled backward off his horse.

Legare looked at Will, nodded, and spurred his horse. Soon, the firing and noise of the assault was a soft mutter in the distance.

Will told Legare, "I feel a terrible coward leaving like this."

"Nay, Sir. 'Tis not cowardice a'tall. We've a mission. Plus, that situation was untenable. I saw Tarleton on his white horse, and his troops were running amok. Huger's men panicked and fled in all directions."

Will spat, "Damn and blast! When will we learn that the British are masters of surprise and deception? I'll bet that they were watching from the woods for a whole day. That would mean they saw us ride in. Once they discover we've escaped, they'll pursue."

Legare said, "Aye. 'Tis all the more reason to canter, at least to Bonneau's Ferry."

~~<>~~

Will and Legare hurried aboard the horseboat at Bonneau's Ferry, and the small troop quickly crossed the Cooper River.

Will pulled the ferryman aside and asked, "Have you seen any British or loyalist troops in the area?"

"Not in the last few days. There were some green-jacketed men – Americans by the sound of them – led by a hard-faced Englishman. That was a few days back...perhaps a week or more. He threatened to hang me if I didn't give them free passage across the river."

"Were they headed north?"

"Nay, Sir. They were heading from the north bank toward the south."

Will nodded. It was as he had feared; Tarleton was scouting this whole area. For it was certain the hard-faced Englishman in a green jacket was Tarleton.

Will looked at Legare, "'Tis a good thing we're on this side of the river. At least for now, we know Tarleton is at Moncks Corner. Unfortunately, he now has some best-quality mounts and will be even more mobile and dangerous."

Clement told the same general story. Clement now admitted the hard-faced Englishman had been Tarleton. He said Tarleton had been back to the Calais Tavern in recent days. He had not taken the ferry across the Cooper but had carefully checked Clement's barns and outbuildings for horses, fodder, and other supplies. This was not good news, for Tarleton was clearly becoming familiar with the entire area.

Will looked at the greasy Mr. Clement and said, "I suppose you were most cautious in not telling Colonel Tarleton anything other than the bare minimum to get him to leave?"

Clement's eyes shifted and settled on Will's forehead. "Oh, no, Sir. I told them nothing."

Will smiled tightly, "Let me be very clear, Mr. Clement. If I learn that you have treated with the enemy, I shall personally see you hang from that ash tree yonder. Do I make myself understood, Sir?"

Clement's eyes darted to the ash tree and went unfocused. He swallowed hard, "Aye, Sir. You are most clear. But I am a great patriot, Sir."

Will bared his teeth in an angry grimace, "I think you are a businessman, Mister Clement. I understand that hanging makes one's eyes bulge out, and in the last instant, you shit yourself. Now have your man take us across the river and be quick about it. I wish you a very good day, Sir."

As they were walking out the door, Clement said, "We have considerable concern about the British warship in the river. I hear they dragged it across the neck from the Ashley River.

Will turned and looked at Clement. "You believe offering that warning somehow makes you trustworthy?"

~~<>~~

The troop boarded the horseboat and left the dock, headed for Charlestown.

375

Legare said, "I've not seen you quite like that, Sir."

Will spat, "Bastard would sell us all down the river. It was abundantly clear that he had been happy to tell Tarleton, and any other English spy, anything they wanted to know. That is, except for letting them have his horses. I'm sure he's hidden away anything of value."

Legare nodded. "Things are getting very chancy, Sir. I fear we'll lose Charlestown."

Will said, "I think 'tis already lost, Jim. They vastly outnumber us. They will force the harbor and then have the city surrounded."

"You think they can get past Fort Moultrie and Fort Johnson?"

Will said, "'Tis a matter of numbers. They charge several ships at the harbor entrance. We fire barrages at them, but we can't hit them all. Some will be hit, but most will get through with minor damage. Consider how quickly guns can be reloaded, aimed, fired, and reloaded. We won't get many shots before they have forced the harbor mouth."

Legare's eyebrows knit together. "I had not thought of that, Sir. 'Tis very grim."

"Aye, Jim. And the city fathers, as well as Governor Rutledge, all know it. But they're clinging to hope, and, last I heard, they were demanding Lincoln keep the troops on the peninsula," He looked at the distant riverbank and muttered, "Where the army will be lost."

Legare said, "This has been my home – the townhouse and our plantations – since my birth. T'will be very hard to leave it. But t'will serve no purpose to lose an army when the town is lost anyway."

~~<>~~

Will and the troop trotted into Lincoln's encampment. Will dismounted, and Cuthbert took Molly to get the saddle off her back and get her rubbed down. Will said, "Thanks, Cuth. We'll stay at the house tonight. I need a bath." To Legare, Will said, "Please join me; the general will want to hear your thoughts about Moncks Corner."

Will and Legare stepped into Lincoln's tent and doffed their hats respectfully. Will reported the facts of Moncks Corner and of Tarleton's movements.

Lincoln said, "So Huger was taken by surprise in the middle of the night? Damn!"

Lieutenant Legare said, "I fear so, Sir. Colonel Yelverton wanted to stand and fight, but I persuaded him that the battle was already lost."

Lincoln's New England accent was strong when he was stressed, "And why did you think that, young feller?"

"Sir, the surprise was total, there were several fires started, and I could see everyone plainly. General Huger was overwhelmed in a very brief time. I saw him order everyone to the swamp near his headquarters tent. I regret that I have no idea of survivors. The horse line looked to be taken almost in the first minute – it was clear the horses were a major objective. Sir, Moncks Corner is no longer a strategic position for us. That avenue of withdrawal is closed."

Lincoln nodded, his jowls shook a bit, and Will could see his age and tiredness reflected in his face. "This confirms the rider who came in yesterday saying the British had taken Biggin Bridge across the Cooper River. They took the baggage train of the Virginia Continentals who arrived last week. Now we shan't have the supplies that were part of that unit's support."

Lincoln beetled his brows and continued, "The news goes from bad to worse, Gentlemen. The British forced the harbor last week. Only Moultrie fired on them and had no effect."

Will glanced at Legare. Legare's expression was bleak. Will's prediction of that morning had already come true.

Lincoln sighed and said, "Rutledge is leaving in short order, and I want you two to escort him. He's going to North Carolina to maintain South Carolina's government in exile, or so he says."

Will's eyes bugged a bit, and he said, "I thought that the Governor was dedicated to staying here and defending the city at all costs."

Lincoln's voice dripped with sarcasm, "He's now *realized* it is *critical* to maintain a government in exile. On the other hand, Gadsden has vowed to remain here, and Rawlins Lowndes will stay with him. Gadsden insists upon being called General. Ah, God, but everyone is a damn general these days. Lieutenant Governor Gadsden is more a politician than a military officer. God knows what high office Lowndes plans for himself in Rutledge's absence. It will surely involve telling me how to defend the city."

Will and Legare did not speak but stood ready to hear Lincoln's guidance.

Lincoln continued, "I know you have ridden these roads, Will, and Lieutenant Legare, you know the countryside and the people. I don't have to emphasize that Governor Rutledge's safety is of paramount importance, and he would certainly be a prize prisoner for the British."

Will nodded, "Yes, Sir. When do we leave?"

"I'm not certain. Perhaps tomorrow. The British continue to build their siege works. Get some rest and prepare to leave. Stand ready for short-notice orders. You won't be coming back because either we'll surrender the city and withdraw, or we'll be beaten and captured."

Will and Legare stood to attention. They turned to leave when Lincoln said, "Once Rutledge is safely away, I shall attempt to treat with the British. 'T'will come to naught, but I shall try."

~~<>~~

Rebecca was happy to see Will and Cuthbert at Will's home on Bay Street. They managed a quiet evening. At least there was still some Madeira wine, cheese, and a loaf of bread. Rebecca got a couple of fish – saltwater trout – which she roasted over the open fire.

Will asked how she had fared in his absence. Rebecca said things were well but lonely. Will left her more money and told her that he would not be back. At least he wouldn't be back for a long time.

Will said, "Remember that Mr. Somersall is your guardian, and he'll take care of you."

Rebecca nodded sadly. "I know. Mr. Somersall, all right. His butler is mean, though. I'll go there if I have to."

Will opened his mouth to say something, but nothing seemed right. So, he smiled at Rebecca. At least, he hoped the face he put on was a smile. Then he went to bed, where he tossed and turned as his conscience raged over his treatment of Rebecca.

The next morning a runner arrived with the message that Rutledge would be ready to leave at daybreak.

Chapter 29 – Rutledge

The morning dawned cold and breezy for April in the Low Country. Will wore his cloak and gloves. He and Cuthbert trotted down the street from Will's Bay Street house to Rutledge's sumptuous home that could easily have been called a palace.

Will had spoken to a lawyer after Mary's death and learned that his modest two-story home on Bay Street was worth more than £5,000. Will considered that he was now a very wealthy man. £5,000 was a king's ransom, but he believed he didn't deserve the wealth. True, he had worked his whole life to become a gunsmith, and his plan had always been to make his own way. He married Mary wholeheartedly and expected to be her husband and little Will's father for life.

As Molly trotted toward Rutledge's palace, Will wondered what his future held. Was there still a plan to move to the frontier? What would be the outcomes of this war? Independence? Defeat and subjugation by the British? Punishment for those who were Continental officers? Mary was gone; Abby was married. It was now Will and Molly. Cuthbert, if he wanted to go, was welcome. But to what?

Will, Jim Legare, his troops, and Cuthbert waited in the stable yard behind Rutledge's opulent house for quite some time before Will walked up to the back door. It was now nine O'Clock, and the day was well along. Will wryly thought, *Daybreak here must mean something different from what it means in North Carolina.*

A dozen of Rutledge's hangers-on were mounted and prancing around the yard. Six slaves and a wagon containing Rutledge's personal baggage awaited.

Will had not reached the door when Governor Rutledge swept out. He was resplendent in white breeches, beautifully polished riding boots with turned-down leather tops, spurs, and a brocade dark brown cut-away coat. His waistcoat was embroidered gold with paisley. A crisp white stock bulged at his throat. Rutledge wore a gray cloak that hung off one shoulder. A magnificent tricorn hat topped the ensemble. He wore an officer's hanger sword as a side arm, and a pistol was tucked into his belt.

As he strode past Will, he said, "Morning, Colonel Yelverton. Let's get moving." This was uttered as if someone else were holding up the outrageously late departure.

Will smiled to himself as he turned to follow Rutledge. For his part, the governor strode into the courtyard, stuck a boot in his white horse's stirrup, and swung into the saddle as though this were a pleasant Sunday ride into the country. Rutledge started to head for the street when Will stopped him.

"Sir, for everyone's safety, especially that of your person, we will ride with two outriders in front, two behind, and yourself in the center. Lieutenant Legare and I will lead the main part of the column. Your orderly and my orderly will be close behind you, Sir."

Rutledge paused as if considering, "Very well. This is a good plan, Colonel Yelverton. May I call you Will?"

"Certainly, Sir. I'm happy to be called by my Christian name. I'm sure you know Lieutenant James Legare. He is in actual command of the troops here. As General Lincoln's representative in assuring your safety, I am in overall command. Jim Legare and I have ridden together several times. We see eye to eye. Should something happen to me, Sir, Jim's guidance is equivalent to mine. Please don't be deluded by his youth; Jim is most capable of conveying you to safety."

~~<>~~

They quickly approached the hard beach where Hibben's Ferry would dock.

Rutledge rushed up to Will. "I thought we'd go across the ferry at Clement's."

Will smiled and said, "Aye, Sir, and we would have, had the British not taken the crossing at Moncks Corner these last couple of days and then forced crossings at Bonneau and Strawberry Ferries. Clement's is suspect because, as you can see, we have plenty of enemy activity in the area. I'm sure you know of the warship dragged across the neck to patrol the Cooper River?"

Rutledge paused and opened his mouth as if to speak. Just then, Hibben's horseboat ferry hove into view and made for the landing at speed.

"Very well, have it your way, Colonel Yelverton. 'T'will lengthen our journey toward the PeeDee area, but have it your way."

Will said, "I believe, Sir, you will be pleased when we are on the far side of the Cooper River. 'Tis true the British are on the north side of the river, but they're not in great numbers yet. This route offers the best chance of success."

Rutledge sniffed and trotted his horse onto the barge.

Will and the troops dismounted. Half of the group boarded while the other half waited for Rutledge's wagon and entourage to get aboard. That process was laboriously slow. The rest of Jim Legare's troops boarded, and the ferry cast off.

~~<>~~

The boat was overloaded, but not dangerously so. The breeze caused a bit of pitching, and a couple of Rutledge's slaves immediately hung over the side.

Will raised an eyebrow at Legare's Sergeant Wilkins, who hurried to get the seasick slaves to move to the other side of the boat and vomit downwind. That was a small relief in an already unpleasant situation. A solid hour of this pitching, bucking drudgery awaited. Will, remembering his senior officer status, turned to face forward. He determined to ignore Rutledge, who strode back and forth as though such activity would speed the slow, pitching boat along.

The time seemed to drag until the last ten minutes when Hobcaw Bluff hove into view, and the slave crew hauled hard on the oars to move the boat with speed toward the ramp.

Will stepped over to Rutledge. "Sir, tis' best to walk our horses off the boat. This landing is a bit dicey with the boat pitching."

Rutledge looked as if ready to dispute this self-evident fact. Then he shrugged and grabbed the reins of his white mare. The boat ground ashore, and he started to walk off.

Will said, "Kindly allow us to establish a security area ahead of yourself, Sir. "'T'will take but a moment."

Rutledge flushed red and appeared ready to object when Sergeant Wilkins and six of Legare's troops hustled off the boat and mounted their horses. Carbines at the ready, they trotted up the road. Two members rode a hundred yards ahead into Hobcaw Point and settled in to watch for a possible attack.

Satisfied that precautions were taken, Will asked Rutledge, "Sir, will you accompany me?" He turned without awaiting a response and led Molly off the boat.

Will walked Molly twenty feet up the small, muddy incline and mounted. Oyster shells crunched under Molly's hooves. Legare and Rutledge walked their horses off the boat and, joining Will, mounted. They waited for the rest of the entourage to disembark before turning and heading off at a slow walk.

Will turned to look at the entire column. *"Damned if we'll make much progress toward Camden tonight with this crew. If Tarleton or his ilk are about, we are truly doomed."*

The bite of salt air mixed with the stink of oysters and marsh grass followed Will and the troop as they headed northeast along the east side of the Wando River.

Rutledge looked at Will hard. "Why have we not simply crossed the Wando and moved along a more direct route?"

"Sir, I'm using the river as a barrier to patrolling British or Tory forces. If we cross the Wando right away, we would be riding directly into the area that the enemy may control. If we ride along the river until it narrows, we can ford and go north, putting some miles between the enemy and us. We will still make progress toward Camden."

Rutledge harumphed but settled into the rhythm of his horse's gait.

~~<>~~

The troop walked along a series of wagon tracks with the dwindling Wando on their left. The goal was to get Rutledge to Camden and ultimately to the safety of the north side of the PeeDee River. Lincoln and other senior leaders believed Camden was still secure from the British, and Huger was reportedly in the vicinity. Will worried that the plodding progress of the wagon, laden with Rutledge's personal property and government papers, would result in the group being overtaken by British or loyalist troops. Knowing that Rutledge would not abide leaving the wagon behind, Will remained silent, and the group trudged relentlessly along.

Nightfall brought the entourage to a spot of sandy high ground with a grove of oaks. It was a perfect camping place. A passable ford was nearby, and Will intended to cross at first light. The water was only two feet deep, and the wagon would handle that.

The men pitched camp, most of them merely putting down a blanket on a pile of grass. A campfire kept down flying insects, though mosquitos were constant companions regardless of any measures. Two of the troopers took on the task of preparing

389

food, though the fare was mostly dried beans boiled with salt pork.

Rutledge had traveled with two servants and a trunk with some prepared food. His servants prepared his food while his orderly pitched a tent and set up Rutledge's cot and field desk where he would eat and work on papers. Rutledge did not invite Will to join him, which was fine with Will. He would rather eat with the troops. Will quietly contemplated the coming day. *"If there's time, I'll see about killing a deer, and we'll have steaks and a roast for the next night. Pork and beans are not the best meal."*

Will checked on Molly. He patted her neck, rubbed her down with a handful of grass, and gave her an apple he had taken from the dwindling supply in the kitchen on Bay Street. Molly crunched the apple contentedly and stamped her hoof. She made soft whickering noises and nuzzled Will with an apple juice-dampened muzzle. Will secretly had carrots and another apple in his saddlebag.

He made sure the rest of the horse line was secure and walked the perimeter of the small sand bluff. He chatted briefly with each of the sentries. He informed Rutledge of the plan to cross the ford at first light.

Jim Legare said, "I'll take the first watch, and Sergeant Wilkins will take the second. I don't want to get surprised."

Will nodded. "I'll be happy to take a watch."

"Not necessary, Sir. We have a plan. Enjoy your sleep."

Will shook out his bedroll and put it on a pile of fresh grass. This bedroll had been his traveling sleep companion since his expedition to Fort Johnston in 1775. Five years of adventures, and there was no end in sight. He smiled a wry smile. In 1775, Will could never imagine what he was doing now. His plan to finish his master gunsmith apprenticeship and move to the frontier had long been deflected. Banastre Tarleton had a hand in that deflection, and Will hoped not to run into him on this trip.

Will drifted into a fitful sleep, his dreams haunted by images of Tarleton's hard face interspersed with his times with Mary together at Bay Street. Images of Mary resting in her family's tomb flitted with memories of Abby Kennedy and his time at Bear Creek when he was still innocent. These dreams drifted through his mind as he realized his innocence was long lost. The beauty who saved his life at the Spring Hill redoubt said, *"Live a good life, Will Yelverton. I did not save you for you to waste it."* He wished he could speak with her. She was a loyalist and unreachable, but he wished for the opportunity to thank her.

~~<>~~

The small entourage crossed the Wando River near its headwaters at dawn the next day. Will had started everyone moving very early, everyone working by firelight to break camp and load the wagon and horses. The water was brown and brackish, and the bottom was sandy and solid. A muddy bottom would have made for an unpleasant crossing.

As with other trips with Legare's troops, outriders and the rear guard were posted, and the group set a faster pace. Will looked around and decided the woods nearby looked ripe for hunting.

He said to Legare, "I'm going to see if I can get us something to eat that's better than salt pork. You're in charge until I get back."

Legare said, "Do you think it's safe, Sir?"

Will said, "Safer than eating salt pork for the entire trip."

Legare grinned. "Bring us back a deer."

~~<>~~

Will let Molly pick along quietly along the edges of the copse of trees he had picked out. Something about that grove of small trees suggested deer habitat to Will. Taking out his .45 caliber rifle, he allowed his English dragoon carbine to hang from its lanyard over his shoulder. Molly stepped over small limbs, and Will could tell she was excited. A deer was probably in the bushes, and Molly was as good a hunter as Will.

Will cocked the rifle and checked its prime. He had already checked the prime on the carbine. This was rattlesnake country, so best to be ready in case of a chance encounter with an angry serpent.

Molly froze, and her ears went full forward. She blew softly. Molly could not speak, but her body language made it clear that their prey was just there.

Will followed her gaze to see the brown back of a deer behind a small green bush. He sat waiting for the deer to move for a clear shot. The wait was not long. Will saw the deer's white tail twitching in agitation. The deer, a young buck, knew something was not right, but he didn't know what exactly the threat was.

Will saw the deer's haunches tighten. It would leap and run any second. Will slowly leveled the .45 and rested the sights about six feet in front of the deer, which burst from its cover in a leap six feet into the air.

WizzzzCraaak! The rifle jolted Will hard in the shoulder. The poor deer landed in a heap, its heart shattered by the rifle ball.

Will put the .45 into its scabbard. He needed to bleed the deer out and gut it before tying its velvety antlers with a rope to drag it behind Molly to the governor's entourage, where someone would skin it and cut it into portions.

Will was swinging a leg over Molly's back to dismount when Molly suddenly jumped and moved six feet. Will almost lost his balance and fell, but he managed to hang on. The singing buzz of a rattlesnake explained Molly's sudden jump. Perhaps the rifle crack or the deer's movements disturbed the rattler. Regardless, it was awake and angry.

Will looked around and saw the snake coiled less than three feet away. Its tongue flicked constantly, and the rattle on the end of its black-ringed tail was a blur. Will froze. Molly was quivering. Both Will and Molly were in striking range of this thick-bodied timber rattlesnake. The snake's head was as wide as a man's hand, and it was quite capable of killing a horse, much less a man.

Will considered his options and knew that the snake would not leave. Rattlesnakes are territorial, and this one would stand its ground. Will slowly moved his right hand to the stock of the carbine, which hung on the same side as the snake. That was a fortunate happenstance. Had the carbine been on the other side, away from the rattler, this would have been much worse. Trying to swing the gun over Molly would have been too much movement, and someone would have been bitten.

It was fortunate that the carbine was primed. Will gingerly cocked the carbine, his hand moving only a tiny bit at a time. Molly quivered and was breathing heavily. Will whispered, "Easy, girl. Easy."

What seemed like an hour passed as Will's slow-moving hand finally reached the stock. Never taking his eyes from the snake,

Will slipped his finger into the trigger guard and gripped the carbine tightly. He would have but one chance to kill the snake.

Will whipped the carbine up one-handed and pulled the trigger just as the snake struck. Boooom! The carbine jumped hard, and Will could not hold it. The ball missed, but the swan shot that Will always loaded along with the ball shredded the snake's head. Nevertheless, the snake's body slammed into Will's boot.

Will thought his leg was broken. He also thought he had been bitten. Molly whinnied and jumped even further away from the snake. Her eyes rolled, and she snorted. Will let go of Molly's saddle and fell to the ground, landing inches from the mutilated snake. The snake was dead, but that did not prevent Will from scrambling hard to get away from it. He also looked wildly in all directions to see if the snake had a mate.

The birds and insects that had flown when the carbine cracked now slowly flitted back to perches in the trees and brush. A small bird landed by the dead snake and, after carefully examining the body, hopped forward to peck delicately at the shredded flesh.

Will took stock. His leg hurt. He turned his boot where he could see where the snake had hit. The boot was intact, with no fang marks. The carbine still was attached to the sling over Will's shoulder, so he grabbed the empty weapon and used it as a crutch to lever himself upright. He tested putting weight on the leg. It hurt but held his weight.

Will hobbled over to Molly and patted her neck. She blew and nodded, her eyes wide and rolling. She nuzzled Will and whickered.

Will hobbled over to the deer and cut its throat. The deer bled readily. Only one or two minutes had elapsed since its death. One or two minutes that seemed like a lifetime. And they were a lifetime because if the snake had struck, Will's life would have been counted in hours.

~~<>~~

Will gutted the deer and rolled it in an oilcloth before tying it behind his saddle. He had decided not to drag the carcass because the deer was small and wouldn't overload Molly. He trotted along, catching up to the column. He had been gone an hour, so finding the column was not difficult.

He rode up, and one of the men whooped, "We'll eat tonight, Sir." Will grinned as another trooper approached and took the deer carcass to ride in the wagon.

Will trotted up to join Legare at the lead of the column. Legare looked over Will, noticing the dirt and a small tear in a sleeve. He said, "I was not aware that deer fought back, Sir."

"Aye, you're right, Jim. But a timber rattler as long as I am tall makes for quite a fight."

"Didn't get bitten, did you?"

"Nay. I was lucky. Killed him just as he struck at my boot. Felt like I'd been hit with a hammer. Fortunately, I blew his head off before he hit me."

Legare said, "You, Sir, are a hard man to kill."

Rutledge said, "Damn irresponsible to go hunting when we have a mission, Will."

"Aye, Sir. Perhaps it was. But we'll eat venison tonight if you'd like to join us. I also have this meat." He pulled the dead snake from his saddlebag and, holding it by the rattle, let it dangle. It nearly reached the ground. Will strained to hold the snake at arm's length. He didn't have to hold it long because Rutledge flinched and quickly turned away.

Will turned back to the column and trotted to drop the snake in the wagon bed next to the deer.

As he rode back to his position in the lead, Will did not notice the grins from several troopers, including Jim Legare.

Chapter 30 – Clermont Plantation

Rutledge's entourage passed the little crossroads of Huger. Will considered this must be land owned by General Isaac Huger's family. He wondered where General Huger was after the rout at Moncks Corner. This was Huger's family land, but the area was quiet. No activity was noticeable, not even a fresh wagon track. Huger was not here.

The small column now swung around the West Branch of the Cooper River. The way ahead was dry but dangerous. Tarleton and his Tory militia were almost certainly in the area.

Will told Legare, "I think Tarleton must be looking for Continental Army survivors from Moncks Corner. Not all 500 troops at Biggin Bridge were killed or captured. Certainly, there were survivors."

Jim Legare said, "We should head northwest and parallel the river. We'll get to the Wateree River in a day or so. Then we can parallel the Wateree all the way to Camden. If I were Huger, I would withdraw to Camden. But regardless of where Huger might be, Sir, I think we have to go to Camden before we move north toward the PeeDee."

Will looked at the map. "I agree. I think the danger is serious until we get to the Wateree. T'won't be safe even there, but better."

Will trotted a little faster to catch up to Rutledge, who insisted on riding at the head of the little column despite Will's best advice.

Will thought, *"You'd think he was Hannibal, and we're his elephants!"*

He said, "Sir, we're proceeding to the Wateree and then to Camden. We do not know where General Huger might be, but we believe he and the remaining troops from Moncks Corner must be in the Camden area. You will be safer there. From Camden, we will head north to the PeeDee region. Charlotte Town might be the best refuge for now."

"I don't seek refuge, Will. I seek a place to set up the South Carolina government in exile. I also seek to recruit militia."

"Yes, Sir. Of course. Charlotte Town is ideal for that purpose."

"Yes, I had already concluded that."

Will said, "I worry that we have no status of Charlestown. Perhaps General Huger will have communicated with General Lincoln and Lieutenant Governor Gadsden."

"Harrumph...Lincoln. Gadsden!" Rutledge trotted a bit faster, ending the audience.

Will grimaced and thought, *I hope I never get to be so sure of myself that I can't listen.*

~~<>~~

Fortune smiled on the governor's entourage, and they spent a quiet night hidden by a copse of trees. A trooper had ridden ahead and recommended the concealed location. Will led the group off the road a mile ahead of the campsite. They trotted through a fallow farm field that was dry and solid enough to take the wagon.

Will forbade more than a tiny campfire sufficient to cook venison stew with some carrots and a few potatoes in the stores in Rutledge's wagon. Fortunately, the supplies had some salt, or the stew would have been bland. The venison was very lean, so the cook jabbed holes in the haunches of deer and pushed in pork fat to lard the meat. Still, the venison cooked for about four hours before it was edible. The stew was falling-apart tender and delicious, especially to tired, hungry men who had eaten beans and fatback for days on end.

Molly was satisfied to have her saddle off and some good grass to crop. She relished the carrot Will smuggled from the camp supply. Will rubbed her down with a handful of soft straw, the remnants of a past year's wheat crop on this unknown farmer's land.

Mindful of Tarleton's bold night attack on Moncks Corner, Will had Legare set extra sentries. Those men wouldn't sleep, but it was better than being dead.

Rutledge griped about not having a tent. To keep him quiet, Will threw a tarp over the wagon to make a wind- and rain-proof shelter for the governor. Will smiled when he heard snores coming from under the tarp. Will thought, *Good. He's like a baby. Beautiful when they sleep.*

~~<>~~

The next day, it dawned dry and cool. Legare said he thought the cold weather was over, and now it would just be some brisk mornings followed by bright sunny days. Another month and late afternoon thunderstorms would make for miserable road conditions, not to mention wet bushes and trees to soak unsuspecting riders.

Will said, "Today is the most dangerous day, Jim."

Legare agreed. "Aye, Sir. We're nearing the Wateree. If we're going to get jumped, it will be here, I think. I've got two outriders in front and behind. I think we should send a couple of outriders on the flanks, as well.

Will nodded. "I know the men are getting tired, but we must be sure of enemy movements."

~~<>~~

The little column made good time and was nearing Camden. The weather held with clear skies and no rain. Clouds were building late in the day, and Will could tell Spring was in full swing when insects buzzed everywhere. Birds feasted on the insects, flitting from bush to tree to the ground.

Will instinctively checked the prime on his English dragoon carbine and the two Branders when he saw one of the outriders galloping back toward Rutledge's column.

The rider pulled up short and, saluting, said to Legare and Will, "Sirs, General Huger and a good-sized group of Continentals are up ahead. They are staying at Clermont Plantation. A gentleman has invited the Governor to stay at his home. The gentleman is Colonel Rugeley, owner of Clermont Plantation."

Will looked at Legare and then the trooper. "How does this Colonel Rugeley know that Governor Rutledge is traveling this way?"

The trooper shrugged. "I know not, Sir. I was scouting when I came across the Colonel and a party of six hunters. They recognized my uniform and offered the governor a place to stay without asking if we were his escort. Perhaps General Huger has told them about the governor?"

Legare said, "This doesn't sound right."

Will was about to send the trooper back, refusing the offer, when Rutledge spoke up, "Trooper, please ride ahead and tell Colonel Rugeley we will accept his gracious invitation." Rutledge turned and trotted ahead as if this were a pleasant Sunday ride in the park.

Legare's words tumbled out, "Henry Rugeley is very much a bloody loyalist. His colonelcy is with the loyalist militia. He's not at all minded to revolution. Rugeley owns a mill and a trading post, and his mill is a major intersection among these back roads. There could be any number of spies and British scouts about. How did he know we were here? A party of hunters? I hardly think so. This is not a good idea."

Will nodded. "I fear we don't have a choice. Rutledge made the decision, plus Huger's at the plantation as well. We shall have to attend but keep an eye on Colonel Rugeley."

Legare nodded. "T'will not go well, I fear."

Will said, "Aye. But we're no longer in charge, Jim. If I'm honest, I can't wait to be rid of his nibs."

Jim Legare grinned his agreement. "Yep. I mean, yes, Sir. I agree."

Will said, "Not necessary for us to be formal, Jim. The situation is that we shall soon all be partisans, I think."

~~<>~~

The small entourage trundled into the yard at Clermont Plantation. Clermont was an up-country South Carolina plantation similar to the one Homer Proctor owned. Will had only been this way once, but he knew the sandy top layer covering a black soil underlayer spoke of excellent crops. The proximity of Camden and the Wateree River meant easy access to ports. Rugeley would be loath to see the colony – State, now – become truly independent of the Crown.

The group dismounted as Rugeley himself burst out the door. "John! John Rutledge! By God, man! 'Tis good to see you. I feared Charlestown would fall with you in it."

Rutledge shook his head as he extended his hand, "My dear Henry! So good to see you. As you can see, Sir, I am not captive in my fair city. We ride for North Carolina and exile, I fear."

Will shot a despairing look at Legare, who muttered, "Well done, Governor. Tell everyone about our destination."

As General Isaac Huger stepped out the door behind Rugeley, Legare grinned ruefully. He glanced at Will and said, "Damn fool wants to be captured."

~~<>~~

Will and Legare were billeted with the troops in the barn. There were perhaps 200 Continentals sleeping in the nearby fields. Will spotted 20 campfires. He thought, *Not wise to have so many campfires.*

The Continentals had sentries out, so Legare let his men rest. Even with some desperately needed rest, Will knew the men would still be exhausted tomorrow. Will worried that Huger's sentries had not been effective at Moncks Corner, so why would they be reliable here?

As officers, Will and Legare were invited to a resplendent dinner of roast pork, greens, sweet potatoes, and apple compote. It seemed Rugeley had a well-stocked root cellar. Will and Legare were well down the table from Rugeley, Rutledge, and Huger.

Two of Rutledge's council, Daniel Huger and John Gervais, had escaped Charlestown and were now reunited with their leader. They sat in close proximity to the head of the table, where they appeared to hang on every word uttered by the great men.

During the conversation, Will learned that Charlestown had fallen. Lincoln and some 5000 American troops were captive. Will wondered where they would all be kept. Gervais related that after the surrender, some fool had put loaded weapons in the Charlestown powder magazine. One had gone off, resulting in a deadly chain explosion that killed dozens. Will wryly thought, *Good job, we inventoried all that powder last month. I hope none of the patriots I worked with were in the blast.*

Also at the table was Colonel Abraham Buford, commander of one of Huger's regiments. Buford was an affable fellow. Leaning over to Will, he said, "I hear you are quite a fighter."

"Nay, Sir. I am but a humble gunsmith who has been put in dire situations where t'was fight or die."

Buford hooted at this and received reproving looks from Rutledge and his staff of hangers-on. Buford appeared not to care.

To Will, Buford said, "This has gone badly from the very start. Now we shall endeavor to get *his nibs* to North Carolina before he becomes too intimately acquainted with a British rope. Tarleton is in the countryside with plenty of horses and some battle-experienced men. He is not to be trifled with."

Will said, "I've had the honor of Colonel Tarleton's acquaintance. Twice in Philadelphia and New Jersey, more recently just outside Moncks Corner a month ago."

"Did you?"

"Aye. A hard man, he is, too. Threatened me with hanging as a spy twice. Most recently, I had the pleasure of holding him at gunpoint."

"Why didn't you kill him?"

"Wouldn't be honorable to shoot him in cold blood. I had no facility to hold him prisoner, so I sent him packing."

Buford said, "I see you're a man of principle, too. I hope your generosity does not haunt us, Colonel Yelverton."

Will nodded. "My friends call me Will, Sir. Tarleton can't wait to hang me. I took two of his pistols. London-made Branders, and fine weapons at that. I took one in New Jersey and its mate at our recent meeting."

This elicited another hoot from Buford. More malevolent looks from the head of the table. And similarly ignored. Colonel Abe Buford was his own man, it seemed.

Rutledge stood and cleared his throat. When all was quiet, he said, "Colonel Rugeley has graciously offered for us to say a few days, and we shall accept. General Huger has taken us under his wing for protection, and *Lieutenant* Colonel Yelverton is relieved of that responsibility with our gracious thanks."

Will smiled an icy smile and held his tongue. Emphasizing the rank of Lieutenant in Lieutenant Colonel was slight. Staying here at all was a bad idea. Remaining for any length of time was downright foolhardy. Will flicked a glance at Legare, whose expression reflected the same thoughts. Will was at a loss for what to do, but Rutledge was now Huger's responsibility ... and good riddance.

The rest of the evening passed pleasantly. Rugeley offered Madeira, port, and an old vintage brandy that Will had to admit was quite good. While Will and Legare drank sparingly, Rutledge lowered his guard and enjoyed the evening to the fullest.

Will thought, *I fear he will pay for this tomorrow.*

But Rutledge paid for it sooner.

~~<>~~

The party broke up at about 10 pm, and everyone retired to their chambers. Will had checked on Molly and thrown his bedroll on a welcome pile of hay. He was tired after several days and was just dozing off when there was a clamor. Will looked out the barn door and saw quite a bit of activity. The main house was ablaze with lights in the windows.

Will quickly dressed; he had only taken off his boots and coat and hurried to the house. As he left the barn door, he told Legare to get the men ready to ride and have the horses saddled. Legare could leave Rutledge's wagon to Huger's men now.

Will entered the house to find a raging discussion between Rugeley and Rutledge, with Huger mediating.

Rugeley said, "Tarleton is 10 miles away and heading this way. He's bringing horse troops, so it is possible he will arrive within the hour. You must escape, John."

Rutledge said, "But, Colonel, our 200 Continentals should be sufficient to defend the plantation."

Looking out the second-floor window, Will could see in the gloom that the troops were now mustering into ranks and marshaling into defensive formations. Will didn't think that 200 Continentals would provide a reasonable defense, especially not against the implacable Banastre Tarleton's British Legion.

Huger settled the argument. "Gentlemen! Governor Rutledge, you must dress and prepare to ride immediately. We simply cannot tarry arguing about what is to be done. Colonel Rugeley, your hospitality and goodwill have been of great kindness to us, and we thank you. We will march immediately for Charlotte Town. Colonel Buford will be in overall command of the march. Colonel Yelverton, you and your troops will join us."

Will hurried to the barn to inform Legare of the developments and ensured everything was in order.

Dawn was breaking as Huger, Rutledge, the governor's councilors Daniel Huger and John Gervais, and Buford led the column out of Rugeley's plantation and struck north to Charlotte.

Will and Legare rode toward the rear of the column, where they ate the dust and smelled the stink of hundreds of men and horses.

Will quietly considered, *"It could be worse; we could be under direct attack by Tarleton."*

He dozed in the saddle as, once again, Molly plodded along with an army.

Chapter 31 – Waxhaws

The small army marched north toward the PeeDee River and Charlotte Town, North Carolina. Everyone saw Charlotte as a haven. Indeed, it being on the other side of the PeeDee was a plus for defensive positioning. The distance between Charlotte and coastal Charlestown would stretch the British supply lines to the breaking point.

Many hard-nosed revolutionaries lived in the Charlotte Town area. After all, the Mecklenburg Resolves in 1775 were an early declaration of independence from Great Britain. The Resolves were drafted in Charlotte Town just a month after Lexington and Concord. A 16-year-old Will saw a copy of the document nailed to the door of Cogdell's Tavern in New Bern. At the time, the idea of independence and a possible war to win it had filled him with dread.

Five years on, Will was no longer filled with a sense of dread. He was filled with a feeling of inevitability, weariness, and sad loss. His heart was heavy, and he was eating the dust of another revolutionary army. An army that trudged along in another desperate endeavor proclaimed to be a key to victory but likely to be just another ignominious defeat.

Rutledge had filled him with scorn for the tragic self-interest of all politicians. True, Rutledge was doing what he could for South Carolina, and at great personal risk. True, also, Rutledge was almost certainly to suffer significant personal financial losses from the war and from his part in leading the State. Still, all politicians were self-interested. Will considered that Rutledge's self-interest was mostly about what would be his legacy. How would he be seen a hundred years from now in the year 1880? What would the books say about Rutledge?

Will snorted quietly, *"Books? Who knows if there will even be books in 1880? Will there even be a United States in three scores and ten years? That's a man's lifetime, so says the Bible. That would be the year 1840. I certainly won't be here to find out, but perhaps I shall live long enough to have children, and they might see. I guess that's the hope of this war, that our children will be free, and liberty will be their watchword, just like ours now."*

Legare interrupted Will's thoughts. "I fear we are moving slowly. If Tarleton's chasing along right behind us, Rutledge and his council will be captured."

Will nodded. "Aye. The governor's blasted wagon, along with the supply wagons for this little army, is ploddingly slow. I was once part of a supply train. They're vulnerable to attack by roving bands of cavalry."

Legare said, "You were?"

Will said, "Aye. I was hired as a gunsmith with the North Carolina Militia in 1776. They were moving to the Cape Fear River to stop the North Carolina Loyalist Militia from taking Brunswick Town and opening up the colony to the British so they could put the royal governor back in power. The Tories failed in North Carolina, and the British came here instead. That was when they were repulsed at Sullivan's Island."

Will continued, "Our supply train was taken by mounted militia, and I was lucky to be riding Molly at the time. I escaped into the woods and got to our militia encampment at Moore's Creek Bridge in time to warn them that the Tories were on our side of the river. We were lucky to win that battle at Moore's Creek Bridge."

Legare looked at Will with new respect. "You've been fighting for almost five years, then, Sir."

Will said, "Aye, it has been a long fight and no end in sight, my friend."

Legare said, "It explains why they have promoted a young man to a high rank."

Will snorted, "I had nothing better to do, Jim. I fell into this because of a woman."

Legare smiled, "Seems we all have that burden, Sir. Mine is Sarah McWhorter. She's a well-born planter's daughter but has no interest in me."

Will said, "I'll bet she has plenty of interest in you, Jim. If that fails, I shall introduce you to Eliza Yonge Wilkinson. She's minded to marry an officer. She was my wife's closest friend."

Legare said, "Perhaps I shall take you up on that offer, Sir. Miss Sarah doth protest too much, as Shakespeare said."

Will said, "Mary uttered that line about Eliza's apparent hatred of me when we first met. That got me reading Shakespeare. Colonel Marion took me to see Mr. Robert Wells, where I saw a new world of books."

Legare snickered, "Sir, I didn't know Colonel Marion was literate."

Will laughed out loud. "Many discount Francis Marion as nothing but a farmer and a fighter, but he's more than that, I assure you. Mr. Wells got me stuck on Homer's *Odyssey*. I've dragged that book all over the South. Still working on it when I have time."

Legare smirked, "I swear that Sarah's daddy is Polyphemus. He's blind in one eye, and every time I see him, I believe he will eat me alive!"

They both laughed.

~~<>~~

An orderly came trotting back down the column to Will and Legare. Handing Will a note, the orderly said, "General's compliments, Colonel Yelverton."

Will read the note and nodded to the orderly. "My compliments to the General. We will join Colonel Buford at the crossroads."

The orderly saluted and left. Will looked at Legare, "General Huger has ordered that Buford and his Virginia Regiments move toward Waxhaws and, if necessary, take up positions there while Governor Rutledge and Huger continue to Charlotte. Huger is taking the remnants of the Moncks Corner regiment. We're with Buford."

~~<>~~

Will rode with Buford at the head of the column now. Cuthbert rode behind with Buford's orderly, and Legare's small unit was relegated to the supply train.

Abe Buford said, "Rutledge, for all his strengths and legal training, can grate on your nerves. I knew him years back. He learned a lawyer's insolence at the Middle Temple in London. I caught that slight snide comment in him calling you 'Lieutenant' Colonel."

Will said, "Aye. When we evacuated him, he had no idea where we were going or how we would get there. We took Hibben's

Ferry out of Charlestown. T'was the only way out of town, and I wanted the Wando River between the Tories and us. He wanted to go to Clement's Ferry."

"I'm not from Charlestown, but I think that would have been right into the teeth of the British."

"Aye. Tell him that."

Buford snorted a laugh. His broad Virginia accent was strong when he said, "Aye. You can always tell the governor, but you can't tell him much."

Will snorted and said, "There were other minor scrapes along the way. He didn't get his way about this or that."

"You got him to Huger safely and did it without loss of life or property. Damned fine show, I think."

Will grinned, "I won't be commanding any South Carolina units for a while, I think."

Another snort. "I hear you got Francis Marion out of harm's way, though I know not where he is. I'm sure he's had to run from his home. It is just a stone's throw from Moncks Corner."

Will said, "Aye. With his leg, he won't be doing much running for a while. He mentioned having plenty of friends he might stay with. What will we do now that Charlestown is lost, and Lincoln's 5000 men are captive?"

Buford shook his head sadly, "I know not, Will. I hear Continentals and militia are mustering in North Carolina. Hillsborough, last I heard. We marched through there on the way south from The Old Dominion. Didn't see much, though. Huger has ordered us to Hillsborough by way of Waxhaws."

Will said, "I can't think of a better idea."

Buford's men – 380 Virginians, plus 40 Virginia Dragoons and Will's little detachment, made about 430 – marched to Waxhaws on the border between South Carolina and North Carolina. They stopped beside a creek and rested.

~~<>~~

An hour passed, and then two. A scout came galloping in from the road to Camden and shouted, "Enemy spotted, Sir. I'd say they're a three-hour march behind us, at most."

Buford stood and looked around the camp. "Let's get on the road; maybe we can get far enough that they won't want to fight."

The 400+ men did not wait for much more direction and rose quickly from their rest. They marched off in good order and once again headed for Hillsborough, North Carolina.

Buford quietly said, "These men have not been well trained. There was no time. We marched from Virginia to try to get to Charlestown in time. It seems we were lucky and arrived just as the city was taken. Otherwise, we'd be in the hold of some prison ship."

Will said, "They seem good men."

"Oh, Aye. They are stout fellows, but I'm concerned they won't hold against Tarleton's experienced cavalry. Some of them have malaria, too. We don't see much of that in Virginia."

Will nodded. "The British have the advantage of money, training, supply, and experience. Their officers have also had training in warfare."

Buford said, "I'm fortunate. I have capable officers, but even the best officer can't hold back panicked men when they break."

~~<>~~

Buford's men had marched a solid two miles when a scout galloped in to say the British were getting closer and that they had spread into advanced units, one numbering some 60 dragoons, another 60 mounted infantry, and a flanking force that looked like another 30 dragoons accompanied by infantry.

Buford called a halt. "Captain Hardy? Have the regiments formed into the battleline and prepare to engage the enemy. The enemy is mounted, so have the men fix bayonets."

The Virginians moved smartly into the battleline, and Will saw the white flashes of steel bayonets in the sun. *If they are as good at stabbing as they are at polishing those blades, we might be all right. I told Tarleton 300 yards was as close as he would get to me.*

With that, Will reached down and drew Josie out of her deer hide scabbard. He checked the prime. Just this morning, he had drawn the load and reloaded Josie with as perfect a ball as he could find in this pouch. The powder was dry, and the priming power was as fine as dust. The clear day had only a hint of a breeze. Josie would kill at 300 yards.

~~<>~~

A lone rider in a green jacket carrying a white flag crested a small rise in front of Buford's arrayed regiments. He rode forward to present a letter.

"Sir, I am Captain David Kinlock. I have the honor of serving with Lieutenant Colonel Tarleton of His Majesty's British Legion. Colonel Tarleton presents his compliments and cordially demands your surrender, Sir. I have the honor of presenting the Colonel's letter with specifics. Sir, you are?"

"I'm your worst nightmare, Captain. I am Abraham Buford, late of the Sovereign State of Virginia."

"It is my honor to make your acquaintance Colonel Buford. May I present you Colonel Tarleton's letter?"

Buford held out his hand, and the captain handed him a folded, sealed piece of paper.

Will noted that the paper was creamy white with some dark specks. Expensive. But then, Tarleton was wealthy.

Buford backed his horse away a few steps.

The captain looked at Will. "May I ask the Colonel's name, Sir?"

Will smiled and shifted Josie a little in his grasp, "It is my honor to meet you, Sir. I am William Yelverton. But Colonel Tarleton knows that. Tell him to remember my promise of 300 yards."

Captain Kinlock looked bewildered. "300 yards, Sir? I'm afraid I am at a loss."

Will said, "Tarleton will understand."

Buford walked his horse back to where Will and Kinlock waited. "Captain Kinlock, please convey this letter to Colonel Tarleton with my compliments. I hope you survive the day, Sir."

Kinlock bowed half from his saddle and said, "A good day, Sir." He turned his horse and trotted off toward the south and Tarleton.

Buford turned to Captain Hardy. "Have the baggage train move off, and then the regiment will continue the march."

Buford handed the note from Tarleton to Will. Will read:

"Resistance being vain, to prevent the effusion of human blood, I make offers which can never be repeated...."

The letter proclaimed that Tarleton had some 700 men, mostly mounted and ready to attack immediately.

Will said, "I presume you rejected his proposal."

"Aye. I told him I reject his proposals and will defend myself to the last extremity."

Will said, "He certainly doesn't have 700 men. We've observed about 200, so we outnumber him. The last time I saw Tarleton, I told him he would not be allowed to get within 300 yards of me."

Buford looked at Josie. "That may very well be the most beautiful rifle I've ever seen. 300 yards, eh?"

Will said, "Yes. When the conditions are right as they are today."

Buford smiled. "Good. Don't wait for orders from me. Kill him."

~~<>~~

The column marched, and the dust cloud became more noticeable. Will and Cuthbert rode at the back of the column, which was even worse for the dust. His English dragoon carbine dangled from its sling, which was uncomfortable. It tended to bob and jerk with Molly's gait. Josie rode on his thigh, much as the carbine usually did. Will noticed that Josie was light as a feather compared to the carbine.

The afternoon wore on, and Will wondered if Tarleton would come on. Will knew Tarleton had gathered the horses from Moncks Corner and had been driving them relentlessly ever since. *The poor horses must be completely worn out,* Will thought.

But no, while the horses were undoubtedly tired and Tarleton was not rushing forward as was his wont, he made contact. It was nearly 3 p.m. when the regimental surgeon, Doctor Richard Brownfield, came galloping up to Will and the elements at the rear of the column.

"Sir, the British caught up to the rear guard. Captain Pearson and five men were captured. I saw Captain Pearson very inhumanely mangled with sabers. He fell off his horse, and the troops continued slashing him even when he was unable to fight."

Will glanced at Cuthbert. "Cuth, go get Colonel Buford."

Cuthbert nodded and wheeled his bay horse to gallop toward the front of the column.

They soon returned with Buford riding up as Brownfield finished telling this tale.

Buford said, "Well, gentlemen, it appears this will be a fight after all. I had hoped Tarleton's horses were exhausted. I don't see artillery. That's good. I've ordered the baggage train and artillery to keep rolling. We'll form battleline here."

Will asked, "Sir, shouldn't we use the artillery?"

Buford looked across the field and squinted. "They only have about 200 cavalry, and I don't see any artillery. T'would be quite an ordeal to unlimber our six-pounders for what I think won't be a long fight. Besides, we'd only get one or two rounds fired before they would be among us."

Will nodded. He had misgivings about this decision. Cannister's shot would wreak havoc on mounted troops as it had on Pulaski at Savannah.

Buford glanced around and said, "Form a single battle line along these woods. Prepare me a white flag in case they want a truce. That cavalry won't stand up to determined musket fire. We're going to wait to fire until they're about 10 yards away. Then, we'll cut them to pieces."

Will had misgivings about this decision, as well. It meant that Buford's troops would have one shot and no time to reload before saber-slashing cavalry slammed into the battle line. These troops were untrained, and the chance of them standing seemed remote.

Will hefted Josie and checked her prime a second time. At least he might get a shot at Tarleton.

~~<>~~

Will looked across the field and saw Tarleton arraying his troops. On the American left, Tarleton's right, there were some 60 dragoons and about the same number of infantry troops. The dragoons wore plumed helmets and green coats. These were Americans, or at least mostly American loyalists of Tarleton's British Legion. Their sabers were drawn and rested on their right shoulders as they moved their horses into formation.

Will could see this would be an all-out cavalry charge, but he also could see many horses had their heads down and were moving slowly. They were bone tired from the long pursuit from Camden.

Molly whickered and stamped her hoof. She pranced a step or two as though taunting the tired horses across the field.

Will leaned down and patted her neck. He whispered in Molly's ear, "We're going to show them a thing or two, girl."

Molly nodded her head and blew. She snorted and pawed the ground.

Will grinned. Molly loved excitement.

Cuthbert sat on his bay next to Will, his fusil loaded with buck and ball. He had two pistols jammed into his belt and was ready.

Tarleton set up thirty dragoons in red jackets in the center. They also carried sabers sloped against their right shoulders. Polished brass helmets glinted in the sun.

On the American right, Tarleton's left, Tarleton himself could be seen prancing his horse back and forth as he arrayed his chosen troops. These numbered some thirty cavalry and a couple of platoons of infantry.

Will wondered aloud to Cuthbert, "I wonder how Tarleton's horse is fresh when everyone else's seems worn out?"

Cuthbert said, "Maybe he was riding another horse, and this one was walking riderless?"

Will shrugged. "Must be nice to be catered to with such niceties as two horses."

Cuthbert grinned wryly, "I think we're getting ready to catch hell, Sir."

Will nodded, "Aye. Don't hesitate if I say run."

Subordinate officers and sergeants dressed the lines and assured discipline across the entire British front. In front of Will, the Virginians lined up in a ragged single rank that stretched quite a distance. Will thought it would be better to have three ranks of about 120 men each so that rolling volley fire might be sustained. The first rank fired and reloaded, the second rank fired and reloaded, the third rank fired, and so on. That approach would have torn into the cavalry starting at 100 yards. Adding artillery with a canister shot would have caused Tarleton to think twice about a frontal assault.

Will wryly thought, *But Tarleton may not be truly sane. Who knows what he might do? It matters not. This will go badly.*

~~<>~~

There was some unseen signal or voice command along the British line, and the line began to walk toward the Americans. Will waited – the British Legion was close to 400 yards away.

In the past, Will had always wrestled with his conscience when it came to shooting an enemy. He was not averse to killing a man who was equally intent upon killing him. But shooting a man from a distance was impersonal and seemed dishonorable. Will made an exception when it came to Banastre Tarleton. Tarleton had singled out Will for some reason and set his cap to see Will hang. He hounded him across New Jersey and now – over a year later – seemed to relish the idea of confronting Will. Well, Tarleton would soon confront a .40 caliber rifle ball.

Will saw the dust kick up behind their hooves as the British Legion and other dragoons began to trot. The infantry stepped up from a quick march to double time. They would be a bit behind the cavalry when the fight started, but they would be no less effective.

Will heard Buford say, "Steady, boys. Let 'em get closer."

He looked for Tarleton and saw the green jacket and black, plumed helmet atop the white charger at the rear of the British left. Tarleton was surveying his troops with calm detachment; their discipline was evident in their near-perfect straight lines.

Some unheard command moved the British Legion to a canter. Will thought, *Maybe 30 seconds until they are among us. Then it will be 'Katie Bar the Door.'*

Now Tarleton was just inside 300 yards from Will. *Time for Josie to go to work.*

Will patted Molly's neck. "Steady now, Girl.

The British Legion broke into a gallop, and sabers flashed as legionnaires leveled the razor-sharp blades at the ragged Virginian line.

WizCRAAAAK! Josie jolted against Will's shoulder.

At the same instant, Tarleton's horse, the magnificent white charger confiscated from some wealthy Carolina planter, stepped up a small rise and took Josie's ball squarely in its eye. A moment later and Tarleton would have been dead. As it was, the horse went down in a lifeless pile with Tarleton trapped beneath.

Buford shouted, "FIRE!" and some 400 muskets cracked. Blinding, burning smoke boiled up from the line, its sulfur stink making Will gag slightly.

Will swore, "Damn! What a beautiful horse." He shoved Josie back into her deer hide case and whipped the English dragoon carbine up. Two legionnaires burst through the line and angled for Will. This was a mistake. The carbine boomed and thumped against Will's ribcage as the buck and ball load pulped the legionnaire's face.

The dead legionnaire toppled backward off his horse as the second legionnaire drew back his saber to slash at Will from his left side. Will nudged Molly with his knees, and she sidestepped. The flashing saber cut nothing but air where Will's head had just been.

Molly's move gave Will just enough time to draw the ancient horse pistol from its bucket holster on his saddle and snap a shot at his legionnaire adversary. The ball missed, but some of the buckshot stung the legionnaire, and he wheeled his horse out of the fight.

Will tossed the horse pistol in its bucket and snatched one of Tarleton's Brander pistols from his belt. He cocked it and held it ready.

Buford said, "They're ignoring the white flag!"

Will said, "What!? What white flag?"

Buford shouted over the din, "I sent the white flag when the volley failed, and they broke our line!"

Will swore, "Jesus! Now Tarleton thinks I shot him under a flag of truce. They'll kill everyone here!"

The British Legion, incensed at what they thought was clear treachery of shooting under a white flag, laid into the hapless Virginians. Sabers flashed; pistols cracked. The infantry following the dragoons burst upon the scene, attacking the Virginians with bayonets.

Buford shouted, "Withdraw! Withdraw!"

Will saw several Virginians throw down their muskets and raise their hands only to be sabered viciously. Will shot at a couple of legionnaires from maybe 50 feet, but that range was too long to be truly effective with a pistol. Will's weapons were all empty except for the .45 rifle. Will drew the rifle from its scabbard; it was now his only defense. Will looked for Buford.

Cuthbert shouted, "He went this way, Sir."

Cuthbert turned his horse to head north, and Will followed.

Will looked desperately for Jim Legare and his troops. They were together and positioned more toward the baggage train, somewhat away from the wild melee of sabers and Virginian blood.

Will saw at least 100 Virginians throw down their weapons and run into the woods. A similar number dropped their weapons and were cut down by furious legionnaires.

A dozen dragoons burst out of the pack and charged toward Will and Cuthbert. Jim Legare and his ten South Carolina troopers rushed to join Will, and a standoff ensued. The legionnaires' horses were spent, and the Continentals' mounts were fresh.

The commander of the legionnaires saluted with his saber. It was Captain Kinlock. He shouted, "I am glad you survived the day, Colonel." With that, he wheeled back to the melee.

Will started to chase Kinlock, but Cuthbert grabbed his arm. "Sir, we can do nothing. We'll just get killed, is all."

Will nodded and tried to spit the gunsmoke taste from his dry mouth, "Damn! Let's find Buford and get out of here."

Thirty minutes later, and three miles up the road, Will found Buford sitting on his horse, pulling together what few troops were emerging from the trees.

"I got them killed, Will. It was a terrible mistake to wait."

Will cuffed the black gunpowder residue from his face, "I got them killed because I shot Tarleton under a flag of truce."

"No, Will. I distinctly heard your rifle crack before the shock of the dragoons hitting our line. I sent the white flag after that."

Will said, "Never mind, Sir. Tarleton will use that as an excuse to hang me at our next meeting."

"You're sure he survived?"

"Aye. I killed a magnificent beast today, but it wasn't Tarleton. It was his horse that stepped in front of the ball just as I shot. Not the first time, either, Sir. The same thing happened with Prevost at Midway."

Buford nodded and turned his horse to head north.

Will looked into the distance, remembering. He thought, *That fight didn't come out any better than this one.*

Chapter 32 – Hillsborough

Buford's surviving troops marched listlessly into the American camp at Buffalo Ford on the Deep River near Hillsborough, North Carolina. Many had lost their weapons. Discarded them is more accurate.

Muskets were very hard to come by. Will remembered that many of the troops defending Charlestown had no muskets. Many of Huger's people at Moncks Corner had no muskets. It was sad to know that perfectly functional guns were cast aside when Tarleton's dragoons burst upon the American lines at Waxhaws.

Will and Cuthbert walked with their horses toward the front of the bedraggled column. Molly and Cuthbert's bay were tired after several days of being on the march. Will was glad that the march had been slowed by the supply wagons, else poor Molly would be exhausted and unable to walk. He thought it was good that the army would be paused at Hillsborough for some time. Perhaps they would be here for weeks. Molly was desperate for a rest.

Will wondered what the next move might be. There was rampant speculation about the next commander of the Southern Department of the Continental Army. Buford said

Major General Johann, Baron DeKalb was marching to Hillsborough with several hundred Maryland and Delaware Continentals. DeKalb was a German and a respected commander. Word was that DeKalb would be named Commander of the Southern Department now that Lincoln was captured.

Rumor also had it that Washington supported a Rhode Islander named Nathanael Greene. Will remembered Greene from Brandywine.

Legare said his highly placed friends were hearing that Horatio Gates would be the commander. Gates was recently the victor at the Battle of Saratoga and a national hero. He was also George Washington's rival for Commander in Chief.

Will did not care who commanded. So far, only Gates had demonstrated much in the way of military skill. Even Washington had not won a decisive victory. It was true that when he was fully apprised of the situation at Brandywine, Washington acted correctly and at once. It was also true that Washington kept his army moving and forced the British to chase him, rarely allowing a full-on fight. But the British got the better of the Americans at nearly every head-on collision. It was a case of training, money, and professionalism of the armies. The British had all three; the Americans rarely had even one.

~~<>~~

The accommodations were acceptable for camp life. Will had a private tent, and Molly was well-kept and had plenty of grass to crop. Will took her a carrot or an apple every day. And every couple of days, Will took her for a ride, so they both got some exercise. Without some exercise every couple of days, Molly became cross and very restive.

Camp life was becoming boring. Will frequently sat in the sun reading his copy of *The Odyssey*. The book was somewhat battered after months of being carried in a saddlebag. Will was determined to finish the book.

He was at the stage of the story where Odysseus had been away for nearly ten years and was returning to his home in disguise to ascertain the situation before making his presence known. Odysseus' wife had suitors and was under some duress to accept one of the men. Odysseus wanted to know if she had been faithful.

Will had a wry look on his face, his mouth turned down, as he considered the similarities between himself and Odysseus. They both had been away at war, leaving their women alone and besieged with suitors. Odysseus had dallied with Calypso for years. Will had been introduced to the pleasures of the flesh by Frances Montravalle.

Will smiled when he thought of Frances. He also felt a stirring in his loins as he contemplated her lying naked, one arm behind her head, right knee bent, relaxing on an expensive feather bed in her Philadelphia townhouse—a townhouse appropriated for her husband, Captain John Montravalle. John Montravalle was never home because he was out dallying with every woman he encountered.

Frances had been quite wanton in her appetites and a patient but demanding teacher. In truth, Will would still be in Pennsylvania had Tarleton not accused him of spying. And why not? Frances could make his skin feel like it was on fire.

Will immediately felt a terrible cheat. Poor Mary was dead less than six months, and here he was daydreaming about Frances Montravalle's rosy nipples and flat, naked belly.

Abby intruded into his thoughts. Abby had become a frequent visitor to Will's unconscious thoughts since Mary's passing. Will admitted to himself that his first true love was Abby Kennedy. Abby was a quiet, unassuming country girl who adored Will.

And now, Abby was married to Zeke Carter. Zeke was an equally simple country boy as Will had once been. Zeke was a good man, and Will was certain Abby had given birth to a wonderful baby for Zeke. Will hoped it was a boy who would grow up strong and confident. Perhaps he would become a gunsmith trained under his grandfather, Alexander Kennedy, the paterfamilias of the Kennedy School of rifle making.

Abby married Zeke because she thought Will was dead. His letters never arrived, and she simply thought her life must move on. But Will's last visit to Bear Creek had been bittersweet. Abby learned that Will was not dead, and Will learned that Abby was married. Will thought of how Abby had given herself to him on his last night at Kennedy's. She had quietly come to his little room in the stable and demanded that he make love to her.

Will found Abby perhaps the best lover of his brief life. Certainly, Frances was like one of Dr. Franklin's electricity experiments – she made Will's hair stand on end. Mary was adventurous and absolutely in love with Will. She showed him that women liked physical love as much as men did, and she had a powerful imagination. Smallpox that took her was equally cruel to both Mary and Will. Will admitted that he loved Mary, and while she was alive, Will thought of no other woman. But Mary was gone, and Abby frequently intruded into his thoughts.

Abby! Her gamine little face and quiet warmth were more appealing than the well-born, educated women he had liked, loved, bedded, and lost. Abby was more his soulmate, and they both knew it. Their only night of love had been astonishingly powerful for them both. More, it had been right. Dishonorable, immoral, sadly furtive, but ... right.

Will had contemplated all these things frequently while half-dozing riding Molly in a column of troops and while encamped at Hillsborough. It was a surprise, then, when Will looked up from The Odyssey to see General Richard Caswell's North Carolina militia marching into camp. An even bigger surprise was seeing Zeke Carter walking along in Caswell's ranks. He carried one of Kennedy's rifles.

Will put down The Odyssey and stood to waive at General Caswell, who inclined his head and grinned widely in acknowledgment. Zeke did not see Will and marched along tiredly with the rest of his company.

~~<>~~

Later that day, Will angled over to Caswell's tent and presented himself.

Caswell glanced up from some papers, stood grinning, and stuck out his hand. "Colonel Yelverton, I presume!"

Will shook Caswell's hand. "*General* Caswell. It seems we've both been promoted since last I saw you."

Caswell said, "Indeed. We've both changed from civilian to military. Last I heard, Francis Marion offered to get you a commission. But I'm surprised to see you wearing silver oak leaves."

Will said, "'Tis a long story, Sir. I am delighted to see you in uniform again."

Caswell nodded with a wry grin, "As governor of our fair state, I was beset with trivia and politics. Now I am beset with fools and politics. Fools who don't want to train or equip an army but who are ready to rush into battle. Politics because everyone is trying to find an advantage."

Caswell looked out at his camp. "I have pulled together this militia from all over the state, and we have provisions. My men are armed, and I've tried to train them. Politically, the quartermasters here seek to poach my supplies, which infuriates me. I've learned that many other units here are short of provisions."

Will said, "I imagine we'll go to South Carolina eventually. Truly, I think we'd rather fight on that ground than on our own native North Carolina soil. Your provisions won't go to waste."

Caswell considered this point. "Aye. We're all the United States now, but I admit to a desire to discourage the British from entering North Carolina."

Will grinned, "Well, you and Lillington and White did it once; I'm sure you can do it again."

Caswell smiled at that memory and asked, "What unit are you with?"

Will said, "I am supernumerary. At the moment, I have no unit."

Caswell said, "How did that happen?"

441

"I was in the 2nd South Carolina Regiment until Lincoln got me promoted to Lieutenant Colonel. A command was unavailable, so he made me Inspector of Armaments in Charlestown. My inspection duties were over, and Lincoln ordered all supernumeraries and injured officers, includng Francis Marion, out of the city. I escorted Marion to his plantation out past Moncks Corner. I was returning to Charlestown for further orders when Tarleton attacked Huger at Moncks Corner. Fortunately, I camped a distance from Biggin Bridge, so we were not directly attacked. We hurried away when we saw Huger and his other commanders rushing to the swamp."

Caswell nodded. "I heard Moncks Corner was a complete mess, and we lost a herd of horses in the bargain."

Will continued, "Aye. I was ordered to escort Governor Rutledge from Charlestown to Camden to meet with Huger, and we accomplished that. I was with Buford when Tarleton caught up to us and attacked Buford's Virginians at Waxhaws."

"Rutledge can be a handful. You saw the massacre of Buford's men?"

Will said, "Aye, people are calling the massacre *Tarleton's Quarter*– in other words, no quarter: a fight to the death. Already, there have been atrocities on both sides since that unfortunate encounter."

Caswell nodded, a sad expression washing over his face. "'Tis a terrible thing, war. I was present when Tryon hanged those regulators at Alamance. That was without honor. No trial, just a rope, a tree, and a rain barrel kicked out from under the poor unfortunate. That said, I am most delighted to be out of the bloody governor's mansion and in the field."

Will said, "Join us for supper tonight? I killed a deer yesterday, and they're making it into a few steaks for the officers and a nice stew for the men."

Caswell said, "I'd be delighted."

~~<>~~

"That's a fine rifle you have there, Zeke."

A startled Zeke Carter looked around to see Will standing there, grinning from ear to ear.

"Maj...er, *Colonel* Yelverton! 'Tis good to see you, Sir."

Will smiled to see Zeke looking healthy. "You've been working in the sun and eating well."

"Abby is a good cook, Sir. But you know that. She and our baby are doing well, too. I named him William Yelverton Kennedy in your honor. We call him Yel."

Will smiled and said, "Not Ezekiel or Micah?"

"No, Sir. The man who saved my life gets first honor. Ezekiel and Micah are for the next 'uns."

Will smiled at Zeke and said, "You do me great honor, Zeke."

Will's heart was heavy, but he was also pleased that Zeke and Abby had a son and Will had a namesake. It was a great honor. Will wondered how much influence Abby had in that plan.

Will sat on a stump and pulled out a clay pipe, offering Zeke some tobacco. Zeke lit his stub of a pipe, and they chatted. The topics covered the rifle-making business and farming near Bear Creek: the turkey hunting last year and the deer hunting in the coming fall.

Alexander Kennedy and Irene were both well. Zeke's father, Micah, had been having heart ailments that made it hard for him to plow, but Alex and Irene's youngest boy, Billy, was more interested in farming than gun-making, so he was helping. David Kennedy was becoming an excellent gunsmith. David had a head for business, so he was slowly taking on many business duties. That freed Alex so he could teach new apprentices. Alex had enlarged the mill.

Will casually asked after Abby and was rewarded with a lengthy tale of how Abby was the mistress of the home now. She had not become pregnant again after little Yel Carter. No other children were yet, but Zeke was proud of little Yel.

Both these pieces of information greatly pleased Will. Yell Carter was a great name! That Abby was not carrying another baby secretly comforted Will, but he knew it was for nothing.

Zeke said, "Congratulations on your promotion, Sir."

Will said, "Thank you, Zeke. It had less to do with skill and everything to do with being in the right place at the right time."

Zeke looked hard at Will, "Don't say that kind of thing, Sir. Begging your pardon. I saw you in a fight, and it scared pure hell out of me. I mean, I'm not afraid of you because you're a kind soul. I can see that. But woe unto the man who crosses you, Sir. And you know, I saw them men follow you. Them other officers would'a got ever one of 'em killed."

They chatted further until twilight.

Will said, "We'll chat again, Zeke. Now I have to go. Caswell's coming to my campfire."

Zeke said, "I like you, Sir if you don't mind my saying. You know how to be easy with people like me and then set a spell with a general."

Will said, "Everybody's the same, Zeke. Caswell's just like you and me. He's just managed to get more work laid on him."

Zeke nodded. "Yeah, but I know why Abby loves you so much."

Will was startled.

Zeke said, "Aww, I done embarrassed you. She said you're like her other brothers, David especially. Makes me feel like we's brothers, too."

Will said, "Aye, Zeke. I am part of the Kennedy family. Now, maybe the Carter clan, too."

Zeke said, "You's always welcome, Will. Er, Colonel Yelverton."

Will said, "Will's fine, Zeke."

As Will walked back to his tent, he thought, *I wonder why I didn't tell him about Mary?* But deep in his heart, he knew the answer.

After supper with Caswell, Will sat in his tent feeling low. Abby still loved him, and poor Zeke, a good man, misunderstood the feeling she expressed. Will resolved to put Abby Kennedy Carter out of his mind.

She named her baby William Yelverton Carter...and they call him Yel, he smiled as he dozed off.

~~<>~~

It was noon when Sam Hawks stuck his head inside Will's tent. "Reckon you don't recognize your friends anymore, now that you're a high-and-mighty Lieutenant Colonel."

Will jumped up and hugged Sam tightly. "Sam! When did you get here?"

"We marched in this morning."

Will said, "I'll be damned! 'Tis good to see you."

"You very likely will be damned, but 'tis all right with me. I'll join you in hell, and we'll give the Devil fits!"

Will laughed. "Have a seat."

Sam and Will chatted about a variety of things. Hunting and fishing in New Bern, drinking at Cogdell's Tavern, Will's surrogate father and master gunsmith Bert Koontz and his wife, Rebecca. Miss Becky had been his mother for seven years of his adolescence. Bert and Miss Becky were doing well, and hearing it made Will glad.

They got around to Noah Harris' parents. Noah's death had hung in the tent since Sam stuck his head through the tent flap.

Sam said, "They were sick when I told them."

Will said, "I'm glad it was someone they know and love. I am so ashamed I couldn't be there."

Sam glanced off into the distance. "They understood. They got the preacher to read your letter. They know you're trying to win our independence."

They talked about how they both missed Noah and how he was their best friend.

Will asked, "How did Dicky Caswell take the news."

"He cried. We were all like brothers. It was hard to tell him, but it had to be done. We drank Cogdell's dry that night. At least we didn't puke in a spittoon like that fool Isiah did."

Will grinned at the memory of Isiah Koontz hurling his drunken guts into a spittoon in the corner of Cogdell's Tavern. "Where's Dicky now?"

"He's still sailing that ship of his up and down the coast. I tried to tell him the British Navy was going to catch up with him and sink his boat. Either that or privateers would do it."

Will nodded. "I don't know what the fascination is with sailing that boat."

Later, after Sam left, Will wondered why he had not told Sam of Mary. But he knew the answer. Mary was gone, and telling Sam about her wouldn't bring her back. It was painful to talk about Mary, so Will avoided it. But he felt he betrayed Mary when he didn't talk about her.

~~<>~~

Will walked across the field toward the militia camp. As he got closer, he heard a familiar voice.

"And lo, the angel of the Lord sayeth unto the Canaanites..."

Will grinned. Benjamin was still preaching. Will came around a tent and saw Benjamin standing on a peach crate, haranguing a group of militiamen. Will smiled an enigmatic smile when he saw that many of the militiamen were paying rapt attention to Benjamin. A correction was in order: The Reverend Benjamin Franklin Yelverton, MG – Minister of the Gospel.

Benjamin finally ran out of energy and breath, saying, "Come on the morrow, my children, and I shall help you find everlasting peace. Amen."

He turned to step off the peach crate and saw Will. "Ah, Will. I'm happy to see you."

Will said, "How did you come to be here? I last saw you preaching in the camp at Charlestown. Did the British let you go?"

"Aye. They were not minded to imprison a Minister of the Gospel."

Will said, "I suppose not. When did you get ordained?"

Benjamin said, "I could not pursue the Anglican Church. As you know, it's now outlawed. Well, not outlawed, but frowned upon. I met an ordained Baptist minister who helped me be approved. I had to study quite a bit, I'll tell you. But how are you, Will? I'm sure your heart still hurts after the loss of your beloved Mary."

Oddly, Will could talk to Benjamin about Mary. Will said, "Aye. But the ache fades somewhat with each passing day. Besides, 'twas God's will, and who am I to argue?"

"Just so, Will. Just so."

They chatted for a few minutes, with Will saying he was proud that Benjamin was now ordained. He also said he was pleased Benjamin was not in some rotting prison ship.

To which Benjamin replied, "Perhaps t'would be a better place for me. The wretched souls on those rotting, stinking, diseased ships suffer, and God's word is the only thing that can help them."

Will wore an ironic smile as he walked back to his tent. Jim and Red, the two slavers who put the fear of God in Benjamin, would laugh for days over the conversion. Ben did not need to know the truth about Jim and Red, the beings he was sure were Angels of the Lord.

~~<>~~

Will was walking toward Sam's hovel when he saw Captain Chuck Black sitting on a stump next to the cooking fire.

"Chuck, 'tis good to see you."

"Will! Er, Lieutenant Colonel Yelverton... My goodness. You have continued to succeed."

"I see you have been promoted, Chuck. Well done!"

Chuck Black smiled. "I had no idea I would be suited to the military. I've always been minded to business and shirking any duties I could get out of."

Will found this self-effacing humor funny and laughed out loud. "Chuck, we're more alike than you might think. I had no idea what I was meant for. But I have a purpose here, and so do you."

Chuck said, "Aye. I have found purpose."

Will said, "You're quite a fighter, Chuck. And I think you like it."

"Aye. I do. I like life and being here with men with the same purpose."

Chuck looked a little hesitant. "Uh, Martha says hello."

"Martha?"

"Yes, Martha came home a few weeks ago. She is still with the sea captain, Manoah Compton. She and Compton put their ship into New Bern and confronted my father."

"That must have been quite a discussion."

"Aye. Father would throw them both in jail, but he couldn't think of any law they had broken. The upshot of the entire thing is that Manoah and Martha now work for my father. They're running cargo for him up and down the coast."

Will said, "That is the life she said she wanted."

"Aye, Will. But she said to tell you she still thinks of you often."

Will grinned. "She always was a puzzle."

~~<>~~

On June 22, General DeKalb and his troops arrived at Hillsborough. The camp population was swelled by several hundred men from Maryland and Delaware. Will was among several senior officers as they conferred. Most hoped that DeKalb was the new Commander of the Southern Department.

That was not to be. A month later, General Horatio Gates rode into the camp with his entourage from New York. Gates was the new Commander of the Southern Department. The Congress considered DeKalb, a foreigner, and Gates had won at Saratoga. That was enough.

The council of senior officers discussed the British consolidation of their control of South Carolina. Militia had abandoned Augusta to the British. British pressure on the Ninety-six District was intensifying. The location of Camden and its proximity to the Wateree River made it a strategic location.

DeKalb presented a letter to Gates from Thomas Sumter, South Carolina's upstate partisan leader. Sumter's message detailed the scattered postings of British forces in South Carolina, listing the strength of their garrison at Camden at 700. Some of the men were sick and recovering.

By the 25th of July, Gates had decided the American army would take Camden. From there, Gates would retake Charlestown and then Savannah.

Will thought this unlikely to succeed but held his tongue.

Apparently, Caswell agreed with Will. The next morning, Will watched as Caswell and the North Carolina Militia marched south toward South Carolina. No one could stop Caswell. He was not under the authority of the Continental Congress, nor was he commanded by the Continental Army.

Gates ordered the Army to march on Camden, South Carolina. It was the 27th of July, 1780, and once again, Will was in an army marching to battle.

Chapter 33 – Rugeley's Mill

Gates rode at the head of the column along with his immediate staff. The presence of several generals – Gates, DeKalb, others – meant that mere supernumerary lieutenant colonels were not sufficiently important to ride near the leaders. That was all right with Will.

Will thought, *At least I'm not at the column's rear, eating the dust, trudging through horse shit, and smelling the stink of marching men.*

He did have the company of some of the other officers. In particular, Colonel Otho Holland Williams was a pleasant companion. Williams was Gates' deputy adjutant, so he rode with Will. He told Will about being held captive in a tiny cell in Boston with a man named Ethan Allen. They shared some 16 square feet of dank, airless room in jail for over a year until Williams was released.

Williams said, "I'm still sick from being in that dungeon. I cough and wheeze, and my bones ache. I doubt I shall ever be over this. At least not during this life."

Williams' leadership of Maryland troops at Monmouth in New Jersey had been exemplary. Williams' troops had gone from undisciplined, ragtag soldiers of indifferent performance to equal or better than other continental line soldiers. Williams was skilled at warfare and had a low opinion of the Camden expedition.

Williams quietly said, "I don't have to tell you, Will, that this part of South Carolina is by nature barren with mostly sandy plains and swamps. 'Tis very thinly inhabited."

Will said, "Aye, Sir. The land is like North Carolina, where I grew up. It will grow things but 'tis hardscrabble living. Few people can farm this land because they don't have the strength. Not enough food makes it nigh impossible to do more in a day than plow a small field. You would think they would hunt, but that requires more strength than plowing. My family is fortunate to own land along the Roanoke River below the falls. We can work the land with some rented slaves."

Williams squinted at a broken-down cabin they were passing. "What few inhabitants we might come across are most likely hostile."

Will said, "The people hereabouts are independent-minded and not easily swayed to war."

Williams had come south with DeKalb. He quietly said, "I wouldn't say this to many, but DeKalb is a better man for the command job. He's more inclined to strategy and less interested in the show. Gates has received great acclaim for Saratoga, but that was over two years ago. That said, he has made me his deputy adjutant general, and I'll have to find ways to support his decisions."

Will said, "Aye, sir. I hope the British are more accommodating than I've found them in the past. We must constantly be on our guard to avoid being flanked. Also, if Tarleton is with the British, he is utterly ruthless and will charge into the heart of our troops. I hope the general knows that Tarleton is Cornwallis' attack dog and is largely without honor. He claims, I hear, that we shot at him under a flag of truce, but 'tis not true. I shot at him before Buford sent the white flag forward. Tarleton ignores that he sent a white flag to parley, and while talks were ongoing, he continued maneuvering his army. Quite disreputable, that."

Williams nodded, "You're the one who shot his horse from under him?"

Will grimaced, his face sad, "Aye. Poor horse. T'was a magnificent white stallion. A half-pace earlier and Tarleton would be in his grave. I shall always regret the horse."

Williams said, "There's more to you than meets the eye, young fella."

~~<>~~

Gates' army rumbled southward but slowly. The weather was acceptable, but August was no time to march an army. Heat exhaustion, the choking dust, and laboring horses made for a miserable time. Worse, Gates had almost no supplies, and his men were constantly hungry.

As was always the case, men on the march had dysentery. This was compounded by poor sources of water and not enough of it when it was available. Men stumbled along in the heat, and their urine was almost black from dehydration.

Will was on the periphery of senior officer meetings and heard Gates' complaints that Caswell had taken the supplies and left him wanting. The way Will saw it, this march was premature and unsupported. Caswell's supplies were not Gates' supplies, and Richard Caswell had marched into South Carolina with the intent of keeping clear of Continental Army politics. Will had known Caswell nearly all his life, and he knew Dick Caswell as not a fool when it came to the political game. War is, after all, politics carried on in a different, more violent way.

Williams told Will that the army was marching to Rugeley's Mill to rendezvous with Caswell. Will thought, *I'll bet that was not General Caswell's idea.*

After a moment, Will said, "I was with Huger and Buford when we overnighted with Governor Rutledge at Rugeley's. 'Tis difficult to know if Rugeley is fully a loyalist or just caught in between. He was frantic to get Rutledge to leave his plantation – Clermont – as Tarleton's Legion was fast approaching. I could not determine whom that was protecting: Rutledge or himself."

Williams snorted, "The politics of this war are impossible to understand fully. Being from Maryland, I don't know Rugeley, but I know his type. Avowed patriots to patriots, avowed loyalists to loyalists. Fence-sitter. Hard to blame such a man because his entire livelihood is in the balance."

Will nodded. "I'll wager he has left the mill and plantation. Needs to be able to deny involvement on either side."

Williams smirked, "Considering that Cornwallis is trouncing us all over the fair state of South Carolina, I'd imagine Colonel Rugeley is supping handsomely at some English table and denouncing us rebels for the scum we are."

Will started snickering, which developed into a full belly laugh. After a moment, Williams joined in. Nearby troops wondered what was so comical that two senior officers laughed so hard.

~~<>~~

The army of some 5000 men was encamped at Rugeley's in the same field as before. The officers liberally used the plantation house as headquarters and accommodation. Already, the small army had emptied Rugeley's well-stocked wine cache, his root cellar, the various foods in the spring house near the mill creek, and all of the milled grain stocks. And that was on the first day.

It was August 6th, and Will, standing well into the background, heard Gates pontificating.

"I shall erect a defensive barrier to Cornwallis north of Camden. He's got military stores and various industries there. He'll be loath to lose those, and so will give battle. More, gentlemen, Lord Cornwallis will not be accommodating of us undoing his year's labor of subduing the South. We must stop him now, or he will march on to Charlotte Town and cut up through Virginia. That would render our fledgling nation impotent and badly damaged."

"We shall not attack but rather plan to defend. Our men are stout of heart, but so many are militia. Against well-trained forces, our men would find themselves outmatched. I would rather defend."

Nods and murmurs accompanied this. Will saw Caswell's expression, which was neutral but betrayed by his eyes, which said, *This is a fool's errand.*

~~<>~~

Will was sitting on the porch at Clermont Plantation house when Francis Marion and a band of disreputable-looking militiamen rode up on their Marsh Tackey horses. The rather rough-looking little horses were tough as leather, suggesting that their riders were just as tough. Each rider wore an oddly shaped, round leather cap without a bill but adorned with a crescent-shaped pewter emblem embossed with one word, "Liberty." Will later learned that this was a miniature gorget – the defiant symbol of South Carolina sovereignty. The single word "Liberty" made clear their cause.

Marion swung down, caught his balance, and limped up the four steps to the porch. "Hello, Will."

Will stood and shook hands, "Hello, Colonel Marion."

Marion smirked, "A colonel without a command!"

Will glanced at the militia. "This it?"

Marion said, "Aye. That is all I can muster. They come when they can and go as they must. They all are farmers and cannot leave their homes for long. The fields and animals keep them busy."

Will tagged along with Marion as he limped into the house looking for Gates.

The meeting was strained.

Gates kept Francis Marion waiting. Marion's leg obviously hurt, and he was in pain standing in the hallway.

When they were finally admitted to the chamber of the great man – the dining room where Rutledge and others had carried on as though there was no war – Gates finished writing something before looking up.

"Ah, Lieutenant Colonel Marion. Delighted to make your acquaintance, Sir."

Francis Marion bowed slightly and said, "General Gates. I come with a modest group of dedicated militia to offer what service I can."

Gates rose and looked out the window. "Modest, indeed, Sir. Yet welcome, of course, welcome."

The slightly sarcastic tone was not lost on Marion, who colored, his neck turning pink. Will knew the warning signs of a Marion explosion but was surprised that Marion held himself in check.

"Aye, Sir. They don't look like much, but they're hell in a fight."

Gates said, "I shall find a good use for you and your men, Colonel. But now, back to business, eh?"

Marion bowed slightly and turned to go; his hook nose wiggled with anger as he walked past Will.

Gates said, "Ah, Lieutenant Colonel Yelverton, is it?"

"Aye, Sir."

"Your business, Sir?"

"I was going to volunteer to join Colonel Marion."

"Ah, admirable. But you're with Colonel Williams and supernumerary. Best stay there, I think."

Will bowed slightly and said, "As you wish, Sir."

~~<>~~

Will walked out of the house and down the steps to find Francis Marion standing by his Marsh Tackey. Will saw that Marion was shaking with fury, his neck crimson.

Marion glanced up and saw Will. "Bastard."

Will said, "Aye. But that's his prerogative."

Marion said, "Oh, 'tis his prerogative, all right. But he lacks the troops to dismiss 40 volunteers simply because they wear rough clothing and are weekend warriors. These men risk homes and hearths to be here! Bloody Hell!"

Will said, "I volunteered to join your band, but *his nibs* refused me."

Marion looked at Will affectionately, "Best steer clear of our little band, Will. 'Tis not political just now to be a militia man of the State of South Carolina."

Will said, "But, are you not still a Continental officer?"

Marion glanced up at the sky as if beseeching some godly apparition, "I know not exactly what I am, Will. It appears the Continental Army has no real use for me. I have been writing to Rutledge about how I might form a militia. So has Tom Sumter. You met him?"

Will nodded. "Very hard man to cross, I'd imagine."

Marion nodded, "Aye. That is true. Sumter is running around in the hill country, playing merry hell with the British and Tories. He specifically did not want to return to military duty, but Tarleton burned his house, and now he is furious. He's fighting mad. They call him the Fighting Gamecock and with good reason."

Will said, "Sumter returned to the Continental Army, then?"

"Nay. He's raised a regiment – well, a band of partisans, really – and hopes to become something more than just a volunteer. So do I. Especially when dolts like Gates lead the Continental Army."

Will could see that Marion was barely controlling his temper. "Sumter's home was at Eutaw Springs, just around Pond Bluff. If they burned his house, I have to imagine they burned mine. I know not. I have been on the run for weeks, and I don't like it one bit."

464

Will decided against mentioning that Gates had defeated Burgoyne at Saratoga. Marion knew this but discounted it in his fury at being dismissed by Horatio Gates.

An orderly came trotting down the steps and rushed over to Marion. "Sir, General Gates' compliments. He asks you to take your men and range out in front of the Army, collecting or destroying all boats on the river. Details are in this note, Sir."

Marion snatched the note from the orderly and then thought better of it. "My apologies, young fellow. Please convey my compliments to the General and say that I shall be happy to comply with his request."

The orderly smiled, "No offense taken, Sir. I shall report your response to the General." He backed away a step and slightly bowed, "Sirs."

Will and Marion both touched their hats, and the orderly hurried away.

"Goddamnit, Will," Marion seethed. "Gates is getting rid of me. Well, I shall seize every bloody boat from here to bloody London itself!"

Will grinned, "That's the Frank Marion I know."

"Aye. T'will be the death of me, I suppose. Listen, Will, keep your head down and do whatever they want. Everyone knows you deserve a command."

Will said, "I care not about command."

Marion said, "One day, you will. Now I need to get on this horse and get out of here before I say or do something that I'll regret. I already regret riding in here."

Marion shook Will's hand. "We'll meet again. Once I have done the boats, I think the Continental Army can go to the Devil, and I shall go to Snow's Island. If things go badly, come there, and find the Britton family or other landholders – the Davises – and they'll help you find me."

Will said, "Aye. Where's Snow's Island?"

Marion said. "East, toward Georgetown. 'Tis a good place to hide in the swamps."

With that, Marion swung up into the saddle and said, "Don't let these fools get you killed, Will."

He spurred the tough little Marsh Tackey and trotted down the road at the head of the ragtag little band, his back ramrod straight.

Francis Marion did not look back.

Chapter 34 – Camden

A few days passed with low activity except for a couple of reports that Cornwallis was reinforcing his troops in Camden. Will heard more than one discussion that the two armies were almost at parity in terms of numbers. Will knew that numbers were not the sole factor. As always, the British, Loyalist legions, and other Tory militias were much better trained and had the advantage of equipment and food. The Redcoats were also typically older men, each with years of brutal military lifestyle and outlook. They were killers by profession.

The situation came to a head on August 14 when Gates had yet another report of more British troops marching toward Camden. Gates ordered the army to march toward Camden. Will did not know if Gates intended to improve his position and build the defenses he had discussed a few days earlier or if this was a rush to a headlong confrontation. But the die was cast, and the armies marched.

The army spent the day breaking camp, and the men got scant rations. Already dysentery was a common malady. The evening meal had little meat and no corn or other grain, but the men scoured an orchard for peaches. Most of the fruit was not yet ripe. This had an unfortunate effect as the unripe fruit gripped the men's bowels.

The army marched down the Great Wagon road – the trace that connected Camden with Charlotte Town – with men frequently falling out of the loose ranks to void their bellies and bowels. The stink was utterly the most powerful odor Will had ever encountered. That included a foul pig farm and abattoir that abutted the road from Savannah to Sunbury. In the months he spent in Savannah and Sunbury, Will learned to avoid that area. Here, there was no avoiding the stink that washed over everyone.

Will again rode with Williams. Will functioned as Williams' assistant, other duties not being assigned.

A few hundred yards back rode General Caswell, his position in the column directed by Gates to punish him for having withheld supplies. Will had visited with Caswell briefly during the encampment, but the business of command kept Caswell occupied.

~~<>~~

The August sun was late in setting, and the army continued to plod toward Camden. Mosquitoes whined, and men constantly swatted them. Several malaria cases had been left behind, but many troops were walking sick. And then there was the dysentery.

Will was glad he had eschewed the peaches and other foul food that made up the army's diet. He had visited Caswell and been offered decent rations, a wonderful respite from the gut-clenching slop available to the rest of the army. Caswell had offered him a militia commission if he would resign from the Continental Army, and Will had demurred, saying it was inopportune just then. But he would consider the offer.

After Marion's mistreatment and Gates' dismissive attitude toward Will, perhaps there was no future in remaining in the Continental Army. A militia command would open more doors in North Carolina after the war, assuming independence was won. If the war was lost, then the hangman would not hang a militia man any deader than a Continental officer.

Will glanced over his shoulder to see a young man with blond hair trotting out of the North Carolina ranks and squatting behind a bush. Zeke Carter had the shits. *Must be more to dysentery than just the green peaches,* Will thought.

The army marched on into the darkness. Occasional curses and thrashing of animals could be heard as man and beast lost footing in the gloom. The Great Wagon Road was only about one wagon wide, and it was easy to step off the track. Getting back on the track was not as simple, and the column occasionally halted while horses and wagons were pulled back out of this or that ditch.

It was 3 am when a sudden fusillade of musketry caused frantic activity in all directions. The firing was from the very front of the column, and Williams sarcastically said, "Seems we have found Cornwallis."

Will nodded in the darkness. "Aye. I hope we have the good sense to disengage and see what daylight brings."

Williams snorted. "Haven't had good sense so far, Will."

Not that anyone could see, but Will's mouth turned down in dismay. *Will this be another drubbing? But this time in the dark where friends kill friends as well as the enemy?*

Soon the firing stopped, and calm descended. Orderlies ran up and down the column, informing commanders that the army would halt until dawn when the army would move into battle formation.

Other orderlies and couriers ran up and down the column with orders. Maryland and Delaware troops to the right, wagon train to remain on the road, Virginia militia to the extreme left, Caswell's North Carolina militia to the near left. Gates and his staff, including Williams and Will, would remain in the center rear. Some 200 Maryland Continentals were held in reserve near Williams' and Will's position with Gates' staff.

Verbal orders from Gates were that the American army would hold along the road, arrayed as ordered with artillery in the center, and use swamps to either side as further defensive barriers.

~~<>~~

Dawn broke, and the Americans hurried to settle into their given positions. Will looked at the sad-looking array of poorly armed, sick, gripe-bellied men, some of whom stood half-bent with bowel cramps. Will's heart hurt as he remembered Noah Harris, sick and unarmed, crawling to get away from the fight at Brier Creek. Of course, Will had killed the gray-haired 71st Regiment Highlander who bayonetted Noah in the back, but that did not save Noah.

Will drew each of his two rifles and checked the prime. He checked the prime on all three pistols and the English dragoon carbine that rode on his thigh. He loosened Uncle Ewan's dirk in its scabbard and glanced at Williams, who checked his sword and a single pistol in his belt. Will wryly thought, *I got to get rid of a gun or two. Poor Molly is carrying a damned arsenal, and 'tis heavy.*

Williams grinned at Will. "I don't need to carry so many weapons when I'm with you, Will. Seems you have cornered the market on firearms."

Will said, "Aye, I'm a gunsmith. Plus, taking these two" – he nodded at the branders in his belt – "from Tarleton was such great fun."

471

Williams said, "I hear you are a dead eye with that rifle."

Will said, "Not so much. I killed Tarleton's horse and not Tarleton. Maybe today I can atone for that error."

Williams said, "Be ready to run, Will. Gates has arrayed his least trained, least experienced Virginia militia on the left. The British will align their most experienced troops on their right. This will collapse from our left. I don't imagine Gates has thought of that, though."

The sun rose slightly higher, and Will saw that Williams was right. Professional troops marched into position on the British right. Green jacket dragoons were in the middle – Tarleton's British Legion. They were opposite the wagon train and the few American artillery pieces.

Will saw Tarleton's horse, a new white charger to replace the poor animal Will had killed. Clearly excited by all the activity, the horse nervously pranced to and fro. It was easily 400 yards, so Will left Josie in her scabbard. Maybe later, Will would make good his promise to shoot Tarleton when he closed within 300 yards.

Will hoped so.

Bastard.

~~<>~~

An orderly trotted up to Williams and Will. "Colonel Yelverton, compliments of General Gates. He wishes you to join General Caswell to observe and liaise as necessary."

Will touched his hat and said, "Compliments to the General. I shall be happy to attend General Caswell."

The orderly left, and Will glanced at Williams, who said, "Caution, Will. Gates knows the militia will be lambs to the slaughter."

Will nodded and glanced toward Caswell, who was on his horse alongside a couple of aides, talking to a company commander and pointing out positions. "General Caswell is a good commander. I hope he can make decisions without being forced to take positions that are weak and vulnerable to attack."

Williams said, "Aye, I hope so too. But remember, the British always follow European tradition and array their strongest troops on their right as a position of honor. The dragoons being in the middle is more a cavalry tactic than an honor. Tarleton needs no reassurance of his position with Cornwallis. Tarleton is the Lord's attack dog, and no two ways about it."

Will said, "Thanks, Sir. Best of luck in this."

Williams said, "In all seriousness, Will, be sure to find an escape path. I believe the British will attack viciously on our left, and the dragoons will be right up the middle with sabers slashing and attacking the supply wagons as well as anyone who accidentally gets in their way. That artillery will fire a few rounds to spook our inexperienced troops, and then t'will be hell to pay."

Will touched his hat and said, "I hope to see you tomorrow."

~~<>~~

The early morning mist cleared as Will and Molly, followed by Cuthbert and his horse, trotted to Caswell's small retinue. Will touched his hat and said, "General Gates' compliments, Sir. He has asked me to be at your disposal and liaise as needed."

Caswell snorted. "Damned, glad you're here, Will. But Gates doesn't give a fig about liaisons. He sent you here, so he has one less field officer to worry about when the bullets fly. I think he probably wants someone to blame if this goes badly."

Will said, "I didn't think you needed any help, Sir."

Caswell said, "Oh, I need all the help I can get. But I don't have a command for you. I keep looking to Brigadier General Stevens with the Virginia militia, and he's having quite a time getting everyone in line. That does not bode well. Ed Stevens is a good man, but his troops are not ready for this. Neither are mine, for that matter. I hope my 1800 men are sufficient to blunt any assault."

474

Will looked at the raggedy Virginia line and had a flashback of Waxhaws and the Virginians who had been mercilessly slashed and battered by Tarleton's men. This situation looked identical.

Will looked over to the American right and saw that DeKalb had arrayed his troops with General Mordecai Gists' Maryland and Delaware regiments and positioned their three guns to command the center.

Caswell's 1800 men were well aligned, and the two guns were set to support the center. General Bill Smallwood's small group of Marylanders was in the center rear as a reserve. This was as good as it would get for the Americans.

Caswell said, "Look yonder, Will. The British have placed Rawdon and his troops on their left, our right. Lord Rawdon is an exceptional commander, and our Maryland and Delaware Continentals will have quite a fight on their hands."

Will looked across the waist-high wire grass and scattered pines that made up the higher ground, the field where the fight would take place. It was difficult ground at best. No real clear field of fire. Dry grass that would catch fire in an instant. He saw green jackets milling about.

Will said, "Tarleton in the center truly worries me, General. He is utterly without principle. He will come after us with a vengeance."

Caswell said, "Look at the discipline of the infantry on their right, our left. They are like clockwork. I really fear for the Virginians."

Will looked across Caswell's troops. He searched for Sam Hawks and Zeke Carter. Chuck Black was easily visible because he was mounted. But Sam and Zeke were just two more militiamen, similarly attired in hunting clothes and broad hats. Finally, Will saw Sam near Chuck Black, which made sense. Zeke was harder to spot, but finally, Will located him with the Hillsborough Regiment. Will thought, *At least they have been in a fight before.*

~~<>~~

Will saw couriers rushing to DeKalb, Gist, and the other commanders on the right. In short order, the Continentals began to move forward. The American guns blazed out and reloaded to boom again. Gates had ordered the attack.

Bagpipes skirled, and fifes trilled as drums rolled down the British right, and the well-trained infantry stepped forward, bayonets glinting in the sun. As they advanced, British guns burst forth with a barrage that cut into the American lines like a scythe.

A few pops of muskets and bangs of American cannons and the Virginians suddenly started backing up until men in the rear ranks were being pressured by front-rank soldiers who scuttled backward in the face of the British bayonets. A loud "Huzzah! Huzzah!" from the British bayonet line and the Virginians broke completely.

Caswell sent word to all North Carolina commanders to hold fast and present volley fire. He also ordered the North Carolina militia to sweep left to refuse the British the opportunity to flank the entire American position.

American guns blasted canister at the implacable Redcoats as they stepped forward. Indeed, a few British troops were killed or maimed, but most walked through the hail of lead as if it were not even there.

Will saw some frantic activity at the front of Caswell's troops. Suddenly, a British round shot from their 6-pound field pieces cut through the North Carolinians. Will saw Chuck Black waving his sword and haranguing his men to stand firm. Will saw Sam Hawks, in one of his lesser moments, turn and run toward the rear.

Zeke Carter was not so fortunate. Poor Zeke, a good man, stood rooted to the spot. Will watched helplessly as Zeke tried to reload the Kennedy rifle. It was a mistake to bring a rifle to a musket fight. Powder, ball, rammer...all slow with a tight patch. Prime and cock.

A round shot from one of the British field guns flew across the two hundred yards that separated the armies' front, bounded three times on the sunbaked August dirt, slashed into the North Carolina line, and killed three militiamen before it decapitated Zeke Carter.

Will watched in horror as a fountain of blood sprayed into the air from Zeke's headless body. Zeke's Kennedy rifle was in his lifeless right hand, its butt on the ground. The rifle propped Zeke's corpse up for a moment until death and gravity combined to topple Zeke into eternity.

Will snatched Josie from her deer hide scabbard, the soft case Zeke's wife, Abby Kennedy, had lovingly made for Will. He checked the prime and looked across nearly 300 yards of the battlefield, searching among the pines and the tall grass for the gun that had killed Abby's husband.

There! It was the third gun, and a burly sergeant was aligning the trail to point the gun at more North Carolina infantry. Will cocked Josie and carefully aimed at the sergeant.

WhizzzzCraaaaak! The artillery sergeant sat on his rear suddenly and then flopped.

Will spat to no one in particular, *"Bastard."*

At that moment, the North Carolina militia broke and ran as Rawdon's troops slammed into the Maryland and Delaware troops commanded by DeKalb on the American right. Will saw

DeKalb unhorsed. It appeared he was wounded. Dead? Will did not know.

Will put Josie in her scabbard and – in a rare moment – drew his sword. He waived his sword and shouted at Cuthbert, "Cuth, try to stop these men from breaking!"

Will put Molly between the Carolina militia and their escape route and slashed around with the sword. "Stop! Stop, damn you! Turn and fight, or they'll run you down and kill you from behind!"

Cuthbert joined in, waving his sword and shouting at the disorganized militia to fall in and face the enemy.

Caswell was similarly broadside to the troops, and Chuck Black was in front of Caswell.

Chuck shouted, "God damn you all to hell! Get back in line, you cowardly poltroons!"

But it was all to no avail. The North Carolina line simply flowed around the officers like rushing water around rocks in a trout stream. A few slowed, but most were frantically rushing toward the Great Wagon Road and Charlotte Town.

Will braved the flow of humanity to wade against the tide toward the British. He desperately wanted to get to Zeke. Zeke's death seemed so unreal that Will was compelled to witness Zeke's body up close.

A lifetime of moments later, Will found Zeke's headless corpse, the Kennedy rifle in his white-knuckled death grip. A militia man was running by as Will arrived.

Will shouted, "You! Yes, you. Give me that rifle!"

The militia man paused, looked at Will, and then at the rifle. "Bollocks! Get it yourself." He turned and ran full tilt toward the rear.

Will considered shooting the militiaman but simply dropped Molly's reins and swung out of the saddle. In one stride, he was beside Zeke's lifeless body and snatched the finely wrought Kennedy rifle. Another bound and Will was on Molly's back. A musket ball whizzed past Will's head; another plucked at his sleeve.

Two Redcoats rushed toward Will. He shot one with the English dragoon carbine, and the man went down on his face, a limp, shapeless form. The second Redcoat grabbed at Molly's reins and tried to pull her head around.

Will leaned forward with the horse pistol and shot the man. The buck and ball load shredded the Redcoat's upper torso, and the man collapsed in a spray of blood and gore. Will, still clutching Zeke's Kennedy rifle, looked at Zeke's body one last time. Zeke Carter was truly dead, but at least one day, Will could give the rifle to little William Yelverton "Yel" Carter and tell of his father's bravery.

Using his knees, Will turned Molly and sought a target. Will saw a British officer doing a fine job driving his troops forward. The officer's reward for a good job was the ball Zeke had loaded in the Kennedy just before his death. Will shot the officer in the heart and only had a second to watch him collapse before a tide of Redcoats rushed him.

Will nudged Molly with his heels, and she picked up a gallop toward Cuthbert, who waited just behind Caswell.

As Will and Molly raced up, Caswell shouted, "We have to leave. Retreat!"

The command was unnecessary. The entire Virginia line had been routed, and the North Carolina militia was in a foot race to overtake them. Will saw Sam Hawks, wild-eyed and weaponless, rushing ahead of hundreds of other North Carolinians.

Caswell said, "Nothing we can do here but stand and be killed. Let's go."

Will and Cuthbert turned their horses and cantered behind Caswell and two of his staff officers.

Will shouted across the melee, "Chuck! Let's go! Retreat!"

Chuck Black, the killing fury upon him, looked wildly about. He slashed his sword at a Redcoat and shouted, "Why? This is just getting good!"

Will shouted, "Come on now! You'll die if you stay!"

Chuck seemed to realize the gravity of the situation and, after one more mad slash with his sword, turned and galloped after Caswell, Will, and the other officers.

~~<>~~

Will and Caswell, several of his officers, and Cuthbert sat on their horses at the intersection of a couple of side roads and the Great Wagon Road to Charlotte.

The Continentals had fought hard before reluctantly giving up the obviously lost fight. Still, Will estimated that Americans wounded and captured numbered around a third of the American force, some 1000 men. Worse, Tarleton had captured eight guns and some 60 wagons of precious supplies.

Tarleton's men were ruthless in sabering infirm, wounded, and civilian wagon masters in the process. Tarleton's legion drove past the wagons and continued a pursuit, bent on killing every American he could find. They finally left off the pursuit, but not before adding to their bloodthirsty reputation.

This action, so soon after the massacre at Waxhaws, gave a lie to the story that Tarleton's men were angry at an American deception of firing under a white flag. Will thought, *No one will ever know the truth of that situation. I know I fired at Tarleton and never saw a white flag until afterward.*

Gates was nowhere to be seen. Colonel Otho Williams was idling under a tree as Caswell, Will, and the others rode up.

Caswell asked, "Where's Gates?"

Williams laconically said, "Good afternoon, Sir. I regret that I know not. I must report he was last seen galloping down yonder road. I would imagine his destination was as far north as his horse would take him. I last spoke to him just before the battle, I advised him to get closer to the actual fight to command the action better, but alas, that would have impeded his escape."

Caswell snorted, "Colonel Williams, you are a master of understatement."

Looking around, Caswell said, "Gentlemen, let's go. This is most ignominious, and we shall all pay the price for this foolhardy day."

Will glanced at Cuthbert and held out Zeke Carter's Kennedy rifle, "Can you take this?"

Cuthbert said, "Of course, Sir. It will be an honor."

Will nodded his thanks.

"I will get it to Zeke Carter's boy one day."

Will nudged Molly, and she turned to follow Caswell.

They headed north toward Charlotte Town.

Chapter 35 – March to Hillsborough

The disheartened group walked their horses north on the Great Wagon Road that led toward Waxhaws and Charlotte. It was slow, but if they mounted the nearly exhausted animals, several would die from the extra effort. As it was, Will worried about Molly carrying his usual war load of rifles, bedroll, fire kit, saddlebags, and other items. Molly's head hung with weariness; Will worried that she might collapse any minute. *Is it time to let her go out to pasture and have a quiet life?*

Caswell's face was flushed. Will looked at him with concern. "Are you well, Sir?"

Caswell brushed off Will's worry. "My physick says I have elevated pulse tension. My blood seems to be under higher pressure than desirable. Says t'will kill me one day. Not today."

Will fretted. "Sir, should you be walking?"

Caswell smiled, "Now don't mother hen me, Will. But yes, the quack says the best for me would be to get more exercise, as he calls it. Marching is exercise outside in the fresh air."

Will nodded but resolved to speak with Dicky Caswell when next he saw him. Caswell's oldest son, Colonel William Caswell, might be available sooner. Will would seek out one or the other. Governor/General Richard Caswell was too valuable to lose from his public service.

~~<>~~

The small band trudged in the late-August heat. Insects buzzed and flitted. Birds kept to the shade, as did the remnants of the North Carolina Militia. The small band of defeated warriors snaked from shade patch to shade patch like a crowd weaving Saturday night drunks. The shade cut the brutal sun, but mosquitos inhabited the foliage and waited to suck blood from every exposed piece of skin. The whine of mosquitoes was part of the larger symphony of nature that was oblivious to the human enterprise of war. Will grinned. It was like Scilla and Charybdis in *The Odyssey*. The sun would redden the skin to the point of pain, or the mosquitoes would chew it to ribbons, turning it red in a different, but no less painful, way.

Days wore on into a week and then two. Walking was slow, but riding the horses would destroy them as assets. Then, what would the army do for transport? Worse, every time a horse collapsed, and quite a few did, who would carry the gear? The wagon train was lost at Camden.

Caswell said, "I hope someone at Hillsboro will take command. We must reconstitute this army if we hope to resist Cornwallis' next offensive. I am certain that will be a thrust into North Carolina. Probably toward Charlotte Town. Right now, we're completely vulnerable."

Will nodded. "For myself, I know not what to do. As a Continental officer, I don't know to whom I should report. I'm certain that there will be someone in authority at Hillsborough."

Caswell said, "Aye. Should be. But who do they report to? Everyone except Washington has a superior officer. Even Washington is beholden to Congress. I imagine that there will be some repercussions from Congress' insistence on Gates over Washington's choice."

"Who was his choice?"

"Ah, that would be Nathanael Greene of Rhode Island. His first name is spelled Nathanael. Sensitive about that, I hear. Vastly better commander than Lincoln, and of course, Gates."

Will said, "We had heard the rumors about Greene. I had the pleasure of briefly meeting Greene at Brandywine. I delivered Washington's order to wheel right to meet the British flanking attack from Birmingham Meeting House. Even in the heat of battle, he was a pleasant gentleman."

"Saved Washington, did you?"

"Nay, but I was among the ones who discovered Cornwallis had marched around our right and crossed two fords, climbed some small hills, and was about to bash into our flank. Washington believed me and others who told him of this threat. He sent me to Greene."

Caswell said, "Will, I've always seen a core of steel in you. You're also smart and capable. I was right to recommend you to my Masonic Brother George Washington. There are greater things in store for you after this conflict."

"But, Sir, I still want to go to the frontier and be a gunsmith."

"Aye, I know that. But the way to success is to capitalize on the acquaintances you have made during your duties – Francis Marion, Colonel Williams, not to mention General Washington, and so many others. You must become a Freemason, as well. A pathway for you is to open a gun repair and manufacturing shop, train some workers, and become more of a proprietor than the man with the screwdriver."

Will said, "But I like wielding a screwdriver."

"Of course you do. I love getting a scythe and cutting in a field. But I didn't amass a fortune by swinging that blade. Instead, I made it by knowing how to swing the blade and assuring that others swung it properly. I hope that makes sense."

Will said, "How would I do that?"

Caswell said, "Did you not inherit a valuable property in Charlestown from your poor, deceased wife?"

Will choked up. "Aye. But 'tis not mine."

"Oh, but it is, Will. Let us set aside sentiment and realize that the home you inherited was gifted by your late wife's father, and he knows 'tis now yours. If the house survives the British occupation, you should sell it and any other property. Do you have any idea of its worth?"

Will looked glum, "I understand such homes are valued at £5,000."

Caswell stopped in his tracks, "£5,000!? My God, but that is a vast fortune, Will. Now listen to me. £5,000 is more than many of our richest citizens might be able to raise. Add the value of your savings on deposit with me, the property you will inherit from the Koontz's, and all the possible war-service land grants you might receive, and you could easily be one of any of the States' leading citizens. My God, but you are modestly among the richest men in America."

It was Will's turn to stop. He looked up at Caswell, who was both taller in stature and a man whom Will admired from childhood. "Sir, will you guide me?"

Caswell smiled and said, "It would be my honor to help you see opportunities. But first, we must win this war!"

They walked on.

Hillsborough looked considerably different from the last time Will had seen it. And that was only about six weeks ago. Men, beaten down from the long marches to and from Camden, poor food, and the absolute licking applied by Cornwallis, Rowden, and Tarleton, sat in small groups. The August heat, the dust of the couple thousand men, and the makeshift hovels and ratty little tents made for a sad existence.

Will did what he always did. He went hunting. Cuthbert went along and killed a couple of deer himself. Will and Cuth would come into camp dragging one or two deer carcasses behind each horse, and the men would fall on the animal with glee, skinning, washing, and butchering. In no time, stews were cooking.

The men were quite adept at scavenging for wild onions. A stock of root vegetables was kept by the Quartermaster, which kept the food from being monotonous. Most importantly, one of the officers from Wilmington had brought a wagon full of salt from his seaside salt flats. Salt was so valuable that there was always a guard on the wagon.

Will did see Sam Hawks, but Sam avoided him. Will thought, *Ashamed of himself, I suppose.*

Will was not the senior Continental officer in the camp. Like many others, he had no unit and no commander. He reported to no one. Confusion reigned supreme, with Gates disappearing and no one appointed to command the Southern Department. Will felt compelled to remain.

Content to rest and let Molly recover from weeks on the road and several desperate fights, Will sat in the sun reading *The Odyssey*. He was dogged in his pursuit of this challenging book. *I will finish this damned thing if 'tis the last thing I do.*

Caswell ambled over. "Hello, Will."

Will scrambled to stand, "General Caswell, good morning, Sir."

Caswell plopped down on a stump, saying, "Keep your seat, Will."

Will relaxed on his two logs arranged into a makeshift chair. "How are you, Sir?"

Caswell looked bleak. "Not terribly well, Will. My blood has really been high, as you can see from my face. Sometimes my head feels like it might explode. But that is not the worst of the day. I just heard the North Carolina Assembly is replacing me with William Smallwood of Maryland as militia commander. Quite ignominious, that."

Will said, "But you're a native son, former governor, and successful commander. They would import a man from another state?"

Caswell looked into the distance, seeing nothing, "You're only as good as your last success, Will. Fail once, and they throw you to the dogs. Smallwood is a Continental officer and has succeeded in several fights since the beginning. He brilliantly covered the retreat out of New York at Camden; his Marylanders held strong until they were forced from the field. My units simply collapsed. So, they've decided to sack me. Of course, I'll be back once the dust settles. But for now, I'm *persona non grata.*

Will looked confused at this last phrase.

Caswell smiled. "Sorry. Too many years as a lawyer. *Persona non grata* means a person who is not wanted."

Will smiled, "That's a big word, but I'm glad to know you will be back, Sir."

"Oh, aye. Politicians are only briefly out of favor. The people will soon demand me back when another fool publicly fails."

Will said, "You're not a fool, Sir."

Caswell looked wistful, "Oh, we're all fools, Will."

Will looked glum and searched for something useful to say.

Caswell relieved the silence, "Now, what I came to see you for is to discuss your wealth and future. That is if I'm not being impertinent to suggest it."

Will was happy to change the subject. "I can think of nothing I'd like better than to have you help me with my situation."

~~<>~~

Caswell had very good ideas, many of which would have to wait until the war ended. Most relied upon the United States prevailing.

Caswell recommended divesting the Charlestown house. Its value of £5,000 was immense and would buy an immense tract of land in a state like Georgia. Will had fallen in love with Georgia and thought that a good idea. He was less enamored of Caswell's suggestion that he must populate a plantation with slaves.

Will abhorred slavery and had taken great risks in getting his former slave, Jack, to Philadelphia. There, Will facilitated Jack's reuniting with his older brother, Caesar. Caesar had been freed years earlier by Will's father, Zech. Buying slaves, and setting up a plantation seemed anathema to Will.

Caswell had also asked if Will wanted to stay in the Continental Army. Will thought his place was to fight for freedom and help establish the Nation he hoped to make his home for the rest of his life. Caswell reminded him that you could still fight for freedom and establish the Western North Carolina frontier. A militia commission was more aligned with those goals.

Caswell had also discussed going west to Tennessee and meeting John Sevier. Caswell and Sevier were speculating on land in Western North Carolina and Tennessee. Will was welcome to join that endeavor. With £5,000, he could be a full partner. This appealed to Will because it preserved his dream of the frontier as well as owning land without having slaves. The militia appealed to Will for the same reasons.

The discussion raged for most of the afternoon. For Will, staying in the Army was an unresolved question but one that demanded consideration.

Will asked, "What shall I do while awaiting a new commander and a new unit?"

Caswell said, "Go to Smallwood as he is the senior Continental Officer present with my compliments. Ask for a furlough for yourself and your orderly, and go home. Or go to Bear Creek. There was a girl there, wasn't there?"

Will looked pensive, "Yes, Abby Kennedy Carter is there. I would have married her, but she married another. His name was Zeke Carter. He was killed at Camden. I retrieved his rifle and wanted to take it to his child to remember his father."

Caswell looked at Will hard, "You still love Abby, Will. I saw it in your face just now."

"Aye, Sir. But t'would be most dishonorable to simply report her husband's death and then expect to take up where we left off before all this war."

"Nonsense! I have lost a wife and mourned as you have mourned Mary. Then I found another and have been happy. 'Tis the way of the world, Will. I must also counsel that Abby will need a husband, and her child will need a father. A rich father would be even better. She will want children, and you will want children to carry your name."

Will said, "Zeke Carter named his child after me – William Yelverton Carter."

"Good! You already have a namesake. 'Tis your duty to raise that boy. He must be educated, and I shall help with the details if you allow me."

Will grinned. "Of course, Sir. Your help has always been most valuable. I'll see Smallwood this afternoon."

Chapter 36 – The Road to Bear Creek

Smallwood was only too happy to be rid of a supernumerary officer and quickly signed a 45-day furlough for Will and Cuthbert.

Will said to Cuthbert, "You know you could go to Georgia rather than go with me."

"Aye, Sir, but the road to Georgia is rife with bandits, loyalists, and all manner of danger. My home in Sunbury is occupied by the British, so there's nowhere to go. I'll be happy to ride with you. T'will be a pleasant distraction after all the fighting."

Will grinned, "Glad for the company, Cuth."

Furlough papers in hand and dressed in hunter's garb, Will and Cuthbert trotted out of the camp about mid-day. Their uniforms were carefully rolled and folded and put in saddlebags on a sturdy pack mule that Will had bought for a Spanish dollar. Highway robbery at that price, but worthwhile if it spared Molly's tired back.

Will thought, *Good riddance to miserable camp life, if only for a brief time!*

He smiled at the prospect of hunting with David Kennedy. They were great friends and very good in the woods together, each knowing what the other was thinking and doing. On the other hand, Will was deeply concerned with the sad duty of reporting Zeke's death to Abby, Micah Carter, and the Kennedy family. He worried that it might make Abby hate him. He also worried that Micah would blame him for Zeke's death.

When Will confided this fear, Cuthbert said, "Sir, you were merely the observer of the sad situation. I saw it, too. T'was nothing to be done."

"Aye, but I don't know that Abby and Micah will see it that way."

Loyalists were abroad in the countryside. David Fanning was the chief culprit. He had been known to waylay riders intending to rob them and demand loyalty to the King. Will considered that it would be difficult to convince someone to be loyal to the King immediately after being robbed, but that was the kind of thinking.

Before leaving camp, Will had learned that Fanning was recruiting loyalists in the Deep River area, south toward Bear Creek. This did not bode well for an uneventful ride, and Will and Cuthbert wore hunting clothes to reduce interest in their passage. Both men rode with loaded weapons to hand.

As always, Will's well-used English dragoon carbine, loaded with buck and ball and an extra dash of powder, rode on his right thigh. Tarleton's Brander pistols and Uncle Ewan's oiled and sharpened Scottish dirk rode in his belt. Josie and Zeke's Kennedy rifles rode in the scabbards attached to Molly's saddle. The ancient horse pistol rode in its leather saddle holster. Will remembered his promise to reduce the number of weapons poor Molly had to tote. He resolved to pass on Uncle Ewan's horse pistol to little Yell Carter. It would be a legacy and help to cut the weight carried on Molly's back. Will also would not take another rifle, the carbine, two Branders, and Josie being sufficient weaponry, he thought.

Cuthbert had his British officer's fusil riding on his right thigh and an array of pistols tucked into various locations. Cuth's sharpened sword hung from his saddle. Unlike Will's officer's sword, which was more of a stabbing weapon, Cuth's sword was a cavalry weapon with a curved blade and thick spine. In the fight at Moncks Corner, Cuth had desperately slashed a Green-coated enemy militiaman as he ran to his horse. Cuth now carried Will's .45 caliber rifle. Will had made it a gift and well deserved.

~~<>~~

They clopped along companionably in the stultifying September heat. The hottest part of the day still lay ahead. Will wanted to put miles behind him. It was some 60 miles to Kennedy's.

499

Although there was a town named Bear Creek in the same southwest direction as Kennedy's rifle works, Kennedy's was also called Bear Creek. Perhaps this was why Will's letters two years ago never arrived. Of course, there was no official mail service, so every letter Will sent was via some form of courier. God only knew if they survived their trip with the letters.

That first evening, Will and Cuthbert made camp in the lee of a small rock ledge. They built a small fire that would reflect off the rocks and provide light. They cooked some fresh venison from a deer Will had killed the day before. After this, their food would be jerky and meat from tonight's supper. The fire kept animals away but would attract bandits. They took turns sleeping, but the night was uneventful.

The following day was, however, different. As they made their way southward toward Lindley's Mill, Will and Cuthbert, saw several damaged farms and houses. Some were burned, others ransacked. It was surprising that much of the damage was recent. Will did not believe the Army was ransacking and burning farms on its march from South Carolina. Indeed, there was foraging for food, but Will's experience was that the Continental Army paid for supplies with vouchers and did not simply take what it wanted. He had not experienced civilian holdings being burned.

Thomas Lindley, Proprietor of Lindley's Mill, came out of the mill building carrying a musket. "Who might you be?"

Will said, "We're travelers heading to Bear Creek to visit my family."

Lindley said, "You're heavily armed for mere travelers."

Cuth replied, "Aye, but lots of burned and pillaged farms means carrying a gun is a good idea."

Lindley pointed with his chin at their saddles, "Not five or six like you have."

Will grinned, "I won't let a bandit take my horse and other property lightly. My friend here is not minded to be robbed, either."

Lindley smirked, "I'd say you need to be better armed than that and fierce fighters into the bargain. Fanning has been hanging about in these parts. His main camp is at Cox's Mill, not far from here. Are you minded to independence or the King?"

Will demurred, "We're minded to getting to Bear Creek, is all."

Lindley stuck a thumb in his own chest, "I'm a Patriot, and I'm damned if those Tory bastards will take my product. I produce flour, grits, and other ground grains like rye and barley. 'Tis not much, but 'tis all I have."

Will said, "I wish you well, and hope Fanning does not molest you."

Lindley glanced around with a vigilant eye. "I'll shoot the first son-of-a-bitch that steps on my land planning to take anything."

Will smiled, "I hope you will be kind enough to let us pass through in peace."

"Aye. You say nothing, but I can tell a Continental soldier when I see one. Go in peace, but be ready to defend yourself. Fanning has been recruiting hereabouts, and you never know when some fool will want to show off his new hat cockade by shooting an unarmed man."

Will nodded, "Good day to you, Sir. And I hope you and yours remain safe."

~~<>~~

The day wore into the afternoon, and the sun began to pound the two riders. Despite the occasional clouds and the frequent shade of tall trees on either side of the road, the heat continued like an omnipresent beast. Sweat popped everywhere, and both men removed their hunting shirts to ride, wearing only light linen shirts, trousers, and boots. It was a small relief.

As they rounded a blind curve in the road, Will saw birds burst from cover about a half mile ahead. Will and Cuth stopped and backed up to shelter in the curve. They waited. The birds had burst from cover on the left side of the road. Soon, more birds flushed out of the brush on the right side of the road. Both bird disturbances were roughly the same distance out. It could either be an ambush or some predatory animal hunting on one side of the road and then the other. Will bet on an ambush.

Will said, "Cuth, let's get off the road and go about a mile west."

"Think those birds flew because there are ambushers in those trees?"

Will nodded, "Aye, the first group that flew was a warning. A second covey flushing made it clear that something was not right."

They trotted across a fallow field that had not been plowed for at least two seasons. Will carefully kept a stand of trees between him and the copse where the birds had flown. They walked their horses down into a little swale in the ground which made it even harder to see them. Once there, they stopped.

Will and Cuth dismounted and tied their horses to a small bush. Still below the swale, Will checked the prime on his carbine and all three pistols. Cuth did the same.

They crawled up on the swale bareheaded so that their wide-brimmed hats would not be visible. Then they watched for a while. Will did not know how long they had waited; he reckoned at least a quarter-hour when three men on horseback trotted out of the nearest copse of trees. Birds flew again, and four more men appeared from the brush and trees on the other side of the road.

Will grinned. When he first came to Bear Creek, he was jumped by two highwaymen and nearly killed. Elijah Wambleeska Hammon saved his life by killing the leader of the pair. Will grinned at the memory of his own inexperience that got him into the scrape as well as Elijah's off-handed ways.

Elijah was a Lumbee Indian. Wambleeska was the Indian name for the white-headed eagle. When Will had time, he would visit Elijah at his village deep in the wilderness near Drowning Creek. Maybe he and Cuth could go there on this trip.

They watched the seven men as they conferred about something. One man animatedly waved his arms toward the road. Others shook their heads. One, apparently the leader, pointed toward the direction Will and Cuth came from, and the group trotted off that way.

Will looked to make sure he and Cuth could not be seen from the road and said, "Cuth, you keep an eye on them from here; I'm going to watch over here to be sure they don't circle back on us."

Time wore on, and both Will and Cuth were sweating heavily from being in the sun when they decided the ambushers were gone. They walked their horses into the shade, where mosquitos hummed incessantly. A sluggish little creek offered drinking water for the horses and a chance to splash water on their hot faces.

Will said, "I think we can get back on the road, but this episode tells us there are highwaymen, maybe loyalists, about."

Cuth said, "Do you think we should consider going across the country and avoiding these roads."

Will considered that for a moment. "I don't know the way, and any creeks or rivers will force us to either a ford or ferry. That's where the trouble will be."

Will gave Molly a carrot and patted her. Her hide was cooler now, and she was ready to move on. Cuth's horse looked refreshed from the water. The mule, on the other hand, was reluctant to move. Will had to jerk its bridle to get it out of the shade. He regretted having to bring the mule. It was a good thing the mule had not brayed and given them away to the highwaymen.

~~<>~~

It was late afternoon on the third day of their journey when Cuthbert pointed out some circling buzzards about half a mile ahead. Will and Cuth left the road and circled to the east around this area, pausing to see what was interesting to the buzzards. Carrion birds will eat any dead animal, so this could simply be a dead rabbit or some other small animal. It could also be dead people.

They came upon the backside of a burned-out farmstead with a dead, half-butchered cow in the yard. Highwaymen must have attacked the farm, killed the cow, and taken some meat, leaving the rest for the buzzards. Already, the carcass was reeking of bloat and rot.

A woman's voice said, "Git, or I'll shoot you both!"

Will looked around at the partially burned cabin, where a woman with white hair and a smoke-stained dress pointed a musket at them.

Will said, "Madam, we are not here to hurt you. Are you all right?"

"I'm not hurt if that's what you're asking, but I am far from all right. My man never hurt nobody, ever, but the Loyalists kilt him deader'n a stone. He's in the back of the cabin, but I ain't got the strength to bury him."

Will said, "We will bury him for you."

"I don't know you, and I damn sure don't trust nobody I don't know."

Will said, "I understand, Madam. Permit me to introduce myself. I am Lieutenant Colonel William Yelverton of the

Continental Army. This is Sergeant Charles Cuthbert of the same. We are on a brief furlough."

The musket wavered a bit as the old woman took in this information. "I heard y'all done got whupped a bunch o' times down in South Carolina."

"Aye, we did take a beating. But the Army will be back, and we shall see to the British."

"Huh. You ain't seen to shit so far. But I gotta trust someone to take care of Isaac. He was a good man and deserves a Christian burial."

Will said, "Do you have kin where you can go stay? This place is ruined."

"Aye, my daughter lives a day's walk that way," she pointed with her chin.

Will said, "We'll be happy to escort you, Madam. We are heading in that same direction."

The old woman leaned the musket on the sagging door frame and said, "Well, I gotta trust somebody, an' you're it. We need to get Isaac in the ground a'fore he starts stinkin' like that cow."

To emphasize this point, a buzzard landed on the cow's ribcage and, completely unconcerned about the human presence, delicately pecked a strip of bloody meat from the exposed flesh.

The burial complete and prayers said, Will and Cuth helped get the woman's few possessions together in a croker sack. They tied the sack on the mule and helped the sad, tired old woman up on the mule's back.

As they walked their horses toward the road, Will asked, "Are you all right, Ma'am?"

"As I said, I'm far from all right, but y'all helped do what had to be done. Now I'll live with my daughter and try not to be a burden. My name is Sarah Wilson. People call me Sally. I ain't never been ma'am to nobody."

Will grinned at this. The old lady had spirit, and that meant she would survive. He asked, "Did you want to take a moment before we go down the road?"

"Hell, no. This here place ain't been nothin' but work since I were 17-year-old. I reckon I'm near 57 now. Isaac was the one who wanted it. He was a good man, but he's dead, and so's this farm."

~~<>~~

Sally's daughter and son-in-law owned a small farm about 10 miles away. The son-in-law was gone to the militia, so Sally's daughter, Honesty, was alone with seven children. Honesty said Sally would be welcome. Honesty also said that David Fanning

508

had been through the area in the last few days and would likely remain nearby.

This was not good news for Will. The chance of encountering David Fanning seemed stronger every mile they rode.

Will and Cuthbert bid farewell to Sally and Honesty. Sally smiled a crooked, gap-toothed grin. "Y'all skeered the pure hell out of me when I seen ya. Damned if you ain't armed to the teeth. But you buried Isaac and got me here. For that, I thankee. I hope y'all kill every one of them goddamn Torys."

Honesty said, "Now, mother. We wish everyone well."

Sally smirked and spat on the ground, "Not them goddamn Tories. Not after what they done to yore Daddy and our farm."

~~<>~~

Will and Cuthbert had enjoyed a mostly uneventful ride. About five miles from Honesty and Sally Wilson's home, a group of Tory militia burst around a curve in the road about a half mile ahead. They were at a solid canter and were closing in a hurry. Will didn't know if he and Cuth had been seen, but they turned off the road and galloped across a fallow field into some trees. They held beneath a small swale.

Will and Cuth quickly checked the prime on all their weapons. Will drew Zeke Carter's Kennedy Rifle and cocked it. If the militia turned toward them, he would shoot with the rifles first to try to cut the Tories' numbers. Cuth had Will's .45 caliber rifle and was ready to do the same.

A few minutes passed with no real activity. Then, Will saw two Tory militia pop out of a small swale near the road. The two Tories rode with a purpose toward Will and Cuthbert. The other group of Tories seemed to continue down the road.

Will looked at Cuthbert, "Cuth, I think this pair is investigating us, and the others will get off the road and come this way about a half mile down. They mean to pinch us in the middle, and we're going to have to fight."

Cuthbert said, "Aye, Sir. You take the left one?"

"Aye. We'll take care of these two and then try to ride past them and out to the road where we can move faster."

Cuthbert looked at the mule. "He is not going to like that."

"Aye. 'Tis a flawed plan, but 'tis the one we've got."

Cuthbert grinned. "Could be worse, but I can't think of how."

Will said, "You take the one on the right, and I'll handle the one on the left."

The two Tories were about 150 yards away and riding in the open. They appeared to fear nothing, and that was a mistake.

WhizzzCraaaak! Zeke's rifle thumped into Will's shoulder as Cuth's .45 cracked. Both Tories went down hard. 150 yards was not a long shot, and the two rifles packed quite a bit of muzzle velocity at that range.

Before the Tories hit the ground, Will and Cuth dragged the reluctant mule to a fast run toward the Tories' horses which were now running riderless in aimless circles. As they passed the two militiamen, Will could see they were dead. Both lay motionless, one with his face in the dirt, the other with arms and legs splayed in an unnatural pose.

Will and Cuth hurried faster and had just made the road when a musket ball whizzed between them.

"Damn!" Will said. "I thought we might get past this."

They rushed as quickly as they could, but with the slow mule, the Tories were overtaking them.

Will shouted at Cuthbert, "When we get to that bend in the road, go straight and get into those trees. We'll have to fight, and the trees will help."

They burst into the copse of trees with heavy undergrowth. Small shrubs, a couple of gnarled oaks, and some scrubby pines helped to obscure the Tories' view. Once in the woods, Will and Cuthbert pulled up short and turned to face the oncoming enemy. Letting his English dragoon carbine dangle from its sling, Will snatched Josie from her deer hide scabbard and thumbed back the cock. Using his knees to guide Molly, he moved behind a small pine and settled Josie on his shoulder.

Only moments later, a Tory popped into view. This was a mistake, but the poor Tory did not know it. He thought his superior numbers were in his favor – there were four of them to the two of Will and Cuth.

WhizzzzCraaaak! Josie jolted Will's shoulder, and then there were only three Tories. The odds were getting better.

The Tories must have separated because two horsemen burst from the undergrowth on Will's left just as he put Josie back in her scabbard. In one motion, Will grabbed the carbine, thumbed back the hammer, and swung it over Molly's saddle.

Boooom! The carbine's recoil snatched it out of Will's hand to dangle from its sling. The unfortunate Tory on the receiving end was hit squarely in the chest by a full load of buck and ball. He slumped onto his horse's neck, blood pouring down the poor horse's hide to spatter on the ground.

There were two Tories left, and one was leveling a musket at Will. Will reached for the horse pistol as Cuthbert's musket banged hard just behind Molly. Molly started, and the Tory fell.

Now, Will had the cocked horse pistol in his hand as the final Tory rushed around a small pine. The Tory's teeth were bared like a wild animal attacking prey, and he was leveling a carbine at Will. The Tory carbine banged, and Will felt a breath of wind as the ball missed his face by a whisker. The horse pistol slammed in his hand as the last Tory, now only feet away, was hit full force in the face, chest, and arms by the buck and ball load. His horse ran a dozen yards past Will, and Cuthbert was ready with his sword to slash at the wounded Tory. But it was not necessary. The Tory's horse stopped, and the Tory slowly toppled to the ground.

Cuthbert put the sword away and dismounted. "Sir, this one is dead."

Will looked at the other two and said, "They're dead, too. I'm pretty sure the one I shot out there is dead. Let's get on the road before their friends come looking for them."

"Do you want to trade the mule for one of these horses?"

"Aye. That damn mule has been nothing but trouble."

Chapter 37 – Arrival

Will and Cuthbert reloaded all their weapons. A thorough cleaning would have to wait until they were less exposed to danger. They dragged the bodies into the swale and kicked dirt over them to keep down the buzzards. It was not a humanitarian gesture. Rotting corpses and a flock of buzzards would alert the Tories to the deaths. That would bring a search party.

Will considered what to do with the horses. If he let them run free, they would also alert the Tories. If he tied them up, they would die from heat, lack of water, and no food. The truly humanitarian choices were to either shoot them or take them. Will could not bring himself to kill any of the poor animals. Five horses would be a valuable trading commodity. The problem would be managing them on the road.

Will solved the problem by attaching the horses' reins to make a long train with the pack horse at the front. This way, Will or Cuth could handle the pack horse and drop the reins if trouble arose. It was still a day's ride to Kennedy's, and there was no telling what would happen.

The group set out on the road, thankful for a light breeze and some shady patches. They stopped a mile down the road and watered the horses at a creek that cut the road. Will and Cuth washed off the dirt and powder residue from the fight. Soon they were back in the saddle.

Will looked over his shoulder frequently and saw nothing coming. The carrion birds had yet to discover the bodies. Will knew the thin layer of dirt would not obscure the stink of rotting corpses, and the buzzards would have a feast by tomorrow. It could not be helped. The only thing to do was to ride through the night. There would be a moon, so that would help. If the dirt kept the buzzards away for a day, then Will and Cuthbert would be long gone.

~~<>~~

Will and Cuth and the valuable horse train cut around the small town of Carthage. There were not many people, but many of them knew Will from his time at the Kennedys. There was at least one lout who had a grudge. He had insulted Abby, and Will had fairly whipped his ass for it—no sense in raising that old specter. The horses would attract undue attention. Will knew this country well enough to ride cross country successfully.

The little caravan intercepted the road to Bear Creek, and Kennedy's a mile west of Carthage. Will glanced into the ditch and saw the top of Caleb Johnson's skull still there. And still looking for all the world like a smooth rock.

Will smiled at that. It was not that he enjoyed killing a man. No, Elijah Wambleeska Hammon had killed Caleb Johnson. What Will enjoyed was that it was not his own skull in the ditch.

Will considered, *This might be the last time I smile for a while. I have a sad duty to perform. I hope bringing such bad tiding to Abby does not make her hate me. Micah doesn't like me already. He sensed that there was a bond between Abby and me. Telling him about his boy's death will certainly not go well. I'm glad I have Cuth to confirm the story.*

It was late afternoon, and Will and Cuthbert were half dozing in the saddle as insects buzzed, birds flitted, and the breeze dropped. The horses plodded in the heat. Will dreaded the next few hours. If things didn't go well here, he and Cuth would simply make excuses and go to see Elijah at Drowning Creek. He hoped Elijah's people would still welcome him.

Will could hear the rush of the mill race that powered the tools in Alexander Kennedy's mill. The soft, rhythmic thump of the mill wheel driving the shafts said Alex was probably in the mill working. Maybe he had some apprentices? That would be good.

The horse train splashed through the creek and slowly plodded into the foreyard of Kennedy's mill. The door opened a crack, and a rifle barrel slid out.

"Who's there?"

"Alex? Mr. Kennedy? It's Will Yelverton."

The door flew open, and Alexander Kennedy stepped into a ray of sun that broke through the trees and landed on the door. He looked like one of the gods described in *The Odyssey*.

"Will?! By God! It *is* you!"

"Indeed, Sir. 'Tis I. This is my friend Charles Cuthbert, and we bring some Tory horses for you to sell."

"Did you know? Welcome, Mr. Cuthbert. Y'all get down off those horses and come in. I have some corn likker in here that Irene doesn't know about."

Will and Cuth dropped lightly to the ground and flicked their reins around a stump that doubled as a hitching post.

Cuthbert said, "It is a pleasure to meet you, Mr. Kennedy. I have heard many good things from Colonel Yelverton about you. Please call me "Cuth," everybody else does."

The three men sat on hard stools next to Kennedy's central workbench. Kennedy poured some potent grain alcohol that was tempered only by being aged in an oak barrel and cut slightly with water from the mill race.

Will avoided the topic of Zeke for the moment. They talked about the rifle business, and Kennedy learned that Cuthbert had started as Will's apprentice in Georgia.

Kennedy said, "After this war, Cuth, you come back here. We'll finish your training."

Cuth said, "I'll do that, Sir. And thank you for the offer."

Alex said, "No need to thank me. If Will thought you were good enough to apprentice with him and to maintain all the weapons for the Army, then that's good enough for me."

A brief silence descended as all three men enjoyed the heat rasping down their throats from the likker.

Alex glanced around the mill and said, "It wasn't to reminisce that brought you here, Will."

Sadness darkened Will's face. "No, Sir. I have bad news." He glanced at Cuth, who put down his drink cup and stepped out the door.

In a moment, Cuth came back in the door carrying Zeke's Kennedy Rifle.

Will took the rifle, nodding his thanks to Cuth. He held it out to Alex. "I'm sorry this is dirty. We ran into some Tories – those are their horses out front."

Alex shot a look at Will, "Shot the Tories, did you?"

"Aye, they were minded to kill us both. They failed."

"This is Zeke's rifle, Will."

"Aye."

A heavy silence descended.

Kennedy raised his eyes to the rafters, "How will we tell Abby?"

Will said, "I thought you and Irene might help with that."

~~<>~~

Alex looked around the room, his eyes filled with tears. "How..."

Will said, "You don't really want to know. But he died a hero at Camden. He stood as the British advanced. Zeke stood bravely as the North Carolina Militia around him broke and ran. He stood, calmly loading this rifle to shoot again. But he didn't get the chance."

"Is there any chance he is still alive and just a prisoner?"

"No, Sir. I got to him just after he was killed but before the British overran the lines. He was absolutely dead, Sir. I took this rifle as something for his boy. A man should be remembered by his son."

Cuthbert spoke, "Zeke was dead, Sir. Will, er, Colonel Yelverton, risked his life to get the rifle. I thought it was insane to ride into the middle of that assault, but well, you know him."

Kennedy nodded, a half-smile on his face. "Aye. He's headstrong, all right."

Alex Kennedy was a pragmatic man and always preferred action over waiting. "Let's go talk to Irene. She'll know what to do."

~~<>~~

Alex went to one of his apprentices, a man Will had never seen before, and asked him to take care of the horses. They would sell for good money next market day in Carthage. Another apprentice would clean Zeke's rifle and oil it to a sheen.

Walking with Alex, Will and Cuth lead their horses to the house. The three men walked slowly.

Alex said, "Will, you know Irene. She'll want to know the details. I'll leave it to you as to what you say."

Will nodded and kept walking toward the house.

Alex said, "Cuth, let's go to the stable with the horses and let Will and Irene talk. You don't mind brushing Molly, too, do you?"

Cuthbert said, "I am Colonel Yelverton's orderly. I'm happy to do anything that helps him."

"That's the second time you've mentioned Will as Colonel Yelverton."

"Aye. He returned from North Carolina in very low spirits. Colonel Elbert had offered him a commission as a major, and he took it. I had been his apprentice at Fort Morris as a private in the Continental Army. I was the first one to see him in uniform when he got off the boat, and I volunteered to be his orderly."

Alex said, "That still doesn't explain how he got to be a Colonel."

"Aye. He saved General Ashe at Brier Creek. He also saved Zeke, Sam Hawks, and a Lieutenant named Chuck Black."

Alex said, "Chuck Black? I seem to remember that Will and Chuck were enemies."

"Ah, well, something about saving a man's life will make him a friend, I think. General Lincoln made Will a Lieutenant Colonel, with all the privileges thereto appertaining, as they say."

Alex said, "My God, but I knew Will was a man of great character. But now he returns to us a Colonel and a war hero. Yet, he's a simple, quiet man. He is not of my blood, but he may as well be my son.

Cuthbert nodded, "Aye. Will Yelverton is the best man I've ever met. Yet, he doesn't know his own greatness."

Alex stopped Cuth as they were walking. "Tell me what happened to Zeke."

Cuth looked up into the trees and took a deep breath. "Ah, God, but 'tis hard to say. Cannonball took Zeke's head clean off. One instant, he was alive and loading his rifle. The next, he was in heaven. He stood, even in death, leaning against that Kennedy rifle, before his body gave up his spirit and collapsed into the blood-stained grass."

Alex said, "Oh, God! How terrible."

Cuth said, "Will went insane trying to get to him. He must have thought Zeke might still be alive and could be rescued."

Alex said, "But..."

"But, of course, Zeke was dead. Will was screaming at the British to come and try to kill him. Something about how Abby was the only woman he'd ever truly loved, and now the British had killed her husband. 'Twas all very confusing. He snatched Josie out of her scabbard and shot the gunner who fired the cannonball. He drew his other rifle and killed a British officer. He was in a frenzy when he jumped off Molly's back and grabbed at Zeke's body, only to be made certain that Zeke was dead. I saw him stop and scream at the sky before he became deadly calm. He picked up Zeke's rifle, and after he knelt by Zeke for a moment, he came back to Molly. I had to drag him out of there, Sir. He was going to go get himself killed."

Alex said, "Thanks be to God he didn't get himself killed. Losing both Zeke and Will would kill Abby, too."

Cuthbert said, "Will lost a wife, Sir. Smallpox. She was with child."

"Will was married?"

"Aye. It's been a long couple of years for Will."

Alex said, "My God, but that is an understatement."

Cuthbert said, "Miss Mary Procter, Will's wife, was a fine woman. Her father is a planter. She left Will a huge house in Charlestown. Sir, Will Yelverton is now a very wealthy man."

They walked on toward the stables. Alex said, "Will lived in the stables for a year; he'll want his room. We'll put you up in the house. There's an extra room after Abby married Zeke and moved out."

Cuthbert grinned, "He may own a house worth £5,000 in Charlestown, but he sleeps in the stable tonight. It's perfect. Will Yelverton doesn't believe he deserves more."

Alex looked at Cuth. "You know, I think you're right. Will is the best man I know."

~~<>~~

Will walked across the yard to Kennedy's door. As he came close, the door popped open, and Irene Kennedy stepped out.

She paused, hands on hips, "What happened?"

Will was startled. "Uh, hello, Miss Irene."

Irene demanded, "What happened? You would not just show up here if all was well, Will."

Will looked stricken. "I, uh, well..."

Irene paused, her eyes sad. Two large furrows appeared on her brow. "Let's go inside."

They walked into Irene Kennedy's well-kept kitchen. Irene indicated the bench by the family table and sat down at the head.

Will asked, "Where's Davy?"

Irene said, "I think he's out in the fields somewhere. It's been dangerous lately, and I think he's trying to hunt without becoming the hunted. But that's not why you're here, Will Yelverton. Now, out with it!"

Will looked around the familiar room. The hearth was still the same. It was where he had first seen Abby sitting and working on some knitting or other. He did not remember exactly what. He just remembered Abby's gamine little face flushing pink when she saw him. He remembered the heat in his own face. And now he had to tell her news that would break her heart.

Will took a deep breath and said, "Zeke is dead."

"I *knew* it! My God, but this is terrible!"

Will's voice broke. "He died a hero, and Abby can be proud to have been married to such a man."

"How did he die?"

"Oh, Miss Irene. You don't want to know."

"Yes, I do, Will. Yes, I do."

"But t'was quite horrible."

"I've seen my share of horrible."

Will wished he could escape. He had dreaded this moment every inch from Camden, South Carolina, to Kennedy's hearth. He looked wildly around the room.

Irene softened. She put her hand on Will's arm, "Will? Tell me, son."

Will whispered, "It was at Camden. A cannonball took his head off, Miss Irene."

Irene Kennedy gasped, "My God! Oh, God, poor Zeke. Poor you, Will, for having to witness that."

Will looked at Irene, a fierce glow in his eyes, "I killed the gunnery sergeant who killed Zeke."

Irene said, "Of course, you did, Will. Of course."

She looked across the room at nothing, just lost in thought. "We have to tell Abby and Micah. T'won't be easy."

Will whispered, "Aye, I know. I have tried to think of what to say all the way here."

Irene sat back in her chair and paused. "We will go together, the whole family. You'll have to tell them, but you won't be alone."

Will nodded miserably. "Zeke called me his brother, and I was glad he was the man Abby married."

As tears ran down her face, Irene said, "Zeke was a good man, but Abby should have married you, and no two ways about it. Don't you ever say that to anyone, but I thought that from the day you walked across that damned threshold."

Will had tears on his face, too. "I would have died before I would let Zeke be killed. There was nothing to do. I was merely present as General Gates' liaison to General Caswell. The Virginians broke and ran, and Caswell's troops followed them. We all tried to stop them from running. Zeke and a handful of others stood their ground. He was reloading his rifle when the British artillery opened fire. Zeke was simply unlucky."

Will looked bleak. "There is no body, Miss Irene. We simply had no time to collect the wounded and dead. I believe the dead were buried where they fell."

Irene said, "We'll get a nice piece of wood, and Alex can carve Zeke's name and dates on it, and we'll put it in the family cemetery. We'll have some prayers. It will be what we can do."

David Kennedy burst into the room. "Ma! I killed a deer. We'll eat well tonight!"

He looked at the small tableau of Will and Irene holding hands and crying. "Oh, God. Will? What are you doing here? What's happened?"

Chapter 38 – Micah and Abby

Irene said, "We have to go tell Abby and Micah."

Will nodded and said, "I brought along my friend and orderly, Sergeant Charles Cuthbert. We'll go wash and put on our uniforms."

Irene said, "Zeke said you were a major in the army. That's most impressive."

Will grinned, "Lieutenant Colonel, now. Not that it matters. The army is in tatters, and I have no command. They were only too happy to give me 45 days of furlough. I expect the only thing rank will get me is a priority in line for the noose."

Irene looked sober. "Will, Micah didn't like it when Zeke insisted on naming their baby after you. Micah didn't like you being here last time. It worries me how he's going to take Zeke's death."

Will said, "I hope he will understand that Zeke volunteered for the militia and his death was not in vain. I still think we can win our independence, or I'd be long gone to the frontier."

Irene asked, "Is that still your dream, Will? The frontier?"

Will looked wan. "I don't know. Many things have happened, Miss Irene. I married, but she died. She was carrying my baby, but smallpox took them both."

Irene's hands flew to her mouth. "Oh, Will! I'm so sorry! Did you love her?"

Will glanced toward the door. "No one will ever replace Abby in my heart, but Mary was wonderful, and I did love her. When she caught smallpox, I was with the army, and I hurried to be there for her. But I was too late. I still pine for her in death."

Irene said, "So many die young, Will. Abby will feel the same way about Zeke. Give her time."

"There's more. Mary Proctor was the daughter of Homer Proctor, a South Carolina planter. His wedding present to Mary was a large home in Charlestown. It is now mine. I should be modest in telling you, but the house is easily worth £5,000. I suddenly find myself wealthy. I don't want it to change me, Miss Irene."

Irene looked into Will's eyes, "It would take a lot more than mere money and status to change you, Will. You are a good man. Many men would glory in their wealth, but you worry that it will change you."

Will said, "I did not come to tell you all about Zeke in hopes of getting back with Abby. We will leave as soon as we have done our duty."

"You'll do no such thing! You'll stay right here and let events take their course. Abby always loved you. She nearly died when you came back here last time and found she was married to Zeke. Let's just let things rest quietly for a while. You have 45 days, did you say?"

"Aye."

"Well, that may be enough time for things to move along, Will. Now go wash; we have to go see Abby ... and Micah."

~~<>~~

Will and Cuthbert went about putting their gear away. Will was happy with the stable, even though Cuthbert said he should stay in the house.

"No, the stable was always my room, and it will be just fine. The apprentices all have a large room in that new cabin outside the main house."

Cuth said, "Mr. Alex suggested I stay in Abby's old room in the house, but Miss Irene said Abby was liable to bring the baby and stay a while after the news. I can understand that. She'll need her mama after the news. There's a bunk in the apprentice house, anyway. That'll be just perfect for me."

They washed at the trough out back and put on their uniforms. Will donned his dress uniform, riding boots with turned-down tops, and silver epaulets of his rank. He put on his sword. As much as he hated that damned sword, he felt he owed Abby and Micah the honor of being fully dressed when he presented the rifle. They walked together to Kennedy's main house.

They stepped in the door, and Irene saw them. She gasped. "My God, you two certainly look, well, magnificent."

Alex and Davy came in and paused. Davy said, "I'm going with you when you go!"

Irene blanched, and she went stiff. Alex looked alarmed.

Will said, "Tis not as glamourous as you might think, Davy. Zeke got killed, and so did Noah Harris, my friend from New Bern. Noah was sick and trying to crawl away from the fight when a Highlander from the 71st Regiment bayonetted him in the back."

Davy asked, "What happened to the Highlander?"

Will's face was serious, "I shot him."

Cuthbert said, "Tell you what, Davy, I'll tell you all about being in the army, and you can think it over. Will, er, Colonel Yelverton, has a different experience being an officer and all."

Will grinned, "Cuth, after today's formalities, we'll leave it at Will and Cuth."

Cuth smiled. "Very well, Sir."

Irene's shoulders relaxed. "Thank you, Cuth. I'm sure Davy will learn a lot from talking to you."

~~<>~~

Alex, Will, and Cuthbert rode horses while Davy drove the wagon with Irene beside him. There was no conversation, and the mood was somber.

It was late in the day when the entourage, led by Alex Kennedy, arrived at the Carter farm. It was a smaller affair than Kennedy's spread. The Kennedys had the factory and water wheel, the main house, the apprentice house, and several outbuildings. Carter had a main cabin, a cabin that was Abby's with the baby, and a small barn. A privy and a smokehouse completed the farm.

Micah Carter stepped out the door holding a musket. "Oh, hey, Alex. What's this big occasion?" He leaned the musket against the cabin wall and stepped out into the sun.

Irene got down from the wagon almost before Davy had stopped it. She hurried toward Abby's cabin, her shoulders square and her step firm.

Micah saw this and said, "What th' hell? What's going on, Alex? Why the hell is *he* here? An' what's he doin' a'wearing that get up?"

Alex swung down from his horse and tied it up. He took Micah aside, and Alex spoke briefly and urgently.

Will and Cuth dismounted and stood quietly by their horses.

His face white as a sheet, Micah tottered over to a chair on the rough porch of his cabin. He sat heavily. After a moment, he put his face in his rough farmer's hands.

From Abby's cabin, a loud, long, and painful scream split the air. The scream trailed off into a series of cries and whimpers.

Micah lifted his head from his hands. Tears streaked his lined face. He stood and snatched up the musket.

"I'll kill you, you son-of-a-bitch! You kilt, my boy!"

Micah fumbled with the cock on the musket and cut his hand on the razor-sharp flint. He sucked on the cut and started down the steps toward Will when Cuthbert stepped between them. Cuth put his hand on the musket, pushing it hard across Micah's chest.

Cuth spoke between clenched teeth, "Don't you move another muscle, Sir. Colonel Yelverton had nothing to do with Zeke's death aside from avenging it by killing the British gunner who killed Zeke. Colonel Yelverton is the most honorable man I know and has come here personally to tell you of the death of your son. He respects you that much, and you owe him the same respect."

Micah searched Cuth's face. "Who the *bloody hell* are you?"

"I, Sir, am Sergeant Charles Cuthbert of Sunbury, Georgia. I am orderly to Colonel Yelverton and privileged to be his friend. I have ridden with him while you and others worked your farms, risking nothing. Zeke marched with him twice. Will saved him at Brier Creek, or didn't Zeke tell you about that?"

"Uh, he done tol' some silly-ass story about ridin' on tha' back o' Yelverton's horse. I never believed a Goddamn word of it."

"Well, you better believe it. Colonel Yelverton saved more than just Zeke that day. And I saw the events at Camden that took your son. Zeke died a hero. Now it is for you to honor Zeke by being brave and acting with dignity as we help you to grieve."

Micah said, "Zeke is dead an' it's the scum like Yelverton who got him kilt! I don't give a shit about them British or them rebels."

Cuthbert spoke quietly, "Don't provoke me, Sir. And have some respect for your son's memory. Zeke volunteered to defend our new nation. Zeke stepped up while others sat in the comfort of their homes. Zeke died trying to throw off the yoke of British tyranny."

"But..."

"No buts, Sir. People like Colonel Yelverton are also volunteers to try to create our nation and throw off the yoke of tyranny.

You may say that you don't care about the British, but if we lose this fight, you will feel that yoke more than you can ever imagine. Even before we win, I will personally assure you that loyalist militias are coming this way. They will kill you and burn your farm if we don't beat them. They will take our young men and force them to join the militia or hang them if they don't."

"Well…"

"No, Sir. No two ways about it. Our lives all hang in the balance, and you have sacrificed a son. Don't sacrifice your dignity by accusing anyone here of having a hand in Zeke's death. Zeke wanted to be where he was. He lies in hallowed soil, fertilized with the blood of patriots. Honor him. Now give me that musket or so help me. I will take it from you and beat you with it!"

Micah looked downcast. "I ain't been scolded like that since I was a young'un. Here, take this goddamn musket."

Micah looked around at the group. "I apologize, Will. Even if you do look silly in that damn get-up. I got corn likker in the cabin. I'm a'drankin' some if'n y'all want to join me."

~~<>~~

Will, Cuth, Alex and Micah went into the cabin where Micah pulled out a jug of fiery distilled corn liquor. He had some wooden cups that they used to drink a toast to Zeke Carter.

Micah, fortified by a second cup of spirits, said, "All right, Goddamnit, tell me what happened."

Will said, "It happened in Camden, South Carolina. We had to stop the British there, or they would already be in North Carolina. Zeke was with the front lines of General Caswell's 1800 militiamen. They fired at the oncoming British assault, and Zeke was reloading his rifle when he was killed. The Virginia Militia broke and ran, and so did most of Caswell's North Carolina troops. Zeke stood his ground and continued reloading. He was killed."

Micah said, "That doesn't tell me much."

Cuth spoke up, "Sir, Colonel Yelverton was trying to spare your feelings. Zeke was hit by a cannonball that skipped across the ground and killed two other North Carolina militiamen. The cannonball hit Zeke in the head. One moment he was alive; the next, he was in eternity. He never knew it was coming."

Micah looked hard at Will, "What did you do? Jes set on that pretty horse o' your'n and watch."

Will said, "I was with General Caswell, and when I saw the situation developing, I rode down to try to stop the troops from running away. That's when Zeke was hit. There was not much time because the British were bearing down on our already broken line, but I dismounted and checked Zeke. He was quite dead; I'm sorry to say. I know it was Zeke because the body's hands clutched this Kennedy rifle."

"That's Zeke's gun?"

"Yes, Sir. I brought it to give you in trust for your grandson so he might have something of his father. It is a small tribute to Zeke that we have this. I fear the bodies of the dead were buried where they fell. We shall never know exactly where Zeke's body lies."

Will held out the rifle with both hands in a formal gesture to present the rifle to Micah.

Micah took a deep breath and rose from his chair. He stood as tall as his hard-worn frame would allow and stuck out his chin. Reaching out with both hands, he accepted the rifle.

"I thank you for this. 'Tis the only legacy of my son and one of small comfort, but your gesture is heartfelt, and I accept. I accept it for the Carter clan as well as for little William Yelverton Carter. We shall treasure it."

Will released the rifle into Micah's hands and, taking a step back, stood tall, doffed his cocked hat and bowed at the waist. Cuthbert did the same.

Straightening, Will said, "Know that your son died a patriot and a hero. With your permission, we will prepare a grave marker and place it in your family cemetery."

Micah said, "That would be appreciated. I can ask the rest of the family to come one day soon. Maybe we can have a little ceremony. You can tell them the story. But right now, I gotta go find a quiet place and cry some."

As he turned to leave the room, Micah looked at Will hard. "You probably ort ter go see Abby."

~~<>~~

Will walked across the yard to the little cabin where Abby Carter and her son, Yell Carter, lived. Abby was barely 20, and Yell was somewhere around 18 months. Will softly knocked on the cabin door.

Irene opened the door. A brief smile flitted across her face. "How did that go?"

"About as expected. Micah's looking for someone to blame. Cuth straightened him out some."

Irene said, "Good. If he hadn't, I would have. Micah is a fool sometimes. Abby is sick at heart. She's lying on her bed trying to understand how she could lose two men in such a short time."

"Two?"

"Yes, you fool. She lost you for dead, and now Zeke. For the longest time, you were dead as far as we knew, and she grieved.

I often found her crying bitter tears over you. She still loves you, Will. You be careful with her tender heart."

Will said, "I still love her, too."

"Don't you say a word of that just now. You just go answer her questions and be yourself."

Will nodded and tapped on Abby's rough wood bedroom door.

~~<>~~

A soft little voice, rough with tears, said, "Come in."

Will stepped into the little room. It was mostly unadorned. The only color was the gingham pattern on the cloth of the bed quilt. Reds danced with blues and yellows. Otherwise, the walls were unpainted logs. A small window was set into one of the walls. It had the rare conceit of four panes of glass, so it let light into an otherwise dim space.

Abby rolled over on the bed. Bloated, tear-stained face and all, she was the most beautiful creature Will had ever seen. The planter-class women of Charlestown could never match her natural, slightly freckled beauty with sandy, curly hair. Her blue eyes sought Will's eyes and held them hard for a long moment.

Will thought, *God help me, but I still love her so. I'm so terrible and disloyal to poor Mary.*

Pushing that thought aside, Will said, "The worst day of my life was when I saw Zeke dead and knew I had to come to tell you."

"I know. Now tell me what happened. Don't spare me, Will. I trust you more than any other person except for Mama. Now tell me the whole truth."

And Will did. He tried to make it less terrible, but that was impossible.

"He really didn't know that hit him?"

"Not at all. Zeke was with the almighty before even the Devil knew he was dead."

Abby nodded. "That's good. I've seen a dog run over by a wagon. The poor creature suffered for the longest time, even though one of the farmers swiftly killed it to end its suffering. I've seen gut-shot deer run for miles with their innards hanging out, suffering every step before they fell and struggled, desperate to get up. 'Tis better to be gone in an instant, I think."

Will nodded. "He's certainly with Jesus, you know."

Abby nodded. "I suppose so."

She looked down at her hands, "I loved him, Will."

"I know that, Abby. He loved you, too. He told me one day, sitting at a campfire, that he was lucky to have you. He was so proud of you and little Yel."

"He insisted that Yel be named after you, Will. Said you saved his life. Thank you for that."

Will made a dismissive gesture.

Abby's cheeks turned pink. "Don't you dare dismiss that you saved Zeke! He worshiped you. He said you were bigger than life, riding on Molly. He said you shot half a dozen raging redcoats as they were killing and maiming. He said you swept up to him, grabbed his hand, and dragged him onto Molly's back. He said you shot several more in a mad run to the river and slashed another one with your sword. By God, don't you try to make it like you're not a hero, Will Yelverton."

Will opened his mouth to speak, but nothing came out. Finally, he squeaked, "I didn't have anything to live for."

Abby rolled back on her face. "Well, now you do. You have a namesake in Yel Carter. Now git. I have to cry over Zeke and then get up from here and continue livin'. I got a baby to feed."

Chapter 39 – Bear Creek

A week passed with Will and Cuth hunting every day with Davy. Will worked in the factory some, honing the skills that he admitted were a bit rusty. Cuth impressed Alex with his skills learned from Will and polished with months of repairing weapons for the Army.

Alex said, "Cuth, like I said, when this fight is over, you come on back and apprentice here. We'll make you a master in short order."

Will grinned at that. "Maybe Cuth and I will go to the frontier and open our gun business there. Governor Caswell says there will be land plenty for veterans after we win this war. He said that every state will most likely have lotteries for large land tracts."

Alex said, "I suppose there will be widow's pensions, too. Abby should consider that."

Will sobered, "Yes, of course. But Abby will want nothing her entire life. I will file papers to be sure she and little Yell have an income. Yell can go to college if he wants. Maybe become a lawyer or doctor."

Alex nodded. "Kind of you, but not necessary."

Will said, "I shall be happy to do it."

~~<>~~

Two weeks later, the entire Carter clan gathered at the Carter family graveyard, where a wooden marker was placed with great ceremony, and Will eulogized Zeke Carter for the hero he was. Will formally presented Zeke's rifle to Micah, Abby, and little Yell. Will and Cuth wore their uniforms, and more than a few of Carter's nieces made certain to simper sweetly in their best country dresses. Nell, a raven-haired beauty with huge blue eyes, was especially attentive to Cuth.

After the ceremony, the clan gathered for that North Carolina tradition called a pig pickin'. A hog was killed the day before, and after scalding and scraping to remove its bristles, it was dressed and put into a pit with a low fire of hickory wood. There, the hog stayed, frequently mopped with vinegar for some 24 hours until the meat fell off the bones. The people gathered and picked the meat from the hog, ate German potato salad and rough yeast bread called Sally Lunn smeared with fresh butter, and drank small beer or corn liquor. Several wives brought pies which were welcomed, especially to Will and Cuth, who had not had such delicacies in months.

Zeke Carter had a remarkable funeral that celebrated his heroism and mourned his loss. Everyone who visited slept in the barn, under wagons or under the stars. Will and Cuth rolled out their bedrolls and slept off the alcohol and heavy food in the air that was beginning to be cool at night.

The next day the gathered family members left except Nell, who begged to stay and "help" with little Yel. After some back and forth, Nell's father agreed to let her stay. Toward the afternoon, it was time to leave for Bear Creek.

Alex and Davy loaded the wagon while Irene played with little Yell. Will and Cuth saddled their horses and said their goodbyes when Abby and Nell came marching out of Abby's cabin, packed to join the group going to Kennedy's.

Micah said, "What's this?"

Abby said, "I need to be with Mama some, Micah. Nell wants to take care of Yel." She leaned forward and whispered something that Will didn't catch.

Micah nodded. "Well, I got work to do around here, so y'all best move on." He walked over to Will and said, "I thank you for the courtesy of coming here."

Handshakes and hugs all around ended the day on a good note.

Will wondered what was going on but decided he would be told if necessary. As usual, he and Cuth rode with loaded guns. Will's carbine was on his thigh and Cuth with his officer's fusil in the crook of an elbow.

The trip was uneventful, and Will took Molly to the stable, where he brushed her down and gave her an apple filched from the table at Micah's. His job done, he went to his little room off the stable and sat on the bed. It had been a good couple of days where people, Americans, found comfort in one another and settled into quiet fellowship.

Will leaned back and considered what he would do when the war was over. The talk with Cuthbert about the frontier had renewed his interest, and the future was on his mind again.

A soft voice said, "What are you thinking about, Will?"

Startled, Will jumped and looked up to see Abby standing at the door to his little room.

"I, uh, I was, uh...that is, I was thinking about the future. I still want to go to the frontier."

Abby's face fell a little. "Oh. I just thought..."

"Thought what?"

"I thought maybe after a little time, we might talk about the future and how it might be for us."

"Oh. Well, I thought you needed time to grieve and consider what you might do."

Abby smiled, "I know you told Daddy you would take care of me the rest of my life and that you would provide for Yel. You said Yel could go to college and be a doctor or lawyer. That would put you in the poor house, Will."

Will smiled, "You should let me worry about that."

"Don't tease me, Will. I know you don't have a pot, and the few hundred dollars you had when you left here must have been used up in all your travels. You would be dirt poor."

"Not exactly, Abby."

"Oh, well, maybe you have a little money and Molly. I saw those horses you took from the loyalists. They will bring some money. But we'd need to spend years getting enough money to set up your gunshop."

Will didn't say anything to this. He thought, *Miss Irene has obviously not told Abby of my wealth.*

He was about to explain that he had been married and about Mary's death when Abby took a step toward him and said, "Then, there's your wife. Oh, Will, I'm so sorry! A wife and a baby and they were taken by smallpox. How terrible for you."

Tears ran down Abby's face. "If only I had waited for you!"

Will leaned forward and put his elbows on his knees, his hands together in an almost prayerful pose. "Don't think like that,

Sweetheart. Mary was a wonderful woman. I was so lucky. I had lost you and felt I had nothing to live for. She burst into my life and took away the darkness."

Abby sat on the bed next to Will and took one of his hands in hers. "Oh, I have been so selfish to think only of losing Zeke. We haven't talked since your first day here, and now I'm embarrassed that I didn't know about this until Mama told me earlier today. Oh, Will, I wish I could make it all better."

Will said, "Caswell said something to me while we were on the retreat from Camden. He said he was married to his first wife, and they had children. He loved her, but she died, and he married Dicky's mother. He said we must move on because so many people die so young."

Abby said, "Richard Caswell is a very wise man."

Will said, "Yes, he offered to help me invest my money."

Abby smirked, "Got to get some first."

Will asked, "How does £5,000 sound?"

"What do you mean?"

Will explained about Mary being Homer Proctor's daughter and that he owned the house in Charlestown.

Abby snapped, "You let me go on about being poor!"

Will said, "You know, I liked myself better when I was poor."

Abby blurted, "I still loved you when I thought you were poor. That you're very wealthy makes no difference. I love you still, Will Yelverton."

Will said, "I have to go back to the war. I only have a month left here."

"I know that. I would expect you to go to war again."

"I won't leave you here without anything, Abby. I have loved you since I walked in the door at your Mama's house."

"I know that."

Will said, "What shall we do?"

Abby looked a little vexed. She said, "'Tis not proper for a woman to propose marriage, Will."

Will looked at Abby. "Is it not too soon? I mean, I would marry you this minute, but what will people say?"

"They'll say you're a damn fool if you don't propose this minute!"

Will dropped to his knees on the hard dirt floor of the little stable room. Looking up at Abby's shining blue eyes, Will said, "Abby Carter, will you do me the honor of becoming my wife?"

"Of course I will, Will Yelverton. Now kiss me."

Will stood and pulled Abby close. He kissed her deeply as he inhaled the aroma of her skin. She had made some form of lavender or other flower water that was soft and pretty.

Abby murmured with exasperation, "I always have to start things!"

She stepped back and pushed the door closed, and flipped the little wooden latch. She pulled the buttons of her simple country dress and pushing it off her shoulders, let it fall to the floor. She stood naked in front of Will.

Will was instantly erect, and he struggled to get out of his boots, shirt, and breeches.

They came together in a rush standing on the dirt floor of the stable, kissing passionately. Abby tugged gently at Will's arm and moved him toward the bed. She found no resistance as they collapsed onto the rough covers, and Will quickly got between her knees.

In one motion, they were coupled, and Abby gasped. "Ahhh, God! Ahhh. I dream about this all the time. I'm so wicked!"

Will whispered, "No, you're not wicked. I often think of you even when I shouldn't. I have dreams that we are doing this, and I awaken having soiled my sheets."

"Well, soil me now, Will. Now, now, now...OhGodohGodohGodohGod..." Abby trailed off as Will exploded inside her.

Later, Will murmured, "You are so beautiful."

"No, I'm not. I'm old and fat. My belly is no longer flat. I have stretch marks on my belly from Yel. I have flat paps. You should run from me while you have the chance."

Will said, "I didn't notice any flaws. But I shall endeavor to examine you more closely."

Abby said, "Oh, so now you're a doctor!"

~~<>~~

The next afternoon, Will was splitting wood in the sideyard when Irene walked over.

As she sat on a stump, she said, "Good. We have a private moment."

Will put down the axe and sat on a stump next to her and wiped the sweat off with a damp rag. "What did you want to talk about?"

Irene said, "Abby told me you asked her to marry you, and she said she would. I'm surprised this happened so fast, but with the war and your short time left, I should have predicted it."

Will said, "She came to me, and we talked about several things. I told her that Governor Caswell said he's been married twice, and it was not disrespectful of him to take a second wife after his first wife died. We agreed that Richard Caswell is a very wise man."

Irene leaned back and hooted a full-throated laugh. "Good. Now we will have to manage Micah."

Will said, "He's a problem, but let me think about it some."

Irene said, "It's possible we might have a double wedding."

"Oh?"

"Yes. You men are so oblivious. Nell coming to visit was Abby's excuse to come here without Micah being aware of developments. Abby and little Yell were Nell's excuse to come here so she could pursue Cuth. She's smitten, and I'll bet he is as well."

Will said, "Oh. Sorry, I'm so dumb. I hadn't thought about anything like that."

"It's how we women trap you, men."

~~<>~~

That night at supper, Will stood and said, "I'd like to announce that Abby and I are to be married. I know it seems rushed, but there is a war, and Cuth and I must get back to it soon. I know it's a terrible imposition, but we would like to have the ceremony as quickly as we can."

Nell jumped up and ran out the door, stifling a sob with her hand. Cuth looked around the group.

Irene said, "Go after her, you dolt!"

Cuth stood and knocked over his chair, stumbled toward the door and mumbled, "Please excuse me," as he hurried after Nell.

Davy asked, "What was that about?"

Irene looked at Will and said, "See what I mean?"

~~<>~~

Will swung up onto Molly and said, "Let's go, girl. We've got a job to do."

As always, he carried his Branders in his belt, the horse pistol, and his English dragoon carbine. Josie rode in her scabbard – the soft deer hide case that Abby had made for him all those months ago. Will smiled when he thought about how she had shyly suggested that something hard and long like his rifle needed a soft and pliable sleeve to protect it.

Molly trotted along toward Micah Carter's farm. It was quiet, and there were few birds flying. The afternoon was warm. September in North Carolina is never cool, at least not during the day.

It was unusual for Will not to notice signs of trouble, but he had other things on his mind. Chiefly, he worried about how he might tell Micah that he was marrying Abby.

Two men on horseback stepped out of the bushes, and one leveled a musket at Will.

"Well, well. What do we have here, Laz? Looks like a yokel who thinks he's safe with that bunch o' guns."

Laz said, "Reckon, we better take them guns."

A coldness settled over Will. His face went blank as he asked, "Is Laz short for Lazarus? As in the Lazarus from the bible, who died and was resurrected?"

"Yup, tha' one and onliest."

Will said laconically, "Well, Laz, I have it that you only live once."

The first highwayman with the musket leveled on Will said, "Ho, ho, ho! Laz, this one's fun...."

Will's carbine took him out of the saddle before he could finish the thought. The jarring boom of the carbine and the cloud of yellow-grey smoke obscured Laz from view.

In one motion, Will nudged Molly left with his knees, dropped Molly's reins, let go of the carbine to dangle from its sling, and whipped out one of Tarleton's Branders. He cocked it, and, as expected, Laz was right where he had been a moment before.

Laz pointed a pistol at where Will had been and pulled the trigger. The pistol cracked, but the ball flew harmlessly into the trees. Will shot Laz in the chest with the Brander.

Laz lay on his back on the ground, looking up at Will, who was still sitting on Molly's saddle. "Wha...who are you?"

"I, Sir, am Lieutenant Colonel William Yelverton of the Continental Army, and I just killed you. Let me know when you are resurrected, and I'll kill you again."

Lazarus, whose last name Will did not know, blinked twice and whispered, "I'll see you in hell."

Will said, "If that's the case, they named you poorly."

~~<>~~

Will tied a rope around each highwayman's feet and tied their horse's bridles together. He dragged the bodies to Micah's farm.

It was not far, maybe two miles. The horses were docile and walked along, ignoring their former owners' bodies.

Will trotted into Micah's yard and found Micah repairing a broken-down fence.

"Damn fools at Zeke's funeral broke this fence. What brings you around, Will?" Seeing the horses and the bodies, he said, "And what the hell happened here?"

Will decided he'd come right out with it. "I came to tell you that Abby and I are getting married. These two got in my way."

Micah walked slowly over to a stump and sat. "Guess it don't pay to get in your way. That musta been what tha' shooting was about. I figured somebody was doin' a bad job o' killin' a deer."

Micah turned sober, "Are ye' lookin' fer my blessin'?"

Will said, "Yes, Micah. I respect you, and Zeke felt we were brothers. I owed you asking for Abby's hand."

"Damn, if you ain't everthang Irene said you wuz. You got a set o' balls on you big as river rocks to come ridin' in here dragging dead bodies and asking fer my blessing. Irene did tole me at the funeral that you'd be marrying Abby. I didn't believe her."

Will said, "Damned if there isn't some kind of plot going on among the women. Well? Do you object?"

"Hell yes, I object. But it won't do a damn bit o' good. That, and I hate to admit it, I respect you, too. I ain't happy with it, but I'll not stand in your way. 'Specially with what done happened to them two."

Will said, "I guess that's as close to a blessing as I'm going to get."

Micah squinted his eyes and chewed on an imaginary item in his teeth. He spat on the ground. "Abby told me she was going to Irene's so Nell could get close to that feller with you. What's his name, Cuss?"

"Cuth."

They musta had something wrong with their teeth when they named him. Well, hell, I don't care if tha' whole damn clan gets married all at oncet. I hope y'all live a long and happy life. How's that fer a blessin'?"

Will grinned, "That's just fine."

Micah said, "Onliest thing: I want to see my grandbaby. Little Yel's 'bout all I got now."

Will said, "I swear you will get to see Yel often. He's the best little baby in the whole wide world."

Micah nodded. "That's all I ask."

Micah nudged one of the bodies with his toe and said, "You done kilt Laz Cabel. Him and that piece o' shit next to him – Jimmy something, can't remember his name – been robbing people for the last couple of years. Reckon we best get to burying them. Hell, I'd throw 'em to tha' hogs, but we done kilt the last hog for tha' funeral."

Chapter 40 – Joy

Will and Micah finished burying the highwaymen and had a drink of corn likker from Micah's small horde.

Micah said, "I didn't like you when you showed up last time. But Zeke came home from Brier Creek and said you done saved him. I didn't want to believe that. But, after what that feller, Cuth, said, I believe it all."

Will said, "Oh, I had a strong feeling for Abby, but when I left, she thought I was gone for good. I was happy for her that she found a good man like Zeke. I was jealous of Zeke but decided he was a better man for Abby than I could be. Abby was lucky to have him and you, Micah. Y'all treated her good."

Micah said, "I love that grandbaby. I'll hold you to the promise that I'll get to see him."

Will said, "I have to return to the war in a few weeks. I can't just up and desert. So, Abby and little Yell will be staying here for quite a while. We have time for the Banns to be read three times before I must leave. That will make us married, and I will make a will that leaves everything to Abby."

Will continued, "I hope I don't get killed, but it could happen. The fact is, Mary, my first wife, left me a house in Charlestown. It's worth a lot. Of course, I can't get to it with the British occupation, but it's there. It means that Yell Carter will grow up to go to college and become a lawyer or doctor."

Micah smiled widely. "Yore havin' money makes you more likable ever' minute."

~~<>~~

Will trotted into Kennedy's yard a happy man. He had reached a compromise with Micah, and soon he and Abby would marry. He saw Cuthbert waiting for him.

"Afternoon, Cuth."

"Good afternoon, Sir. I trust your meeting with Mr. Carter went well?"

"Aye. He helped me to bury two highwaymen who tried to rob me. We talked, and he blessed the marriage. That was a relief."

Will paused and said, "Last I saw, you were hurrying to catch up with Miss Nell."

Cuth looked sheepish. "Aye, and I caught her, too. She's agreed to marry me. Would a double wedding be acceptable?"

Will grinned widely. "Of course, a double wedding would be fine with me. I'll ask Abby, but I doubt there will be any problem. There won't be much of a ceremony there being no minister hereabouts. But we were planning to have the Banns read three times and then have a small ceremony, a handfasting."

Cuth exhaled in relief. "Good, I've been holding my breath for hours."

~~<>~~

With no real meeting hall for a church, Will had the Banns posted in Carthage three times over the next three weeks. Lowden's Tavern was the center of community for the area, and the Banns for Will and Abby and Cuth and Nell were posted for all to see. If there were any objections, then they must be made by seven days after the third posting. The handfasting ceremony was not a truly legally binding marriage, but it was recognized as the public announcement of the union of two people. It informally recognized the posting of the Banns. Will could have found a county ordinary and paid the £50 license fee, but it seemed unnecessary.

The weeks went by with blinding speed.

Each day, Will and Davy hunted. Cuthbert preferred to spend time at the factory learning skills required to build guns. Alex said that Cuth was a natural and would make a good gunsmith. Will agreed.

Supper frequently consisted of something Will or Davy shot. It was moving into fall, and deer and turkey were active. One day Will and Davy dragged a bear home. It had not been easy to kill, requiring each hunter to shoot it. Irene said the meat would be good but greasy. She was right. It also had a strong flavor that few in the family liked.

Alex said that the hide would make a good rug after it was tanned and washed.

Little Yell Carter had taken to Will, calling him Da. That was no surprise because both Will and Zeke had been fair. Will looked enough like Zeke, and no one objected to Will being Da to little Yell. Will loved the little fellow and called him 'Little Man.'

Nearly every night, Abby quietly stole out of the main house and came to the stable. She was passionate, letting Will know that she loved him. The lovers exhausted themselves, exploring each other. More than once, Abby cried when she realized that Will would have to leave shortly after the wedding.

Abby also confided that while she was leaving the house, Nell was entertaining Cuth, who sneaked in from the apprentice's bunk room.

Will thought that Irene pretended not to notice any of these activities, but she secretly smiled at him.

~~<>~~

The day of the weddings approached. It was late September, and the weather promised to cooperate. No rain and pleasant temperatures. No one objected to the Banns.

Will, Davy, and Cuth killed a hog and went through the preparation ritual of scalding, scraping, dressing, and cooking over a slow fire. They sat up all night laughing, drinking hard cider, sneaking an occasional cup of corn likker, and mopping the pig with vinegar. The result was three hungover young men and one perfectly barbecued pig.

Everyone washed before the ceremony, and Will and Cuthbert donned their full uniforms. They were resplendent in their blue Continental Uniforms. But these elaborate uniforms did not outshine the beauty of Abby and her cousin-in-law, Nell.

Abby had a new dress made of lovely dove-gray fabric that Irene had gotten two years ago at the Carthage Fair. Irene had enough peach-colored fabric to make a beautiful dress for Nell. Each girl had a matching bonnet and carried an oriental fan. Irene had bought the two fans several years earlier at the Carthage fair in expectation of the potential for an occasion precisely like this.

Irene pulled Will aside. "I kept all this back when Abby married Zeke. I didn't think anyone would notice the quality or value of any of these things. The Carters are not the most cultivated lot."

Will grinned. "Nobody ever accused me of being cultivated."

Irene dug a finger into his ribs. "You're far more a gentleman than you think, Will."

~~<>~~

The gathering was very boisterous, with young people joking and laughing. The elders started drinking early. As a distant cousin said, "You can't drink all day if you don't start in the morning!"

Several of Nell's relatives were present. Her parents were very pleased about Nell marrying, but one or two commented on how quickly Abby was remarrying. Will overheard Irene say, "There's a war going on, and there's no time to tarry; young people who love one another should hurry up and marry." Will smiled at this bit of country wisdom and poetry. He loved Irene all the more because of it.

Irene, along with Will's real mother, Mandy, and his other adoptive mother, Becky Koontz, had helped him maintain a path to success all these years. Will's biggest soft spot was for his Aunt Patience, who had loved him with a gentle heart all her life. She was gone now, but Will knew she would approve of this marriage. He resolved to visit Aunt Pat and Uncle Ewan's graves and tell them about Abby and Yell, for Yell would soon be his son.

Will had a moment behind the stable where he could reflect. He thought of Mary and their unborn baby. He wished them both peace in Heaven. He told her about Abby. He hoped she approved and that she knew he was happy. He thanked her for their time together and prayed for her and the baby's souls. It was all he could do.

~~<>~~

The two brides faced their grooms, both couples radiant in their finery. The men looked resolute and brave. The women were astounding in their dresses; their cheeks were pink with a mixture of health and rouge carefully applied.

There was no minister, so Irene stood in. She asked everyone to pray that both couples would be happy. She said:

"Will and Cuth are to be their families' husbands, fathers, leaders, and patriarchs. They are to be kind and loving, firm, and faithful. They will support their families with sober hard work and provide for everyone equally. They will defend home and hearth."

"Abby and Nell are to be good wives who love and obey their husbands, mother their children, manage the home and hearth, and keep the family in good times and bad."

"Now, each couple shall join hands, right hand to right hand, left to left, as I bind you together with this cord."

Irene took out a gold braided cord with small tassels on end and looped it around Cuth's wrists, then across Nell's. She took out a red cord braided with silver thread and looped it around Will's wrists, then across and around Abby's.

"The Banns having been posted for three weeks and no objections and these two couples having agreed to be married and having been handfast before the people gathered here, I declare them to be married."

"Will and Cuth, you may kiss your bride."

There was a cheer and applause.

Alex stood and said, "Come congratulate the two couples and then let's eat. There's a pig to pick!"

~~<>~~

That night, Cuth and Nell shared Abby's room. Alex and Irene offered Will and Abby their room in the house, but Abby said, "I'd rather stay with Will in the stable. It's always been his place, and now I'm his too."

Alex looked puzzled, but Irene smiled and said, "That sounds right."

Davy said, "Y'all keep the racket down out there so the horses can sleep," and earned a hard look from Irene.

Later, both exhausted from a long day and vigorous sex, Abby said, "I have wanted this moment forever. You are the true man for me, Will. I will love you until I die."

Will smiled as he looked around the little stable room and down at the beautiful, naked woman of his dreams cuddling in his arms.

He said, "I have lived in many places, but none match this little room for feeling like home. It feels like home because you are here, and even though we're in a stable, it's our little place. I love you, Abby, and I love Yell, too."

Abby said, "You had better come back to me when this war is over. Do you still want the frontier? Or would you want to live in Charlestown?"

Will said, "I wish I knew what I wanted. I've got you, and that's the main thing. Governor Creswell says that as soon as the war is over, there will be plenty of land to be had. With our wealth, we can afford a plantation. That would mean owning slaves, and I won't be a slave owner. The frontier has become a darker place of foreboding with the war. I heard Sevier and a group of men came over the mountains and shellacked the British at King's Mountain. I wish I had been there to share in that victory. We've lost so many times."

Abby said, "You'd rather have been there in a battle than here with us?"

"No, but you know what I meant. My place is with the Army and helping win this fight. I didn't want this war, but By God, I shall see it finished!"

Abby said, "Here is where you belong. At war is where you must be ... for now. Those are two different things."

~~<>~~

Three days later, Lieutenant Colonel William Branch Yelverton and his orderly, Sergeant Charles Cuthbert, rode out of Kennedy's yard. They were once again journeymen on the road to Hillsborough to rejoin the remnants of the Continental Army's Southern Department.

Will was sad that he wouldn't get to see Elijah on this trip. But there would be more trips to this part of North Carolina, and Will was sure he would see his friend again.

A rider had passed just yesterday and told the news of the war. Washington had appointed Major General Nathanael Greene to command the Southern Department of the Continental Army.

South Carolina was still in chaos, with the British consolidating their hold on the state. There was every possibility of a renewed British invasion of North Carolina. Now there were rumors of partisan attacks harassing the British at every turn. The partisans were operating from the deep South Carolina swamps. They were led by a general named Francis Marion.

It was a new day and a new war, and Will Yelverton was riding toward it.

Epilogue

"That's how it happened, Kenny. Of course, it's not everything. Some things I don't remember."

"That's how you and Grandma Abby got hitched?"

"Yep. Your Uncle Yel Carter is Grandma Abby's first baby by her first husband, Zeke."

Kenny looked puzzled, "Where's Uncle Yel now?"

"Your Uncle Yel is down in Florida."

"Where's Florida?"

"Boy, you are full of questions. Florida is a long, wide peninsula that sticks off the bottom of the United States. Spain owns it. They started it as a colony and then had to give it to the British. The British lost it back to Spain at the end of the Revolutionary War."

"Why isn't Florida part of the United States if we won the Revolutionary War?"

"Well, Kenny, it's not that simple. See, a treaty – an agreement between countries – ended the war and gave us independence.

But Spain had helped us win that independence and they wanted Florida back. T'was only right that they got their wish, which was part of that treaty."

"What's it like in Florida?"

Will looked off into the mountains that marched into the distance. "Oh, 'tis different than here. 'Tis hot and wet. There are swamps with alligators and snakes. There are beautiful, white beaches with sand as far as you can see. The ocean surrounds the whole of Florida except for the part attached to Georgia."

"I'd like to go to Florida."

"Well, maybe you'll visit your Uncle Yel one day."

Kenny paused, "Tell me about what happened after you went back to the Army, Grandpa."

Will grinned, "Oh, that's a long story for another day, Kenny. I'll tell you soon, though."

THE END

Watch for the fourth book of Will Yelverton's adventures coming soon.

Journeyman: A Brighter Sunshine of Their Own

In Congress.

The DELEGATES of the UNITED STATES of New Hampshire, Massachusetts-Bay, Rhode-Island, Connecticut, New-York, New-Jersey, Pennsylvania, Delaware, Maryland, Virginia, North-Carolina, South-Carolina, and Georgia, TO

William Branch Yelverton, Esquire

We, reposing special Trust and Confidence in your Patriotism, Valor, Conduct, and Fidelity, DO by these Presents, constitute and appoint you to be *Lieutenant Colonel* of the Army of the United States, raised for the Defense of American Liberty, and for repelling every hostile Invasion thereof. You are, therefore, carefully and diligently to discharge the Duty of *Lieutenant Colonel* by doing and performing all Manner of Things thereunto belonging. And we do strictly charge and require all Officers and Soldiers under your Command, to be obedient to your Orders as *Lieutenant Colonel*. And you are to observe and follow such Orders and Directions from Time to Time, as you shall receive from this or a future Congress of the United States, or Committee of Congress for that purpose appointed, or Commander in Chief of the Army of the United States, or any other your superior Officer, according to the Rules and

Discipline of War, and the instructions herewith given you, in Pursuance of the Trust reposed in you. This commission is to continue in force until revoked by this or a future Congress.

November. 15. 1779

By Order of the Congress

Samuel Huntington   President

Attest. *Char Thomson Jun*

The Siege of Savannah

The Siege of Savannah was among the bloodiest battles during the American Revolutionary War. Savannah, Georgia, was held by the British, who took control of the city in 1778 (see *Journeyman: Heart of Tempered Steel*). The Americans, led by General Benjamin Lincoln, and French forces led by Compte Giscard d'Estaing, failed to recapture it in the fall of 1779.

The Franco-American force consisted of around 5,500 troops, while the British force numbered around 2,500. Many aspects of the Siege of Savannah are too in-depth to cover here. However, both the British and the Americans were surprised when the French appeared off the coast of Georgia in August 1779. The French set about disembarking a large army consisting of French troops, a mixed force of Haitian volunteers and slaves, animals, and artillery. Meanwhile, General Lincoln rushed some 2500 troops from Charlestown, South Carolina, to Savannah. The French and Americans took two weeks to get in position.

The French built siege works – mainly digging a series of trenches zigzagging toward the British lines. Meanwhile, the British frantically completed their defensive lines, sank derelict ships in the Savannah River Channel as barriers to Naval invasion, and deployed about 100 guns all along a line surrounding the city. When the Franco-American force was finally ready to launch their attack on the city they faced a well-entrenched British army, which had ample time to fortify its positions.

After a prolonged siege, the Americans and French launched a poorly planned and equally poorly executed assault on the British positions on October 9, 1779. The attack was to commence before dawn with a feint toward the southern side of the British line, while the main thrust was at the Spring Hill Redoubt on the western side of Savannah.

The Spring Hill Redoubt was a defensive fortification built by the British during the Siege of Savannah in 1779. The redoubt was located on a slight hill overlooking the Savannah River, and it was an important strategic position for the British army and anchored the British right. The redoubt was constructed along the road to Augusta in the spring of 1779, in preparation for the expected American attack on Savannah. The redoubt, essentially a square fortification made of earth and timber and reinforced with palisades and a ditch, would withstand infantry assaults.

Confusion reigned as French and American forces blundered in a swamp, hindered by pre-dawn darkness and inadequate guides. The attack was finally launched well after sunrise with devastating consequences. American and French units marched across some 500 yards of the prepared battlefield and avoided defenses, including ditches and abatis (tree trunks bristling with sharpened branches) before they reached the actual line that included the Spring Hill Redoubt. The attack was repulsed with heavy losses, and the American troops were forced to retreat. There has been speculation that the British were aware of the Franco-American focus on the Spring Hill Redoubt and reinforced militia units with seasoned British regulars.

The spirited defense of the Spring Hill Redoubt was key to the British holding Savannah. The American and French commanders launched several attacks against the redoubt, but they could not breach its defenses. Several Americans attempted to plant the 2nd South Carolina Regiment Flag on the redoubt. These included the legendary Sergeant William (Wilhelm) Jasper and several lieutenants. All were killed, and the British captured the regimental colors. The redoubt was pivotal in the British victory which ended the American attempt to recapture the city and cemented British control of Georgia for the remainder of the American Revolutionary War.

In all, American casualties at the Siege of Savannah totaled 244 killed, 584 wounded, and 120 captured. British losses were 155 killed, wounded, or missing. But these figures do not truly reflect the significance of the American loss at Savannah. The Siege of Savannah was a significant strategic setback for the American cause, as it demonstrated the difficulties that the American forces faced in trying to take on the better-trained and better-equipped British army. Strategically, the British controlled Savannah for the remainder of the war. The Siege of Savannah also set the stage for the British Siege of Charleston (Charlestown), South Carolina, the following year.

One interesting aspect of the Siege of Savannah is the participation of Haitian soldiers on the American side. At the time of the battle, Haiti was still a French colony known as Saint-Domingue. The French governor of the colony, Jean-Baptiste de Vimeur, Comte de Rochambeau, had dispatched a force of 500 free black soldiers and 500 enslaved black soldiers to assist the Americans in their fight for independence. Jean-Baptiste Chavanne de La Giraudière, a French officer, commanded this group of Haitian soldiers.

Despite the defeat, the Haitian soldiers significantly contributed to the battle and demonstrated their courage and commitment to the cause of freedom. The participation of Haitian soldiers in the Siege of Savannah is an important reminder of the contributions of black soldiers to the American Revolution, which is often overlooked in history books. It also highlights the important role that Haiti played in the fight for independence in the Americas, both during the American Revolution and later during its own struggle for independence from France.

The combined allied forces' failure also illustrated difficulties in coordinating with the French, who had a mind of their own about warfare, regardless of the conditions faced in North

America. Nevertheless, the battle also highlighted the bravery and courage of the American soldiers who fought in the face of daunting odds.

While Will Yelverton is a fictional character, his experience of the Siege of Savannah symbolizes the brutal fight and the courage required to charge against the better-trained and better-equipped British defenders who were entrenched in a nearly impenetrable series of fortifications.

Today, few elements remain of the British defensive line around Savannah. The Spring Hill Redoubt has been excavated and rebuilt and is part of the Savannah History Museum. The Savannah History Museum is located in the old Central of Georgia Railroad complex in downtown Savannah. Ironically, much of the Revolutionary War battlefield lies under rail lines, depot buildings, and roads constructed over the almost 240 years since the Siege.

Davis, R. S. (2021, February 22). Black Haitian soldiers at the siege of Savannah. *Journal of the American Revolution.* https://allthingsliberty.com.

Clark, G. P. (1980). The role of the Haitian volunteers at Savannah in 1779: An attempt at an objective view. *Phylon 41* (4).

Elliott, R. F., & Elliott, D. T. (2009). Savannah under fire. *Coastal Heritage Society.* Savannah, Georgia.

Jones, G. F. (1979) A note on the victor at Springhill Redoubt. *The Georgia Historical Quarterly 63* (3).

Lawrence, A.A. (1951). *Storm over Savannah: The story of Count d'Estaing and the siege of the town in 1779.* University of Georgia Press.

Rogers, T. G. (1997). Siege of Savannah during the American Revolutionary War. https://www.historynet.com/siege-of-savannah-during-the-american-revolutionary-war.htm

Siege of Savannah. (n.d.). *George Washington's Mount Vernon.* https://www.mountvernon.org/library/digitalhistory/digital-encyclopedia/article/siege-of-savannah/

The Siege of Savannah: September 16-October 18, 1779 at Savannah, Georgia. (n.d.). https://revolutionarywar.us/year-1779/battle-of-savannah/

NB – There are many, many more references available on this extremely important fight.

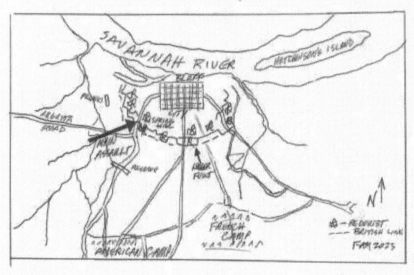

SIEGE OF SAVANNAH, 1779.

The Siege of Charleston

The Siege of Charleston was among the most pivotal actions of the American Revolution. The city's defense was robust but ultimately inadequate, and the British took the city. The loss of Charleston opened South Carolina, and indeed the entire southern colonies, to British control.

The siege began on April 1, 1780, and lasted six weeks. However, the invasion of South Carolina began shortly after the successful British defense of Savannah. In January of 1780 the British army approached the Savannah River with several thousand troops embarked on a flotilla. The British, under General Sir Henry Clinton and Lieutenant General Charles Lord Cornwallis, landed on Simmons' Island (now called Seabrook Island). They began an inexorable march toward Charleston.

Among the various units deployed by the British was the British Legion, Commanded by Lieutenant Colonel Banastre Tarleton. The British Legion was made up of American (Tory) volunteers and had a reputation in New York and New Jersey for being fierce fighters. Tarleton also had a reputation as an aggressive commander of the mixed dragoon (mounted infantry) and pure infantry troops. They would become a major factor in the Revolutionary War in South Carolina.

Charleston is a city on a peninsula, with the Ashley River on one side and the Cooper River on the other. Americans hoped the city would be an unbreachable citadel with the addition of a defensive work stretched across the 'neck,' the narrow part of the isthmus to the north of the city. Ditches, a massive stone 'horn work,' and numerous redoubts and batteries were erected, mounting over 300 guns facing enemy forces from all sides. Ultimately, these defenses were useless because the city fathers and Governor John Rutledge could not withstand the ferocious British artillery barrage that preceded the threatened assault.

By Mid-April 1780, the British had surrounded the city and cut off supply routes in and out of Charleston. The British had superior numbers and firepower and bombarded the city with artillery. Many artillery shells fired into the city were 'hot shot' – heated cannonballs that set fire to structures. The American forces, which were poorly supplied and lacked sufficient reinforcements, could not hold out against the British assault.

On May 12, 1780, the American forces surrendered to the British. More than 5,000 American soldiers were taken as prisoners of war, making the siege one of the largest military surrenders in American history. The loss of Charleston was a significant blow to the American cause, as it gave the British control of the South and disrupted American plans for a southern campaign.

The Siege of Charleston was also notable for the participation of many African American soldiers on both sides. The British offered freedom to enslaved people who fought for their cause, and many African Americans joined their ranks. Unfortunately, many former slaves were used for forced labor, such as digging ditches for fortifications and other similar tasks. At least one British Commander, Lieutenant Colonel John Simcoe, was sympathetic to the plight of slaves, unlike many others who simply sought to entice the slaves to desert plantations to inflict economic hardship on rebel plantation owners.

National Park Service. (n.d.). The Siege of Charleston 1780. https://www.nps.gov/articles/siege-of-charleston-1780.htm

Siege of Charleston, March 29-May 12, 1780. (n.d.). https://revolutionarywar.us/year-1780/battle-of-charleston/

The American Revolution in South Carolina. (n.d.). The Siege of Charlestown with order of battle. https://www.carolana.com/SC/Revolution/revolution_siege_of_charleston.html

Related Actions to the Siege of Charleston

The Battle of Monck's Corner, northwest of Charleston, was a critical fight in the campaign to subdue Charleston. Tarleton and his British Legion routed American General Isaac Huger's troops in the middle of the night on _____. Huger was defending Biggin Bridge over the Cooper River with some

500 troops, many of whom were mounted, but only about half of the troops had muskets.

Tarleton secured the bridge and captured hundreds of top-quality mounts for his legion. The capture of the bridge finalized the isolation of Charleston, and Tarleton was desperate for horses because most of the British Army's horses had not survived the lengthy sea crossing from New York south to Savannah.

The Siege of Charleston was a turning point in the American Revolutionary War, and it demonstrated the difficulties that the American forces faced in the southern colonies. Nevertheless, the battle remains an important chapter in American history for its status as a significant loss that shifted the South Carolina front in favor of the British.

Harris, C. L., & Baxley, C. B. (2021). Tarleton tightens the noose around Charleston Neck: Biggin Bridge April 14, 1780. *The Journal of the Southern Campaigns of the American Revolution 18*(2).

NB – The above reference is an excellent, detailed account of the fighting in South Carolina after the British defense of Savannah. It covers more than just Biggin Bridge.

Escape of Governor John Rutledge. South Carolina Governor John Rutledge escaped the city in mid-April 1780 and his travels toward North Carolina were as described in

Journeyman: Honor Fades Not. Rutledge was an honorable man, but his stance to defend Charleston – backed up by his council, including Lieutenant Governor Christopher Gadsden – effectively trapped Lincoln and the 5000 American troops.

Waxhaws. Rutledge's escape and his pursuit by Tarleton, including the pause at Rugeley's Clermont Plantation, are described in *Journeyman: Honor Fades Not.* The escort included Brigadier General Isaac Huger and Colonel John Buford. Huger and Buford separated for unknown reasons, with Huger taking Rutledge on toward Charlotte and Buford heading toward Waxhaws.

The fight at Waxhaws was as described in the novel. Poor leadership decisions, such as forming a single line and withholding fire until the very last instant, all but assured a loss. During the battle, someone did, indeed, shoot Tarleton's horse, and the horse landed on Tarleton's leg. Simultaneously with Tarleton's horse being shot, Buford sent forward a white flag. The British Legion troops were incensed at what they thought was Tarleton's death and doubly infuriated by the belief that Tarleton had been killed under a flag of truce. This led to the terrible massacre of American troops.

Tarleton's troops' massacre of American troops was termed Tarleton's Quarter, meaning take no prisoners. Tarleton later commented that the unfortunate shooting of his horse led to "...a vindictive asperity not easily restrained" (Tarleton, 1787, p.

32). This is an understatement for the slaughter that set a pattern for the war in South Carolina.

Tarleton, B. (1787). *A History of the Campaigns of 1780 and 1781*. Dublin, Ireland.

Map: Siege of Charlestown, 1780

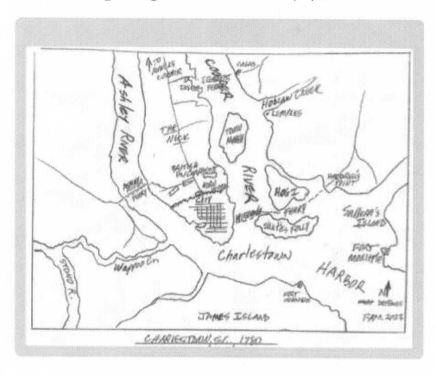

587

The Battle of Camden

The Battle of Camden was a significant engagement of the American Revolutionary War that took place on August 16, 1780, near Camden, South Carolina. The battle was fought between American forces commanded by Major General Horatio Gates and British forces under the command of Lieutenant General Charles Cornwallis.

The American forces, which included both regular soldiers and militia, were poorly trained and equipped. Gates, who had won a significant victory at Saratoga, was overconfident and made several tactical errors, including dividing his army into three parts.

Washington had sent Major General Johann de Kalb to attempt to relieve the Siege of Charlestown. However, de Kalb was too late to save Charlestown. Congress appointed General Gates to command, and de Kalb fell under Gates'.

The British, on the other hand, were well-trained and well-equipped, and they had the advantage of superior firepower. Cornwallis had fresh troops, and he was eager to engage the Americans in battle.

The two armies blundered into one another in the dark. They disengaged and set up to fight the next morning. American troops were sick from having eaten unripe fruit and many were unfit for combat.

The battle began early in the morning of August 16, 1780. The American forces, which were disorganized and poorly positioned, were quickly overwhelmed by the British advance. The battle turned into a rout, with American soldiers fleeing in all directions. The British forces, particularly Lt Colonel Banastre Tarleton and his British Legion, pursued the retreating Americans, inflicting heavy casualties and capturing many prisoners.

General de Kalb ably led the forces of the American right but was mortally wounded and died a few days after the battle. This was an unfortunate loss for the patriots because de Kalb was among the more capable American commanders.

The Battle of Camden was a devastating defeat for the American forces, with more than 2,000 casualties and the loss of much of their supplies and equipment. The defeat severely weakened American morale and allowed the British to gain control of South Carolina.

However, the battle also highlighted the need for better training and discipline among the American forces, leading to the appointment of new commanders who were more capable. General Horatio Gates fled the battlefield on horseback and was not seen again in the Southern Department. Major General

Nathanael Greene was appointed to command the Southern Department. Greene's leadership blunted Cornwallis' success and contributed to the ultimate failure of the British Southern Strategy.

Despite the defeat at Camden, the American forces continued to fight on. However, much of the fighting in South Carolina was now done by guerilla forces under the command of militia Generals Thomas Sumter and Francis Marion.

Isenbarger, D. (2006). Battle of Camden. In William S. Powell. *Encyclopedia of North Carolina* (https://uncpress.org/book/9780807830710/encyclopedia - of-north-carolina/).

Piecuch, J. (2013). Repercussions of the Battle of Camden. *Journal of the American Revolution.* https://allthingsliperty.com.

Water, A. (2020, September 14). The mysterious march of Horatio Gates. Journal of the American Revolution. https://allthingsliberty.com/2020/09/the-mysterious-march-of-horatio-gates/

Zucker, A. E. (1966). *General de Kalb, Lafayette's Mentor.* Chapter 14: Washington sends de Kalb to rescue Charleston: Congress appoints Gates. University of North Carolina Press.

Recent events at Camden. In 2022, the remains of 14 Revolutionary War Soldiers were discovered on the battlefield at Camden, South Carolina. In September 2022, the area was excavated and remains were recovered. The archeology team conducting the excavation believes the bodies include 12 Patriot Continental soldiers, one loyalist soldier, and one British soldier of the 71st Regiment of Food, Fraser's Highlanders. Many of the remains were discovered buried only inches deep in the sandy soil dotted with pines and tall grass, just as it was on the day of the battle in 1780.

Examination of the remains is now complete and attempts to identify the remains continue. The South Carolina Battleground Preservation Trust conducted a reinterment ceremony in April 2023 with the participation of the United States Army, the British Army, and other units. These young men died fighting for the causes they believed in, and the reinterment ceremony was conducted with great reverence. Interested readers can find full videos of the event online.

Mejia, J. (2022, November 11). *Remains of fourteen Revolutionary War soldiers discovered at Camden Battlefield.* WOLO, ABC Columbia, SC.

South Carolina Battleground Preservation Trust. (2023). *Camden burials: August 16, 1780 & April 22, 2023, Honoring heroes.* https://www.scbattlegroundtrust.org/camden-burials.

Biographies

Admiral Comte d'Estaing. The French Count d'Estaing, whose full name was Charles Henri Hector d'Estaing, was a prominent military leader and naval commander of the 18th century. He was born on November 24, 1729, in the city of Ruvel, in the region of Auvergne, France.

D'Estaing's family had a long history of military service, and he followed in their footsteps by joining the French Navy in 1746, at the age of 17. He quickly rose through the ranks, and by the time of the Seven Years' War (1756-1763), he had become a captain.

During the Seven Years' War, d'Estaing played a key role in several important naval battles, including the Battle of Lagos in 1759 and the Battle of Quiberon Bay in 1761. He also participated in several successful raids against British shipping in the Atlantic.

After the war, d'Estaing continued to serve in the French Navy, and in 1778, he was appointed commander of the French fleet that was sent to aid the American colonists in their fight for independence against Great Britain. He arrived in North America with a fleet of 12 ships in July of that year and was immediately tasked with the important mission of capturing the British-held island of St. Lucia.

D'Estaing's first attempt to capture St. Lucia was unsuccessful, and he was forced to withdraw after a fierce battle with the British. However, he returned a few months later with a larger fleet and was able to successfully capture the island.

D'Estaing's next major engagement came at the Siege of Savannah in 1779. He led a joint French and American force in an attempt to capture the city of Savannah from the British, but the attack was unsuccessful, and d'Estaing was forced to withdraw after suffering heavy losses. D'Estaing's slow disembarkation of his troops, followed by slow deployment and an overly courteous request for the British surrender, permitted the British the crucial time to develop defenses and draw in reinforcements.

With supplies running low and disease spreading through his ships, d'Estaing ordered an attack on the ground. While American troops were not well trained and were poorly equipped, d'Estaing's failures of command and decision-making were core to the failure of the Siege of Savannah. D'Estaing personally led the attack and was severely wounded. He returned to command before he fully recovered.

d'Estaing continued to play an important role in the American Revolution, providing crucial naval support to the American forces in several other battles, including the Battle of the Chesapeake in 1781. d'Estaing's ships were part of Compte DeGrasse's fleet that prevented the British Navy from rescuing

Cornwallis' army at Yorktown. Cornwallis' army was left without support and surrendered to the Franco-American armies, effectively ending the American Revolution.

After the war, d'Estaing returned to France, where he continued to serve in the Navy and was eventually promoted to the rank of admiral. D'Estaing's legacy as a commander is one of great courage and skill.

As a member of the nobility and someone close to the King, d'Estaing was prosecuted during the French Revolution. He was guillotined on April 28, 1794, at the age of 64. Before his execution, d'Estaing reportedly wrote, "After my head falls off, send it to the English, they will pay a good deal for it!" It was a sad end for a man whose entire life had been in the service of France.

Jean Baptiste Charles Henri Hector, comte d'Estaing (n.d.). https://en.wikipedia.org/wiki/Charles_Henri_Hector_d%27Estaing

Horatio Gates was a prominent military officer and statesman who served during the American Revolutionary War. Born in Maldon, Essex, England in 1727, he spent his early years as a soldier in the British Army before emigrating to Virginia in 1772.

At the outbreak of the American Revolution, Gates joined the Continental Army and quickly rose through the ranks due to his military experience and leadership abilities. He served as a brigadier general under George Washington, and played a key role in the victories at Saratoga in 1777, which is considered a turning point in the war.

However, Gates' military career was not without controversy. He was accused of plotting to replace George Washington as commander-in-chief of the Continental Army, and his leadership during the Battle of Camden in 1780 was widely criticized for being ineffective and leading to a devastating defeat.

Despite these setbacks, Gates remained active in politics and served as the governor of Virginia from 1786 to 1788. He also supported the ratification of the U.S. Constitution and was elected to the U.S. House of Representatives in 1790.

Throughout his career, Gates was known for his intelligence, organizational skills, and ability to inspire troops. He was also a skilled military strategist and is credited with developing the tactics used at the Battle of Saratoga, which helped to secure a crucial victory for the Continental Army.

In addition to his military and political career, Gates was also a successful farmer and plantation owner, and played an important role in the development of agriculture in the southern United States.

Horatio Gates passed away on April 10, 1806, in New York City. Despite the controversies that surrounded his military career, he is remembered as a skilled strategist and a key figure in the American Revolution. His legacy continues to be celebrated today, particularly for his contributions to the development of military tactics and agriculture in the United States.

Gates, Horatio. (n.d.).

https://en.wikipedia.org/wiki/Horatio_Gates

Sergeant William Jasper was a soldier in the Continental Army during the American Revolutionary War who is known for his bravery and heroism. Jasper was likely born in Germany about 1750 and immigrated to Philadelphia as an indentured servant. Researchers believe he escaped his indenture and ran to Georgia. He then joined the 2nd South Carolina Regiment of the Continental Army in 1775.

Jasper is famous for his actions during the Siege of Savannah in 1779. During the battle, Jasper and his comrades attempted to raise an American flag over the Spring Hill Redoubt. Jasper was mortally wounded in this attempt. A statue in downtown Savannah commemorates his bravery and patriotism.

Before the Siege of Savannah, Jasper earned a legendary place in South Carolina lore. During the 1776 attempted British invasion of Charleston, the flagstaff at the fort on Sullivan's Island (later named Fort Moultrie) was shot down by British fire. Without hesitation, Jasper picked up the fallen flag, tied it to a makeshift pole, climbed the rampart, and held the flag high in the face of heavy enemy fire. Jasper's actions inspired his fellow soldiers, and he became a symbol of bravery and patriotism during the Revolutionary War.

There is considerable evidence that Sergeant Wilhelm Jasper frequently went behind British lines to capture prisoners for interrogation. It is claimed that he entered occupied Savannah, passed himself off as a deserter, and conveyed false information to the British defenders. The incursion with Will Yelverton in Journeyman: Honor Fades Not is fictional, but it is highly similar to other incursions where Jasper and his friend, Sergeant Newton, captured British officers and returned them to American lines for interrogation.

Jasper's bravery earned him a reputation as a hero of the American Revolution, and he became a beloved figure in South Carolina. Today, Jasper's legacy continues to be celebrated, and he is remembered as a symbol of American courage and determination.

Shenawolf, H. (2018). Sergeant William Jasper: American Revolution's celebrated hero at the Battle of Sullivan's Island. *Revolutionary War Journal.* https://www.revolutionarywarjournal.com/william-jasper-gallant-soldier-celebrated-hero-at-the-battle-of-sullivan-island-yet-little-is-known-of-his-life/

Jones, G. F. (1981). Sergeant Johann Wilhelm Jasper. *The Georgia Historical Quarterly 65* (1).

General Benjamin Lincoln was born on January 24, 1733, in Hingham, Massachusetts, and was the son of a prominent landowner and politician.

Lincoln began his military career in the colonial militia and quickly rose through the ranks due to his leadership abilities. He was appointed as a major general in the Continental Army in 1777 and played a key role in several important battles, including the Siege of Charleston in 1780.

Despite being captured by the British during the Siege of Charleston, Lincoln continued to serve in the Continental Army. He, along with many other senior Continental Army officers, was exchanged by the British and was subsequently instrumental in the American victory at the Battle of Yorktown in 1781. He was also involved in negotiating the surrender of British forces under General Charles Cornwallis, which effectively ended the war. Because the British had humiliated Lincoln at the surrender of Charleston, Lincoln was detailed to receive the British surrender at Yorktown.

After the war, Lincoln served as the Secretary of War under the Articles of Confederation and played an essential role in establishing the U.S. Army and Navy. He also served as the lieutenant governor and then governor of Massachusetts and was a strong supporter of the U.S. Constitution.

Despite his many accomplishments, Lincoln's legacy is somewhat overshadowed by the controversial surrender of his army at the Siege of Charleston. Many criticized Lincoln for his decision to surrender, arguing that he should have fought to the end. However, others defended Lincoln's decision, pointing to the difficult circumstances he faced and the fact that he was able to save many of his soldiers from certain death.

Benjamin Lincoln passed away on May 9, 1810, in Hingham, Massachusetts. Despite the controversy surrounding his military career, he is remembered as a skilled military leader and an important figure in the early years of the United States. His legacy continues to be celebrated today, particularly for his contributions to the establishment of the U.S. Army and Navy.

Francis Marion, also known as the "Swamp Fox," was a South Carolinian of Huguenot descent (as were many other members of the planter class). He was born on February 26, 1732, in Berkeley County, South Carolina, and spent much of his early life working on his family's plantation.

Marion spent much of his life in the military, serving in the South Carolina Militia during the Cherokee wars before joining the Continental Army in 1775. He was quickly promoted to captain. Marion served alongside equally famous Sergeant

William (Wilhelm) Jasper at Fort Sullivan (later Fort Moultrie) during the failed British invasion of Charleston in 1776.

Marion was promoted to Lieutenant Colonel and commanded the 2nd South Carolina Regiment of the Continental Army. He was among the leaders of the failed assault on the Spring Hill Redoubt at the Siege of Savannah. After the failed siege, Marion led remnants of the 2nd South Carolina back to South Carolina where they prepared for the British invasion.

As described in *Journeyman: Honor Fades Not*, Marion injured his leg jumping from a second-floor window to avoid a drunken party. Along with other incapacitated and supernumerary officers, Marion was ordered to leave the city prior to the siege. He repaired to his plantation at Pond Bluff near Eutaw Springs, but was forced to leave.

Still recovering from his injured leg, Marion brought a small group of volunteers to General Gates' headquarters prior to the Battle of Camden. Gates rejected Marion and his volunteers, directing them to interdict boats along the nearby Wateree River. After Gates was beaten at Camden, Marion began organizing a militia to fight against the British.

Governor Rutledge promoted Marion to Brigadier General in the South Carolina Militia. Marion's militia was known for its guerrilla tactics, which involved quick strikes and hit-and-run attacks against British forces. He and his men often took refuge in the swamps and forests of South Carolina, which earned Marion his nickname, the "Swamp Fox."

Marion's tactics were highly effective, and he was able to disrupt British supply lines and communication networks, as well as capture important British outposts. He played a key role in several important battles, including the Battle of Eutaw Springs, and was instrumental in the American victory at the Battle of Cowpens in 1781.

Despite his success, Marion was not without controversy. His militia was accused of using brutal tactics, including attacks on unarmed civilians and prisoners of war. However, Marion maintained that these tactics were necessary to defeat the British and secure American independence.

After the war, Marion served in the South Carolina State Senate and was a strong supporter of the U.S. Constitution. He passed away on February 27, 1795, at the age of 63.

Today, Francis Marion is remembered as a skilled military leader who played a crucial role in the American Revolution. His innovative tactics and determination helped to turn the tide of the war in favor of the American forces, and his legacy continues to inspire generations of Americans.

After George Washington, Francis Marion has the distinction of being the namesake of the second-highest number of places in the United States. There are numerous references describing the life of Francis Marion. That said, none truly capture the essence of this reclusive man. He is buried at his brother's plantation, Belle Isle, in Berkeley County, South Carolina.

Below is a tiny sampling of the many available writings on Francis Marion. The books by Stephen Smith are of particular interest.

American Revolutionary War Continental Regiments. (n.d.). *South Carolina Regiments in the Continental Army.* https://revolutionarywar.us/continental-army/southcarolina/

Crawford, A. (2007). The Swamp Fox. *Smithsonian Magazine.* https://www.smithsonianmag.com/history/the-swamp-fox-157330429/

Smith, S.D. (2021). *Francis Marion and the Snow's Island Community: Myth, history, and archaeology.* United Writers Press. Asheville, NC.

Smith, S.D., & Dougherty, K. (2022). *Leading like the Swamp Fox: The leadership lessons of Francis Marion.* Casemate Publishers. Havertown, PA, & Oxford, UK.

Brigadier General Francis Marion. (n.d.). *The American Revolution in South Carolina.* https://www.carolana.com/SC/Revolution/patriot_leaders_sc_francis_marion.html

Casimir Pulaski was a volunteer Polish cavalry commander who served with Washington and later in the Southern Departmant. He is often referred to as the "Father of the American Cavalry."

Pulaski arrived in the American colonies in 1777, after meeting with Benjamin Franklin in Paris. He immediately offered his services to the Continental Army, and he was quickly put in charge of a cavalry unit. Under Pulaski's leadership, the cavalry unit was able to inflict significant damage on the British army.

One of Pulaski's most significant contributions to the American war effort came in the Battle of Brandywine in September 1777. Pulaski's cavalry played a critical role in holding back the British advance and buying time for the American infantry to retreat safely. This action was recounted in *Journeyman: The Bridge.*

Pulaski continued to serve the American cause throughout the war, and he played a significant role in the Siege of Savannah in 1779. Pulaski led a charge against British forces during the battle, but he was mortally wounded in the fighting and died shortly afterward.

The American forces highly valued Pulaski's bravery and military expertise, and he is considered one of the most important foreign military leaders who helped to secure America's independence. He is remembered as a hero of the

American Revolution, and his legacy continues to be celebrated today.

It is of interest to the reader that there are many locations in the United States named for several of the key historical players in *Journeyman: Honor Fades Not*. Marion is the second most honored American with place names after George Washington. Jasper and Newton are honored with numerous counties and places. Pulaski is a town name frequently seen on road signs – Florida, Georgia, Virginia, to name a few.

Charleston River Ferries

During the 1700s, river ferries were an important mode of transportation in and around Charleston, South Carolina. These ferries provided a vital link between the city and the surrounding areas, allowing people and goods to travel more easily between different parts of the region.

The operation of river ferries was typically handled by private individuals or companies, who were granted a license by the colonial government to operate a ferry service on a particular route. These ferries were typically small boats that could carry passengers, animals, and goods across rivers and other bodies of water.

One of the most important ferry routes near Charleston was the ferry between Charleston and Sullivan's Island, which provided a vital link between the city and the important military fortifications on the island. The ferry was operated by a series of private individuals and companies throughout the 1700s and played a key role in the defense of Charleston during the American Revolution.

Other ferry routes in the area included Hibben's ferry between Charleston and Mount Pleasant, and the ferry between Charleston and James Island. These ferries were important for transporting goods such as rice, indigo, and cotton, which were major cash crops in the region.

Despite their importance, river ferries were not without their challenges. They were often affected by weather conditions and could be disrupted by storms and flooding. In addition, many ferries were operated by private individuals who may have prioritized profits over safety, leading to occasional accidents and incidents.

Despite these challenges, river ferries were a vital part of the transportation infrastructure of Charleston and the surrounding area during the 1700s and played an important role in developing the region's economy and society.

In *Journeyman: Honor Fades Not*, Will Yelverton extensively uses various ferries in the Charlestown area. He also participates in the critical defense of the Ashley River Ferry during the 1779 British incursion into South Carolina. The ferries are identified in the map of Charleston provided.

References

The following is a *partial list* of references used in writing Journeyman: *Honor Fades Not*. The work is not an academic endeavor, so these references informed the story and set the historical stage as a backdrop to the story of Will Yelverton in South Carolina. Every effort was made to follow history and to set events in the actual timeline of the American Revolution, particularly in the context of the British Southern Strategy of 1778 and later. That said, this is a work of fiction, and it is possible that events may not line up precisely with historical chronology.

The references are in alphabetical order.

Anonymous. (n.d.). The Battle of Camden. *American Revolutionary War 1775-1783*.

Anonymous. (n.d.). The Siege of Charleston: March 29-May 12, 1780 at Charleston, South Carolina. *American Revolutionary War 1775-1783*.

Anonymous. (n.d.). The siege of Charlestown with order of battle. *The American Revolution in South Carolina*.

Brown, W. (1968). The American Farmer during the Revolution: Rebel or Loyalist? *Agricultural History 42*(4), pp. 327-338.

Cashin, E. J. (1999). *The King's Ranger: Thomas Brown and the American Revolution on the Southern Frontier*. New York, NY: Fordham University Press.

Clark, G.P. (1980). The role of Haitian volunteers at Savannah in 1779: An attempt at an objective view. *Phylon 41*(4), pp. 356-366.

Coleman, K. (1958). *Fighting after the siege of Savannah: The American Revolution in Georgia, 1763-1789*. University of Georgia Press.

Davis, R. S. (2006). A frontier for pioneer revolutionaries: John Dooly and the beginnings of popular democracy in original Wilkes County. *The Georgia Historical Quarterly 90*(3), pp. 315-349.

Davis, R. S. (2017). The murder of Colonel Dooly of Georgia: A Revolutionary War mystery. *Journal of the American Revolution*.

Davis, R. S., Jr. (1984). Colonel Dooly's Campaign of 1779. *Huntington Library Quarterly 47*(1), pp. 65-71.

Davis, R.S. Jr. (2021). Black Haitian soldiers at the siege of Savannah. *Journal of the American Revolution*.

Dibble, E. F. (2001). Religion on Florida's territorial frontiers. *The Florida Historical Quarterly 80*(1), pp. 1-23.

Dobein, J. (2008). *A sketch of the life of Brig. Gen. Francis Marion*. Project Gutenberg eBook.

Elliott, R. F., & Elliott, D.T. (2009). *Savannah Under Fire, 1779: Identifying Savannah's Revolutionary War Battlefield*. Savannah, GA: Coastal Heritage Society.

Ferrari, M. C. (2011). Charity, folly, and politics: Charles Town's social clubs on the eve of the revolution. *South Carolina Historical Magazine 112* (1/2), pp. 50-83.

Gilman, C. (1839). *Letters of Eliza Wilkinson during the invasion and possession of Charlestown, S.C. by the British in the Revolutionary War*. New York, NY: Samuel Colman.

History of War. (n.d.). Benjamin Lincoln, American Revolutionary General. www.historyofwar.org/articles/people_benjaminlincoln.html

Jensen, M. (1970). The American People and the American Revolution. *The Journal of American History 57*(1), pp. 5-35.

Jones, G. F. (1979). A note on the victor at Springhill Redoubt. *The Georgia Historical Quarterly 63*(3), pp. 377-379.

Jones, R. (2011). *Before they were heroes at King's Mountain.* Winston-Salem, NC: Daniel Boone Footsteps.

Joyner, C. (2011). *Remember me: Slave life in Coastal Georgia.* Athens, GA: University of Georgia Press.

Landers, J. (1984). Spanish sanctuary: Fugitives in Florida, 1687-1790. *The Florida Historical Quarterly 62*(3), pp. 296-313.

Landers, J. (1989). Black frontier settlements in Spanish Colonial Florida. *OAH Magazine of History 3*(2), pp. 28-29.

Lewis, J.D. (2015). *The known patriots at the Battle of Kings Mountain.* https://www.carolana.com.

Little, B. (2019). The massive, overlooked role of female slaveowners: It's estimated that 40 percent of slaveowners may have been white women. *History Channel.*

Lynch, W. (2014). The Georgia refugees turn the tide against the British. *Journal of the American Revolution.*

Lynch, W. (2016). Daniel McGirth, Banditti on the Southern Frontier. *Journal of the American Revolution.*

Olson, G. D. (1970). Thomas Brown, Loyalist Partisan and the Revolutionary War in Georgia, 1777-1782. *The Georgia Historical Quarterly 54*(1), pp. 1-19.

Piecuch, J. (2013). Repercussions of the Battle of Camden. *Journal of the American Revolution.*

Robertson, H. (1974). The second British occupation of Augusta, 1780-1781. *The Georgia Historical Quarterly 58* (4), pp. 422-446.

Saberton, I. (2019). Midsummer 1780 in the Carolinas and Georgia – Events predating the Battle of Camden. *Journal of the American Revolution.*

Searcy, M. C. (1983). 1779: The first year of the British occupation of Georgia. *The Georgia Historical Quarterly 67*(2), pp. 168-188.

Siebert, W.H. (1929). Loyalists in East Florida 1774-1785, vol 2. *University of Central Florida Libraries STARS.*

Simner, M. L. (2022). Emergence of the French alliance: The beginning and final phases. *Journal of the American Revolution.*

Swager, C. (2012). Elijah Clarke (Part II). *KCBA: The Battlefield Dispatch 1*(3), pp. 2-5.

The American Historical Review (1899). *The Siege of Charleston: Journal of Captain Peter Russell, December 25, 1779 to May 2, 1780.* Oxford University Press.

Williams, S. C. (1941). Colonel Elijah Clarke in the Tennessee country. *The Georgia Historical Quarterly 25*(2), pp. 151-158.

Wood, B. (1992). White women, Black slaves, and the law in early national Georgia: The Sunbury Petition of 1791. *The Historical Journal 35*(3), pp. 611-622.

Acknowledgments

In any writing project, the author is only one of the players. I am fortunate to have many friends who are kind enough to also function as helpers. They all help as beta readers, consultants on history and military operations, consultants on writing, and advisors on the business of being an author.

I extend my sincere thanks to the following people who have been invaluable in my journey as an author. All dear friends.

- My wife Deri encourages me daily and serves as my primary beta reader.

- Ms. Karen Brady, who has become my de facto editor.

- Colonel Mat Matecko, USAFR (Retired), who stays on the lookout for marketing opportunities.

- Colonel Rick Davis, USAF (Retired), writing critic and sounding board.

- Dr. Bob North, long-time friend and beta reader.

- Dr. Lyn S. Heck, my collaborator, and creative advisor.

Special thanks to John Greene, a friend and brilliant beyond his years. He singlehandedly developed marketing plans and successful ad campaigns that have put my books in the hands of many more people than I could have ever imagined.

Randell Jones, award-winning author of several histories of the pioneer era and militiamen in the South during the Revolutionary War—and a fellow Georgia Tech grad (we survived!)—offered his generous counsel on book design and reference sources. He has made me better at the craft of writing.

Visit Randell's website at:

https://www.DanielBooneFootsteps.com.

Griff Hosker is a renowned English author of historical fiction and a most generous friend in the gift of his time and advice. Griff has kindly given me the value of his counsel on how to manage the business of being an author. Visit Griff's webpage at: https://www.griffhosker.com/

Danny Morrison at Amazon ProHub, my publisher.

Jack Robert Pearson who made his debut in this world in May 2022. Jack is the best grandchild in the entire world and is the inspiration to tell stories that he may one day read.

I am sure there are others who deserve thanks. If I missed anyone, please know you are valued and appreciated.

FAM

Author's Biography

Frank A. Mason is the pen name for retired USAF Lieutenant Colonel Bob Amason, PhD, who also served as a college professor for 25 years. As an officer in the USAF, Mason flew as a crew member on B-52s during the Cold War, served as a flying training instructor, and directed high-level staff organizations over 22 years of his early adult life. A college professor from the late 1990s to the present, Mason's alter ego earned degrees, including a Ph.D., from two of the nation's top five public institutions. He had the privilege of mentoring hundreds of doctoral students at three institutions. He is a member of the Sons of the American Revolution. Several of is patriot ancestors rode with Francis Marion.

The *Journeyman Chronicles* books narrate the adventures of Will Yelverton, a young gunsmith caught in the vortex of the American Revolution. The present book is number III in the *Journeyman Chronicles: Honor Fades Not.*

Four Women of the Revolution is a story of courage and resilience inspired by actual events and is a companion to Mason's *Journeyman Chronicles* series of novels.

Frank A. Mason is also the author of a series of modern suspense novels featuring the reluctant hero, Mac McCall. The first Mac McCall novel, *Blue-Green for the Grave,* is available on Amazon. Look for the second Mac McCall novel, *The Bronze-Wound Lament* coming in 2023.

Frank A. Mason's novels are available on Amazon.com and other booksellers.

Journeyman Chronicles Series

Journeyman: The Bridge

Journeyman: Heart of Tempered Steel

Journeyman: Honor Fades Not

Historical Novels

Four Women of the Revolution

Mac McCall Suspense Novels

Blue-Green for the Grave

The Bronze-Wound Lament (coming in 2023)

Writing as Bob Amason, PhD

"November Wind." Personal story in Randell Jones' Anthology, *Twists and Turns* (2022, Winston-Salem, NC, Daniel Boone Footsteps).

"My Father's Photograph." Personal story in Randell Jones' Anthology, *Lost and Found* (2023, Winston-Salem, NC, Daniel Boone Footsteps).

Made in the USA
Middletown, DE
25 July 2023

35700931R00368